THE
BELT OF
GOLD

THE BELT OF GOLD

CECELIA HOLLAND

Alfred A. Knopf

NEW YORK

1984

THIS IS A BORZOI BOOK
PUBLISHED BY ALFRED A. KNOPF, INC.

Library of Congress Cataloging in Publication Data

Holland, Cecelia. [date]   The belt of gold.

1. Byzantine Empire—History—Irene, 797–802—Fiction.
2. Irene, Empress of the East, 752?–803—Fiction.
I. Title.
PS3558.O3486 1984   813'.54   83-48854
ISBN 0-394-52791-7

Manufactured in the United States of America

FIRST EDITION

THE
BELT OF
GOLD

: 1 :

She had kept silent until now, but when they brought a horse to her, saddled and bridled, the stirrups tied up neatly over the seat, Theophano said, "Shimon, I cannot ride."

The big Jew yanked the saddlecloth straight and brought the stirrups down. "Theophano," he said, "get on."

"I cannot ride, Shimon."

"It's only a little way. Would you approach him on foot? You must ride, as if you were an aristocrat."

"I am an aristocrat," she said. "Get me a chair. You said we had an hour—go into Chalcedon and hire me a chair."

Shimon gave her a long meditative stare. He had the long sad face of his people, deeply graven with lines, and although he never raised his voice it made her quail a little to risk his anger. But if she was to gull Targa, and secure the precious list of names he was carrying, then she had to dominate the circumstances, and she meant to begin doing so now.

"The best chair you can find," she said. "Now. Hurry; we have little time."

Shimon stared at her a moment longer, expressionless. She made her face implacable. The Basileus had a look, when to argue or complain would rouse the Imperial wrath and make the very mountains quake, and Theophano put on such a look now, facing Shimon.

It succeeded. He turned away, shrugging, and beckoned to one of his men. Theophano throttled down a sigh of relief. No need to let him guess he might have refused her with impunity. She walked slowly away, down the road, her gaze sweeping the horizon.

There was little horizon here to sweep. Through the brown hills the road wound down in coils over the slopes; parts of it were visible for miles, but most of the roadcourse lay hidden in the folds and laps of the land. There was no water here. Even the burgeoning spring brought only the timidest haze of green to the rocky soil, slashed with gulleys as if by a great knife. The tough thorny brush that sprouted among the rocks was as colorless as the ground itself.

She walked up and down along the side of the road, kicking at pebbles with her embroidered slippers. How strange it was, to be outside Constantinople. She had spent her entire life in the City, and everyone had always told her that there was nothing of any interest elsewhere, but she had not believed it. Now she saw it was true.

Shimon brought her a clay flask of wine. "Will you need a cup?"

She laughed at him, at this new diffidence in his voice. "I think I can manage." She took the flask, the clay still damp enough outside to cool the wine within, and lifted it to her lips. Carefully. She wore a white dress and it would not do to blazon it with a long red wine stain down the front.

As she drank, Shimon spoke to her in a low voice.

"Remember. Targa has seen you with John Cerulis, on the most intimate possible terms with him. You have the money with John Cerulis's seal on the purse. You must get him to give you the list quickly, before he can think it over."

"I understand."

"Targa's no fool. But he wants the money."

"Yes, Shimon."

The Jew sighed. His forehead was dappled with sweat. "Where is that chair?" He walked away, his arms swinging; he wore a long striped coat, like a Persian trader's; under the arms great wedges of sweat darkened the cloth.

At the trot, the chair arrived, elegant enough for a rented vehicle; six bearers carried it, but Shimon paid them off and sent them back to Chalcedon, and ordered some of his own men to strip down to their underclothes. Theophano pulled the curtains out and flapped them in the breeze to get rid of the smell of must. There weren't enough cushions even to cover the bare wood of the bottom. Laying her cloak down on the floor, she climbed in, piled what cushions there were behind her, and drew the curtains closed.

A moment later the chair rocked from side to side, as the inexperienced bearers got hold of the poles, and lurched up into the air. There was an explosive oath from behind her. She leaned back, the air already too close, the stale smell stuffing up her nose. Accompanied by the shuffling of the feet of her bearers and the escort, she jounced away down the road.

She thought again of what the Basileus had told her. The list that Targa was bringing, for which John Cerulis was prepared to pay well, must not reach his hands; she and Shimon were to do everything possible to divert the list to the Basileus. Everything possible. The Basileus had said those words with special force.

It was hot in the chair; her clothes were sticking to her. When she sat up and squirmed around, trying to get more comfortable, she unbalanced the load, and the bearers shouted, and one of them thumped the side of the chair in protest. She pulled the back of her dress away from her skin, feeling cooked lightly in her own juices.

"There." Shimon stuck his face in the side of the curtain. "There he is. Are you ready?"

Her hands flew to her hair; suddenly she yearned for a looking glass. "I am ready." Her heart raced. Quickly she felt under her cloak for the purse. She sat upright to keep from creasing her dress. The scent. She had forgotten it; she fumbled in her cloak and found the little vial of essence. She always wore this scent when she was with John Cerulis and the fragrance might be the perfect detail necessary to convince Targa.

Not foolish, Targa, as Shimon said. She wondered how much he would have given her to know what she knew, that John Cerulis was aware that Targa, his chief spy in Baghdad, took the money and orders also of the Caliph. She daubed the scent on her wrists and the insides of her elbows and over her throat.

"Targa!"

That was Shimon, outside, shouting. She sat rigid in the cushions, her backside numb and aching from the hard floor, while the unseen bearers took her into the middle of a great dusty thumping and tramping of hoofs: Targa's party. Putting her hand on the curtain, she pulled it back.

"Aha." Directly before her, the Persian spy sat on a black horse. Seeing her, he split his beard with a white grin, and swept his arm down in an ebullient bow. "The glory of Christendom has come to attend me. I am blessed above all men."

"Targa," she said, and leaned on her elbow, reclining a little, showing him the opulent curves of her body. "John Cerulis has sent me here with urgent news for you. The Basileus has ordered out the Imperial Guard to watch for you on the road and to seize your person and all your goods and men when you reach Chrysopolis." With a flourish she produced the forged letter and held it out to him.

Targa reached for it. The exuberant good humor that usually ruled his face was draining away; now he looked angry, his eyes sharp, and his cheeks sucked in. He glanced at the letter. "What is this?"

"The Patrician has sent me to warn you, and to exchange this—" She turned, fumbling around in her cloak for the money, and held out the purse to him. "For the list you are bringing to him."

"He sent you? Why you?"

"Targa," she said, "who better? Who would suspect me? Now, swiftly, give me the list, take your well-earned reward, and get you gone again to Baghdad, before the troops of the Basileus descend upon us."

His eyebrows worked up and down. Behind him, his train clogged the dusty road, donkeys packed with goods, five or six drovers on horses. He made no move toward the heavy purse she was proffering. "Really. Is the matter so urgent? Often have I dreamed, Theophano, of a moment's dalliance with the loveliest of all the lovely women of Constantinople."

"Targa," she said, exasperated, "only a man would think of sex under these conditions. The list."

He grunted. "Would that I understood the attractions of such as John Cerulis for such as you." Gracelessly he took away the purse and from a bag on his horse's saddle removed a piece of paper.

"Now," he said. "Here it is." He waggled it at her, and his irrepressible smile was back, dividing his curly black beard with the stained white of his teeth. "One final payment, perhaps—a kiss from those ruby lips?"

"Hold!"

She jumped, startled, at the shout behind her. It was Shimon, now mounted on his mule, twisting to look behind him. He wheeled around again. His eyes were wild, his mouth open round and wide.

"Fly! Fly! Here they come—"

Targa jerked his head up. Shimon's mule reared up, spinning on its hind feet. Theophano stood in the chair, leaning out the side, and looked down the road.

In three orderly lines, fletched with rows of upright lances, a troop of soldiers was galloping down on them. Now the other men saw them, and Shimon, his mule under control, was gathering his own.

"Run—into the hills! Run—"

Targa said, "Those are John Cerulis's men. Why are you afraid of them?"

"They are after you," Theophano shouted. She snatched the list from his fingers. "He knows you betrayed him to the Caliph. Hurry—escape!"

He blinked at her, his face fierce with suspicion. "Then why are you—"

Her bearers were taking her swiftly away down the road. She shouted, "Run!" Ducking back into the chair, she yanked the curtains closed again.

She could hear her bearers panting; the chair bounced and jiggled so that she had to hold on with one hand to the frame. "Stop," she screamed. "Stop!"

They stopped. She slipped under the closed edge of the curtain and dropped into the road. Shimon on his mule lunged up before her.

"Here." He put his hand down toward her, to pull her up behind him, but she leapt back.

"No—I have the list—you go! Take the chair, as if I am still inside—Lead them off!" She darted off the road, down into the ditch.

Shimon straightened up. His men were packed close around him, wild-eyed; they turned to look down the road, where the troop of soldiers was now hidden behind a curve of the hillside, and some of them yelled in fear and pushed on up the road after Targa and his donkeys and his men, who were now swiftly disappearing in the other direction. Shimon bellowed an order, and they moved off in a body after Targa, the chair jouncing and fluttering in their midst.

Theophano crouched down in the ditch, looking around her. There was nothing here to hide behind, and she stuffed the list into the bosom of her dress and scrambled up the steep bank on the opposite side from the road and ran through the brush toward a ravine a hundred yards away.

In the shelter of the yellow bank, she sank down as small as she could, her arms around her knees. Targa and Shimon and their men were hurrying away up the road in a disorderly mass. The chair, curtain closed, fluttered along in their midst, a gaudy fragile ship upon a stormy sea. She licked her lips. Somehow she had to get back to Constantinople, on foot, by herself, without being caught.

A low rumble reached her ears, and she shrank down against the crumbling alkaline earth. Around the curve swept the troop of horsemen at full gallop, thundering up the road.

Shimon and Targa and their men were still in sight, and seeing them, the ranks of soldiers yelled and spurred on, swinging down their lances to the level. A scream of despair went up from their victims. Theophano caught her breath. She knew Shimon and his eight men were armed only with belt knives; Targa, being a merchant, would carry little more than that. They were struggling away up the road but the horsemen were on them now.

The soldiers never faltered. They slammed into the disorderly little mass and trampled over them. The chair went down like a sinking ship in the midst of the bodies. Theophano jammed her fist against her teeth, her heart hammering. She saw them dying and thought not of them but of their mothers, of their women, who would mourn them. The horsemen trampled right over the chair; their horses crowded around it, and she saw their lances jab and jab down through the filthy cotton curtains. Now they would know she was not there. Turning, she ran up the ravine.

"She's not here."

Karros leaned out from his saddle, peering into the debris of the chair. "What do you mean? Where else can she be?" The scraps of wood and cloth and cushions that littered the road gave him no clues. He straightened up, yanking his horse's head around.

His butt hurt. He was a city-soldier, Karros, and riding on horses in the countryside did not amuse him. He kicked his mount forward, around the mess in the road, past the crumpled bodies of those of Targa's men foolish enough to have resisted, over to the tight-packed crowd of prisoners.

Targa saw him coming and pushed forward, his arms tied behind him, his face dark with anger.

"Karros! What in the hell are you doing?"

"Out of my way, traitor." Karros kicked him in the face as he rode by.

The other prisoners faced him in a mass, their faces sullen and fearful. Karros looked among them and saw only male faces. How could she have gotten away? He twisted in his saddle again, looking all around him, first through the crowd on the road, his men and his prisoners, and then, slowly, methodically, scanning the bleak hillsides around them.

She had been here. She had been here when he and his troop set on them. Why else would they have brought a chair? He wheeled around again, back toward Targa.

The Arab merchant was lying on the road, his face split down the middle by the kick Karros had fetched him; he rolled over, groaning, and the blood dappled the soft dust under him. Karros crooked his finger at one of his men.

"Strip him. And find his horse. Turn out his wallet, everything."

While his men did this he rode around the tight clump of prisoners, searching through them with his eyes. If they found the list here, then Theophano's escape meant nothing, a minor annoyance. But if the list were missing—

On the road now Targa squirmed naked, and the soldiers were laying out the contents of his clothing on the ground. Karros dismounted to pick through it; there were the usual incidentals a man might carry with him—a brass key, a hoofpick, some loose coins, and at the end of the line, a purse.

A purse heavy with money, and sealed with a familiar seal. Karros loosened the strings and spilled out a few coins and found them newly minted irenes, their edges still sharp. He swore.

"Where in the hell is she?"

The soldiers were tearing apart the packs from Targa's horse. Karros bellowed to them to strip the other prisoners, to search their horses. Restlessly he walked up and down the road, his mind on the boil. It was hot and he hated riding, but if he came back without that list, his master John Cerulis would deal with him harshly. How had she escaped? She had to have the list—the money proved it, surely, that she had exchanged it for the list. His gaze traveled slowly over the bleak brown hillsides. She had to be out there somewhere.

He turned to his horse. "You, you, and you, come with me. The rest of you know what to do." Four men ought to be able to handle a single girl. In fact, he could imagine some very satisfying ways in which four men could handle a single girl. He waved to the others to keep on with their search, and with the three soldiers on his heels trotted away down the road, looking for some sign of where she had gone.

Theophano's clothes were ripped from the thorny brush and her feet hurt. She struggled on up the slope and over the top, panting at the effort.

From this high point, she could see down the road a good long way; she stopped, catching her breath, and straightened up to look around her. The road would take her off to Constantinople, if she followed it in this direction.

If she went back, within a few hours she could reach Chalcedon. In Chalcedon there would be food, water, wine, fresh clothes, and a way to make her plight known to the Basileus, who would then rescue her. Perhaps. But she dared not take that chance, not with the precious list now safe within the bosom of her dress, against her skin. She pressed her hand against it, glad. She had done what her Basileus had ordered. That lifted her heart like a jolt of strong wine.

She had to get back to Constantinople. She would lay the list into the Basileus's hands herself, or die in the attempt.

That gave her strength, and she started away down the slope again. Unfortunately the strength did not last very long. As she clambered downhill, the bleak, sunblasted slopes rose up around her as if they would swallow her entirely; the road disappeared; the flat, leathery-leafed brush tripped her and caught at her clothes and clogged her path. At the bottom of the hill she sat down, exhausted.

For a moment she was still, limp and empty of thoughts. The dust smelled bitter. Behind her something rustled in the brush, and she heard a twittering of birds.

She longed for Constantinople. For the comfort of her place in the Palace, her silken sheets and her bed, clean clothes. To bathe; to drink cool wine. Something good to eat. She imagined a baked fish on a bed of spinach and eggs. Her mouth watered.

Why had she ever come out here? Irresistibly tears drew into her eyes.

She cursed herself. She was a fool, a silly girl, as the Basileus often called her, and she deserved no pity. She had wanted this. A woman born of her rank was offered few choices in her life: she could become a nun and pray all her life, or she could marry and bear babies, immured as surely as a nun in the women's quarters of her husband's house. She could wait upon the Empress. That was Theophano's choice, and she had seen that as the opportunity to do other things as well, to serve the Basileus, to do deeds of great import. She had asked for this.

Do it, then, she told herself. Do it, and do not cry, and do not yield. What can happen to you, after all? You will be uncomfortable for a while, but in the end, if you persevere, you will be home again, your task fulfilled. Do it.

She got up, squared her shoulders, and faced the countryside. That way was Constantinople. All she had to do was keep walking.

Yet as she looked on the barren hills her heart sank again, and she felt again the shameful burning of her tears. Her hand rose to her breast. Even the soft crumple of the paper there could not spur her forward. She could not go on.

She started down again, to sit some more, and weep. But as she sank down her eyes detected a sort of smoke climbing into the sky, from beyond the hill she had just descended. It was a plume of dust. They were chasing her.

She sprang up. She knew who it was who chased her: the wretched Karros, surely, John Cerulis's bully boy. If Karros caught her, she would suffer a good deal of indignity. Lifting her skirts up out of the brush, she raced away toward the next slope, toward the road and Constantinople and safety.

2

"God, I hate churches," Hagen said. "When we get home again, I'm never going inside another church. I've earned so much absolution, anyway, these two years, that when we get home, I'll sin for free the rest of my life."

"Be quiet," Rogerius said.

They had left their horses in a grove of trees at the gate, and now, approaching the little stone church, they unbuckled their sword belts and laid their weapons down on the uncovered porch at the door. Hagen went first into the church. He pushed back the hood of his cloak; inside the church, the jingle of his pilgrim's bells sounded noisy and irreverent.

The church was very small, six steps from door to altar. Fresh whitewash covered the walls and the dome. Disappointed, he saw that there were none of the magnificent pictures here that he had gotten used to finding in such places in the Holy Land. On the curved wall behind the altar was a plain cross of wood. With his brother beside him, Hagen knelt down to pray.

Rogerius crossed himself, pressed his palms together, lowered his head, closed his eyes, and gave himself up to devotions. Hagen shifted his weight from knee to knee, already restless. It was part of their penance that they could not pass by any church on their road without stopping to pray, and he was heartily sick of it. It irritated him that his brother, who had done the deeds for which they were now repenting with as much initial enthusiasm as Hagen, had become so passionately godly as a result. In as few words as possible Hagen asked for God's protection on their journey—they were still half the world away from home—and began to look curiously around him.

This church was little different from dozens of others they had seen in the twenty months they had been on pilgrimage. The ceiling was domed, and two little windows cut the side walls. A few stubs of candles were stuck onto the altar rail a few feet from him. This close to Constantinople, many palmers probably came by this way, going to and from Jerusalem. He wished there were some pictures to look at. His knees already hurt.

Then the door behind them opened and a single figure hurried into the church, and Hagen glanced keenly around.

He did not want either his horse or his sword stolen while he was reconciling himself to Heaven. But the hooded figure kneeling down at the altar was a woman.

A pretty woman. She tipped up her face toward the cross; her skin was smooth and pale, her cheeks brushed with color that had not come from God; her black hair swept back under her hood from a deep peak above her brow. She crossed herself in the Greek fashion and, turning, cast a look back over her shoulder at the door.

As she did so, she saw Hagen staring at her, and swiftly she lowered her eyes, and the color on her cheeks took on more the hue of nature. But she did not pray. Instead, crouched forward, she twisted to look behind her again, back toward the way she had come in.

Hagen looked where she was looking, and Rogerius nudged him hard in the side with his elbow. "This is a church," his brother said. "Pray."

Hagen ignored him. The door stood halfway open, and through the gap he could see several men on the porch and hear their muttered voices. He shifted his attention to the girl again; she was biting her lip, staring straight ahead of her, her hands tightly gripped together, and once again, while he watched, she threw a look of fear behind her at the door.

"What are you doing?" Rogerius asked.

With a nod of his head, Hagen indicated the girl; he got up and walked back through the church to the door.

He was a tall man, Hagen, even for a Frank, and when he went out the door, the several men standing there on the porch backed up quickly to let him through. They were Greeks, by their beards and leather armor. There were four of them. Hagen kept his eyes on them, reaching behind him for his sword belt on the porch, and standing there to buckle it on. The weight of his sword made him smile. He put his hands on his hips and smiling faced the four Greeks, who edged together into a tighter pack and pretended not to notice him.

"Here to talk to the Lord?" he said; he had learned a lot of Greek, in the course of the pilgrimage.

The four men shuffled their feet. One of them, a fat man who wore rosettes of red-dyed leather on his shoulders, turned his head and without meeting Hagen's eyes said, "On your way, barbarian."

"Oh, no," Hagan said. "You go on yours."

The Greeks moved, their feet crunching on the stone porch and the single step, their leather armor creaking. The man with the red rosettes turned to one of his fellows and said, "Go in and get her."

That man started toward the door. Hagen took a step after him, and the other Greeks swung to face the big Frank, and the door flew wide open and Rogerius stood there.

Shorter than Hagen, stockier, he filled up the doorway, and seeing his brother involved in this dispute, he put his shoulder to the door frame and looked the Greeks before him up and down.

"What's this?"

Hagen reached behind him for his brother's sword, the belt wrapped around the scabbard, and held it out to him. "These city people are after that girl in there." He spoke Frankish.

"Oh," Rogerius said, and glanced over his shoulder into the church. He slung the heavy brass-studded belt around his waist. "Well, that's too bad."

"Look," said the man with the red rosettes on his shoulders. "You two don't know what you are doing. Don't get yourselves into trouble here. That woman is no concern of yours."

"Walk," Hagen said, and put his hand to the hilt of his sword.

"I'm warning you—"

"I'm warning you, fellow. I've been all the way to Golgotha and I have a lot of currency with God, and I don't mind spending a little of it to rid the world of a few of you backwards-signing Greeks."

Rogerius was looking at him, his forehead creased; he did not speak the language as well as Hagen. Behind him, suddenly, the girl appeared.

The Greeks saw her just as Hagen did, and as one man they lunged toward her. She was behind Rogerius, and when the Greeks jumped toward him, he stepped sideways, blocking their way. His sword leapt out of its scabbard with a clash of iron. Hagen swung around, putting the four Greeks between him and his brother. He whipped his long sword free, and as ever when he felt its power in his hands a heady passion filled him and he roared with exultation.

The Greeks scattered, two to the left, two to the right. The man with the red rosettes cried, "Away! Stand off—" None of them drew a weapon. Still backing away from the two Franks, they circled off the porch and banded together again in the churchyard.

"We'll get her later," the fat man with the red rosettes said to the others, and herded them swiftly away. Looking back over his shoulder, he shouted, "And you, too, barbarians! Don't think you've gotten away with anything."

Rogerius laughed. "What cowards." His sword slithered back into its scabbard.

Hagen watched the Greeks, who were leaving the churchyard; there were several horses tied to the trees a hundred yards away, in the opposite direction from the two Franks' horses, and the Greeks mounted up and rode off at a brisk trot. Slowly Hagen put his sword up. He disliked drawing it without bloodying it; he imagined the sword to go hungry. Turning, he looked beyond his brother at the girl.

She was gone. "God's bones," he said, and pushed past Rogerius into the church.

At the side of the church, the girl was struggling to climb out the narrow window. Her cloak hindered her and she flung it down, and Hagen bounded across the church and caught her around the waist.

"Let me go!" She twisted violently in his grasp and tried to hit him. He held her arms down against her sides; she was light as a child, and he held her without effort. She smelled wonderfully of roses. Rogerius picked up her cloak from the floor.

"What is happening here? Hagen, put her down. She won't go anywhere."

"You think so?"

"Put her down," Rogerius said.

Reluctantly Hagen lowered the girl down onto her feet, and Rogerius hung the cloak around her shoulders again. She looked from one to the other of them. In spite of the thick paint on her eyes and lips and cheeks, she was very pretty, and rich, too, by the weight of metal in her ears and around her neck. Her clothes were torn and filthy but her skin was white as cream, and her hair black as ebony.

She said, "I suppose I should thank you for saving my life."

"I suppose you might want to," Hagen said. "Were they trying to kill you? Why?"

"I don't know," she said.

"You're lying," Hagen said.

Swiftly he translated what she had said into Frankish, and Rogerius shook his head, exasperated. "She's lying."

"See? He agrees with me," Hagen told the girl, "and he's nowise as clever as I am. Come along with us. A church is no place to talk about things like this, and we are armed men now."

The girl looked from him to his brother, and under her silk bodice her breast rose and fell in a deep noisy sigh. She walked toward the door with an air of being taken prisoner, and the two Franks followed her out.

They crossed the open yard toward their horses. The girl looked keenly down the road in both directions, obviously searching for the four Greek soldiers; she held her cloak tight over her breast with both little fists. Hagen wondered how she had come here. Her thin embroidered shoes, battered now, were worthless for walking. Probably the four Greeks had made off with her mount.

He said, "My name is Hagen, and this is my brother Rogerius. Our father was Reynard the Black. We are from the Braasefeldt, in Frankland, and we have been on pilgrimage to the Holy Sepulcher."

"Tell her we mean her no harm," Rogerius said, "and that God must have sent us to help her, because clearly those other people did mean her harm, and so she should be forthcoming with us."

Hagen repeated this in Greek. The girl listened with no warmth in her expression, but when he was done, she put up her hand and brushed back a stray tress of her hair from her forehead and nodded to them both.

"Very well. I owe you my life—perhaps a good deal more than my life. My name is Theophano. I am a handmaiden of the Basileus Autocrator, whom God protects."

Hagen looked at his brother. "She says she's a servant of the Empress."

"Well, she's rich enough, look at the jewels around her neck."

Hagen had already assessed her jewelry; he had killed people, during his bad days, for less than she was wearing, although of course he killed no women. He said, "What are you doing out here by yourself, Theophano? Why were those men after you?"

"I can't tell you," said Theophano. "But I will pay you to take me to Constantinople. I'll pay you splendidly."

"We are going to Constantinople anyway," Hagen said.

"I'll pay you," she said again.

Rogerius swung up into his saddle. Hagen said, "You would pay us best by telling us why you are in trouble." His hands on her waist, he lifted her up behind his brother.

"You must believe me. I have done nothing wrong. Those men are enemies of the Basileus, whom God protects."

Rogerius was looking impatiently at Hagen, and obedient to the look on his face Hagen told him what the girl was saying. Turning to his own horse, he stepped up into the saddle and gathered his reins, and side by side they started along the road.

"Don't harass her," Rogerius said. "She's been through enough difficulties, can't you see that?"

The girl sat behind him, her arms around his waist, her breast against his back. Hagen saw that his brother's sympathies were engaged—Rogerius was quick to defend small, weak creatures. Hagen licked his smile maliciously wide.

"Do you want me to carry her?"

"No, no," Rogerius said.

"Then you could look at her all you will. As it is, only I can see her."

"I will carry her," Rogerius said firmly.

"She's very pretty. Much prettier than the one in Bethlehem."

"What do you think her trouble is?"

"Us, now."

"Do you think she's really one of the Empress's women?"

Hagen shrugged. They had come through Constantinople on their way into the Holy Land, and he had learned there of the Empress Irene, who ruled in the Greek lands, alone, with no husband, although she kept the man's title of Basileus Autocrator. She had the reputation of being a she-wolf. She had taken the throne by force from her own son, whose eyes had been put out.

He turned to Theophano again. "Whose men were those who were after you?"

She looked gravely at him, her arms around his brother's waist, her wide blue eyes candid as a baby's. "I cannot tell you. Please, trust me."

"We saved you, didn't we? Now the master of those men will bear us a grudge. We have to protect ourselves."

"Such heroes as you must have no fear of anything," she said.

Hagen put back his head and laughed a loud laugh. He told Rogerius what she had said, and Rogerius smiled wide and glanced over his shoulder at her, chuckling.

"Why are you laughing at me?" she asked, her pride clearly touched.

"Heroes we are not, my lady," said Hagen. "We came on this pilgrimage because otherwise we would have been hanged, in Frankland."

Her eyes grew wider. She shrank back away from Rogerius. "But you are men of gentle birth."

"Our blood is as noble as any family's in Christendom—the King is our kinsman. That was why we had the choice between hanging and pilgrimage."

"Then you have chosen wisely. God will save you. God will help you cleanse your souls."

Hagen shrugged; he was keeping watch around them, as they travelled, for the four Greeks. He decided he liked her. In spite of the paint and the lies and her being Greek to begin with, he saw something honest and solid in her. He told Rogerius the trend of their conversation and his brother looked over his shoulder at her with a protecting and tender expression that made Hagen snort.

"You are probably right, about Rogerius," he said to the girl. "Since we saw the places where Christ walked and died, he has been steadily becoming more and more holy. It's getting hard for me to keep company with him."

"He speaks no Greek?" She peered at Rogerius over his shoulder.

"Very little."

"Yet he has a kindly face."

Rogerius looked down over his shoulder at her again, and she smiled at him.

Hagen turned forward again. Rogerius's new saintliness had not extended to a life of chastity. He had always done well with women; he would do well with this one too. Shut out of their company, Hagen cleared his throat, reproved himself for envy, and pointed up ahead of them, where the road wound over the barren hillside.

"That looks like a good place for an ambush. I'll go make sure her friends aren't waiting for us." With a nudge of his heels, he lifted his horse into a gallop down the road, toward the curve in the distance, where great stones crowded up against the way.

The barbarian knight's cloak was of some coarse stuff that smelled of horses, but his face was noble, almost gentle, although of course not Greek. Theophano trusted him. She liked him better than his brother, perhaps because of his brother's insistence on asking questions. And she remembered how Hagen had caught her and held her against her will.

Now Hagen was going on ahead of them. Theophano slipped her hand inside her cloak, down under the silk of her tunic, and fingered out the list of names.

If John Cerulis's men came back in force, two knights would not stop them, even these two, with their great swords and their air of joy in fighting. She would have to give herself up to save lives. What was important was the list. If Cerulis's men found it, many more would die than Theophano. She leaned forward toward this knight who spoke little Greek and therefore certainly did not read Greek and held out the paper to him.

"Please," she said. "Hide this."

His brother had said he was of a holy bent. She had to trust him; she did trust him. He looked down at her, unsmiling, and took the paper.

"Hide it." She pronounced the words slowly and exactly, nodding to him, and he understood. He understood better than she had hoped; he looked ahead of them toward his brother, now only a speck on the road between the great grey high-piled boulders, and without even unfolding the paper to look at it, he slipped it away inside his tunic.

Theophano sighed, relaxing. She smiled at him, and with the worry eased from her mind she saw that he was a handsome man, in his way, rough and without graces, but full of vigor. His body was pleasantly large and solid under the rough cloak. She leaned her cheek against his back, her arms around his waist.

"Theophano," he said, caressing her name with his voice, and his hand clasped hers above his belt buckle. She smiled, her face against his back. Love knew all languages. The brother was coming back. She moved her fingers against her new friend's palm, a little promise in the touch.

She had heard that the hair of the western barbarians was blond, and Rogerius's hair was the gold of wheat, Hagen's almost white. As they rode on, they talked back and forth. She learned that they had been on pilgrimage for the better part of two years, going to the holy shrines of Syria and Palestine, and rather timidly she asked what sins they had committed to require so great a penance. That got from Hagen another roaring laugh, but no answer. She remembered the yell with which he had drawn his sword, and shivered. Men like this were best avoided, used only when necessary, paid promptly, dismissed at once. She would have to get rid of them, once she was safe in Constantinople, before they could embarrass her before the Basileus.

As soon as the thought formed, she was ashamed. They had saved her from the despicable Karros—more important than herself, they had saved her mission, however inadvertently. She should not be thinking of getting rid of them, but of rewarding them somehow, for their service to her and to the Basileus.

The road wound down the hillside before them, switching back and forth across the steep slope; the brother on his bay horse was far ahead now, galloping easily along before a plume of dust. She pressed her cheek against the harsh cloak of the man before her. That same rude power and lack of refinement that would have made them into fools at court would save her again if Karros tried to seize her from them. She saw the deeper lesson in that. God measured the value of men; she accepted what God sent to her, gladly and without judgment.

The knight before her murmured something to her. His hand pressed warm over hers. She smiled against his back. God would not mind if she gave this handsome and courageous knight the only reward she had to bestow. He spoke little Greek, but that was no hindrance, once they got past talking. She tightened her arms around his waist, pressing her cheek to the warmth of his back.

"Theophono," he said, crooning out the syllables. She smiled and shut her eyes, feeling very safe, at least for a while.

They stopped for the night at an inn beside the dark sea. The wind out of the west was blowing a storm down on them, and the waves were breaking on the rocks of the shore with a crash and hiss like a great boiling cauldron. The inn stood outside the little white town of Chrysopolis, where the ferry took on passengers for Constantinople, across the narrows that separated Asia from Europe.

Besides the common room, there were several smaller rooms on the second floor, which the innkeeper let out to overnight guests, and this night there were few travellers. Hagen and his brother and the girl Theophano hired a room all to themselves.

It would have mattered little to Rogerius and Theophano if they had been surrounded by strangers. They saw only each other. Somehow over the afternoon's ride their wordless companionship had ripened to a precipitous lust. From the moment he lifted her down from his horse, Rogerius touched her, his arm protectively around her shoulders, his head inclined toward her. Hand in hand, the two stood smiling like idiots while Hagen paid for their room, and, in the room, they leaned together, their gazes locked, almost breathless, until Hagen said something only half-worded and went out and left them alone.

It made him angry. He liked women; he loved his brother; but he had been riding all day long and wanted to get his weight off his feet and rest. Now he had to wander off through the inn looking for something to do, while his brother and this Greek slut bounced the bed around. In a sour mood, he went down to the common room and bought a jug of wine.

The common room was filling up with people—travellers and local folk—drinking, calling for food and for their friends. Alone, lonely, Hagen took the jug and went out behind the inn, off through the sharp-smelling pine trees, down through rocks and beds of fallen needles to the shore.

The wind was blasting in over the water. The sun was going down. Out across the black water, whitecaps danced and leapt as thick as stars in the sky of a clear night. Hagen sat down on a rock and pulled out the cork from his wine and took a long full drink of the wine.

Tomorrow they would take the ferry to Constantinople. That meant they were halfway home, because from Constantinople they could take a boat to Italy, and Italy was in the hands of the Franks. By Christmas they would be back at the Braasefeldt.

He drank more of the wine, remembering the great hall that his grandfather had built, with the skulls of bear and deer nailed to the rafters, the hearth of massive stones, the smell of meat roasting. The sound of Frankish voices. To hear his own tongue again! To taste beer again, real beer and not the thin insipid stuff these Easterners brewed. To eat the bread of home again—

He had plans, for when he reached home again. In alien lands, among strangers night after night, he had talked to Rogerius about Braasefeldt. They would build dikes all along the river, raise a mill, drain the marshes for farmland. No more robbery, no more feuds, no more going around looking for trouble and looking out for it, too, hands ever at their sword hilts, drawing at shadows. If he had not learned to pray as well as Rogerius, he had at least learned not to sin.

The wine tasted bitter but it relaxed him. It fed his lonely melancholy. Looking back, he saw now that he had wasted his youth in drunken brawls and getting revenge on his enemies. Avenging his father's murder had been necessary, although Reynard had been so bad a man it was inevitable that somebody would slay him; but most of the other feuds and quarrels Hagen had pursued with such single-minded devotion had been only excuses for frivolous crimes. Now he was ready for a quiet, honest life, ordering his serfs, protecting his borders, fighting the wars of his king. Marrying. Raising a brood of little boys with white hair and hot tempers, and little girls, too, to marry off into other families, to make alliances against his enemies. He was tired of being an outlaw. He wanted respect, connections, and honor.

The sun was gone. The light was bleeding from the sky. Already the sea was dark as the waters of Hell. He got up and walked unsteadily along the rocky shore, kicking stones into the water. The waves surged up and broke over the teeth of the rocks and spread their sloppy suds out and drew back, rattling and banging the cobbles of the beach. There in the west, pure and bright, the evening star shone like a drop of heavenly fire. The jug was empty. Turning his back to the wind, he trudged onward toward the inn.

He went in through the back of the yard, where cats fought over a mountain of garbage, and circling upwind of the stench, he headed for the side door into the inn. Halfway there, he stopped dead in his tracks. Off in the front of the inn, barely in sight around the corner, stood a man in leather armor, holding the reins of a group of horses.

Hagen recognized him at once: it was one of the Greeks from the little stone church. He broke into a run toward the front of the inn. His room was on the far side, in the second story. Just as he reached the corner of the inn, the other three Greeks from the church burst running out the front door.

The leader, the fat man with the red rosettes on his shoulders, saw Hagen and yelled. He leapt up into his saddle, whipped his reins out of his friend's hands, and charged straight at Hagen. The two men behind him were slower; one was dragging his leg.

The horse bolted down on Hagen, who dodged to one side, coming up against the wall of the inn. Wrenching his mount's head around, the Greek with the rosettes spurred it at a gallop toward the gate, and without waiting around for his men fled away down the road. The others were scrambling into their saddles and turning to follow. Hagen ran into the inn.

The common room was packed with people. He had to fight

through the press of bodies to the stairs. There, the crowd eased; he went up the stairs two steps at a time and raced down the narrow corridor. The door to his room stood halfway open. Hagen shouted his brother's name and rushed into the room.

The bed was all pulled apart, the covers strewn halfway across the room, and the window shutters were thrown wide open. The only occupant was Rogerius, who lay naked in the middle of the room on his back, a great puddle of blood spreading across the floor. Hagen knelt down by his brother and lifted him, and from the first touch he knew that Rogerius was dead.

Still, he lifted him up carefully, to keep from hurting him, and held him in his arms, his mind stuck, waiting for his brother to come alive again.

A shadow across the door brought his attention that way. The innkeeper, spitting out an oath, strode into the room.

"Who did this? Who are you people?"

Hagen was struggling with himself; he loved his brother more than any other creature alive. Slowly he got himself to carry Rogerius across the room to the bed and lay him down there. A great wound in Rogerius's chest smeared blood all over Hagen's clothes, and there was a wound in the side of his neck also, a wound given from behind.

The innkeeper was pressing after him, shouting, "Who did this? Who did it?" With a sharp twist of his head Hagen faced him.

"Get out of here."

"This is my inn!"

"I don't care; get out of here before I kill you."

The innkeeper's jowls sagged. Slowly he backed up, away from Hagen, into the crowd of curious gawkers that now packed the doorway and the corridor outside. Whirling, the innkeeper drove them all out of the room again. The door shut.

Hagen took the patched and ragged sheet from the floor and laid it over his brother's body, and knelt down and said some prayers for Rogerius's soul, still fresh from life. He imagined the soul a white moth that fluttered up and up toward Heaven, burdened down by the weight of sin, and he sent his prayers to it like helping wings. Slowly, as he ran out of holy words, a red tide of rage drowned the white vision. He began to weep. Clutching his brother's hand, he cried and swore and thought about the four Greeks who had done this.

He thought about Theophano. She had not been with them when they ran out of the inn, and on the evidence, he guessed she had gone out the window.

He mastered himself; he opened the door, and finding the innkeeper outside in the hall he beckoned him into the room.

"What is this?" the innkeeper said. "I keep a decent establishment here. Things like this are very hard to explain to the authorities."

"You didn't see those soldiers come up here?"

"Of course I did! You can't miss four heavily armed men, tramping into your establishment and—"

"You didn't stop them?"

"I didn't know what they wanted! Obviously they serve someone important, with uniforms like that—"

"Did you recognize their uniforms?"

"I didn't see them for very long—they just walked in and made straight for this room. They must have spied on you, somehow—they came in right after you left, in fact."

Hagen was breathing heavily. He felt as if a great chunk of his body had been torn out. If he had not left—if he had been here when they came—he could not bring himself to look on his brother on the bed.

"The girl," he said. "The Greek girl who was with us when we got here. Where is she?"

"Now, listen to me, you're full of questions—"

"I want a graveyard. And a priest."

"I want some answers!"

Hagen's temper slipped and he cocked up his fist, ready to knock the innkeeper to the ground; the Greek backed away a few steps. His palms rose between them. "Now, listen, don't get yourself in more trouble."

The Frank lowered his hand. It did no good to strike at this man, anyway, who was innocent. Like a fluttering in his brain his brother's soul cried to him for revenge. He gathered himself, aware of being alone in a strange and treacherous place.

"I need a priest. A graveyard. I will dig the grave." He turned toward the bed where Rogerius lay, and gathering up his brother's scattered clothing began to make him ready for his burial.

There had been times in the past he had expected to do this for

Rogerius, other times when he had thought Rogerius would do this for him. Even so he was unready. He wished that he had died with his brother, rather than do this.

He touched the body's cooling flesh with hands that trembled. Memories overwhelmed him. As boys, two years apart in age, they had fought all the time; he remembered chasing his brother with an adze around the courtyard, remembered Rogerius, still in a long shirt, hitting him in the face with a rock. Gradually they became friends and set to fighting everyone else. Their mother had died in childbed when Rogerius was born; their father, merciless in all his other doings, doted on his sons and let them do as they would. After Reynard died, they came to depend on each other even more, and as Reynard had taught them, side by side they stood against the whole world, and asked for nothing more than a chance to win.

Now he was alone. He had never expected to be alone, even in the worst of times.

While he was pulling Rogerius's shirt on over his head, a folded piece of paper fell out of the sleeve. He opened up the paper and stared at the lines of ink marks on it. He could not read, but he recognized Greek letters. Theophano must have given this to Rogerius.

Theophano. She had brought this on him and his brother.

He steadied himself, feeling dangerously light and thin, as if he were stretched out around a great swollen boil of grief. He knew he would have to be careful. He was not afraid. He understood fighting; he had always taken a deal of comfort from the simple discipline of feud and counterfeud, blow struck for blow taken. But this was not his own country and these Greeks, he had marked before, were of a different order from Franks. He would avenge Rogerius, but he would have to walk like a cat to do it, keep watch like an owl in the night, and be ever mindful of his own ignorance, if he wanted to survive.

When his brother was dressed and laid out straight, his hair brushed, his hands folded on his breast, his eyes decently shut, Hagen knelt down again, but this time he did not pray to God. This time he spoke to his father, Reynard the Black.

He apologized for letting Rogerius be killed, since as the elder brother he had been responsible for him, and he swore, by an oath so old that the words were strange and his tongue went slowly over them, that he would pay the blood debt. He did not cross himself afterward. There were things best kept without Christ. Getting up, he went out to find shovel and pick and dig the grave in the dark.

In the morning, he buried his brother in a churchyard near the Sea of Marmora, among the dead of an alien people. This hurt him with an absurd sharp hurt, that Rogerius should lie until Doomsday with a crowd of Greeks, and for long moments he could not bear to walk away from the grave and leave his brother alone there.

At last he went away up the road through the dark pine trees, along the foot of the hill, and went to Chrysopolis. There he found the ferry boat and bought passage for himself and his horses over the straits to Constantinople.

With the wind so high, the crossing took the whole afternoon and most of the night. The darkness and fog hid the great city from view. At last, as the dawn spread its white veil across the sky, the sea quieted, and the mist began to rise.

Hagen stood in the bow of the great ungainly barge with his horses. The other passengers crowded on the deck around braziers of coals and shared their cloaks for warmth. The storm had subsided and the air was as still as water in a jar. Hagen's face was clammy from the dawn mist, his fingers numb on the bridles of the two horses.

At first, in the feeble early light, the great towering promontory on which the city of Constantinople stood was only a vague sensation of mass to his left. The billowing flame of the lighthouse on the very tip of the cliff faded like the stars into the pallor of the day. The barge on its groaning sweeps crept along the shore and slowly turned north, butting into the harbor.

They called this harbor the Golden Horn. A finger of water, it lay protected in the lee of the cliff, the narrow way into it made narrower yet by breakwaters and heaps of rock linked together by chains. When the barge finally turned inside this mouth, the men at the sweeps gave out a cheer and crossed themselves and thanked Christ for their deliverance.

It was a wonderful harbor. Hagen had marked that when he came through here on his way to Jerusalem. In the long, shallow inlet ahead of him, now beginning to glow with the first true daylight, ships lay by the hundred. He saw the fat-bellied bottoms of the Venetians side by side with the narrow wedge-prowed ships of eastern sailors, the tilted sails of dhows, red and orange and striped, and the swollen-waisted river-going longships of the north. Little harbor boats danced between them and the shore, unloading, reloading, carrying supplies back and forth. Hagen narrowed his eyes, looking among this city of ships for one he might take to Italy.

The sun was warming his face and hands. He straightened, his cold-stiffened muscles soaking up the heat of the day, like a tree that wakened from the grip of winter. Now his gaze turned to the city itself.

It shocked him. It had shocked him when he first saw it and he should have been ready this time, but even so his first clear look at it made him draw a deep breath, fascinated, his eyes caught, his mouth falling open.

The mist still hugged the shoreline and veiled the lower slope. From this indefinite lightless mass of grey rose up layer on layer of buildings, climbing the steep cliffside in ranks, up into the sun, until at the top of the cliff, in a blaze of sunlight, the white marble buildings of the Palace stood up against the blue vault of the sky, and the golden domes of the churches there glittered like holy flame. They seemed closer to Heaven than to the earth, those great white and gold buildings on the clifftop, as if they had been placed there by the hand of God, and from them the rest of the City seemed to depend like the broad and graceful sweep of a cloak. Along the spine of the promontory, leading back to the mainland, were more churches, domed in gold and silver; a row of white columns fletched the spaces between them. That was their central street, which the Greeks called the Mesê. Here and there among the rounds of the domes, sweet to the eye as the curve of a breast, a spire stuck up boldly into the blue of the sky, so that the horizon was a jagged march down the ridge toward the undistinguished hills below.

The rest of the City fell away in patches of garden and trees, masses of buildings one on top of the other, the streets plunging among them like goat tracks, or spreading wider and gentler into marketplaces on the flats, down to the crowded shoreline.

Even at the edge of the sea they had not stopped building. The whole long beach was cut with causeways and breakwaters of stone, forming little shelters for the boats, and out along these moles were more buildings, shacks and warehouses and even churches, lapped by the mild waves of the Golden Horn. Now, with the full day upon them, these walkways teemed. Men with handcarts hurried down to the water's edge, and rows of half-naked slaves carried bundles from the ships standing at the wharves back into the City. He saw covered cushioned chairs on rails, supported by brawny men, swaying along the harbor-side street, and now, for the first time, the sounds of the place reached them, the cries and yells, the songs of the workmen, the scream of the sea gulls, the tramp of feet and the patter of donkey's hoofs, blended into a featureless roar that—he knew, from his past experience here— would never cease, not even when night fell, like the life-sounds of the City itself.

The barge was nosing into its berth in the harbor. The other passengers, as one man, lifted themselves and their goods and their babies and rushed forward into the bow, crowding together, their voices raised in excitement. Hagen's horses laid their ears back and swung their broad haunches threateningly toward the crowd, and the other passengers shrank away, avoiding them. The barge rocked under their weight. The prow touched the wharf, padded with plumped sacks hanging in nets of rope from the pilings, and a cable hissed uncoiling through the air to the boatman waiting on the deck.

The crowd screamed and pressed forward. Hagen did not move; he had seen before what happened now, and knew there was no reason to try to get off. Scream and struggle as they might, none of the others left either; two shouting officials forced them all back on to the barge and came on board, carrying tablets of wax and sharpened reeds to write with, and made everybody form lines, and began to ask questions.

Hagen had already mastered this part of it. When the first of the two officials came quickly along the line, making a preliminary order in the swarm of people, Hagen gave him a bribe. At once they passed him through, ahead of all the others, let him off the barge with his horses, and took him to their chief, who had a room at the head of the dock.

"You are a barbarian?" this man asked, writing down the answers on a piece of paper.

Hagen had kept his papers from the last time. He pulled them out of his purse and laid them on the work-scarred table before the official.

"My king is Charles. My bishop is Adelhardt, and my overlord is the Count of Frisia. I am going home from a pilgrimage to the Holy Land, and my first purpose is to find a ship here to take me to Italy."

"You are alone?" the officer said, surprised. "Well, well. You speak fair Greek, for a barbarian. You have no goods you mean to sell here?"

"No," Hagen said brusquely. They had asked him and Rogerius that before, and it still insulted him.

"How much money are you carrying with you?"

Hagen had counted it on board the ferry. "I have eighteen bezants, about sixty dinars, and twenty-five silver pence." He spread it out on the counter and let the officer look for himself. Carefully the man wrote this all down. Hagen watched with distaste. It was beneath his birth to pay so much heed to money.

He said, "I have a message for someone at court. How would I go about delivering it?"

"You won't be able to do anything about that until the day after tomorrow," said the Greek. "Tomorrow is a race for the Golden Belt. Every soul in Constantinople will be in the Hippodrome. Name?"

Hagen told him his name, and the Greek made reference to a tattered list on the wall. "What horse-races?" Hagen asked.

"In the Hippodrome. You should go, if you can still get in—no visit to Rome complete without the games."

"Why do you people insist on calling this place Rome? I've been to Rome, it's on the far side of the world."

"It's not a matter for the barbarian mind. I am giving you twenty days." The officer wrote on a piece of paper and heated wax over a candle and put a seal on the corner. "If you haven't found a ship by then, come back and I'll see about giving you another twenty. No buying or selling of goods without licenses, please." The Greek held out the sealed paper. "Good day."

"Good day." Hagen took the paper, which they would expect to have back when he left, and went out.

: 3 :

The city Byzantian, which Constantine the Great had called New Rome, and which everybody else called Constantinople, had mothered forty generations of men. The towering wedge-shaped cliff above the Bosporos commanded the sea route between the steppes of Asia, source of gold and silk, jewels and spices, and the Mediterranean; as well, it dominated the connections between the valley of the Danube and the highlands of Anatolia, from the dawn of time centers of metal-working and trade. Long before Byzas the Greek built a permanent settlement there, in the seventh century before Christ was born, the site of Constantinople had been a place of power.

Thus Byzantium was already old when the Emperor Constantine, his choice confirmed by oracles, walked around the site with a pack of architects and masons, and laid out his new capital. After years of civil war and rival claimants to the throne, he had at last reunited the great Empire of Augustus Caesar, which enclosed the entire Mediterranean world—which, as if to emphasize its utter dependence on the Middle Sea, stubbornly resisted all efforts to extend it east or north beyond that drainage: an empire taking name from the city of Rome, but no longer confined to the character of Rome, or to its traditions. It was to get away from those troublesome traditions, most annoying being the expectation of republican rule, that Constantine was removing the center of government east, to his new city, where with a free hand he could shape the Imperial destiny to his own notions.

The East offered positive help in this regard. In the East, the king was a god, whose will had the authority of godhead. No senate, no raucous mob, no irritating pre-existent body of law could defy him. In Constantinople, laying out his palace, his state buildings, his gardens and his places of worship, Constantine meant to make himself omnipotent.

To this purpose also he chose a new religion. After generations of ridicule and oppression, the Church of Christ would become the sole faith of the Empire. Everybody would worship one God, in one way, according to the word of the thirteenth apostle, the companion of Christ, the voice of God on earth, the Emperor in Constantinople.

In the terrible generations to follow, Constantine's foresight was vindicated. The western provinces of the Empire crumbled into decay and were overrun by Visigoth and Vandal, Hun and Lombard; Rome itself fell time and again until only the shell of her glory was left, but Constantinople endured. The barbarians sent armies against her so great they covered the plains like swarms of locusts, but they could not penetrate her defenses. Attila lived and died, and Alaric, whose sword weighed out the ransom of the weeping Romans, and lame Gaiseric, in whom Carthage at last had her revenge, and Theodoric the Ostrogoth, who wanted only to be Roman himself, and their trumpery ambitions died with them and turned to dust, while Constantinople endured and grew mighty. Even when disaster struck, as when the Emperor Valens died under the hoofs of the Visigoths' horses at Adrianople, the City was invincible.

She was an idea, the City, an idea like Justinian's, a perfect world order, a universal Christian empire; for a little while at least Justinian even recovered the old western provinces of Africa and Italy, and the Empire reached around the Middle Sea again. Then, because a eunuch took insult at a woman's slight, the Lombards took back most of Italy. And the Arabs came.

The desert bred them, as if the grains of sand turned into warriors, and the hot blast of the wind drove them in a wild irresistible whirl across Africa and up through the Holy Lands, where an unfortunate dispute over a subtle matter of doctrine made the people ready for a new master, who possessed a clearer statement of what God had in mind. The Empire shrank like a puddle in the sun. Africa was lost again, and Egypt and Syria, the Arabs coming on and on, driven by their simple credo and their seemingly limitless numbers; they reached the shore and built ships, took Cyprus and Sicily, and then one day there they were, before Constantinople itself, expecting to have it all.

Some said the Virgin walked on the walls of the City during that siege, and by her motherly smile and the touch of her hand gave heart to the defenders; others, more practical, attributed the success of the defense to the new weapon, Greek fire, blown through hollow tubes onto the Arab ships, which then blazed on the water like the hecatombs of old. The Arabs failed. Came back again, fools, not knowing the will of God when they saw it (although they mouthed great speeches about the will of God), and were beaten again, and again and again, and each time as the baffled minions of catastrophe withdrew, the Empire grew a little stronger.

There was no peace. There was a balance—the Arabs struck, the Empire struck back, and where their strengths were equal, a boundary appeared, but as ever, with one enemy subdued, another appeared. From the north came the Bulgars, a great grunting people without even a true king, pushing down into Thrace and Illyria and Greece. Then the Emperor made a terrible mistake.

The Emperor—Basileus, he was called, in Greek, the Latin tongue having ceased to serve the Empire around the time of Justinian—was equal to the apostles, but even Peter made mistakes; and in the face of the Arabs with their sublimely simple faith, the Emperor Leo the Isaurian was tempted irresistibly. He would simplify Christendom as well. He decreed that all idols and images of God and the saints were blasphemous and were to be destroyed.

Like a whirling maelstrom, the iconoclasm nearly pulled the whole Empire in after it. Perhaps there had been abuses of the images of saints —in the eastern provinces especially, where icons had often stood god-parents at christenings—but the people loved them, and cleaved to them. Within a few years of the decrees of the iconoclasm, Constantinople had lost most of Greece and all that was left to it of Italy, and the rebelling populations of the Empire were making government impossible.

Yet the Emperor would not relent. Nor did his son Constantine yield to reason, but closed up the monasteries that were the champions of the icons, and seized their wealth, and the icons were broken or covered over with whitewash, so that the Church of the Holy Wisdom itself looked like a poorhouse. The monks fought back with the fervor of those for whom death meant salvation, and the Arabs and the Bulgars took the opportunity so advanced to attack the Empire again, and it seemed that all would fall into chaos.

One among the Imperial court kept faith. One saw the true way. At eighteen years of age, the Athenian noblewoman Irene, named for the goddess of peace, was chosen from eighty others to marry the Emperor Leo IV. While her husband lived she could do nothing but wait and watch and suffer with the rest of right-thinking humanity. But in her thirtieth year Leo died, leaving their son Constantine a mere baby, and Irene became regent and took the government into her own hands.

She bought off the Arabs with a great tribute, and sent her generals into Macedonia to hold back the Bulgars, and she struck down the decrees of the iconoclasm, and all over the Empire people rejoiced. The women brought forth from their dower chests and cupboards the precious images they had been hiding; the whitewash was scrubbed off the walls and domes of the churches, and once again people could look up and see the face of God.

The boy Constantine, growing older, grew impatient as well, and would have ruled. He sent his mother away, and ruled very badly. Still Irene kept faith with those that mattered. She spoke soothing maternal words to her son, and he allowed her back from her exile, and she saw what ruin he worked and knew what must be done. With the help of monks and officers of the court, she convinced Constantine to divorce his wife and marry another woman, and when he did, she used the unpopularity of that marriage to dethrone him. His eyes were put out with hot irons, and Irene ascended the throne, not as regent, not as empress, but as Basileus Autocrator, Equal of the Apostles, Ruler of the World.

In the year 802 after the birth of Christ, Irene was fifty. Her magnificent blonde hair was thick and lustrous as ever; the brilliant grey-green eyes for which the Emperor's son had chosen her from among eighty of the most beautiful women in the Empire still made men dream and quote poetry and search the lexicons for adjectives that always seemed too tame. In the Palace of the Daphne, where Constantine the Great had tread, she walked with a sure step, and the diadem with its pendants of pearls fit her as well as it had Justinian and Heraclius.

Now she said, "What does this Pope of Rome? Does he presume to tell me what to think in matters of religion? Pagh." Opening her fingers, she let the letter drop from her hand onto the tufted Shiraz carpet.

"Basileus, Chosen of God," said the scribe, bowing so that his nose touched the floor.

Along the wall, gorgeous in their court clothes, stood a row of her officers, who whenever she glanced their way bent like blades of grass before the wind in elegant submission. Irene walked the length of the room, her step firm, and her head high. She had been sick all the night through, but she could master that. She mastered everything else, and she would master the crushing pain in her chest as well. It was gone now anyway, leaving only the memory, which was almost as bad.

"Tell him," she said, "that since he is so benighted that he would crown some barbarian as emperor of the West, he clearly has no insight into truth of any sort, not even in the most earthy and unpretentious matters, much less doctrines of the most high. Tell him to read the Credo of Constantine, and he will see there, most clearly, that the Son sitteth at the right hand of God, which means to any with sense that the

Son is subordinate to the Father, as it is even in the most primitive households."

They all murmured, in one voice, "Yes, Basileus, Chosen of God," and among them the Parakoimomenos, the Grand Domestic, lifted his hands and said in his sonorous voice, "Glory to God on the Highest! Glory to the Basileus whose mind is suffused with the glory of God!"

Irene stared at him a moment, her face expressionless. The office of the Parakoimomenos was reserved for eunuchs, the earthly angels; he was splendid to look upon, taller than any other, with a brow like a marble statue.

"With the letter to Rome send someone who is capable of good judgment in such matters. I would know more about this collusion between the Bishop of Rome and the Franks."

"Yes, Basileus, Chosen of God."

They dipped and swayed, their brocaded coats glittering. Irene paced back up the room.

"You may go."

One by one they came and knelt down and kissed the floor at her feet—Nicephoros was the last, her treasurer—and went out. As the door shut behind them, the chief lady-in-waiting got up from her chair in the corner and came forward.

"You must sit down."

"Helena," said the Empress, "I will see Theophano now."

"That stupid child," Helena said, between her teeth. "Sit down, I beg you, mistress, I beg you."

"Do I look ill?" Irene said swiftly.

"No, no—but—"

"Then send me Theophano."

Helena sighed. She had been in Irene's company for thirty years, since the day they sat together in the Hall of Chimes, with the other beauties of the bride-show, and waited for the Emperor's son to make his choice among them who should be his wife. Helena's black hair was striped with grey and her face was formed in the soft folds and wrinkles of age; looking into her face, Irene knew herself still young by contrast. The lady bowed and backed away, and at a nod from her head a page leapt to a little door in the back of the room and opened it.

Through it came Theophano. She had arrived at the Palace late the night before, considerably disheveled, but now she came forward suitably dressed to face her Basileus, her hair wound in sleek black coils on her head, her mouth painted to a delicious curve, her cheeks highlighted with Egyptian rouge. She knelt down at the feet of the Empress and pressed her forehead to the floor.

"Augustus, Protected One of God, I have failed you."

"So I am told," Irene said. Helena, who disliked Theophano, had brought her the whole sordid story, along with a potion, at three in the morning.

"I have no excuses," Theophano said, into the carpet. Probably she was crying; she had a lamentable tendency to excess emotion. "I am foolish and weak and I erred."

"You should never have involved barbarians in this, Theophano."

"Augustus, I had no choice—John Cerulis's men were about to take me prisoner, and I had the list. The Franks saved me and the list from them."

"Yes," Irene said, between her teeth. Helena was hovering nearby, solicitious as a nurse, and she waved her away. "But now you don't even have the list, do you."

"Augustus, have me put to death. I cannot bear the agony of failure."

"Where is the list?"

"I gave it to one of the knights for safe-keeping, and when John Cerulis's men burst in on us, I could not recover it. I had to run for my life. Oh, I should have died." Theophano moaned. "I have failed you. Oh, Augustus, have me blinded for my crimes, cast me out entirely—"

"Foolish you certainly are." The Empress went closer to the window. In the garden below, laid out in a series of concentric squares of roses and gravel paths, the exact center was a sundial. Several hours remained before she had to appear in the Hippodrome and declare the race for the Golden Belt. "But you meant well, and I forgive you, Theophano. You may rise."

Theophano stood up, her hands on her thighs. "Augustus, Beloved of God, your kindness is a blessing from Heaven. I swear to you, I shall be worthy of your generosity—"

"Yes, yes, my girl. You will always do your best." It would have been best if she had died with Shimon, especially since she had mishandled the list. If John Cerulis's soldiers had overcome the barbarians, they certainly had the list by now. She waved away Theophano, still brimming over with promises, and with a gesture dismissed her. The girl's voice ceased abruptly and she hurried out of the room.

Irene walked the length of the carpet. This was her personal library, long and narrow, lined with books. The silk curtains over the windows painted the sunlight as it streamed through the eastern side of the room and laid strips of transparent purple and yellow color over the heavy cream-colored carpet, a gift from the upstart ruler of Merv and Baghdad. In the end window, which the early sun as yet only grazed, hung a string of silver bells that chimed as the wind turned it. She stood listening to this random music, thinking of John Cerulis, who wanted her throne.

He would be there, in the Hippodrome, in the enclosed box his family had kept for generations. When she came out into the Imperial balcony, he would bow, and she would lift her hand, accepting his greeting, while in the background his people and her people killed one another.

His people did. Her people—possibly she should not have used Theophano, who was young and more passionate than wise. Of course that had been her credential, her willingness to supply passion in the right places.

Damn that list. Who had it now? She imagined the barbarians finding it, musing over it like apes with the tools of Archimedes, using it thereafter for an outhouse wiper, that precious piece of paper that had cost so much in blood and time and Irene's concentration.

She turned around, abrupt, decisive, putting that image out of her mind. It was time to do other things. With a clap of her hands, she summoned her pages out of the corners, ready for her commands.

⁙ 4 ⁙

Race day. He knew it as soon as he woke up, before he even opened his eyes.

He got out of bed, his body so charged with excitement that it seemed an effort to keep his feet solidly on the floor. His servant brought him his clothes. In silence Michael allowed himself to be dressed. His body felt like a cold case for the fiery life within. The servant who put clothes on the case and the other servants who brought in his breakfast and opened the windows and took away his chamber pot were only shadows at the periphery of the world.

In what he always thought of as his mundane life, he was a prince, with obligations at court. Dressed in his court clothes, he walked from his quarters in the Bucoleon Palace, an old rambling building at the very tip of the Imperial Rock, up the terraced slope to the Church of the Holy Wisdom, where with thousands of shadows round him he heard the Word of Christ and received communion. He prayed for the continuance of the Empire and good health and long life for his cousin the Basileus, but he asked for nothing for himself. He knew that he needed no help from Jesus Christ to win.

Outside the church, on the porch, his uncle Prince Constantine met him. They did not speak, but Constantine took Michael's hand and wrung it with a fierce grip and looked into his eyes and nodded, and Michael saw his excitement and managed to smile at him. Constantine was too old to race anymore, but once he had driven in the Hippodrome, although never with the success of his nephew Michael. He had won once or twice—one year he had taken two challenges for the Golden Belt. Now he lived through Michael, advising him, helping him with the horses, thrashing out strategies, keeping quiet when—rarely, but sometimes—Michael lost.

They went back down through the Palace grounds toward the lower entrance to the Hippodrome, but before they reached it, a page came from the Empress and ordered Michael into her presence.

He could not argue; all that did was waste more of the precious time she was already stealing so much of, so Michael went off immediately to the Daphne Palace, which was in any case hard by the Hippodrome wall.

His cousin was waiting in her morning chamber, surrounded by her women, who were preparing her for her appearance at the races. While they brushed her hair and smeared cream on her cheeks and put on bits of jewelry for her to examine in her mirror, Michael stood before her, listening with no attention to her long rambling discourse on the necessity of serving the Empire.

Michael had no interest in serving the Empire, and very little interest in his cousin Irene, and all the while she talked, he clenched his fists against the pressure to be gone that swelled unbearably in his veins and muscles. He could feel nothing but the longing to go to the Circus, to change these jeweled silks for his charioteer's leather coat and cap, to take the reins in his hands, to drive the four half-wild horses out on to the raked sand. To see beside him the other fiery teams, the white-ringed eyes of his rivals. To race. To win.

His cousin said, "Michael, you are not heeding me."

"Your pardon, most excellent and adored lady." Michael bowed.

She smiled at him. The women who tended her were piling up her thick fair hair in curls and tendrils above her forehead; a tall dark-haired older woman thrust a diamond comb into this mass to hold it all in place. Irene was fifty, but she was still the most beautiful woman Michael had ever seen. Her eyes were wonderfully green, their direct and artless expression making a lie of her Imperial detachment. She said, "Will you win today, darling?"

"Yes."

"What of Mauros-Ishmael?"

Michael pressed his lips together, considering what he might say to this, but his face revealed his thoughts adequately enough; the Empress laughed, cool and lilting, like a girl's laugh. She took a scarf from her sleeve.

"Wear this on your arm, darling—perhaps it will bring you the favor of the Divine Judge."

"Most mighty lady."

Taking the scarf, he went down on his knees before her, as ceremony demanded, and bowed his head to hide his face from her; he knew she did not give him this token from love or kindness. It was a signal to someone, part of the endless game of intrigue and deceit she played. Often she involved him in some way, as she did now, which he had to put up with, part of the annoyance of being a member of the Imperial family.

He left her. With six of his cousin's servants attending him, he walked away through the Daphne Palace to the two-story tower called the Kathismus, which housed the narrow stairway leading from the Empress's private quarters to the Imperial balcony of the Hippodrome.

At the entrance to the Kathismus, Irene's servants left him, and he climbed the stairs alone. The door at the top was open, and he walked forth into the Imperial box.

The silk curtains were still drawn, the great floating silk ceiling of the pavilion was in place, the full sun shining through, filling the balcony with violet light. He parted the curtains. There far below him the track lay, an ellipse of golden sand, split down the center by the narrow spina of brick. Along this center island, centuries of emperors had set up trophies to their glory; at the far end of the spina, red in the sun, was a sandstone needle someone had long ago pillaged out of Egypt, and closer stood another column of porphyry, and there almost directly opposite him a bronze column wrapped around with three serpents, tongued and fanged. Standing there, looking down the dizzying swoop of seats to the track, Michael thought, again, how deceiving it was to be emperor.

He climbed down through row on row of stone benches, down to the level of the track, and walked along the sand a little way, to the curve in the wall, where two doors of wood opened into the stables under the southwestern end of the enormous structure. The guardsman there saluted him as he passed.

"May God be with you, Prince—my money is."

The Hippodrome was built on the edge of the same bulging rock that lodged the whole Palace, but the hillside there being insufficient to support the whole length of the circus, the southwestern end had been built up with a huge curving wall of brick. Inside this wall were the stables for the racehorses, as well as, in another section, the Imperial menagerie.

From the doorway off the track a ramp led down into the dark cavernous smelly barns. Only a few lanterns lit the place, because of the threat of fire, and by each one stood a boy whose sole duty was to tend the flame and keep it where it belonged. The air, heated by a hundred bodies, was sharp with ammonia and sweet from the cooked grains of wet mashes. The horses were eating now, and from every stall came the steady champ-champ of their jaws, their snorting and sighing, the clunk of hoofs on the wooden walls, and the whispering swish of their tails.

Michael went through the first of the five corridors, into the broad open area where all five met, and where the equipment rooms were, and there turned into the third corridor, where his horses were kept.

The four animals he would drive today were eating the small measures of grain they were given on race mornings. They stood in their adjoining stalls, their heads deep in their feed buckets, and Michael could hear the sweep of their tongues on the wood, licking up the last grains of oats. He leaned over the door of Folly's stall and the big bay gelding darted its head at him, its teeth snapping an inch from his hand. The horse's sides already gleamed with a fine sheen of sweat.

"He knows," said the horse's groom, Esad, who came by Michael with a bucket of water. Setting the bucket down, he unlatched the stall door and swung it open, murmuring in a soft voice to his charge.

Michael went on; Folly was less liable to strike out when Esad was alone with him.

The next horse was the mare, Rayda, a Persian-bred, as mild as milk. Even she was excited today, and rubbed her head against Michael's arm. Her eyes glowed. He pulled on her long forelock, which her groom kept braided.

Beyond her in the next stall the black horse Demon was banging on the wooden wall and nickering; when Michael put out his hand to him, the black horse whirled around in his stall, half rearing. His mane rippled like a sea wave.

"Happy, old boy? This is your day, isn't it?" Michael patted the thick black neck.

In the last stall, the fourth horse of his team stood hipshot, his head drooping, asleep. Nothing ever excited the Caliph. Michael looked in to be sure the big grey gelding had eaten all his grain and backed away to leave the horse to his own ways of making ready for the race.

Down the row of stalls, Demon reared up, braying a war cry that rang away down the corridor, and drew a rush of stablemen. Michael walked off. The grooms could manage these petty excitements better without him. He still had to inspect his harness and his car, which superstitiously he did with his own hands before every race.

The cars were housed in a room at the front of the stable, in the wide, dirt-floored area where the corridors met, which the racing people all called the Apron. The stablemaster, having heard that he was come, waited at the door to open it for him, and while he struggled with the lock, Michael glanced around him, casual as a falling leaf, toward the Apron's far side.

Over there, in front of the second corridor, they were already drawing their car up and down the aisle. Four men pulled on the traces, while a fifth went along on hands and knees, packing grease around the axle turnings. Off to one side stood a man who stared frankly across the wide room at Michael.

When the Prince's gaze fell on him, this man smiled, a broad toothy grin, and waved at him.

Michael glared coldly back at his rival. Mauros-Ishmael acted sometimes as if this were all some great joke. Suddenly Michael wanted to crush the younger man, walk on that smile, and laugh at his agonies. A trickle of sweat ran down his spine. He fought off a violent surge of panic: Mauros-Ishmael was young, strong, a brilliant driver, and he had a magnificent team. The terror subsided. Cool and calm again, Michael stood far above it all, and ready. He knew he was going to win.

He was still looking at Mauros-Ishmael. It seemed hours had gone by while their eyes were locked together in this piercing stare. Now one of the grooms was pulling on his arm.

"My prince—you dropped this."

It was the yellow scarf his cousin the Empress had given him. Michael stuffed it into his sleeve and went toward the storeroom, to look over his car.

⋮ 5 ⋮

Having nothing else to do, Hagen did not mind waiting for hours to get into the Hippodrome. The crowds amazed him. Some of these people, the ones at the head of the two lines, had waited for days to get the best seats; they brought food in baskets, jugs of wine, blankets to sleep on. Their voices were strident with excitement. Their children climbed and ran and fought and wailed around their knees, while the parents argued at the tops of their voices over the various drivers and teams of horses. All around Hagen, the Greeks made bets with the fervor of men seeking Heaven. They swore and laughed and sang songs in honor of their favorites, and hated anyone who disagreed with them.

There were two factions, Hagen gathered, from what he overheard, and everybody in the waiting crowd wore his faction's colors, blue or green. They banded together, all the greens in one line, all the blues in the other. Two teams in each faction raced today. The Blues had some local hero, a driver who seemed to be related to the Empress, and also had brought in a team from Nicomedia; and the Greens were putting up a team from Thessalonica as well as their home team from Constantinople, whose driver was named Mauros-Ishmael, Black Ishmael.

Since Hagen had by chance come to stand in the Blue line, he heard wonderful things about the Prince, who was the favorite to win. The bet-takers, working their way up and down the line, were calling out the odds on their teams, and Prince Michael was never offered at more than one to one. Being champion, he wore the Golden Belt, which was the object of winning the race.

The lines clogged the whole street outside the Hippodrome and wound away into the City. The high brick wall of the racecourse curved around to the southwest, and the street travelled along its foot, going steeply downhill, and at the foot of the hill opened out on to a flat wide pavement. All along this way, the Hippodrome wall was cut into a series of arches, leading into caverns and alleys and rooms beneath the wall.

Here, the whores sauntered up and down, and Hagen, wandering around while he waited for the racecourse to open its gate, saw more than one man pay his penny and take what he had purchased in the shadow at the back of an arch.

Here also were rows of cages and fenced enclosures, full of extraordinary animals. Hagen had seen a giraffe in Antioch, but he had never come upon an elephant before, and he stood on his toes to look over the wall into its pen, amazed at the size and weight of this beast that before he had known only in tales. A swarm of little boys scrambled up the wall and threw scraps into the elephant's straw, and the vast creature groped among the wisps with its long nose and neatly picked up tiny bits.

While Hagen stood gaping at this, a wild-eyed man in a hooded cloak gripped his arm and whispered in his ear. "I can tell your future!"

"What?" Hagen asked.

"I can tell you the future! Will you be rich? Will you live to a great age? I have the secrets of the cosmos—here!" The man tapped his forehead. "Two irenes."

Hagen grunted at him. He wasn't sure he wanted to know the future. "Leave me alone."

"Wait! Are you married?" The man seized his hand and tried to turn the palm up. "You will marry an heiress. A fortune shall be yours! You will be emperor—"

"Get away from me!"

"One irene!"

Hagen cocked his fist. The soothsayer ducked away from the threatened blow. "Half! A farthing!"

Hagen laughed at him, turning away.

"Ten pence!"

Still laughing, the Frank walked off, away from the animal pens, back toward the crowd waiting to get into the track. As he climbed the slope, a man in a monk's robe hissed at him from the shadow of an arch.

"You! Pilgrim! I have pieces of the True Cross—"

Hagen ignored that. Ever since he came through Italy people had been trying to sell him relics. Behind him, the monk cursed him in a voice much thickened with wine.

Finally, at noon, the lines began to move, creeping forward, two sluggish ropes that wound up the hill and through the double gate. Once inside, the orderly lines dissolved as people battled for the good seats and shoved and pushed and elbowed their way on to the great stone benches that rose like a frozen wave above the long sides of the racecourse. Hagen separated himself from this confusion as soon as possible and climbed up to the top of the circus, where he could see everything and still be by himself.

He was tired; Rogerius haunted him. Everything he did reminded him of other times when he had done the same thing with his brother there beside him. He found himself listening for his brother's voice. Out in the City, once, passing a little old Greek church, he had nearly gone in, because Rogerius would have insisted on it.

Now he sat down on the very top bench of the Hippodrome and stared out across the flood of strangers and wished Rogerius were here.

It was a beautiful racecourse. The oval was covered with coarse sand; down the center ran a low wall of brick, studded with curious shafts of stone and statues of people and animals. Up here, at the top, there were more statues. The whole top tier was crowded with them, old, battered, in no order, some reduced to pieces of pieces, an arm, a foot, a horse's head. He roamed among them, fascinated by the variety and number of them. Below him, the living, raucous crowd rapidly filled up the whole Hippodrome.

He had never seen so many people all in one place, not at the Marchfield where the lords of the Franks assembled to give and hear counsel; not at the hostings of King Charles; yet those numbers had been marshalled up by great effort for grand purposes, and these people had come in off the streets, to see a horse-race.

Rogerius would have said something about that. Hagen clenched his jaws tight against the sudden renewed ache in his heart.

Off to his left, the awesome sweep of the benches was broken. From the middle of the crowd rose a sort of square tower built up out of the wall. A huge silky pavilion topped it. This must be where the Basileus would sit to watch the race. Hagen walked closer along the top tier of the racecourse wall; from this height he was above even the floating purple silk canopy, and he saw easily into the space beneath it. There seemed to be no one inside it, although ranks of armed guards were slowly filing into place along the outside of the square wall that supported it.

These were men wearing leather armor, like the men who had killed his brother. He found himself standing taut, with fists raised. He reminded himself that he knew nothing of this place—he had no understanding of the course of events that had caught him and Rogerius up momentarily and ground his brother's life away.

Down on the racetrack, a few of the spectators had climbed the wall and dropped to the sand, and one took a string and made it into a sort of bridle for the other and pretended to drive him up and down past the benches of onlookers. A swelling roar of approval greeted this performance. Flowers and pieces of bread sailed out of the stands onto the track, and people applauded and crowded and cheered and shouted derisively.

Now other people were scrambling down from the benches onto the racecourse. Tumblers did flips and handstands up and down the sand, and someone tried to climb the stone column at one end of the central ridge.

The day was wearing on. The sun burned hot, and still the Imperial box was empty. All around the crowd, people began to clap in unison.

Swiftly the hand-drumming spread, and everybody turned to peer at the pavilion, with its billow of purple silk rising and drifting on the wind from the sea. The rhythmic applause swelled to a thunder, all hands together.

"Come forth!" they shouted, a hundred voices at once. "Come forth, O Radiant One, Glory of the World, our pride and our hope! Come forth, come forth—let the races begin!"

Nothing happened. Hagen walked closer to the canopy; where he walked stone men and beasts packed the ledge so densely that he had to squeeze between them.

"Come forth, Joy of Christ—Protected of God, come forth!"

Now Hagen was almost directly above the Imperial balcony, and he could see people inside, moving around behind the drawn curtains. He squatted down on his heels, close enough now that he knew he would be spotted if he did not conceal himself a little.

The purple silk fluttered. For a moment longer, the pavilion curtains hung closed, and then abruptly a fanfare blared out from the brass throats of a dozen horns. The rippling drapery was thrown back, and out on to the expanse of white marble at the front of the box walked a woman dressed all in gold.

The crowd howled at the sight of her. They tossed their hats and baskets and empty wine jugs into the air and waved their arms, while the horns blasted, and drums rolled, and at the edge of the pavilion the golden woman raised her hand and made the Sign of the Cross over them, first to the left, then to the center, then the right. Her clothes shimmered. The sunshine struck her gown and surrounded her with a dazzling nimbus of reflected light. Her face itself shone like gold. With two little pages around her to spread out her glittering skirts, she took her seat in the center of the balcony.

Now more horns tooted, and the whole crowd shifted its attention from the Basileus to the racetrack, every head turning. The noise dropped to a hush of excitement, like the slack of a wave, and then mounted again to a shout that rocked the Hippodrome. The chariots were coming out on to the track.

There were four, all in a line, each drawn by four horses. They went decorously around the track, showing themselves to the crowd. The cars were only large enough to hold the man who drove the team. The horses were big, strapping beasts, with long thin heads, and legs like deer. They snorted and danced in their harness, the little cars jiggling along lightly on their heels, comical afterthoughts to the power of the brutes that drew them.

Hagen admired these horses. The two stallions he had now were Syrian-bred; he and Rogerius had bought them in Aleppo, and he was determined to get them back to Frankland, even if it meant paying out all his money for their passage to Italy, so that he could breed them to his Frankish mares. But the horses from Aleppo were mules compared to these racehorses.

Below him, now, the four little cars lined up side by side. The crowd fell still. On the side of the racecourse, a man stood with his arm upstretched, holding a flag.

The flag fell. A trumpet blew. The horses surged forward down the track, and from the great crowd watching a yell went up that washed away all sound and left Hagen with his ears ringing.

The horses swept down the track, the cars flying at their heels, fighting for position to take the sharp curve on the inside track and save some ground. In the turn, the cars swung out on one wheel, the drivers leaning hard to the left to keep the flimsy vehicles from overturning. The cars lurched back and forth, banging into one another. Teetering on the verge of a crash, one skittered along sideways through the whole turn, and the crowd screamed for every bump and wobble.

Now they were racing down the far side of the track. In the lead was a driver in a blue cap, leaning forward over the rumps of his team, the reins in both hands, urging them on with his whole body. Around his upper arm was a rag of some color other than blue; Hagen wondered what that meant. In the far turn, the blue driver swerved his team around under the noses of the horses running second and straightened his car out down the middle of the track as a flying team of greys and blacks ranged up alongside.

The crowd doubled its huge voice. Below Hagen's vantage point, people wept and prayed, clung to one another and beat the air with their fists.

"Prince Michael! The Prince—The Prince—"

"Mauros-Ishmael! Ishmael!"

"The Prince! Michael! Michael!"

The fool who had cried out for Mauros-Ishmael was quickly beaten to the floor by the people around him. Hagen stared at the fight, amazed, and when the nameless Greek lay bleeding on his bench, Hagen looked around at the Empress Irene in her pavilion.

She sat canted forward, her face taut, hawklike, her gaze on the race. Her fists were clenched on her knees. Her cheeks blazed like a maid's in the marriage bed. As the crowd around her shrieked, its ardor rising to its climax, Irene herself raised her voice in a wild animal cry, and heaved in her place, her arms pumping, urging on the teams that hurtled toward the finish line, and then, the race over, she sank back as if exhausted, limp and sated in her chair.

Hagen looked past her. A flock of women surrounded her, but among them his eye caught on only one, a tall girl with black hair, who stood with a mirror in her hand, staring down at the track. A blue ribbon floated from her ebony hair.

Theophano. So she had gotten back here, somehow—run away, left his brother bleeding, and made her way back to safety and high position, with no thought probably for the man whose death she had caused. Hagen bit his lip, forcing down a wild vengeful rage.

The crowd was settling down again, quieting, the low murmur of ordinary talk picking up, a giant rumble of careless conversation. The race had unified them; without it, they fell into chaos. Here and there in the spreading disorder, several other fights became obvious, and among their fellows people ate and stretched and walked about.

Hagen glanced into the Imperial pavilion again. It was certainly Theophano, sitting there on a stool just behind the woman of gold.

Now a tremendous roar went up from the crowd, and he jerked his gaze back to the racecourse. Clowns and tumblers had rushed out on to the sand to perform. Music struck up, so far away that Hagen could detect only the insistent throbbing of the drum. In among the stone people, crouched on the ledge above it all, he settled down to watch and wait.

"The star-blessed little bitch," Karros said. "There she is, safe and sound, looking as if she'd never set foot outside the Daphne."

"Really." John Cerulis lifted his head and turned his gaze on the Basileus and her attendants, less than thirty feet away from him.

The Basileus was watching him. He smiled at her and bowed his head and made an elaborate gesture of subservience with his right hand, and there under her purple silks she returned his smile, and raising her arm made the Sign of the Cross in his direction. John touched the corners of his mouth with his scented handkerchief, his guts gnawed by the worm of envy: what right had she to be where he so longed to be?

None of this discontent showed on his face. He was a spare, tall, hollow-chested man in later middle age, his clothes elegant, his grey hair polished to a silver sheen, his every mannerism evidence of his excellent breeding and perfect education. He was Basileus in every particular but one: he could not wear the purple. It was an oversight on the part of the Creator that he had been working hard to amend for the last twenty years of his life.

"Well," said Karros, clasping his hands behind his back, "she can't have that list of names, anyway. The last I saw of her she was going out the window, and she didn't have enough clothes on to hide a pimple. She must have hidden it somewhere on the road."

He was still staring at Theophano, in the Empress's entourage. Abruptly Karros's face stiffened, his gaze sharpening, and quickly he jerked his whole body around to put his back to the pavilion.

Intrigued by this indication of alarm, John Cerulis adjusted his seat slightly, to look around him again at the pavilion. Nothing in the scene there seemed enough to provoke such a response. Beyond the Imperial box, up on the highest level of the Hippodrome, a slight movement caught his eye: there was someone up among the antique statuary stored on the upper level. Cerulis glanced at Karros again, but the fat man was relaxed now, his hands clasped behind his back, rocking up and down on his heels and toes. Whatever had bothered him had not apparently bothered him very much.

Perhaps Theophano had seen him. The slut. John Cerulis raised his handkerchief again to his lips, smiling.

"Here comes the second heat," Karros said, eager.

The four teams were rolling out on to the track. Prince Michael led the way, since he had won the first heat. John Cerulis noticed again the bright scarf fluttering on his arm.

"There, you see? He's involved in some sneaky business."

Karros said, "I don't understand that."

"Someone does, you fool. Didn't I tell you to find out what he's up to? Why must you fail me in everything?"

"Most Noble, I've talked to Michael himself at great length sometimes—I swear to you, nothing concerns him but horse-races."

"Then why does he send secret signals to his followers? No! You've been duped again, Karros, you fool." John kept his voice mild. This was why he was not emperor, because he had the use only of silly and ignorant men who could not understand what they were seeing. "I'm telling you, go make friends with him, and find out what he intends."

"Yes, Most Noble."

Cerulis placed himself more comfortably in his chair, smiling. He tried to smile always, since people were always watching him, and it would not do to betray any mood less than perfect serenity. The chariots were lining up for the start of the next heat. He leaned on his elbow, smiling, to watch.

One of the horses on the team from Trebizond was refusing the start. Rearing and pitching, it backed away from the ribbon in spite of the whip and the shouts of the driver. The groom assigned to lead the Trebizonders into place was approaching warily, his hands out.

Because the Trebizond team had finished last in the first heat, they had the inside position for this one, and so the race could not begin until the horses were settled. Mauros-Ishmael calmed his raging heart.

Kept his eyes forward, his hands firm on the reins. He felt, as he always felt before a race, that he was made of fire.

Now the crowd began to scream and chant, stamping their feet. The colors of the teams fluttered in the air. Ishmael's wheelhorse tossed its black head, impatient; Ishmael felt the action through the reins and his fingers opened and closed, giving and taking rein, the man and the horse perfectly tuned together.

Before them lay the track, the sand gleaming, furrowed by the rakes. The shadow of the Hippodrome wall cut across the straightaway halfway down its length; the whole far end was deep in the shade. In the sun, the crowd rose up like a mountain, howling and cheering and all moving at once, all watching him.

Hot all over, his blood burning in his veins, his eyes boiling, he longed for the explosion of the start.

Now the inside team's flanker was calming down. For an instant it stopped plunging, its head thrust up high, its nostrils pumping the air in and out, and the grooms bolted to the side walls. The starter raised his flag. The crowd hushed, gathering its breath.

The flag dropped, and the ribbon fell away. The bronze horns blared forth two notes, and the crowd's thundering cheers drowned the rest. Needing no cue from Ishmael, the horses flung themselves forward down the stretch of sand.

The inside team's flanker had chosen exactly that moment to rear again, and so the Trebizonders lost the start. Ishmael with his greys and blacks bolted out into the lead, half a stride ahead of Michael on the right, a horse's length ahead of the team on the left. Before the surging horses had even steadied their stride Ishmael was urging them sideways, toward the inside track, left open by the faltering of the Trebizonders.

The roar of the crowd, the rattle of wheels and the pounding of the horses' hoofs blended into an indefinite thunder that was like hearing nothing at all. The four heads of his horses bobbed in unison, their braided manes laid back on the wind of their passage, spume flying from their necks and mouths. He tightened his inside hand and the big black wheeler responded, edging closer to the spina, pinching off the team between them and the inside, charging toward the open sand ahead.

"On! On!"

That was the driver of the team on Ishmael's left; he went to the whip, lashing his horses, trying to keep them up and hold Ishmael out. Ishmael's horses needed no whip. They knew racing as well as their driver. With the black wheeler guiding them all into the open track inside, they slackened stride just a little, just enough to keep team, and forced the horses in their way to shorten up or crash.

Losing ground with every stride, the inside team faltered still more, and Ishmael swept on ahead of them. Now Michael was racing up fast on the outside, urging his team out ahead of Ishmael's, now leading by a neck, now by half a length. Ishmael gripped his reins tight, giving his horses the strength of his arms and shoulders to steady them. Michael was straining for the lead, but the turn was on them, and Ishmael had the inside track. Gripping the wheeler as short as he could, he sent on the flankers in a burst of speed, whirled around the turn in perfect rhythm, and came out of the curve ahead of Michael by a clear length.

They charged down the straight and Michael went for the lead again. His horses surged up alongside Ishmael's car, their long lean heads flat as blades. Ishmael leaned into his outside reins and his flankers moved out sideways a little, forcing Michael wide, holding him off. The horses raced together, two teams side by side, buckle to buckle. For long strides they raced even. The crowd was screaming their names, some calling the drivers by name, some calling the horses, its passion like a whip. Ishmael himself screamed. Through the reins he knew the splendid unfaltering strength of his team, and there beside him Michael's horses and the Prince himself were racing with the same power, the other half of this little world, locked into an eternal contest at the peak of life.

The turn swept at them. Ishmael leaned his horses into it, asking the flankers for more speed, drawing the wheeler in a little, but he asked for too much, or did it wrong. Their rhythm broke. They lost something, a failure of concentration, trembling back through the reins into his hands, so that for precious instants he drove not a single pulsing power but a collection of separate and contending wills. Faltering, they went wide, forcing Michael also wide.

Under Ishmael now the car rocked up onto the inside wheel. He leaned out hard toward the outside, trying to bring it down. The car lost its track entirely and skidded, swinging hard toward the wall. The horses had to slow; Prince Michael surged out ahead of them, while Ishmael, sobbing with desperate fury, worked his horses down and got his chariot firmly under him and turned them straight again.

The other three teams were already entering the next turn. The race was lost. Ishmael flung his whole heart and mind forward and sent the horses hurtling after, down the passage of the sand.

They responded. Impossibly far behind, the four horses leaned into the harness and stretched their legs into the rushing wind. Flying down the straight into the turn, they gathered themselves like an arrow drawn to the full might of the bow. Hopeless. Yet they raced on.

This time, without other teams there, they executed the turn perfectly. Coming into the straight beyond it, they were eight, no, ten lengths back. Ishmael's hands gripped the reins so tight the blood striped his palms. He wept and called to his horses, his voice lost in the wind and the roar of the crowd, and straining for every inch, for every instant of speed, the team crept into the gap between them and the others, narrowed it, and at the far turn, closed it.

This was the last turn. Ishmael held them close against the spina, to save everything he could for the straightaway. As they wheeled into the turn, he prayed for help, and help came.

Swinging around the turn, the Thessalonian team, on the inside just ahead of Ishmael, began to drift wide. On the outside the Trebizonder driver screamed at the errant racers and lashed at his own horses, but to no purpose. The Thessalonian horses veered out across the track, leaving the inside open, giving Ishmael just enough space to fit through.

The horses saw the opening and needed no command from him. Flattened to the task, their haunches bunching and thrusting in powerful coils, they forced their way through the opening. For a moment the heads of the Thessalonian team bounced even with the wheel of Ishmael's car, but then, drained by the effort, they stopped. Falling back, they took the Trebizonders with them, and now Ishmael stretched out his team alone in pursuit of Michael.

It was too far. The champion was already halfway to the finish line, the yellow scarf on his arm flapping, the crowd standing to welcome him, their darling, into his place of victory. Ishmael bent over his horses' rumps, begging them for more, weeping for their useless courage, and they raced up closer and closer, now fifteen yards behind, now ten, now five. Then they swept over the finish line, Michael first, Ishmael nowhere.

The crowd loved it. They stood on the benches and cheered until the whole Hippodrome reverberated, and clouds of flowers and bits of food and paper and even small coins rained down on the track and on Michael, his horses, Ishmael, and his horses. Ishmael let his team slow as it would. They were tired and came back quickly to him, snorting and sighing. They knew they had lost. With heads drooping, their flanks streaked with salty drying sweat, they walked back toward the stable gates.

Michael was touring the Hippodrome. Having won two heats he had won the day's race, and he carried his golden belt at arm's length over his head, showing it off to the crowd. Ishmael passed him going the other way, and for an instant they looked at each other. Ishmael raised his hand in tribute, and Michael nodded, distant, aloof, took his gaze away, and went on.

Ishmael felt all eyes on him—all jeering, contemptuous eyes, all laughter, all the world's scorn falling on him and his horses. Another cheer for Michael sounded, a blow struck on his heart. He bowed his head. The grooms were waiting at the stable door, and he gave up the horses into their care.

He slipped down from the car, tired, his knees quaking, his wrists and shoulders stiff and sore. He had sand in his eyes and in his mouth and hair and nose. Blind in the darkness of the stable, he stumbled down the corridor into the Apron, banging into gear and people. Once inside the shelter of his team's equipment room, he shut the door on the rest of mankind, and sitting down on a trunk began to cry like a child.

⋮ 6 ⋮

"Now he is leaving," Theophano said; she stood by the rail of the Imperial box, looking down at the enclosure where John Cerulis had been sitting.

"Pull the curtains," said Helena, the chief lady-in-waiting.

As if she gave the order to herself, she went forward to draw the great silk curtains closed. Theophano stepped back, her hands at her sides. John Cerulis frightened her; he was like a serpent, impossible to predict or placate, and now he was her enemy.

The Empress would protect her. She thanked God for giving her into the protection of the Basileus, whom Christ Himself had chosen.

Irene was gone now, with the others of her party, since the race was over. Helena had fastened the curtains into place, and stooping gathered up the Empress's cloak and a stray earring and went into the back of the box, to the door that opened on to the stairwell to the Daphne.

"Bring your lute. She'll want music after dinner. And don't forget those sweets here or they will draw the ants." Helena bustled out of the box and disappeared down the dark stairwell of the Kathismus.

Theophano loitered in the pavilion, fixing the back of her hair, which had come loose. She was thinking about the horse-race. Michael had won again, which delighted her, although they were no longer lovers. Maybe she would talk to him after dinner, and if he showed interest, go down later to the Bucoleon for the drinking and celebration. She stuck a hairpin into the coiled mass of her hair and fingered a heavy curl into place.

Behind her the silk curtain ripped with a long hissing sound that sent a shiver of horror through her. She whirled.

In through the long rent in the curtain a man was coming, and she snatched up her lute and leapt into the doorway, to block it with her body. An instant later she dropped the lute.

It was the big white-haired Frank. He climbed in across the chair of the Empress herself and faced Theophano, his eyebrows cocked up.

"Well, well, pretty, remember me?"

"What are you doing here?"

"I want to talk to you, pretty."

He was coming toward her; she reached behind her for the door into the Kathismus and pulled it closed and set herself firmly before it, a barrier between this savage and the Empress. "I warn you, there are guards at the foot of this stair!"

"Are there really!" He came up beside her and took hold of her arm. "Then you tell me right now and here what it is I want to know."

"What do you want?"

"Who killed my brother?"

She licked her lips; he was hurting her arm, and by the look on his face he intended to hurt her more if she did not cooperate with him.

"I can't tell you—it is business of the Empress." The brother was dead, then. She had hoped he had somehow fought off the attack. Then abruptly a pain daggered through her arm, wiping out all thought of Rogerius.

"Tell me!" He twisted her wrist around behind her.

"I can't—I can't—" She sobbed, her upper arm and shoulder a fiery agony. "Please—"

"I don't believe you. Why should my brother's murder be any

business of the Basileus? Tell me, damn you, Theophano, I will break off your arm if you don't."

She was sinking down onto her knees, limp and helpless. He let her go, and she cried out with relief; he gripped her by the front of her dress and yanked her up again onto her feet to face him.

"You won't tell me unless she allows it? Then take me to her."

"No! Heavens—"

"Why not? Are you afraid of what she'll tell me?"

Her arm dangled, numb and useless. She pressed her back against the door. "She is the Basileus! You—you can't—" She surveyed him, his battered boots, his rustic leggings of rough knitted cloth, his coat like the hide of a wild animal; she imagined him in the presence of the Basileus, and almost laughed. "No. You are not worthy."

"Yet my brother was worthy enough to die?"

Theophano dragged in a deep breath. She saw a certain sense in that.

"I'm sorry about your brother, truly."

"Then help me get revenge for his murder."

She had involved him in this. Rubbing her arm, now tingling painfully alive again, she faced the unpleasant truth; she was responsible for this, and an uncouth barbarian had the right of her.

"Very well," she said. "I'll take you to her."

This would cost her much, perhaps even her place with the Empress, but grimly she forced herself to admit that it was all her own doing. "Come along." She opened the door and led him into the Palace.

Helena said, "I would feel safer, mistress, if we had an army to call upon."

"Would you," said the Basileus. Helena had attended her for thirty years, and had earned this freedom of opinion by her loyalty and self-lessness. "I would not. There is no safety in relying on force, my love."

"John Cerulis has an army."

"Fortunately it is scattered over Thrace and Macedonia."

"But he will summon it here, mistress, and hold us up to ransom, and the price of our lives will be your power."

Irene laughed. She reached out and caressed her maidservant's forearm. They were sitting in the evening room, at the rear of the Daphne Palace. Through the great window at the end of the room, she could see out on to the torch-lit terrace, where the fountains showered streams of diamonds into the jasmine-scented air. Night had come. The long day's labor was done. Irene sprawled across silken cushions, her women fussing around her, and looked forward to hours and hours of leisure and self-indulgence.

"It is better to rely on Christ," she said, "since it was Christ who gave me my throne, and only Christ can take it from me. If I raised an army it would surely lead to war; fighting always brings on more fighting; an army often runs off ahead of its purpose, dragging in its wake those very people who ought to be leading it."

The little girl Philomela, sitting beside her, lifted her round young face in an adoring smile at these words. The Empress fondled the child's cheek with her free hand. The other hand lay on Philomela's knee, where the little girl could massage creams into the skin and paint the nails with gold.

"Nonetheless," Helena said, "I think you ought to rid us once and for all of John Cerulis."

"You panic easily, Helena."

Two of the other women were setting up the table for supper; the jet-black man whom the Caliph had sent her as a birthday gift waited beside the door with a tray of food. Where was Theophano? The Empress's intuition bothered her and she never lost time trying to verify the judgments of her sixth sense by the laborious exercise of reason. Something was wrong.

"Theophano must be in difficulty. Someone go find her."

"Mistress, Nicephoros is here, outside—"

"Oh, Nicephoros." Irene waved her hand in the air, wafting away the mention of her treasurer, who always wanted to complain to her about money. "I'll see him in the morning."

"In the morning is the procession from the Well, and then after that the Saint Matthew's Day Mass in Holy Apostles'—"

"Well, I'll see him in the afternoon, then. Find me Theophano." She leaned forward a little, to let another woman comb out a vagrant tendril of her hair and pat it into place. A subtle aroma reached her nose and she sniffed. "Ah, delicious. Octopus in cream." She beckoned to the black man to bring the food to the table.

He stepped forward, leaving the door, and an instant later the door flew open.

All the women screamed. As if they moved on wheels and springs, they rushed together into the center of the room, to make a wall of their bodies between their mistress and whatever danger threatened. The black man leapt away, his mouth an O of alarm.

But it was only Theophano who came in, looking rumpled. "Mistress," she said, and went to her knees. "Mistress, this is all my fault—"

Into the doorway behind her a stranger stepped.

Irene stood up. With a gesture she dispersed her women to the sides of the room. "Who are you?"

The strange man walked calmly into the center of the room, looking around him. "Very beautiful," he said. "This is very nice."

Theophano, still on her knees, reached up and gripped his hand and tried to pull him down beside her. "Down on your face, you lout—that is the Basileus!"

He did not kneel. He braced himself easily against the tug of her hand on his arm and faced Irene, a big, square man in foreign clothes, his hair white and thick and curly as sheep's wool.

He said, "I am Hagen, lady, the son of Reynard the Black, of Frankland. Men call me Hagen the White. My king is Charles. I mean you no harm, lady, but I have urgent questions of your serving girl here, and she will not talk to me without your permission."

"Oh," Irene said, understanding everything at once. She walked leisurely across the room toward him, taking in every detail of his appearance. She liked men, and this one pleased her by his size and evident strength. His straightforwardness she also enjoyed. It was the salient characteristic of men, refreshingly uncomplicated, unlike the subtle and oblique minds of women, and was, she thought, the chief reason for marriage, each finding its perfect equal in the other.

She was past needing marriage, or even sex. Nonetheless she intended to enjoy this encounter. She walked once all the way around the big Frank, looking him up and down, and went to sit before him again; one of her women rushed up with a little spindle-legged stool for her.

"Well: ask," she said, with a gesture toward Theophano.

"I want her to tell me who killed my brother," Hagen said.

"Does she know? Theophano?"

"Not precisely, mistress," said the girl, still crouched on the rug. "I ran away—I could see that even so mighty a man as his brother would not hold off four of John Cerulis's men for long."

"Who is that? John Cerulis?" asked the Frank quickly.

"An enemy of mine," said Irene, and smiled, because suddenly she saw possibilities in this Hagen the White, uses for him multiplying steadily through her imagination, like a series of doors opening. She fixed her eyes on him.

"Tell me, my dear, are all Franks as handsome and well formed as you?"

He put his head to one side, his blue eyes pensive. He said, "My lady," in a voice quivering with suspicion.

"I'm sorry. I didn't mean to be forward. Clearly your ways are more sober than ours. But the proposition has been advanced that your king and I should marry, and bring the western provinces into the Empire again."

"My lady, I only want to know who killed my brother."

"Well, that's easy: John Cerulis. Or his men did it, anyway, obeying what they took to be his will. I would even venture to guess that their leader was a certain Karros. Theophano?" She glanced at the girl, who nodded. "Yes. Does that satisfy you?"

"Karros," said the Frank, with purpose in his voice. "Yes. Thank you."

"And tell me now what you intend to do."

"Nothing that will trouble you, lady, if these men are your enemies."

"Enemies, yes, but they are also my subjects, and I will not suffer them to come to harm at the whim of a barbarian."

"They killed my brother," he said.

"And you seek revenge. That's certainly simple enough. Do you plan simply to kill them, or have you more complicated measures in mind?"

He stood there a moment, his gaze on her, his brow furrowed in thought, which, being a barbarian, he could not have much practice in. Or perhaps he was having trouble understanding her Greek; he spoke the street language, and she spoke court Greek. She lifted one hand. "I will dine now, before the food is cold." Swiftly, their silk clothes rustling, her servants hurried to bring her a plate.

The Frank said, "I am sworn to avenge my brother. That means the death of those who killed him. That is our way, in Frankland."

"You have made that clear."

"I realize that here you do things differently."

One of the women knelt down, holding the plate so that Irene could survey the food upon it; everything was laid out in the shape of a fish, because it was of the sea's larder, and because the only true nourishment was the Body of Christ. The rings of the octopus in their sauce formed the scales of the fish; strips of marinated eggplant were the fins, and colored fruit the eye and gills and the sea around it all. It was a shame to disturb it, but she was hungry, and she reached for the spoon.

"Here we trust in the judgment of Christ our Lord, and strive for mercy in our dealings with others." Gently she removed one of the scales and began to eat.

"Yes," he said, malice in his voice like a rock in the grass. "Here you put out the eyes of your own children."

The women gasped. Theophano reached out and struck him, which he ignored. Irene ate the mouthful of the white octopus and laid the spoon down.

"Ah," she said, the food swallowed. "Don't try to duel with me, my dear, you will fall victim to the simplicity of your sex and race and also to your shortcomings in the language. Yet I will answer your remark, because I see you do not understand the ways of Rome."

"Make me understand."

"When I had my son blinded, I committed an act of mercy, because otherwise I would have had to kill him. Alive and whole, he would always have been a threat to me, the center of plots against me, and therefore a threat to the Empire itself. But a blind man cannot rule, and so I have put him out of danger."

"Surely you had another choice, which was to leave him the Emperor, as he was."

"No," she said swiftly, and put down the spoon, and waved the dish away. Intense, fierce, she leaned forward toward this barbarian whose physical excellence was so in contrast to his shallow understanding. "No, I did not have that choice. He was weakening the Empire. He was destroying the City of Christ. That cannot be allowed to happen.

Constantinople must not fall. Troy—Athens—Rome itself—the tide of barbarism has swallowed them all. Only Constantinople remains. But the barbarians are ever at the gates. We must defend and protect with every guile, every craft, every dedicated power in us, with no thought for ourselves, because when Constantinople falls—"

She flung up her arm, as if to strike, and her lips snarled; she saw in this brute before her the eternal enemy of her City.

"When Constantinople falls, then night will come, finally and forever, night without end."

Around her, in the hush after her voice ceased, her women smiled on her, adoring, themselves made great in her. The barbarian was impressed. She saw it in his eyes. His wide mouth lost its smile. Now he even took a step backward, and went down on one knee to her.

He said, "Hail to you, Basileus, and glory to your City."

She nodded, pleased with this natural tribute from a creature unschooled in flatteries. He was falling into her power. She saw uses for him that made her hungry to control him.

She said, "You have my blessing, Hagen. God has sent you here. You must see that the death of your brother is but part of something much, much larger, in which you should tread warily, lest you do damage utterly beyond your ken."

He said, "I have sworn a blood oath, lady. Yet I will give heed to you."

"Excellent. In due course, I tell you, in Christ's name, your oath shall be fulfilled. Your brother's blood was spilled in my behalf, protecting this innocent young creature whose tasks are mine, and I am aware of my duty to you."

She put out her hand to him; he was supposed to kiss her seal-ring. Instead her long white hand disappeared into his in a hard clasp that let her feel every rough callus on his palm.

"Done," he said, as if they had made a bargain, and he got up off his knee.

"Now, come talk to me about your King Charles, who I understand now wants to call himself emperor."

She gestured; her servant brought her the dish of octopus. The big Frank folded his arms over his chest and looked around him at the room.

"He was crowned emperor in Rome," he said, as he surveyed the place. "In the way of things, he will get whatever he can take and hold. As for myself, I only call him King because I have to—he is of no better blood than I am, Charles. His father was only the chief of the royal household, until the Pope came over the mountains."

"Oh? Where is the real King, then?"

"They threw him into a monastery," he said, and smiled at her. He had a way of smiling that suggested more intelligence than he had yet evinced to her. "Here you blind them, there we cut their hair off. It's the same thing."

"I doubt it much." She hoped her women were attending to this, since it proved her point about force as a means of statecraft. "Why was the deposed King superior to Charles, in your view?"

"His blood was royal. Charles's birth is no better than mine."

"You keep saying that."

"I mean it," he said.

"But your blood doesn't matter, does it, compared to the individual quality of the man? Charles has the name of being an exceptional man, for a barbarian."

He stared at her a while, his arms folded over his chest, and the lids of his eyes lowered. He said, "Meaning that you are not of the blood royal, lady?"

She grunted. Too late, she saw that she had lost some prestige with him, violating some arcane barbarian idea about kings. She pushed away the half-eaten dish and gestured to her women, who rushed in around her, tending her hair, her clothes, her cosmetics. In the center of this bustle, she faced this brute she meant to domesticate and said, "Meaning things are not so simple here as they are in your fens and woodlands. Theophano. You will escort our new friend to suitable quarters and see that he is attended as befits one whose birth is equal to a king's." She gave Hagen a level stare, annoyed with herself; had she had him believe she was descended from the gods, she could have gotten anything from him. "You may attend us in the morning ceremonial."

He bowed his head to her, saying nothing. Theophano already stood at the door behind him, impatient to get him out of here, and he turned and went after her. The door shut.

Irene said, "God, my only Glory. How can this Charles hope to manage with men like that around him?"

Helena brought her a cup of wine. "I thank God we are Romans."

"He was sent to remind us why we must keep the City safe," said Ida, who stroked one hand over the Empress's hair and down her shoulder, a loving, possessive caress. "You were wonderful. Even he felt it."

Irene sipped the wine. "Nonetheless I feel he is insufficiently impressed."

Helena said, "He is a barbarian."

"Such as he have served Rome in the past." Irene put out the cup and someone took it. "Clearly God sent him to me, as Ida says. Glory to God."

"Glory," they murmured, "glory, glory," but their eyes were on Irene, and not on Heaven.

Following after the girl Theophano, Hagen thought back over what had passed between him and the Empress. He had carefully avoided making any promises to her, but somehow she was giving him space in her Palace, making deals with him, inviting him into her following. Her whole manner toward him made him uneasy.

Still, it was shelter, and he had learned some names: John Cerulis, and someone named Karros. He went after Theophano across a dark courtyard and down three wide shallow steps onto a terrace.

This was a garden, adorned with statues and a fountain, and all around it torches in iron standards held back the night. He followed Theophano through the yellow haze of the torchlight. Other people moved past him, some carrying dishes or books or jugs from the fountain, others idle strollers, who stared at him with curiosity bright on their faces.

The Palace was huge. At the edge of the terrace, he paused to look behind him, and saw the great curved wall of the Hippodrome looming up in the darkness, connected by the tower of the Imperial balcony to the many-leveled building he had just left.

The ground sloped away across the whole headland; retaining walls and buttresses and pavements tamed it all into a descending sweep of terraces. Besides the sprawling Palace behind him, other buildings studded the grounds. Open walkways connected them, some bordered with gardens, and others with rows of white columns. The fountain before him was made in the shape of a great fish that spouted water from its back, and other monstrous shapes formed some of the columns of the building directly before him.

The people who swarmed through this complex seemed somehow too small for the place, as if it had been made for giants. The torches fluttered in the wind with a hissing roar of flame. Music sifted through the air, and somewhere nearby people were laughing. Hagen stood still, enjoying the sight, moved again to admiration of these people who had the grace and good luck to live like this.

Theophano came back to him, frowning, impatient. "Are you coming?"

"Yes, yes." He went after her along a walk of brickwork. "We don't have anything like this in Frankland."

She gave him a look of pity mixed with amusement. "I can see that very well. Come along."

Opening a door, she led him into a large empty hall, half-lit by candles on the walls. "This is the Triclinium. This is where we eat."

All the tables and benches had been shoved back off to one wall. At the far end of the room from Theophano and Hagen, a man with a mop was sloshing water over the black and white tiles of the floor. Theophano crossed the hall swiftly to the far side, Hagen on her heels.

"Why did you run away, at the inn?" he asked. "Why didn't you come and get me so I could help Rogerius?"

"I was naked!" She shook her head; her hair ribbon fluttered over her shoulder. "I looked for you, I did, really, but I had no clothes on, and it was I they wanted—I had to escape. I had some thought of leading them off, but it all happened too fast to make plans."

She led him across a semicircular pavement, another fountain in the center of it, where people were crowded on benches, talking, walking up and down, hailing one another. Someone called to Theophano as she passed and she raised her hand in answer without slackening her steps. In the wall at the far side she opened a door and stood aside to let Hagen through.

"You are fortunate the Basileus likes you. That was most presumptuous of you, talking to her the way you did. It's an offense to everyone. I wouldn't talk like that to your little barbarian King."

"I don't see any offense in talking honestly to anybody, even a Basileus."

They were inside a long corridor that led off through the dark. On one side was a series of doors, and on the other the wall was broken up into great windows that let in the light from the terrace outside. Theophano went swiftly along the corridor opening each door as she came to it, looking through and moving on. After she had inspected three or four rooms this way, she found one she liked and went in, motioning to Hagen to follow her.

"Here. You can stay here, if it suits you."

The room was large and airy, the wall opposite the door being open to another terrace; the golden light of more torches outside spilled into the room, showing Hagen the square lines of a table and the foot of the bed. He nodded. "Help me find a candle."

Instead, she clapped her hands, and at once a man with an embroidered coat appeared from the corridor, bowing. She gave him crisp orders and he hurried off. Theophano loitered in the doorway, her hands behind her.

"Did you—" Her voice quivered. "Bring my clothes?"

He sat down on the bed. The light from the terrace glowed on her face, gilding her cheekbones and nose, leaving her wide-spaced eyes deep in the shadow. "As it happens, I did. They're in my packs, at the inn where I was staying. What about my horses? Where can I stable them here?"

"Oh—take them to the Hippodrome." She discarded that topic with a little twitch of her right hand, which dove away immediately behind her again. She touched her lower lip with her tongue. He thought, She wants to ask me something, but she's afraid of telling me too much, and guessed it was the paper he had found that was on her mind. He smiled at her.

She said, "Well, I'm glad you did. Did you bring—my shoes, too?"

He said, "I brought everything."

She moved a little, bringing her face more fully into the light; her eyes were bright with a sudden desperate interest. The servant came in with a candle, a pile of linen, a jug, a bowl, a chamber pot. Quickly he dispersed these things around the room.

"Good night," Theophano said, but she did not go.

Hagen got up and went to the far wall, which opened on to the terrace beyond. The air was warm and smelled of the sea. A door stood ajar under a hanging drapery, so that he could close the room if he wished. From here he could see all the way to the tip of the headland, where a lighthouse stood, its great flame curling and leaping into the night sky.

"Will that be all, my lord?" the servant murmured.

Hagen glanced around him. Theophano had gone. He nodded to the old man behind him. "Yes, thank you."

: 7 :

He had the list. She was sure of it, as sure as if he had told her outright.

She walked down the slope past the Triclinium, through the grove of mulberry trees that fed the palace silkworms, her hands winding together as she thought. If she could retrieve the list somehow she might restore herself in the Empress's sight.

With the help of some of the guards she could probably take it back by force. She imagined that, the fighting, and remembered with a cold shiver the fierce fighting in the little room of the inn at Chrysopolis and knew at once that was not the way. Besides, he had said something about his packs; he did not have the list with him, and in fact from the way he had phrased things she guessed he understood, in some dim brute fashion, that the paper was of value, and would conceal it.

At the edge of the mulberry trees, she paused to look down over the lawns and gardens before her. The large important buildings of the Palace were nearly all above the place where she was standing; this area below was given up to pavilions and fountains and walkways among the plantings. At the very end of the whole complex stood the Pharos, with its tossing head of flame.

Down there also was the Bucoleon, the little old ramshackle palace that Prince Michael occupied. A screen of tall cypress hid it from Theophano's view, but she imagined she could see the faint flicker of torchlight, and hear the sounds of laughter and music.

Her spirit leapt. She needed that, some amusement, some respite. Her intertwining hands parted. Gathering up the skirt of her gown, she hurried down past the cypress, down toward the lights and joyous sounds of the party.

Hagen saw her go. He stood near one of the fountains on the level above her and watched her, light-footed and graceful in her white gown, running away through the line of cypress trees.

He drank some water from the fountain and wandered off, looking curiously all around him. There were few people outdoors now, in the full night, but the rings of torches that lit up every garden and courtyard still blew like red-gold rags in the wind off the sea. He found a tiny pavilion of white columns, half-hidden in the middle of a garden whose voluptuous waxy flowers were wide open to the wind, casting a perfume so thick and sweet it rolled his stomach. Inside the little pavilion was nothing but an overturned chair, and near the way out, a glove too small for a man's hand.

He drifted away across a broad pavement, studded with strange trees in stone pots, and went down three steep little steps onto another walkway. No one stopped him; no one challenged him. As he walked through the darkness, he saw a few other people, a servant climbing up from a fountain, a girl who darted out of the bushes, giggled, and raced away on bare feet. Apparently, anyone who wished could roam at will through the palace complex. He opened doors and peered into dark hallways, saw empty rooms full of things worth stealing, but there were no guards.

Were they so trusting, or merely sure of themselves? Carefully he shut all the doors behind him.

Twice the walks he followed led him out unexpectedly on to some parapet that overlooked the sea. The second time he leaned against a railing of stone and looked west.

In Rome he had seen the wreckage of buildings like these, huge archways, walls, broken columns, monstrous remnants of an age of heroes. The current occupants of the Holy City lived among them in smoky hovels and were chopping up the marble to burn for lime. King Charles had said, "This was the real Rome, what's left of it, and not—" and waved away toward the Lateran palace, the Pope's residence, with a sniff of contempt. Hagen had not understood it then. Now he understood.

She had mentioned Rome, and other places he had never heard of. Troy, and some place whose name he had forgotten. He imagined suddenly that once the whole world had been ordered within the walls of cities like this one, where the people lived like this; but it had gone now, all but Constantinople, because—

He did not want to think about the reasons why. The people here thought the barbarians had ruined it all, and he was a barbarian, to their eyes.

To his own, now. He knew himself a different man from this, a creature from the outer darkness, whose clumsy hands could only break, not build.

In the west the twin stars, the Gateway, as his people called them, were disappearing into the mist along the horizon; soon they would be washed in the limitless sea. Here, he supposed, they called them something else, the right name, a name lost to him, or never known. He felt alone and out of place here, less than a man.

That feeling drove him on, walking along the narrow, steeply descending walk. The sea had splashed it, making the stone slippery under his feet, but he did not slow; he plunged through the gap in a hedge, and came out on a windblown lip of rock below the lighthouse.

The flames in their brass bowl hissed and thundered above his head. He went by the lighthouse, plowing through a tangle of brush, and there before him was an open courtyard full of people.

He stopped. In the hazy torchlight, half a hundred men and women sat or stood around a semicircular pavement, drinking, laughing, leaning on one another. In the center of the pavement was a statue, so worn and cracked with age he could not easily make out the subject: two great breasts locked in a lewd embrace. Behind the torchlight was a long low building half-buried in the brush.

As he stood there watching, a man with a grey beard walked into the midst of the other people, and they crowed and clapped and gathered around him, and striking a pose, he began to speak in rolling tones. The words were Greek, but strange and oddly accented, like the speech of bards, and Hagen had to go down closer to hear it better.

The Greeks sat down in a semicircle around the man who was speaking—or reciting, Hagen guessed, certainly performing in some way. He was telling a story about a band of men taken prisoner by a one-eyed giant, and that held Hagen's interest; he loved tales about monsters. In Jerusalem once he and Rogerius had spent the whole night buying wine for a drunken monk, who repaid them with stories of giants and pygmies, black men and yellow men, men with two heads, men with their faces in their chests, men with one leg, who hopped about and when the sun shone bright held a huge foot over their heads as sunshades.

The monster in the Greek story was less interesting. The crafty leader of the captive band burned out the giant's eye with a fiery stick, and tying his men under the bellies of the Cyclops's sheep, he got them past the monster and out of the cave. There were other Cyclops living nearby but the leader of the Greeks tricked the poor blind creature and no one came to his help. The poem ended in a patter of applause. Hagen turned to go, and then he saw Theophano.

He stopped where he was. She was standing near the doorway to the old building behind the courtyard, with two or three other women. These women all moved closer together, and he saw that in their center was a man.

Tall and massively built, the man came out into the courtyard, ignoring the women, who hung on him adoringly. Even Theophano was gazing on him with a look of rapture. Hagen grunted, half-amused; where was all that pride now? Having never seen Prince Michael before at a close distance, he recognized the man as much by his haircut as anything else; unlike the other men who wore their hair loose and flowing, this one had his head close-cropped, so that the charioteer's cap would fit. Around his waist he wore the heavy golden belt of the champion.

He paid no more heed to the worshipful women around him than to the air he breathed. Theophano gave up. Drawing back, she remained a moment with her wistful gaze upon him, her hands at her sides, and turned away. Watching from the shadows, Hagen thought she was the most beautiful of them all; had he been Michael, he would have taken her into the house and let her prove her adoration. Her black hair was gathered up in a cluster of ringlets at the back of her head, secured by a long ribbon that fluttered down over her shoulder. If he tugged on the ribbon, Hagen imagined, all that perfumed hair would come tumbling down—

She felt his look upon her; she raised her head and saw him there.

He backed up a step, embarrassed, as if she could see what he was doing to her in his mind. She was coming toward him. He began to move away, back into the darkness, but she smiled, and the smile held him. He stood waiting for her, at the edge of the shadows.

Theophano crossed the courtyard, circling the people who listened to Romulos recite Homer; she wondered what Hagen was doing here. She realized she was foolish to believe he would stay neatly put away in the room she had found for him. If Michael saw him here, the Prince would chase him off. Michael never let strangers stay within the bounds of his palace.

"Hello," she said. "What are you doing here?"

"Looking around. Should I go?"

"Well—" She thought of the list he had; she should be trying to get it back. Not tonight. Tonight she wanted to do nothing but enjoy herself. "No, no," she said. "Stay and have a cup of wine, listen to the poem."

"I've been listening," he said.

"Oh? Do you understand it?" She moved sideways a little, toward a stone bench under the trees, and he went with her. Perhaps he was lonely. She could give him a little companionship, she decided; after all, he had saved her life once. She beckoned to a servant with a tray of wine cups. Hagen sat down beside her.

He said, "The Greek's a little odd. It sounds beautiful."

"You think so?" That surprised her; it seemed a refinement beyond the barbarian mind.

"Yes. But my sympathies are with the Cyclops."

"They are! But why?"

"He's a barbarian, like me," Hagen said.

"Oh, it isn't like that."

At once she saw that it was, that poor old Polyphemus groaning in his cave was the popular figure of a barbarian, hairy and strong and stupid. "Nobody is killing me!" Hagen was not stupid; Hagen resented it, and with good reason. She wondered, unsettled, if she had been rude to him, condescending, and was ashamed of herself. She put her hand on his, where it rested on the stone bench, and sought words to make it better between them.

"But you are more like Odysseus, aren't you—wandering the world on your way home." There, that would serve. She smiled, pleased with herself, her tact, her generosity. "Do you have a pretty wife at home, too, weaving all day and picking it out again at night?"

Under her hand, his hand moved, turning over, and he gripped her fingers. "Why, are you looking for a man? I saw you trying for him." He nodded out across the courtyard toward Michael.

She yanked her hand out of his grip, her ears hot with embarrassment. "Michael doesn't love anyone but his horses."

"Michael is a fool," Hagen said. "You're much prettier than a horse." He caught her by the hand again, his long smile on his face, his eyes bright.

"I'm not sure that's a compliment." With some difficulty she freed herself from his grasp.

"Who the hell are you?"

Absorbed in the talk with Hagen, she had not seen Michael coming up to them; she started all over, and Hagen took her hand again.

"Oh! Michael," she said. "You frightened me."

The charioteer stood before them, his feet widespread, his chest thrown out, his hands on the golden belt at his waist. "Who the hell is this? What are you doing bringing peasants into my house?"

Hagen did not get up; he sat there looking Michael over at his leisure, all the good nature gone from his face. Alarmed, Theophano got swiftly to her feet, remembering how on the porch of the church on the Chalcedon road Hagen had drawn his sword against four men.

"Michael," she said, "he is the guest of the Basileus—"

"I don't want the low-born here!"

Hagen got up. He was even taller than Michael, seeming slender next to the Prince's heavy-muscled chest and shoulders. He said, "What's wrong, horse-boy—can't you bear the competition?"

Theophano pushed in between them, her heart pounding. "Please, can't you have some courtesy—"

"Get out of my house," Michael said, and wrapped his arm around her and pulled her around behind him.

The big Frank grunted at him. "You've got a cheap courage, horse-boy. I suppose it goes with the language."

He turned away, walking off, long-strided, unhurried, going away through the trees. The Prince snarled something under his breath. His hand slipped down Theophano's arm and left her.

"Michael," she said, "that was crude and boorish."

Suddenly there were tears in her eyes; she saw more of the barbarian in Michael now than in Hagen.

The Prince laughed at her. There was a rough edge to his mirth; he glared over her head at the absent Frank. "You can do better than that—consorting with peasants."

"He's not a peasant! He's a Frankish nobleman. He is the Basileus's guest."

"He's half in love with you."

"He is not. He knows no one else, he was lonely."

"I won't have you giving yourself to men who don't deserve you, that's all. Come on with me."

"I wasn't giving myself to him. I—"

"Theophano, keep your voice down, you're attracting attention."

She bit her lip, aware that he was right: everybody was looking at them, she was making tomorrow's gossip. She saw no virtue in being Roman if people still behaved like brutes.

"Come," he said, soft. "Get yourself under control."

"Pagh." She jerked herself around and walked off, her face hot, and went away into the dark.

⋄ 8 ⋄

In the brilliant sun of the desert, all things seemed simple, divided sharply into light and dark, just as the radiance of Christ divided up the works of men into salvation, pure as sunlight, and sin, as black as night.

Daniel had been six years sitting in the desert, eating thorns and brambles, while the pitiless purity of the sun burned away his doubt. Now he was ready. Now he was going to Constantinople, his flesh hallowed as a vessel for the message of Christ.

He had walked for three days, coming down from the treeless rock-strewn mountainside where he had been transformed, before he reached the first town in his path.

This was an ancient village, made of small stone buildings and hovels of straw and twigs. In the center stood a little domed church, shaped like an octagon. It was evening as Daniel approached, and the village women in their black shawls were drawing water from the well. In the distance the serrated ridges of the mountains were luminous with the pink sundown, and in the pastures behind the houses, the goats bleated to be milked.

Daniel was taller than most men, thin as a vine after the years of fasting, and all who saw him stopped to stare as he passed. He did not stop. With his staff in his hand and his single threadbare garment clutched close over his breast, he paced through the village straight to the church.

Inside, the village priest and his boy were making ready for the evening service. The boy at the altar was setting new candles into the candlesticks on the altar and the priest, a weary man in middle years, his head bald as a stone, stood in his pulpit turning the pages of the Bible.

Daniel walked into the center of the church and stopped and turned slowly to see the whole interior.

The building looked very old. Perhaps it had even served once as a place of pagan worship. The tile floor was worn down here and there to the underfloor by the feet of the pious; the ceiling was newly painted, a blameless white, but on the wall behind the altar, where all the faithful had to see it, a face had been made with mosaic chips, two faces actually, a mother and a child.

When his gaze fell on these false images, these demonic representations of that which could never be represented, Daniel gave out a scream of real pain. The boy at the altar whirled, several of the white candles dropping from his hands to the floor. Daniel strode toward the icon, raising his stick. When the boy rushed toward him, Daniel struck him hard on the head and walked over him.

The priest cried, "Stop! Stop—"

Daniel climbed up onto the altar, wielding his stick with both hands, and struck at the icon on the wall. His foot slipped on the altar cloth and he fell on one knee and knocked down some of the candles, and was trying to rise again when the priest caught his arm and pulled him away.

Daniel swung the stick awkwardly backwards and banged the end on the top of the priest's head. "Blasphemer! You worship idols here— idols!"

The priest went down on all fours; blood streamed down over his bald head and down his cheeks, and he swayed there, like a dog, gasping for breath and snorting, dazed. Daniel climbed down from the altar and rushed out of the church again, into the square by the well.

The women gathered at the well had clearly heard the turmoil in the church. They were clustered together, staring and muttering to one another. When Daniel came running out of the church, many of the women screamed. He rushed in among them, scattering them out of his way, and seized the first water jug he saw and overturned it into the street.

The women screamed again, and like a flock of birds scattering away from a child throwing stones, they shrank away from him, darting off in all directions. Some made the sign against the Evil Eye. Daniel tipped over another water jug and another, and beat the water into mud with his feet, and gathering up two handfuls of the mud he ran back into the church.

As he went in he saw that the men of the village were running in from the fields and their houses, drawn by the screams of the women.

He ran up the center of the church. The priest was getting up, pulling himself to his feet with one hand on the altar. The blood shimmered on his face. Daniel ran past him and flung the mud full into the face of the idols, one handful at the woman, one at the child.

The villagers were crowding into the church behind him. He swung around to face them.

"Idols! You have worshipped idols—made sinful idols and icons to give your prayers to, when you must pray to God! To God Himself and no other—for has He not told us, *I am*—"

The crowd began to clamor, drowning his sermon, and he had to raise his voice to a bellow.

"I am the Lord thy God, thou shalt have no other gods before Me!"

"He's muddied up the Virgin! Look!"

"He's right—the Word of God—"

Here and there among the crowd people were going down on their knees.

"Look what he did to the picture!"

"God sent him to us."

Some prayed, but now from the crowd three or four men burst

forward, coming at Daniel with their hands out and their teeth bared. He whirled up his stick, ready to fight for the Lord's sake, and gave the first to come within range a good crack across the face. Then other men poured from the crowd, and women, too, some to attack him, and some to defend him, and all got to fighting in the middle of the church, before the altar.

In their midst the priest began to weep, and held up his hands to Heaven, crying for God's help. All around the back of the church people knelt in prayer as if their friends and neighbors did not go on beating one another there before them. In the midst of this turmoil, Daniel felt God urging him to leave, and he did so. The doorway was packed with weeping, praying women, who watched the struggle inside and wrung their hands together, and he had to bully his way through them. Outside, in the deepening grey dusk, he drank the bitter water of the well and took the road again for Constantinople.

The ceremonial robe weighed on her like a suit of chains; the head-dress hurt her neck to wear. Irene stood straight and still as she could, her hands pressed together before her, her eyes on the door with its heavy bronze panels. In a few minutes she would walk through that door and into the Church of the Holy Apostles and there before thousands of her people she would reaffirm the mysterious and ancient relationship between God and this City, and there could be no mistake, no misstep, nothing to mar the perfection of the ritual.

She said, "Parakoimomenos, you may approach me."

The Grand Domestic shuffled forward; he wore only his court costume, no ceremonial gear, since he was here to watch and not to take part. "Augustus, Chosen One of God, command me."

"This holy man in the desert," she said. "What do you know of him?"

The eunuch's noble white brow rumpled quizzically. "Augustus, Chosen One. A holy man? I know of no such a one."

"I had a message last night, from the drungarius of Paphlagonia—"

Beyond the bronze doors, the drums thundered, and like a war-horse at the sound of trumpets, she wheeled around, her head rising. "Find out," she said. "You who know everything, Parakoimomenos, do not disappoint me this time." The doors were swinging open, letting into this little room the blaze of lights from the altar.

"Augustus—"

With a short chop of her hand, she sent him away; there was no time now to speak with eunuchs, or concern herself with the holy man. Before her lay a test, another of the many tests that God had placed in her path, and she girded herself to meet it.

"Hail, O Chosen One of God!"

She advanced through the doors into the church, and the roar of voices met her, a thousand throats yielding up praises. In the midst of dozens of her servants, each costumed in a fortune in gold and gems, she paced forward into the blaze of the candlelight. Before her, the great church shimmered with gold, on the walls, on the columns that divided off the space, on the clothing of the celebrants, on the magnificent altar. She fixed her eyes on the Crucifix, at the head of the altar, and with measured steps advanced down the aisle toward it.

On either side of her, the packed bodies of the multitude swayed and dipped down to their knees. From each the incantation rose, in perfect order, a single superhuman voice.

"God, hear us! God, have mercy on us! God, protect us!"

Ahead of her, at the altar, the Patriarch was waiting, with three ranks of lesser priests. At her approach, they knelt down, and from them also the chant sounded.

"God, defend us from the barbarian! God, preserve Thy truth in us! God, uplift us with Thy grace!"

The Patriarch raised up the image of the City, a miniature building made of solid gold; he lifted it up above his head, and the thousands of candles showered their light on it, and the people went down on their faces before it.

"God, receive us into Thy hands."

The Basileus had reached the altar. With the people prostrated around her, she lifted her arms until the gold-plated wings of her robe were extended, took the image of the City from the Patriarch, and raised it at full length above her head. It was so heavy her arms trembled. If she dropped it, Constantinople itself would fall. She forced her arms to raise it high into the air, where all could see it, and opened her throat and shouted the chant.

"I take my City into my hands!"

"Amen! Amen! Amen!"

"I receive my people into my protection!"

"Amen! Amen! Amen!"

She turned, the golden image on her fingertips, her muscles on fire at the effort; with every passing second the weight seemed to double, the strain to drag irresistibly on her arms.

"I renew my spirit in my City!"

"Amen! Amen! Amen!"

"Here is Christ, Basileus!"

"Amen! Amen! Amen!"

The chorus echoed and echoed again in the great dome above her. She lifted her eyes to it; there in the concave surface the face of God Himself looked down, Pantocrator, the Judge of All. Her arms were numb with weakness. Still she supported the whole City on her fingertips. God had chosen her again, and her triumph gave her strength beyond herself, Basileus.

She faced the altar again, and started forward. The Patriarch and his priests stepped to one side. In solemn march, she advanced to the altar, and there, only there, allowed herself to lower her arms, to bring the great weight slowly down onto the altar, to lay it there for another year.

"Hail, Basileus! Hail, Christ, our Ruler!"

She raised her arms again, buoyant without the golden City. Her spirit flew up like a winged dove. God had chosen her again. The Caliph could threaten, and John Cerulis spin his plots, but she was invulnerable as long as God maintained her.

"Hagen has the list," Theophano said. She lifted off the heavy golden robe like a shell, freeing the warm woman inside.

"He does? Are you sure?"

"He as much as told me so."

Irene shook her hair out, stretching her arms, the ceremonial robes falling away from her. The other women were in the next room still, getting more clothes for the Basileus, and Theophano was alone with her for a moment. She swept a gauze dressing gown around her mistress's shoulders. When she reached forward to fasten it at the throat, her arms were around the Basileus's neck, and Irene turned her head swiftly and kissed her.

They laughed. Theophano withdrew her arms, her gaze lowered, warm and happy in the intimate moment. Irene stood up, paced across the room, and shut the door, so that the other women would stay out.

Sitting down on the stool, Theophano looked up at her mistress, aware now that some furthur task would be expected of her. Irene came back toward her and her hand passed swiftly over Theophano's head in a light caressing touch.

"The list matters nothing, so long as John Cerulis does not have it," she said. "What matters is his plot against me, which he surely will not abandon simply because he has not got the list. I must know more details of that plot."

"Alas," Theophano said. "I learned nothing of it."

"Yet you were a member of his intimate company," the Empress said. "Could you not somehow inveigle yourself back into his good graces?"

Theophano's heart stopped; she felt cold all over. She said, "Oh, no, mistress, he will never believe me again."

"You could tell him that you had to do what you did, to preserve your good standing with me, but that you are sincerely in his service, and mean to betray me to him."

"Oh, mistress, he will never believe that."

Tap-tap, came a discreet little knock on the door, Helena wanting to come in: tap-tap-tap.

"One moment," Irene called, and leaning down took Theophano's hands in hers and looked into her face.

"You must. My love, for me, will you do it?"

"Oh, mistress—" Theophano laid her cheek against the Basileus's hand. "I would do anything for you, you know it, but—"

"I shall rescue you, I promise. God will not abandon you, if you do His will. I shall not abandon you. But we must have knowledge of his plans, or we shall all be destroyed, and the Empire with us."

Theophano gathered breath. She was frightened of John Cerulis and the idea of putting herself into his power again turned her heart to ice. The hands on her hands were warm and soft and loving, a mother's hands. The womanly face that looked down into hers was soft with love. She could not fail the Basileus now. Lifting her eyes, she said, "I will, mistress."

Irene leaned down and firmly kissed her lips. "Stay by me a while longer, we shall discuss ploys to use against him."

She called out, and Helena came in, on her heels the Parakoimomenos. Theophano drew back into a corner, struggling with her tangled feelings.

To serve the Empire: she wanted nothing more. She fixed her mind on that, the one worthy goal.

Before her, the Empress had risen, restless, her hands unceasingly moving. The Parakoimomenos had prostrated himself when he entered, and now he rose to his knees.

"Augustus, Chosen One of God, glory of the Empire!"

"Yes, yes, yes," Irene said. "Speak." She drifted away up the room toward the window.

"The holy man in the desert, Augustus, is a hermit named Daniel. He is coming this way, along the Paphlagonian highway, causing damage as he goes—"

"How?" The Basileus wheeled. The sunlit window behind her turned her into a featureless shadow.

"He preaches a new breaking of the images, Basileus. Wherever he goes, some of the people heed his words and obey him, and then the others are drawn into the strife to protect their churches."

"Has he followers?"

"Some. Not many. Some say he is mad, given to visions, inspired to prophecy."

The dark figure before the window spun around again, giving off flashes of light from the gold ornaments in her hair. "Very well. We shall keep watch on him."

"Yes, Augustus, Chosen One of God."

"He is no danger, unless he attracts followers."

"Yes, Augustus, Chosen One of God."

"See to it."

The Parakoimomenos prostrated himself again. From the corner Theophano looked on with a new quaking of her heart. The Grand Chamberlain was in charge of the household of the Basileus, nothing more. He had no right to duties outside the Palace. Why was she giving him such powers? Now he was coming to his feet, his body submissively bent, his hands together. Neither man nor woman, what strange lusts manifested themselves in him? And Irene was giving in to him, giving him what he wanted. Theophano turned her head away.

"Now, for contrast," Nicephoros said, and shuffled through his stacks of paper. Until his appointment to the office of treasurer, the accounts of the Empire had been kept on wax tablets and sheets of horn, but he had reorganized the procedures, made the scribes use paper, and went over all the books himself. He produced a sheaf of accounts from the stack on his left.

"In contrast, Augustus, to the frail condition of your own finances, let me present the finances of the monastery of Studion."

"Studion," she said, startled, and walked quickly toward him. "What relevance have the monks to any of this?"

"If the Augustus will condescend to read through these—"

The Treasurer laid out sheet after sheet of the figures, in his own precise Damascene hand; she glanced at them and with a sweep of her arm scattered them onto the floor.

"Damn you, Nicephoros! Why show me that? They are rich! They are monks, God makes them rich, and I cannot touch any of it —why do you show me that, when I am poor, to tempt me? Or to taunt me, damn you?"

As she shouted, she strode up and down the room faster and faster, another form of temptation. Yesterday she had led the sacred procession to Saint Anthony's Stone, and at the effort of the long walk the crushing pain in her chest had come back. All night long she had lain in her bed unable to sleep. Now the pain was gone, and she walked, she worked her body, pushing, pushing, because it frightened her, and when things frightened her she knew no other answer than to defy them.

Nicephoros was bowing at her from the desk, his nose skimming the heaps of paper. She walked straight up before him. "Well?"

"Basileus, I see no reason why the monastery of Studion, and the other havens for the holy monks, should not contribute somewhat to the running of the Empire—"

"Render unto Ceasar," she said. "The monks have suffered enough, in the past days."

The monks had put her on her throne. She had promised them—especially the monks of Studion, the greatest monastery in the City itself—that she would not tax them.

"As you wish, Augustus."

The papers littered the thick tufted rug beside the desk. She stared down at him, bemused; the monks kept their accounts utterly secret. "How did you find these figures?"

Nicephoros slid off the stool and knelt down to recover his notes. "I deduced them, Basileus, from information available to me from other sources."

"Then you don't really know how much money they have."

It was mad, that the Empire should tremble on the verge of bankruptcy, while this household of celibates ate off gold plate.

"My sources are reliable," said the Treasurer.

Her intuition told her he was right; Nicephoros, methodical, intelligent, loyal, laid his reputation on nothing he could not verify a hundred ways. She went back to the window.

"I do not see how we can separate the monks from any of their treasure, Nicephoros."

He murmured a few rote phrases. She rubbed her hands together. Today, as usual after an attack of the chest pain, she felt vigorous, alive, brimming with vitality; yet it was not a triumph over the pain, but a partner with it, this high hot energy that would not let her rest. She felt herself teetering on a pinnacle; like a whirling top, if she ever stopped moving, she would fall. She looked out the window into the garden.

There below her, in the rose garden, was the Parakoimomenos, talking with Helena as the chief lady-in-waiting plied her loom. The Empress rubbed her palms together until the skin warmed like a fire.

When the pain came, she could do nothing but lie down. She was vulnerable, then, as a rabbit in a mown field. Of all her ministers, these two, Nicephoros and the Parakoimomenos, were most dangerous to her if they perceived her weakness—Nicephoros because he controlled the finances of the Empire, the Parakoimomenos because he controlled her household.

She had to leash them, somehow. Below her the Parakoimomenos was gossiping with Helena, whose tongue would eventually slip, and yield up the secret of her mistress's weakness; behind her Nicephoros was writing something on one of his sheets of notes.

She could set them against each other, which would be easy enough, since they were already rivals for power, and by nature hated each other. And she knew them, both men, very well. She could devise traps for them that their own characters would lead them into.

Her body was nagging her again, to walk, to move, to use up the overflowing energy rising through her. To use herself, and see how much she could do, how far she could go, how hard she could work, before the pain struck her down again. To find her limits.

She paced up the room. "Well, Nicephoros? Surely you have some ways in mind to tap this gold reserve at Studion?"

"Yes, Augustus."

"Excellent," she said. "I shall hear them eagerly. Go on."

⁙ 9 ⁙

"You should go to the ceremonies," said Constantine, taking off his cloak.

Prince Michael grunted at him. "Folly needed to be soaked."

"By the true nature of the Trinity, Michael, you can't tell me you spent the afternoon soaking a horse's leg. You know, there's more to life than horse-racing." Constantine went down the aisle of stalls to Folly's and leaned over the door. The horse snapped at him, its ears flat to its neck. "Is it any better?"

"I don't know. He's getting old, I guess—I think maybe there's something going wrong in the leg, or maybe in his shoulder." Michael went after him. The grooms were gathered at the far end of this aisle, probably dicing, and the horses were munching through their hay. There was nothing to do until dinner and Michael was bored. He leaned over the stall door and indicated the dark bay flanker's near foreleg.

"See? There he is, pointing his foot out again. I hate to see him do that, I think he's going unsound."

"He looked good enough during the race."

Michael sighed, chewing his lip, his eyes on the black foreleg, which the horse held slightly extended forward, the weight resting on the tip of the hoof. Constantine was right. The horse had raced well, but then this morning he had come up lame.

"How went the ceremony?"

"She was perfect." Constantine's voice softened, breathy with sentiment. "I love that ritual, and she has the gift for it, you just feel God's hands around you."

Beside him, Michael leaned into the stall and unbuckled Folly's halter. That was what happened to a man when he stopped being able to race; he got soft and spent his mind on rituals. Might as well go into a monastery, Michael thought, and took the halter off the bay horse.

"I keep telling them not to leave their halters on at night." He swept his gaze up and down the four stalls where his horses stood, champing through their afternoon. "They ran Ishmael's Khorasan horses right off their wheels."

"On that track they'd give their lives for you. You have the hands of Castor. Still, when I was racing, we'd have given you a run for it."

Michael shut off his ears. That phrase recurred in his uncle's speech several times a day, and he had heard all the stories that succeeded it. He stood watching Folly point his forefoot, worrying about the horse, about replacing him, about having to destroy him, whom he loved. Constantine rambled on about some long-past challenge series. Somewhere in the next aisle, a man yelled.

Michael paid little heed to that, but a moment later the yell came again, closer, and he looked up. One of Ishmael's grooms ran around the corner, all agape, his eyes wild.

"Prince, my prince—Esad! He's fighting in the back with some wild man from the steppes!"

Michael swore under his breath. "Damn him, let him get beaten up. He's always taking on people he can't handle."

The groom danced up and down before him; he was very young. "Master, this man's going to kill him."

Constantine hissed between his teeth. "I don't believe it." But he and Michael went at a trot down the aisle.

In the back of the stable was another door, leading into the Palace grounds; down here someone had brought in two strange horses, country-bred, and opened the top of the door to give them some air. In this row of stalls, half a dozen of the grooms from the racing teams had cornered the owner of the horses and were exchanging some hot words with him. Chief of the grooms was Esad, who fought all the time, but when Michael and Constantine got there, no one was fighting. The stranger sat calmly enough on top of the door of the first of his horses' stalls, smiling, calmly returning the sharp insults the grooms were hurling at him and his horses.

Michael stopped short, a hot spurt of anger threading through his veins. It was the man who had been flirting with Theophano at the Bucoleon, the night before.

To Esad he said, in heavily accented street Greek, "Look, horse-boy, in my country only the slaves fight with their hands. If you want to fight me, go find a sword."

"Oh?" Esad threw out his chest and strutted around a little. He was a big, strapping fellow, a Canaanite, covered with crisp black hair, lantern-jawed and ham-fisted. He did not notice that Michael and Constantine had come up behind him. "If you're as good at sword-fighting as you are at buying horses, I don't think I'll have much to worry about. Come down here and fight me, outlander, if you have the guts."

The other grooms cheered him on, snarling and hissing at the stranger. They were always willing to make brave talk for someone else. Esad pranced up and down the aisle again, while the big barbarian, fair as Esad was dark, kicked his heels against the side of the stall and smirked at him, and then Esad went to the wall and took down a long whip.

"Well, if you won't come down, we'll have to chase you out, hah?"

The other grooms muttered and backed away in a rush. One or two of them looked alarmed. Michael crossed his arms over his chest. The big white-haired barbarian had sounded tough enough the night before at the Bucoleon; it would be interesting to see if he could act up to his talk.

Esad uncurled the whip and stroked it across the floor. "Come out here and take your punishment," he said, purring, his eyes glinting, and snapped the whip at the barbarian.

The white-haired man came down from the door of the stall in a single fluid leap. He dodged the first curling snap of the whip, and when Esad jerked it back up over his shoulder, the barbarian lunged at him and caught the end of the lash.

Esad yelled. He pulled on the butt of the whip, and the white-haired man gave him some slack and then yanked back hard, dragging Esad forward onto the tips of his toes, and with a quick coiling motion of his arm looped the bight of the whip around Esad's neck.

Michael gave a hoarse cry. He plunged into the midst of the crowd and got between the barbarian and his groom, who was making horrible half-throttled noises. Michael's hand closed on the whip an inch from the barbarian's. Face to face, chest to chest, they stood with the whip gripped hard between them.

The white-haired man's eyes opened wide. "Where the hell did you come from?" he said, but he let go of the whip, and backed up a few feet.

Michael cast the whip down. He looked quickly over his shoulder to see that Esad was safe. The other grooms knelt around him, helping him unwind the whip from his throat. Michael faced the barbarian again.

The barbarian hitched himself up onto the top of the stall door again. The horse inside it came up to nuzzle him.

"What brings you into this?" he said to Michael. "No women to impress here, are there?"

"Look," Michael said, and poked the barbarian in the chest with his forefinger. "Stay away from my grooms."

The barbarian struck his hand down. "Keep your hands off me."

They glared at each other. The other grooms were carrying Esad away, his hands to his throat, where the red weals showed like necklaces of blood. Michael stooped and picked up the whip and rolled the lash in his hands. He hated this barbarian with an intensity like white heat. He was the champion; he had won the awe and respect of everybody in Rome, and now this common brute, hardly a man at all, was sneering at him.

"Get out of here," Michael said. "Get those nags somewhere else. There's nothing for you here but trouble."

"Thank you for the warning."

"If you have any brains at all you'll heed it."

The big man made no answer, but his nasty smile said he had no intention of leaving the Hippodrome. Michael went away down the aisle.

"What happened to him?" Ishmael leaned out to see the groom Esad, stumbling into the tavern in the arms of several other men, among them two of Ishmael's grooms.

"He got into another fight," one of these called to him.

Ishmael laughed, easing back onto his stool. Michael's head groom was forever fighting and getting beaten. He turned back to the man who was paying for his wine.

"When will there be another race?"

"When the Basileus declares one." Ishmael was watching Esad stagger into a chair at the back of the tavern. The skin of his throat had peeled back like the rind of an orange, and he could barely keep his feet.

This tavern lay down the street from the Hippodrome, and the racing teams all spent much of their free time here. From his place near the wine tuns, Ishmael could see twenty men he knew, most of them crowding around Esad, demanding the story of his battle wounds. Bits of horse gear hung on the walls; above the wine tuns, on a hook in a rafter, dangled a dusty leather belt, studded with gold plates, that some long-ago champion had won in the challenges. Legend said that when that belt came down, the Hippodrome walls would crumble and weeds grow on the track. Legend also said the plates were brass.

"He's one of the Prince's men, isn't he?" said Karros, who was sitting across the table from Ishmael. Picking up the wine jar, he filled Ishmael's cup again.

The charioteer took a deep drink of the wine. John Cerulis's bully boy had sought him out for some reason, and now maybe he would find out what it was. "Yes, he's the head groom."

"He's a hero to the multitude, Michael is."

"True. Anybody who wins is a hero. As long as he goes on winning."

Karros stroked his beard. He was Armenian, or a good part of him was, and his curly black beard betrayed his Eastern blood. For a man who made a living being tough, he looked a little soft, his stomach swelling over his belt, his neck and upper arms sagging and plump and pale. He cocked his thumbs, his leer showing wide-spaced yellowing teeth.

"You'd love to have it, wouldn't you. Just once."

"Hunh." Ishmael pushed away the wine cup, which was empty anyway. "Do you have something to say to me of any consequence?" Once would not be enough. Never enough.

"You know the race yesterday?"

"Yes, I think I remember something happening yesterday in the Hippodrome."

Karros smiled humorlessly at him. "Michael wore a color on his arm during the race."

"Did he? I don't remember."

"He did. A yellow scarf."

"Maybe for luck." Now, his memory filling in, Ishmael did recall, as he raced his team hopelessly in the dust of the Prince's car, a yellow scarf fluttering like an insult in his face.

"Why now? He's never used a luck charm before. You don't think it was a signal?"

"I don't know what it was, Karros. Why don't you ask him?"

Karros's lips twisted in a wry grimace. The whites of his eyes were tinged with brown.

"Think of this, Ishmael. He's the darling of the people. If he wanted to be emperor, nothing could stop him."

"'Emperor,'" Ishmael said, astonished. "You're crazy, Karros. Whose idea is that?"

"The yellow scarf—it's a signal to his supporters, we think."

"Horse dung." Ishmael looked suspiciously into Karros's face, wondering where he got such stories; he blurted out, "Why would he want to be emperor, when he is Champion of the Hippodrome?"

Karros said, "You race drivers see the world a little narrow, don't you think?" He nodded toward the door. "Here comes the man himself. That was one hell of half of a race, that last heat."

Ishmael's temper slipped. "Thanks for the cup." He jerked himself up onto his feet, glared at Karros, and went across the tavern to the big table at the back where Prince Michael usually sat.

Michael had stopped to speak to Esad, who was feeling his throat and talking with a rasp. Ishmael waited until the Prince turned away from the injured groom.

"What happened to him?"

Michael went on toward his table. "He talked too much to the wrong man. Sit down and share a jar with me."

Ishmael pulled up a stool to the scarred wooden wheel of the table. The lamp hanging above it smoked in billows and the ceiling was black with soot; the shadow of the lamp fell on the table. He fingered the deep marks on the worn surface of the wood, where generations of patrons had idled away their time with their knives. "Where did Esad get into this fight?"

"At the stables. There's a stranger in the back, there, a white-haired man; have you seen him?"

"He has two Syrian stallions—a bay and a black? Yes. He looks very rough in harness. Whose man is he?"

Michael had already signalled the tavern's serving girl, who brought a double-handled jug of a very fine western wine over to the table and set down a cup before each of the charioteers. "Apparently he is in the service of the Basileus. Maybe he's one of her spies."

Ishmael fingered his cup. Karros had pumped him full of drink already, and he disliked being tipsy. The notion of spies beguiled him. Karros was right: he looked too little at the world outside the Hippodrome. That reminded him of the yellow scarf, and he glanced at Prince Michael.

The other man's eyes rested speculatively on him. "Have you heard anything about this new team from Caesarea?"

"I've heard he's very daring, but his hands are a little heavy."

"What are his horses like?"

"Ferghana crosses, probably."

The other teams did not interest him much. He knew he could beat any of them in straight heats. Ishmael had won the right to race for the Greens of Constantinople in a summer-long competition in which he had not lost a single heat; he knew himself the best, and was not worried about the need to qualify again for the championship series. All the teams but Michael's had to fight for a place in the track with the champion; the qualifying heats would be run over most of the summer, according to the whim of the Basileus.

"When will you and I race again?" Ishmael asked.

"Before the hot weather's done, certainly." Michael leaned back, his long arms outstretched on the table. His white tunic, of the finest, softest silk, could not conceal the perfect structure of his chest and shoulders; his upper arms were as thick as a lesser man's thighs. When he fluttered his fingers, the great muscles of his forearm jumped. "The harder the summer, the more often the races." He shook his head at Ishmael. "You will never beat me, you know."

Ishmael straightened, his back tightening. "Someday."

"You will never beat me."

Affronted, Ishmael got to his feet; the stool scraped on the floor. Worse than losing was hearing about it all the time. He walked off a few steps and wheeled.

"Michael!"

The whole place fell quiet. Everybody looked around.

"*Prince* Michael," said the man at the table, correcting him, calmly.

"That yellow rag, Prince, that you were wearing during the race, Prince—what did it mean?"

The other driver laughed. "A present. From a female friend." His teeth were white against the cropped black beard. He drank his wine down and put the cup on the table.

Ishmael went to the door. On the way, he passed Karros, still sitting alone at the table by the wine tuns, and paused to speak to him. "There. You see?"

"He wouldn't say in front of everybody, would he," Karros said.

"I yield," Ishmael said. "There is no answer." He walked out to the street.

Karros lingered on in the tavern as long as he could, which was most of the day, drinking and listening to gossip. He liked this kind of work; what he did not like was going back to his master without some definite word on the intentions of Prince Michael. He held his drink well, so that in midafternoon he was only slightly drunk when a street urchin ran in with a note for him on scented paper.

The scent was familiar to him. He knew who had written it even before he unfolded the paper and saw the firm strokes of her writing. When he read the words, he began to smile.

She was a meddler, the little bitch; now she thought she could meddle again. Swiftly he got up from his table, collected his cloak and the shoes he had kicked off under his chair, and went out the door into the street.

It was near nightfall. Outside the tavern, the whores were gathering, ready for the evening's work. Karros plowed through them without even a glance. He had promised himself, once, that when Theophano had lost the protection of the great, he would take her himself. Now she was asking for it again.

He went up past the public baths, to a little church on the slope there, surrounded by the tenements of the poor. A swarm of workmen and housewives were waiting in the churchyard for the mass to begin. Karros went by them and in through the front door.

The church smelled of stale incense. The priest's boys were running irreverently up and down under the dome, taking candles up to the altar, and on the way back playing some game, skidding over the smooth floor, and giggling. When Karros came in they pulled themselves up into an exaggerated sobriety of pace. He went around to one side, outside the ring of footed columns that supported the dome, to a bench where a woman was sitting, her face heavily veiled.

It was Theophano, pretending to pray. Karros sat down beside her. Her perfume excited him.

"Good evening, Theophano." He licked the salty taste of sweat from his lips, remembering the last time he had seen her. "You are much more clothed than you were at the inn in Chrysopolis, my dear."

She crossed herself, silent, as if she did not hear him. He could make out nothing of her face behind the veil.

He tried again; he said, "Lying down with sweaty unbathed barbarians these days?"

She seemed not to hear him at all, and for a moment, his stomach suddenly giddy, he wondered if she were the wrong woman—if he were making some horrible mistake. But then she sat back on the bench, lifted her veil, and faced him, her heart-shaped face perfectly framed by the mass of black gauze, her blue eyes guileless.

She said, "Tell me, Karros, is the Patrician discouraged with me?"

The fat man blinked at her, taken off-stride by this unexpected question. "You want to come back to him?"

Her eyelashes fluttered; new color bloomed in her cheeks. Karros cleared his throat. He knew he should talk her into thinking she would be welcome. John Cerulis would give much to have her within his power again.

He said, "I believe he loves you, my dear—he will forgive anything to one he loves."

Impossible to get that through his lips without stumbling. He patted his mouth with his fingers, wishing he had not drunk so much.

She said, "Then you think he will have me back again?"

"I shall make the way straight for you." He wondered why she was doing this. Certainly on orders of the Empress. But what difference did it make? Once within John Cerulis's grasp, she would never escape again.

She said, "I had to go with them, you know—I really do want to serve the Patrician, but Shimon dragged me off to meet Targa. And then those Franks—"

"Oh, yes, my dear. I saw how much you struggled against the Franks."

Her eyes widened; in a voice that quivered with false feelings, she said, "I don't know how to thank you for that, Karros—had you not come in just then, I fear he would have raped me."

Karros laughed out loud; people were filing into the church, now, and his boisterous mirth drew pointed looks. He settled himself. Up at the altar the boys were lighting the candles. Karros put his hand over his mouth.

"Those barbarians." He remembered the man he had thought he had seen, on the top tier of the Hippodrome, a man he never wanted to see again. "You don't happen to know where they are now?"

"Well, as it happens—"

"Yes?"

"I don't, actually." She smiled at him, sweet as a child. "Have you seen them since Chrysopolis?"

"I thought—" He frowned, watching her closely; did she really not know that one of them was dead? "I thought I saw the big one at the races the other day. Probably I was wrong."

"I have seen neither of them since the inn," she said. "I have no desire to do so, either, and nor should you—they were little more than common criminals, those two." She gathered up the veil in both hands.

"Tell the Patrician John Cerulis that I shall present myself to him soon, and hope to recover a place of grace with him."

"It shall be my privilege." Karros leered at her, delighted; this news would quite make up for his failure to learn anything about Prince Michael. "If you were to bring him the list, he would certainly welcome you with every honor."

"The list is gone," she said. "Think no more of that." She lowered the veil over her face. Karros got up, expecting her to leave the bench past him, so that he could brush up against her, let her feel his body, but she backed up to the other side and went out that way. Disappointed, he tramped off through the mob toward the door.

: 10 :

The Empress had a map of the world, woven of silk threads with an emerald to mark Constantinople, and a great white pearl to mark Jerusalem; the sea was the blue of lapis lazuli, the Empire was of gold, and the rimlands of earthen brown and green. Nicephoros, coming early into the council room, saw this beautiful work displayed and went up to the wall where it hung to admire it.

He was of Syrian blood, the Treasurer of the Empire, born near Damascus; he had been brought to Constantinople as a baby, when his parents fled the oppression of the Caliph, but the authority of his blood still marked him, in the dark hue of his skin, his great hook of a nose, and his passion for numbers. As a boy, sitting cross-legged on a terrace before his tutor and his tutor's cane, he had suffered through Homer and Pindar, struggled with geography and astronomy, and gloried in the work of numbers. In their abstractions he found a peace beyond controversy, and their clues to the fundamental relationships between apparently disparate things seemed to him revelations of the order of the cosmos.

What that order was, he had never come to grasp; it was enough, usually, to know that an order existed. Especially in the administration of the Empire, it was a necessary belief that beneath all chaos there was pattern, even if comprehension of it were beyond the reach of men.

He stood before the map, seeing in the arrangement of the colors a problem in geometry; the door behind him opened, and he wheeled, ready to prostrate himself. But it was only the Parakoimomenos.

The tall eunuch advanced through the room with stately pace. His skin was white and smooth as goat's cheese. "Nicephoros," he said. "Perusing the book of the world, are you?"

Nicephoros greeted his colleague with a bow. "I am assured we are here today to discuss matters of war and barbarian government. I wished to refresh my understanding of the details of the earthly frame." He sniffed. The Parakoimomenos wore a subtle fragrance he could not identify, disturbingly feminine. It suited the council room, its cushiony gold and white luxury.

"The Basileus may not appear today," he said. His voice vibrated musically in the bellows of his chest.

"Oh?" Nicephoros raised his eyebrows.

"I understand she passed the night very poorly." One long pale finger reached out and picked at the pearl of Jerusalem. His fingernail was perfectly oval, the color of a moonstone. In a hushed voice, the Grand Domestic said, "You know she is unwell."

"I know no such thing," said Nicephoros, and glanced over his shoulder.

The eunuch laughed richly at this response. "Oh, but she is. Perhaps it is a passing thing, a mere indigestion, or a touch of female troubles— in spite of all, we must remember that she is still a woman—"

He sniffed; his black eyes glowed hotly a moment. Nicephoros said nothing. It was never wise to trade confidences with a eunuch, or with a complete man, for that matter.

"She has never named an heir," said the Parakoimomenos. "Perhaps the moment is upon us when that must be done."

Nicephoros said, "She will never name an heir," and promptly clamped his lips shut, vexed with himself for letting out such a revealing comment.

"Oh? Why ever do you say that?"

The Treasurer shrugged, turning away. "Merely a passing thought, my dear fellow. Think no more of it."

"No, no." The Parakoimomenos pursued him sedately back across the room. The piles of carpet silenced their steps, as if they walked on clouds. "Your opinion in such matters is ever acute and edifying, Nicephoros—please, amplify your remarks."

Nicephoros bowed to him, hands pressed palm to palm. "I would not take your precious time with my ignorant daydreams, my dear Parakoimomenos."

"Oh, but—"

The door swung inward again, and several more of the Imperial staff swarmed into the room; the Parakoimomenos, thwarted, stood back from Nicephoros, and went to greet them, and Nicephoros sat down, much relieved. He pinched the bridge of his enormous bony nose between thumb and forefinger.

The Empress would never name an heir, because to associate anyone else with her in the Imperial dignity would give her enemies one more angle of attack. He raised his head, facing the map again, his hands in his lap. For that reason also, if she were ill, she would do all necessary to conceal it. For that reason, to suspect her of illness, even rightly, or to pressure her to name an heir would be to provoke her suspicions; Nicephoros had no desire to find himself the target of his Empress's suspicions.

The Parakoimomenos knew all this as well as anyone. Why then was he muttering into men's ears? Nicephoros glanced across the room at the eunuch, who in the midst of the crowd of officers went from one to the next, pressing hands, talking in his melodious voice. Eunuchs were not supposed to have ambitions for themselves. But then neither were women.

Now she was here, among them as suddenly as if she had dropped from Heaven. Nicephoros sprang to his feet and at once went to his knees. She strode into their midst, her coat of gold and pearls all asparkle in the lamplight, and turned in the center of the room, and Nicephoros lay down on his face at her feet.

"Hail, Basileus, Augustus, Chosen of God!"

Some of the others had not even seen her; gaping, they were caught on their feet as in a great rustle of their clothes the men sank to the floor and raised their voices to her. Lifting his head, Nicephoros saw her smiling down at him.

Had she set the Parakoimomenos on him to test him? Perhaps that was it.

"You may rise," she said, in her cool voice. She walked restlessly around the middle of the room, her garments swishing and swaying around her. If she were ill, it lay lightly on her; she was full of energy, her face bright with life, her eyes snapping. Nicephoros and the others rose and arranged themselves around the room according to rank, the Parakoimomenos foremost. She went along the rank and spoke or smiled to each one, and put out her hand, and each man bowed and touched her hand—this was a little private ceremony of hers; she did it always. A womanish thing: she trusted her sense of touch to find out falsehood. Nicephoros pressed his fingers to her fingers and her smile fell on him like a lover's look. He lifted his head, his spirits suddenly high.

"Excellent," she said, when she had seen them all. "Now. What is the news from Europe? Drungarius?"

The Grand Drungarius stepped forward and flexed his arm in a military salute. "Basileus, from Stauriakos comes word that he is steadily recapturing those villages along the coast of the Adriatic that were lost three winters ago. The Bulgars are fleeing back toward their mountain strongholds. But it is piecemeal work, Basileus."

"Ah. Bit by bit we shall recover what is ours," she said. "Very good. You may write to our general Stauriakos and tell him we are pleased."

"He needs money, Basileus."

"I shall take that under consideration."

"Basileus, Stauriakos is a brilliant general—if we sent him more men and more money he might drive the Bulgars completely out of the Empire in a matter of months! I—"

"No," she said, and turned her back; she went to the map on the wall and laid her hand on the hand-shaped landmass of Greece. "He does well. Bit by bit, this is how to win wars. That way, we always know what it is that we have won, and if we lose, we lose only a little. Let Stauriakos do as he can with what he has."

Also, Nicephoros thought, to concentrate so much power in the hands of one man would make him a rival for her throne. She distrusted armies and always had. Soldiers would not obey a woman, they would always seek to put a man in her place; she had no choice but to stand alone.

"Now," she said. "Nicephoros, you have some report on the finances of the Empire?"

He cleared his throat; he felt all eyes turn on him. Stepping forward, he faced the Empress and said, "Basileus, the most diligent of the tax-collectors have not been able to make their quotas this year. Besides the poor harvest, the plague has broken out in Paphlagonia and Chaldia again and people are fleeing from the villages there."

Behind him the others murmured at the mention of the plague, and the Empress glanced around the room and came a step toward Nicephoros.

"The bearer of bad tidings, Nicephoros. The more galling is it that we must somehow amass the tribute for the Caliph, whose emissary is to arrive here in a little while to receive it."

Nicephoros saw no reason to speak on this matter. He knew there would be very little money for the Caliph, but he knew also that the Basileus meant to do rather more than give the Arabs money. He backed up, returning to the protective company of the other men.

"The Caliph is sending us the Emir Abdul-Hassan ibn-Ziad," she said, "whom many of you will remember from the last embassy here from Baghdad, a genial man, a son of the Barmakids, that industrious and farsighted family that does the Caliph's practical work for him. While he is here—" She turned smoothly toward the map again, and putting out one red-painted fingertip directed their attention to Baghdad. "I intend to seduce him."

Some fool behind Nicephoros actually gasped. Nicephoros laughed; some of the others hushed the fool in a barrage of hisses, and the Empress wheeled, her clothes a dance of fiery glitter as she moved.

"What! Bardas Therias, do you not believe I am capable of it? No, my good fellow, I meant it as a figure merely." She paced forward, her hands before her, a smile curving her lips. "He has been here before, he speaks our language—somewhat—and he has learned a little of our ways. This time, we shall show him what a man's life may be like. Let him see what it is to be Roman, and he will not want to be anything else."

Around Nicephoros, the men murmured their rote praises of her. Nicephoros glanced behind him, looking among the ranks of officials for the Prefect of the City, whose task it was to manage the affairs of the City of Constantinople itself; the Prefect had not yet appeared, although his report would be called for next. The Empress was facing her map again, her mind still fixed on her plans for the Barmakid ambassador.

"They have wealth, in Baghdad," she said, and put her hand out toward the blue of the twin rivers. "Mere wealth will not bend his mind toward us. In his own country he may have anything he wishes, anything he can conceive of. It is our superior uses of our wealth that will infect him with that disease most useful to our purposes—civilization. Nicephoros."

The Treasurer bowed, spreading out his hands in gestures of submission. "Basileus."

"You have travelled to Baghdad—you know what in our City will compare most favorably with his own. You will escort ibn-Ziad about Constantinople."

"Basileus," Nicephoros said, alarmed; his duties already consumed every daylight hour. The Parakoimomenos was bending forward also, urgent, intent.

"You may speak," the Basileus said to him.

"Basileus, Augustus, Chosen of God—" The eunuch's flexible tall shape bent in several bows as elegantly as a palm tree yielding to the blast of the wind; in the course of his obeisance he advanced himself several feet closer to the Empress.

"Basileus, the most noble and glorious Nicephoros is already much involved in the problems of the taxes and the money difficulties of the Empire—am I audacious in suggesting that this largely ceremonial duty of escorting the Arab visitor be lifted from his shoulders and placed on one with more idle moments at the disposal of his Augustus?"

She smiled at him; her smile extended to include Nicephoros, now caught in a painful conflict: dealing with ibn-Ziad was a chore he wanted neither for himself nor for the Parakoimomenos. The Empress's eyes sparkled. Surely she enjoyed making rivals of these two men.

"You shall share the task," she said. "Nicephoros shall bring his experience, the Parakoimomenos his own resources; in no way then can our objective confute our efforts. So be it."

The officers chorused, "So be it," and many patted their hands together in a polite applause. Nicephoros bowed, accepting the task, hiding his expression. The Parakoimomenos should never have thrust himself forward; yet that was a trifling lapse of decorum compared with her allowing him to dictate his will. She had slighted Nicephoros, giving him an important duty and then taking it away, even if he had not wanted it. His guts churned. He hated the Parakoimomenos, and it was wicked of her to force him into company with the eunuch. And where was the City Prefect?

Not here. Nor did she expect him here, because she was now moving on to some other problem of the government, eliding smoothly over the gap where the report on the affairs of the City should have been.

Nicephoros straightened. He was a servant of the Empire; he wore the belt of service to the Basileus, and whatever the Basileus wanted was the will of God. He had no right to these poisonous sentiments against the Parakoimomenos. The eunuch was another of the belted men, his colleague, his helpmate. Besides, he had no testicles. Nicephoros folded his hands together before him, pressing subtly against the front of his coat, reassuring himself with the witnesses of his manhood. He lifted his head. The Empress needed him. He would serve, as he always had, with no thought for himself.

After the meeting in the council chamber, Nicephoros went out to the courtyard called the Phiale of the Greens, a spacious terrace in the Palace grounds, where a fountain of fanciful shape showered the air with its cooling moisture. It was the first true summer day of the year, and the heavy, windless heat oppressed the spirit and laid waste to the body's resources of strength and energy; the walk down to the terrace left Nicephoros damp under the arms and down the back. The cool of the fountain was a benediction. He sat down on a stone bench at the side of the terrace and prepared to eat his midday meal.

The terrace was paved in rounds of grey stone, with the spaces between filled in with red and green and blue pebbles. Doves and pigeons in busy swarms hurried over this ground; over the low wall that surrounded the area grew a profusion of wild roses. Looking on it was a tonic to Nicephoros's spirits, and he sat a moment, his hands on his knees, smiling at this pure and unaffected beauty.

The pigeons, bold as bandits, hurried in a clucking waddling rush toward him. He broke off a corner of his luncheon bread and crumbled it up and scattered the bits around his feet, and laughed to see the birds fight over this largess. Besides the bread, he had brought a piece of cheese wrapped in a wine-soaked cloth, a little jug of the same wine, some olives and pickled mushrooms. While he was arranging this repast on the bench, his friend the City Prefect appeared.

"Good morning, my dear Nicephoros. You won't mind if I join you?"

Nicephoros looked up, surprised; he had assumed his friend was ill. "No, of course—sit with me. We missed you, at the council."

The Prefect pulled his coat skirts up around him and sat down. He was a younger man than Nicephoros, a native of the City, tall and handsome, with curly dark hair and a splendid beard and a ready, charming smile; in his rapid rise through the government to his present eminence this rare and delightful mixture of ingratiating charm and impeccable refinement had been more valuable than any genuine skill at administration.

"Nicephoros," he said, with no more preamble, "may I ask a favor of you?"

"Ask me, Peter."

The Prefect was poking into Nicephoros's lunch; he nibbled an olive and nodded, pleased.

"Ummm. Not bad. Is the cheese as good?"

"Try some," Nicephoros said patiently.

"Thank you." The aristocratic fingers of the younger officer went hard at the block of crumbly cheese, which gave off its briny fragrance like a protest at this rough treatment. The Prefect leaned on his arm, a pose no less pleasing for the studiousness of its effect, the folds of his coat sleeve falling precise as mathematics to the tight-fitting cuff. "The presidents of the Guilds have come to me with a huge petition, Nicephoros, asking for a whole long list of changes in the laws of commerce. God's Judgment, you would not believe it without reading it—they want nothing less than the overthrow of the entire economy." The Prefect lifted his eyes to Nicephoros's, his look candid as a baby's. "It's a catastrophe. She will never agree to a word of it."

"Tell them so," Nicephoros said.

"Nicephoros, I cannot do that. It's not so easy as that. You know the Guilds—how hard it is to get them to do anything in concert? This petition took them weeks to draw up. Every single page is signed and sealed with every single president's name. I can't simply throw it into the scrap basket and say, 'Not this time.'"

He was eating the cheese in great chunks; Nicephoros watched another toothsome piece travel to the Prefect's lips and disappear within. What he was saying made sense. Through the Guilds of Constantinople, the Basileus regulated every detail of commerce—who bought what and at what price and for what purpose; under normal conditions, these rules provided for the smooth functioning of industry, allowed a decent living for everybody, and brought the Basileus sufficient income in taxes to support the court. Unfortunately conditions in Constantinople were seldom normal. The iconoclasm had aroused the people to unnatural passions, which even now surged powerfully into evidence at the least excitement, and the steady shrinking of the Empire itself over the past century had lost the City Guilds important markets and sources of raw materials, while driving thousands of new people into the City. The Caliph's court in Baghdad had come to contend with the Romans for the raw materials of civilization, the gold and wax, gems and incense, wood and furs and slaves, forcing all the prices up.

"She has to see it and make some answer," the Prefect said. "Nothing less is appropriate."

"I agree with you," Nicephoros said. The cheese was gone. He put the jug of wine before his friend. "What I cannot as yet perceive, Peter, is what favor you require of me in this context."

"I can't face her, Nicephoros."

"Peter."

"I mean it!" The Prefect leaned toward him, as if shortening the distance between them intensified the force of his words. "I cannot take this petition to her, Nicephoros."

The Treasurer laughed, disbelieving and amazed; but the expression on his friend's face moved him to the yet more amazing understanding that the Prefect meant what he said.

"She terrifies me," said the Prefect, and his voice sank. "And you know—you know, Nicephoros, she cannot grant the changes. She will think me a fool, or worse, for proposing them."

Nicephoros drank some of the wine; he turned his gaze away, toward the fountain's pleasing sprays. As certain as he was of the Prefect's real alarm at facing his Basileus, the Treasurer was just as certain that the reason for it was not what he said it was.

"Will you take it to her? You could say that—it does fall as well within your province, after all, and perhaps is better explained to her—defended to her from your point of view. Nicephoros. Please?"

"I shall do what I can. Have the petition sent to my secretakoi."

Into the handsome face of the Prefect rushed a warm glow of relief. "Nicephoros, what a wonder you are! I shall never be able to repay you."

"I'll think of something, Peter, have no fear of that."

"Anything, Nicephoros—any extravagance I can secure for you. Only name it."

Nicephoros grunted. None of this tasted sweet to him. He reached for the wine again. "Look—there is Prince Michael."

The Prefect turned. The wall behind the bench where the two men sat fell off on the far side ten feet to a walkway through the dense hedges that lined the Empress's mulberry orchard. Along this walkway two people were walking, hand in hand—a girl and the charioteer.

"He's certainly a greater driver than any other I've been privileged to witness," Nicephoros said.

The Prefect was staring glumly down at the Empress's kinsman. "I wish he would lose."

"Oh, do you? I wouldn't be so quick to look for Michael's downfall. The mob adores him. The Empire itself will tremble when he loses."

The Prefect turned around, putting his back to Michael, who was walking directly behind and below them now, his feet crunching the gravel. "Yes, but the odds they give on him are dirt-low."

"Ishmael has an extraordinary fire and style. He'll win against any but Michael. Bet on him."

"The odds on him are just as low."

Nicephoros was eating the pickled mushrooms, which, in keeping with his high-bred tastes, the Prefect disdained. "Gamblers only win in their dreams, Peter. Tend your purse in your waking hours."

The Prefect scratched his nose, muttering under his breath. "You'll talk to the Basileus?"

"Yes, yes."

"You're a lovely man, Nicephoros."

"Yes."

"Augustus," the Parakoimomenos said, in his mellow tremulous voice, and reached out to tap a line in the letter they were drafting, "Is it not perhaps unduly—shall we say—provocative? to mention Africa among the Imperial provinces?"

"I thought that over quite some while," Irene said. Helena was doing her nails. The Empress sat sprawled on a low divan covered with red and blue and green pillows of silk, the Parakoimomenos beside her on his knees on the carpeted floor, the letter between them. This corner of the day room was the only quiet one. The Empress's nameday was fast approaching and crews of workmen were hurrying to redecorate this room and the rooms around it for the celebration, and even now three half-naked men were struggling to hang a chandelier from the ceiling at the end of the room to match the one already in place above the Empress's head. The rest of the furniture was covered with drapery to protect it from the dust. Irene could have gone elsewhere to work but she wanted to supervise the redecorating herself, to avoid any un-pleasantness later. Now she watched as the men teetered off balance on a ladder and one another's shoulders, the huge heavy candle-holder swaying in their midst.

"However," she said, returning to the matter of Africa and the letter to Alexandria, "Africa was indeed a third part of the Empire, in the days of Augustus, and with God's help will be part of the Empire once more, when we have recovered it from the Arabs. To leave it off the list would seem to surrender even hope, would it not?"

The Parakoimomenos pursed his lips. "Perhaps. Still, this may not be the most appropriate moment to insist on such things."

"Pagh." She waved her hand at him. "If we say it often enough they will believe it." In the doorway, just beyond the workmen, who had succeeded in hanging the chandelier, a page appeared, and behind him, Nicephoros. She sat up.

"Now, what do you suppose he wants?"

The Parakoimomenos looked where she was looking, and rose at once to his feet. "The most excellent Nicephoros? You did not summon him?"

"He asked for entry." She suspected what was Nicephoros's business. Nonetheless it suited her to keep the rivalry between him and the eunuch on her left as lively as possible short of bloodshed and poison. "I cannot guess what he wants. Would that he were as open with me as you are, my angel."

The Parakoimomenos swelled at the caress of her voice. She smiled to herself; with one hand she gestured Nicephoros across the cluttered room toward her.

He knelt down and pressed his face to the floor at her feet. The Parakoimomenos watched him with the avid intent of a hawk watching an unwary mouse, and indeed, when Nicephoros rose, he spared no look for the eunuch, ignoring him entirely.

"Augustus, Chosen One of God, I ask your leave to present to you a petition from the Guilds of Constantinople."

From his coat he took a sheaf of papers, which he bent down to lay at her feet. Irene put her shoe down on it. She had known this was coming.

"Really, Nicephoros. This is not your office, is it? Where is the Prefect of the City, whose responsibility such a matter must be?"

"Augustus, Chosen of God, the Prefect and I discussed the matter, and we concluded that the issues that force the Guilds to plead with their most beloved Basileus for recourse might be better elucidated from my perspective."

She tongued her lower lip; her gaze slid to the Parakoimomenos, and she smiled and put out her hand to him.

"If you will be so good—go and find out where our refreshments are? Helena, you may go with him and help."

The eunuch's mouth drooped. With a bow and a series of eloquent gestures he backed away from the couch, lingering as long as he could; Helena swept right by him, her skirts trailing off the divan. A pillow rolled after her and the Empress caught it and put it back where it belonged.

"Now, Nicephoros," she said, "you know this will not do."

"Augustus." On one knee, he gathered up the petition and put it firmly beside her among the silks. "I assure you, the sufferings that these words represent are as real as—"

"No, no, no," she said. "I shall read the petition, that isn't what I meant. It is the Prefect whose little foot doth not fit his shoe. What's wrong with him?"

"Augustus."

"He has been avoiding me. Something is wrong, Nicephoros. He's taking bribes, or subverting the government, or plotting my overthrow —what is it?"

The Treasurer's face, saturnine by habit, was rigid as a mask. "Augustus," he said, his voice off-key, and cleared his throat. The Prefect was a friend of his. Everyone befriended the Prefect, even the Empress, who liked his handsome looks and his splendid taste in jewels and clothes. Nicephoros gave a little shake of his head, putting off the concerns of friendship, and his gaze met hers.

"Yes, Augustus. I marked it myself. There is something gone wrong."

"Very well." She sat back. The Parakoimomenos was rapidly returning, his long legs striding through the door from the terrace, his coat sinuous around his knees. She said to Nicephoros, "Find out what it is."

"Augustus, I wish the burden of spying on this man could fall on other shoulders—"

"Nicephoros, do it."

The Parakoimomenos reached them, overhearing this, and with many bows to her and to the Treasurer he overflowed with protests.

"Augustus, Nicephoros already is so heavily overworked—allow me the honor of taking whatever of his tasks I can."

Nicephoros stood up, his face flushing, his eyes sharp. "I will do as my Basileus orders."

She nodded. "You will indeed. And soon, Nicephoros." Her unsmiling gaze turned sharp on the eunuch. "Did I not send you on some errand, my angel?"

"Basileus, the cook refuses to serve the meal in this room, because of the dust."

Helena was coming into the room now, and overheard this; she nodded, her hands clasped, her mouth pursed as if her lips clasped one another also.

"God's True Nature." Irene plucked at the huge pile of the petition. It would take her hours to read it, and she already knew what it said; her spies in the Guilds had been relaying her news of this for months. One of the pots of nail paint had tipped and was spilling purple onto a red cushion and she threw it irritably onto a pile of rubbish near the door. "Who rules here, the cook or me?" The chandelier was up; now the men would begin to hang the new draperies on the walls, and there would be a lot of dust. She knew the cook was right. With no grace she yielded, getting up, pushing aside the men who leapt to help her as if she were an old lady. Helena bustled around her straightening the long gauze oversleeves and the embroidered skirt of her dress. "Come on, then, I'm hungry," Irene said, and went out on to the terrace.

"I shall have to see Nicephoros after the reception," Irene said; she was crossing the courtyard of the Daphne toward the Octagon, the robing room, to be dressed for the meeting with the presidents of the Guilds, and half her court hurried along with her, receiving orders and obeying them. "No, no, Helena, not that one, the green one. Where is that damned Frank?"

At top speed she strode at the door in the brick wall of the Octagon, and a page leapt to open it for her. She burst into the Octagon without even faltering in her step; a volley of orders sent her people radiating into all parts of the building to fetch her ceremonials. In the center of everything, she stood with her arms outstretched and let Helena peel off her coat and robe.

"There he is." Off by the wall in the midst of other men she saw a white head. "Bring me the Frank." She stooped slightly, to let the women slip the robe of purple onto her arms; Helena knelt down before her to fasten the clips.

A page led the tall barbarian up before her; he lowered himself down on one knee in deference to her. Someday she meant to see him on his face at her feet, but not now.

She said, "My dear Hagen, are you enjoying the hospitality of Rome?"

"Augustus," he said, "you are most generous to me. I hope now you are ready to let me have the men who killed my brother."

"Well, we are proceeding in that direction, in any case. You know that John Cerulis is behind it all."

"So you told me."

"I want you to go to his palace—he lives near the Forum of Theodosius, on the Mesê, that's the central street leading north—and keep
watch on him, and see if he leaves the City, and if he does, you will
come back and tell me."

On her left, Ida, on her right, Helena raised up the robe of golden
net above the Empress's head, and she moved backward to let them put
it on her; when she emerged from the center of the dress, Hagen was
frowning at her.

"Augustus, I don't see why—"

"You aren't being asked to understand," she said, exasperated; her
people always did exactly as she told them, with no questions, and it was
annoying to have to train him now. "If you wish my help in achieving
your revenge, you will yield up control of the matter to me. I see everything, you see only your small place in everything. Now do as I say.
Cerulis may be getting ready to leave the City, after all, and it's he you
must destroy, which you cannot do if he is off in the countryside somewhere. Now, go."

Forward to her now came the six noblemen whose ritual task it
was to put on her purple slippers. They knelt in rows before her, and
Hagen got up and backed away. She watched him go, her heart per-
turbed. He had no respect of place. She wondered how the barbarians
managed to survive if their social order were so chaotic. Still, he was
going. She had shown him good reason to keep watch over Cerulis, and
if he lost patience and attacked her rival, that might have its advantages
as well.

They put the slippers on her feet, and now, accompanied by the
chanting of monks, the chief officers of her court advanced with the
Imperial diadem. Irene fastened her eyes on it. This was the chief emblem of her power, the only thing save God that she knelt down to, and
she put her hands together as if in prayer and went down on her knees
on the cushion that Helena had laid before her and bowed her head.

The diadem was formed all of jewels and pearls in the shape of a
flat cap, from which flaps of pearls and garnets, emeralds and blue
diamonds hung down over her hair and her cheeks. When she raised
her head under its weight, she was Basileus, and all the people in the
room around her went down on their faces before her.

She rose, smiling. The monks began their chants again, this time
at a higher pitch, and swiftly the court formed up ranks at the door,

each hurrying to his appointed place. In step, as one body, they marched out the door, and Irene followed them, surrounded by her women and her guards.

They walked up the hill to the Magnaura Palace, where all such receptions were held. On the far side of the building from the door through which Irene entered, she knew the presidents of the Guilds of Constantinople were waiting, each in his official dress, in his place in line. They could not enter until she was ready, and she marched after her court into the huge empty room.

The Magnaura was drafty as a barn. Its walls stood up high as a church, the ceiling vaulting over like a replica of Heaven, the floor of green and white veined marble giving off a clammy chill. The walls were hung with tapestries from all over the world, and busts and statues of the great emperors of the past lined the two long walls. The throne took up the entire west end of the room, two seats side by side, encrusted with gold and cushioned with velvet. From one seat Irene would give audience. On the other seat lay an open Book of Gospels.

Beside this emblem of Christ, the real ruler of Constantinople, Irene took her place, her hands in her lap. The rest of her court arranged themselves around her. On her left, three rows of men with long coats stood, each with his rod of office laid in the crook of his arm, and on her right, her guards formed up in three rows, each man standing with his feet exactly one arm's length apart, his left fist clasped to his armored breast, his right hand, gripping his axe, swung up to hold the great curved blade over his right shoulder.

Before these, the lesser officials ranged themselves, their posts prescribed by half a thousand years of tradition. All averted their eyes in deference, faces turned at the proper angle to the ground, and waited.

Now here came the presidents of the Guilds, come to ask her for what would help them little enough in the short view of things, and ruin them all in the long.

The Guild presidents shuffled in through the doors in worse order than the courtiers, having less practice at it. Most of them walked with their heads bowed down between their shoulders. They wore rich coats, past knee-length, aping the style of court dress, which was called the Hun coat, from a time when barbarians had dominated the Imperial service. Their feet were shod in velvet boots. These clothes were passed down from each president to his successor and some were as old as

Irene's own ceremonials. They advanced into the center of the hall and formed up their ranks and in a ragged sort of timing they went down on their hands and knees before her and pressed their faces to the icy marble floor.

Irene looked out over them a moment, letting them feel the power of the Basileus. She knew that most of the City's trades were suffering through a series of poor years, this latest being the worst. Nicephoros, gifted as he was at these things, had explained why to her, and made her see that the problem was not one that needed her interference. But the Guilds, which controlled industry in the Empire, wanted her to let them raise the prices they charged for their goods, reduce the wages they paid to their workingmen, and lower their standards of manufacture, and they claimed that otherwise they would lose so much money that they would be unable to continue their trade.

She lifted her hand and made the Sign of the Cross over them, and they responded with the words that centuries had hallowed, the words that had greeted Constantine and Justinian and Heraclius.

"Hail, O Basileus, Beloved of God, Augustus, Equal of the Apostles, from whom comes all, in whose name all is done, Hail, Hail, Hail."

She answered, as Constantine had, in a voice made louder by the hollow of the great room around them.

"Welcome, Romans, and give tongue to your thoughts, advise me and request of me, in the name of Christ our Lord, amen."

Their orator crept forward a little on his hands and knees.

"O Basileus, Augustus, Chosen of God, we beg of you that you give us the grace of a hearing."

There began the long summary of their tribulations. Too many people, not enough money, no place for them all; the Arabs, the Jews, the Italians competed unfairly—

The litany of complaints went on and on. The orator had a gift for rhetoric, and couched his speech in terms as fanciful and elegant as poetry, but even so the matter began to beat on her like a rain of stones. Why could they not be content with what they had? They never once mentioned salvation, the priceless treasure they received by virtue of their birth, which the Arabs, for all their gold and myrrh and zealous over-work, could not aspire to.

That reminded her of the holy man, whose name she knew now: Daniel. He was coming toward Constantinople, and he was preaching very disagreeable ideas, such as the perfect union of the soul with God, and the superfluity of the Church and the City and the law, when the soul belonged utterly to God.

She knew that John Cerulis had sent men to observe this dangerous ecstatic. If John Cerulis could manage to find an interpreter of God's will who would proclaim him emperor, then his lies could cloud the minds of men and lead them into a terrible crisis.

She was true emperor. She knew that. More than for herself, she trembled to think of the consequences for her people and the Empire, should they desert God and Irene, and follow John Cerulis. Therefore she had sent Hagen the Frank to spy on John Cerulis, and she meant to plant Theophano there as well.

In the meantime, the presidents of the Guilds were huddled before her waiting for her answer. The orator had done. Silence filled up the Magnaura Palace. The Basileus sat absolutely still for a long while, letting them all wait for her.

They knew what she would say. Had she not said it before, over and over—did they not come here to be told again what the truth was? And the truth did not change with the price of gold and silk and wax and wood. The sinner did not go to mass to hear that for his sake sin would now be virtue.

She said, "My people have come before me, and I have heard them. My heart is moved to pity by their lamentations. Yet I must deny them the swift and easy ameliorations that they seek."

Crouched before her, they kept their faces to the floor, but from some of them, rising above their bowed backs, came a tremulous sigh.

"We belong to the Empire," she said, and saw again, as if in the air some vision formed, the wonderful image of salvation that was Constantinople. "We belong to our Empire, whose order was set down by God, and made manifest by the laws of Constantine and Theodosius and Justinian. They gave us the perfect City. If now God chooses to test our hearts, we must prove our hearts worthy, and not change the order of God. To change is to fail. To keep faith is to survive. So be it. I have spoken, Basileus, Irene, Augustus, Equal of the Apostles."

For a moment, in the cold echoing chamber, there was silence. She trembled with the intensity of her vision. It was true, and unfaltering she would serve that truth, though she be the last, the only one to do so. Now from the people crouching at her feet came their own assent to the truth.

"We hear, and we shall obey, O Basileus."

The Chamberlain came forward with his staff and rapped the butt hard on the floor. "Blessed be the name of the Lord our God!"

"Blessed be the name of God, and long life and salvation to our Basileus." And one by one they inched forward on their knees to kiss her shoe and the hem of her robe.

The Guild presidents, in their antique coats, walked in formal steps from the throne room, their heads bowed, their hands together; as soon as they crossed the threshold their sedate and orderly lines broke and they rushed in a yammering mob on the Prefect of the City, standing in the antechamber.

"She denied us!"

"We can't go on like this—you must do something—"

They swarmed around him—he was at the end of the anteroom opposite the guards—and drove him backwards to the wall; and there, shouting and furious, they held him fast and screamed their problems in his ears.

"Please—please—"

His voice was drowned in theirs. "We need help! There is no work —no money—" "I have not paid my workmen in more than six months—" "I have not taken a nomisma of profit in over a year!"

"Please," he cried, and smiled, trying to look each furious red face in the eyes. This placid kindly look and his smile usually won people over to him, but the Guild presidents, old men all of them, were caught up in the full fury of their own little crisis. They were actually leaning on him, and his back, pushing to the marble wall, was beginning to throb. Then, to his incalculable relief, he saw Nicephoros coming across the antechamber.

"There," he cried, and thrust his arm out in a gesture as noble as any statue's. "Here comes the Treasurer of the Empire to deal with your questions."

They all turned, their voices falling silent for an instant, to see the angular figure of the Treasurer marching into their midst. Three of his secretakoi accompanied him. The Prefect used this lull to abandon the wall and make for the refuge of Nicephoros's side, where he caught his friend's hand in a hard grateful grip.

"My God," he murmured, "you've been my own redeemer, Nicephoros. I hope you have something to say to these people."

The Treasurer shrugged, a gesture he had from his Syrian ancestors. His dark face showed no light or easy humor. In the Prefect's grasp his hand was cold and limp as a day-old fish. His eyes swept the mob of the presidents, now facing him with the hostility and expectation by which they had pinned the Prefect to the wall.

"Now, hear me," Nicephoros said. "The Basileus has spoken, and has made clear what our duties are to the Empire and to God."

The mass of old men cast up a single groan.

"However," Nicephoros said, in a ringing voice, and paused. Beside him, the Prefect looked swiftly down the antechamber. The Imperial Guard was filing out of the throne room, their axes shining in their hands; one or two looked curiously in this direction. A servant with an iron lamp standard came quietly up the long room and put the lamp down and swiftly lit it. "The Empress," Nicephoros said, "cannot hear the pleas of her people without ears of pity. Therefore she has commanded that your burdens be eased somewhat by the following."

The Prefect relaxed, smiling. He took a moment to admire Nicephoros's statecraft. It was the Basileus who had insisted on duty to the state; it was the Empress whose heart went out to them. A nice touch; the Prefect knew he would use that sometime in his own work. Nicephoros turned to take a slip of paper from one of his underlings. The lace collar of his coat had etched a line of red across the back of his neck.

He said, "We shall allow the complete remission of your taxes, those owed from previous years and those owed for this year. In addition the Prefect shall issue you licenses to buy bread at a special rate. And finally the Empress will guarantee that you receive the materials for your crafts and industries whether or not you can sell the finished product."

The presidents murmured, their faces raised toward Nicephoros's; was it relief that made them pale, or merely the light from the lamp standard?

"In return," Nicephoros said, "we shall expect that you will distribute your available resources even-handedly, care for those among you who are suffering the most, and keep all your workmen at their benches and looms and in their shops, busy."

A necessary corollary: busy people did not collect in mobs in the streets and riot against the state.

"If we all give whatever we can to one another," Nicephoros said, "and take only what we must to live, then we shall survive this trial. When God sees how we uphold His Word, He shall be moved in our favor, and surely will bestow on us again those favors by which He has distinguished us above any other men. Go, now, and keep the Word of God and the commands of your Basileus."

"Amen," they cried, in one voice, their faces softened with relief. Not much relief, to be sure; not what they had wanted; but the method of its presentation had satisfied them. The Prefect admired this very much, and when the crowd had dispersed a little, and he and Nicephoros were alone together beside the lamp standard, he said so.

"Really," Nicephoros said, and gave him a cold look, "you respect appearances too much, Peter, and perhaps care too little for that understructure of performance that maintains the surface. I shall have to see you sometime soon, and speak with you in depth."

"Ah," said the Prefect, alarmed.

"Not now. I have many pressing engagements. I shall send a page to you to arrange a meeting time. Good day."

"Nicephoros," said the Prefect. But the Treasurer was going. Alone beside the lamp standard, in the glow of the light, he wound his hands together and tried not to think about what Nicephoros wanted to say to him.

It wasn't fair. He had never really wanted to enter the Imperial service; his father had insisted on it.

That would not salve Nicephoros's sore temper, should the Treasurer discover what the Prefect had been doing with some of the Imperial money at his disposal.

The light surrounded him like a protective shell. Everyone had gone away now, and the Magnaura seemed empty. He too had important meetings to attend, great work to do—after all, he was one of the officers of the Basileus, and in the City itself none was higher than he. He struggled to find comfort in these facts, but the nagging alarm remained, a worm in his guts. If Nicephoros knew—or guessed—then she knew too. Or guessed.

It wasn't fair. They leapt to the rescue of a few starving artisans, sweepers and bakers, goldsmiths and workers in ivory, but they would not take pity on him, who was one of their own.

It had always been easy for him to feel sorry for himself, which may have been why nobody else ever bothered. In a rush of courage, he left the shell of the light, and hurried toward the door.

⁝ 12 ⁝

Obeying the Empress's orders, Hagen went out into the City to find the palace of John Cerulis. He took one of his horses and rode out along the Mesê, the great street that ran from the Chalke gate into the Palace down the backbone of the promontory that supported Constantinople, away to the north to the mainland.

The Mesê was relatively flat, following the gentle descent of the ridge; the rest of the City fell away from this spine on either side—on the right, down to the sun-gilded bustle of the Golden Horn; on the left, through gardens and orchards, clumps of buildings, and a series of walls, down to the shores of the Sea of Marmora. On the side facing the harbor, the slopes seemed gentler, but he thought it was only because there were more houses there. Their flat roofs and whitewashed stone walls covered the earth like a crust, and even their gardens grew in pots and hanging baskets; the streets swarmed through this tangle in twists and turns, up and down, the buildings sometimes pressing so close to the street that they overhung the walkways and made passage impossible for more than one person at a time.

On the other side, where there were fewer houses, the streets were straighter and wider. He rode down along between palm trees like clumps of feathers on sticks, looking around him for some sign of John Cerulis.

He was hoping to find some district in this place where all the mighty lived, a cluster of palaces, or even a place fenced off from the common herd, but in Constantinople there was no such tidy order. Down each street he rode he found some great building that might have been a palace, side by side with the smaller houses of smaller people, and sometimes even hard by the decrepit many-storied buildings that housed the poor in swarms, like a hillside full of caves.

He turned a corner and came on a street that plunged away from him down a slope so sheer the houses were built out from it on stilts of stone; at the bottom, at the land's end, the sea laid down its hem of surf. Hagen drew rein. He would never find what he was looking for this way.

He hooked his leg around the pommel of his saddle and looked around him, no longer trying to force some order on this place, but letting it present itself to him as it would. No use trying to see it as a larger version of Aachen. He could walk around Aachen in half an hour and see everything. Even Rome was small and simple compared with this.

The buildings around him gave him very few clues. In the half-collapsing tenements down to his right there were no windows on the street; all the houses offered nothing for the passerby but a blank wall to look at. Like a woman who veiled her face, this mystery made him angry and unbearably curious. They came out, these people, they seemed to live in the streets, clusters of them on every corner, around every fountain, their voices drowning the cries of pigeons. He rode up to the nearest of these groups and asked for directions to John Cerulis's palace.

To his surprise, the old man he spoke to knew at once, and gave him detailed instructions, pointing, making turns with his hands. Hagen went off obediently down the next street, turned right, turned left, and stopped again, puzzled. He was lost again. The old man had told him to go straight here but there was no street to take him straight. He asked another man on the corner.

Once again, this fellow knew exactly where John Cerulis's palace was, and gave him directions, this way, that way, go up here, pass by the church—when he mentioned the church, he crossed himself—down the slope, past the garden, turn left at the fountain. It all seemed clear enough. Hagen rode off again, got about half a mile on, and lost his way again.

He felt like a fool. The City around him seemed to be laughing at him. Were they sending him wrong? The blank walls of the houses around him infuriated him. Pass the church! On every street corner was a church. He sat on his horse's back watching the streams of people that came down the hill by him; as they went past the old domed church across the way from him, they all crossed themselves, and some genuflected, without breaking stride. A donkey jogged along the street, tiny under a mountain of hay, a paper hung around its neck like an amulet. He went on to the fountain just beyond the church and asked again.

Like this, up and down, he went patiently through Constantinople. The City was all contradiction. The people were friendly to him, unceasingly helpful, smiling, cheerful; but the winding streets, the blank walls, threw him back like a magic kingdom to which he did not know the charm. Yet by degrees he fought his way closer and closer to where he wished to be, until at last, when he asked a little child in the street, the child ran ahead of him around a corner and pointed.

There, across a triangular courtyard, was a long wall with a gate in it, and by the gate a myrtle tree. Beyond the wall he saw the roofs of other buildings. The child was looking up at him expectantly. Hagen fingered up a coin from his wallet and dropped it to him, and the little boy leapt into the air, nimble as a juggler, and ran off.

Nothing distinguished the outside of this particular place from any of a hundred others he had seen in the course of the morning. Hagen rode slowly around it, looking in over the wall when he could. The wall contained a number of buildings, their roofs tiled in red clay tiles; he could hear people inside working and talking, and, coming on the front gate, which stood open, he watched as a group of elegantly dressed Greeks arrived in curtained chairs carried by poles on the shoulders of half-naked men. Through this gate he could see a courtyard, where many people worked. He itched to go inside, but on either side of the front gate stood soldiers, and so he went back around the palace to the gate by the myrtle tree.

A wagon loaded with firewood was rolling slowly in through the opening in the wall. Hagen dismounted and tied up his horse to a branch of the myrtle and went in after the wagon as if he were one of the workmen.

The wagon lumbered into a little kitchen yard, and there men sprang to unload it. Hagen went past them, into the great courtyard at the center of the palace complex.

On all sides were buildings, one or two of them having several stories, connected by covered walkways. The courtyard itself was full of servants, women at their looms, scullery wenches cleaning the pots and spreading out the linen to dry in the sun. Hagen went through an open doorway into the largest of the buildings and found himself in a lavishly decorated room like a great hall.

This place was as magnificent as the Palace of the Daphne, although much smaller. The walls were covered with panels of gold worked in relief with religious scenes, and the furniture was inlaid with shell-pearl and jewels. Sumptuously dressed men stood in lines before a door to the right, and all around loitered John Cerulis's guardsmen, wearing the short leather-skirted armor that the men had worn who had killed Rogerius.

Obviously they expected no danger. They drank from leather jugs, talked and gambled and paid no heed to what went on around them. Hagen walked right by them and no one even hailed him.

He went into the kitchen and helped himself to one of a heap of loaves on the table, took a wedge of cheese from a rack against the wall, and went out again to the courtyard to eat. One or two of the women at work around him gave him curious looks but no one asked him what he was doing there.

It was very clear to him that John Cerulis was going nowhere in a hurry. With all these people waiting to see him, and all this house-hold bustle around him, it would take the effort of days to uproot him. Hagen finished his lunch, admiring the orderly business of the court-yard around him, the women at work, gossiping, and the men waiting for work. A little naked baby wobbled up to him on wide-spread feet and leaned against his knee and begged for food, and Hagen put a bit of cheese on his knee and the little boy took it gravely and went away. Hagen got up and left.

He saw no purpose in returning to the Palace, where the Empress would have some other errand for him. He rode his horse up through the narrow streets toward the crest of the ridge, and there turned down along the Mesê and rode off through the City.

On this main thoroughfare most of the trade of Constantinople was done, either in shops in the colonnades on either side, or in the great squares strung along the Mesê like jewels on a necklace. There were three of these squares, each one lined with little shops and stalls, and

crowded full of traders and merchants and people buying goods. Hagen
steered wide of these crowds. Unused to large groups of people, he preferred to watch everything from a distance.

He could not buy anything here anyway; he had not the money
for it. The prices wanted for these goods astounded him. He saw that
the buyers all were haggling over their purchases, leaning across counters
piled up with cloth or pots or glassware, but even so they paid more
for a piece of wax, here, or for a clay pot, pretty as it was, than he was
used to giving for a night's lodging and a good meal, on the road. He
saw a woman in a chair borne by patient, stupid-looking men, who
carried her from one stall to another, where she was buying up silks,
spending more for each roll of fabric than Hagen had ever paid for
anything in his life. At another stall she stopped and bought each of her
bearers an orange.

Hagen went on, curious in spite of himself. He drew rein to let a
string of camels pass by him through a narrow archway. The City
beguiled him. He did not want to like it; it was too different from his
home. Yet it trapped his interest, as women did, by glimpses and suspicions and hints. Each little street that wound away down the hillside
or around a corner seemed a promise. The blank walls of the houses
made him ache to know what went on inside.

He stopped in the square where they sold beasts, to watch a drover
of oxen bargain with a customer; the great dun-brown dewlapped brutes
lay on the straw behind the two men, chewing their cuds, their wide-
spread horns tipped in brass. The two men were using a language he
had never heard before, but their gestures were perfectly meaningful to
him, and when one man turned and saw him watching, he gave Hagen
a broad wink.

In a narrow street just off the Mesê he found a row of cobblers'
shops, and went from one to the next hoping to get his boots mended
cheaply. They all charged exactly the same price, and each one tried to
sell him a pair of new boots first, although his own were still good
enough to mend. He settled on one at random. The cobbler examined
his boots closely, eyebrows raised, picking at the long Frankish stitches,
and smelling the leather.

"Not deer," he said, "or cattle leather, either, by my nose."

"Bear's hide," Hagen said. "Off the bear's belly."

The cobbler's eyebrows waggled up and down. "Interesting." He fit the right boot down over his lathe and peeled off the sole with a short stubby knife. "I suppose a man who walks in bearskin concerns himself just as much with the True Nature of Christ?"

"Hunh," Hagen said, startled.

The cobbler bent to look through a bin of leather pieces. His voice rose past him like smoke. "Because I can promise you, barbarian, that unless you understand that the Son partakes of exactly the same attributes and nature as the Father, you shall never see the Kingdom of Heaven."

"Amen," Hagen said, which seemed safest.

"Yes, indeed." The cobbler fit a piece of leather over the foot of the boot and scooped up a handful of little nails, which he popped like a handful of grapes into his mouth. "Because the Son existed in the Father always, since God is perfect—" He spat nails into his palm as fast as he spoke, a word, a nail, the word flying to Hagen's ears, the nail to Hagen's bootsole, the hammer tap-tapping without a pause in rhythm. "Yet God could not diminish Himself, and therefore when He yielded up the Son from His own substance He did not give up anything of Himself—"

Tap tap tap. Hagen watched the nails disappear into the leather. "Amen," he said, wondering how tight these boots would be.

"And since the Son also is perfect, of the substance of God, He could not have been partial in any way, but must partake of all those attributes that are undeniably the attributes of God, that is—"

"Amen." Tap tap tap. Without a break in his discourse the cobbler lifted the boot up off the lathe and twisted and flexed it in his hands, found it good, and with his knife trimmed away the extra leather, working with a master's fleet deft gestures.

"Eternity, truth, justice, goodness—these are the attributes of God."

"Amen," Hagen said.

The other boot went down over the lathe, and the cobbler continued his discourse; Hagen had lost track of his line of argument, if he had one at all, and merely said "Amen" whenever some comment was wanted of him. When the boots were done, he put them on his feet.

"Ah."

"Good?" the cobbler asked, smiling.

"Very good."

"If a man's feet are comfortable, the rest of him is comfortable," said the cobbler, and took the money, gave him change, made the Sign of the Cross at him, and blessed him in God's name. Hagen went back to his horse, at the side of the street.

God dominated every life in Constantinople, not just the cobbler's. There were churches in every street, some magnificently domed in gold, with doors of brass, and some mere huts with crosses on their roofs, and still the preachers overflowed into the streets, took up posts on walls and corners and on the tops of columns, declaiming passionately on matters of Faith. At the fountains, where the women gathered to draw water and exchange gossip, old men sat on stone benches tossing crumbs to the pigeons and damned one another to Hell for confusing the coterminous and the coeval. Even the little children, chasing their hoops and balls through the side-streets, teased one another in the name of God.

He stopped to let his horse drink at a fountain, and sat in his saddle laughing at a little band of boys who fought and swaggered in the square. Through them came a little troop of women, in the black shawls all the married women wore, with jars for the water, and he drew back to let them reach the fountain. Among them was a girl with un-bound hair. She caught his appraising look on her and her cheeks flushed and she lowered her head, and then flashed him a sidelong look as sweet and merry as any harlot's. Hagen coughed, amused.

When the women had gone, he drank from the fountain and sat down beside it, thinking of the girl he had just seen. As he sat there something splashed on his hand. He looked down. His hand rested on the mossy stone base of the fountain's shell-shaped dish, and near his thumb now he marked a hole in the stone, full of black water. Above it, the fountain's dish was cracked. As Hagen watched, a drop of water slowly formed at the foot of the crack, growing from a bead to a great tremulous dark ball that hung impossibly long from the stone.

Abruptly it burst, streaked down into the dark hole below, and cast up a spidery web of a splash. Hagen put his finger down into the hole, and could not touch the bottom.

How many years had this slow drip worked, to hollow so deep a hole in the stone? For the first time the weight of the years of this place impressed itself on his mind. No wonder these people fixed their minds ever on eternity. While their City decayed around them, they consoled themselves with the struggle for a matchless purity.

Yet as he looked around, ready to despise them, he saw again how beautiful was Constantinople, although the work of time and change; how well fashioned were their lives, although the work of delusion.

He had no truth so excellent as their delusion.

Once again he felt himself utterly alone without his brother. Mounting his horse, he rode slowly back toward the Palace.

He went into the stable under the Hippodrome. While he was putting his horse away, he saw that his packs had been gone through.

He realized at once who had done it. His temper brimmed over, although he had foreseen this and left nothing of value in the stable. All his money and the Greek paper he carried in his clothes. Still he got his sword from its scabbard and stormed off through the stables, looking for the grooms, but the racing teams had already gone home for the night. Only a few guards and the dozing nightmen were left, scattered here and there in the vast subterranean barn.

He walked in through the back door on to the Palace grounds and went up toward the building where he was housed. The sun had gone down. The sky was a deep lavender, and a violet mist was rising from the sea; the great marble buildings on the top of the headland above him seemed to be floating on the clouds. He stopped to admire this, pleased in spite of himself.

Gradually, as he stood there, his senses opened to the place around him. He could hear laughter and low voices to his right, beyond the hedges that marked the edge of the rose garden; behind him someone was playing on a pipe, not making music, but going through little strands of notes, practicing, or exploring. He could smell the spicy sauce they put on all their food, and when he sniffed deeper he picked up the toasty aroma of bread, and his mouth filled up with water and his stomach growled.

Now, off to his left, a door opened, and he moved swiftly to put a hedge between him and whoever was coming out.

Two women emerged, carrying bundles of linen. From the open door behind them came a gust of damp, warm air. The door slammed. The two women, sighing over their burdens, went up the stair to the next level of the grounds.

Hagen knew what was in the building they had just left; he had come on it the first night he was here, when he had walked over the whole place. It was a little bathhouse. He had swum in the bath the first night. Now he turned his steps that way again.

The door was unlocked, as it had been the first time. The room was utterly dark. He could still smell the smoke of candles in the air. Groping along with his feet, he brought to mind his first visit and remembered where the edge of the pool was and found it with his toes. He peeled off his clothes, left them in a heap on the tiles and dove into the warm, perfumed water.

It was delicious on his skin, better than the baths at Aachen, which smelled foully of sulphur. He floated around on his back in the darkness, his arms sculling the lukewarm water; he sank down completely under the surface, his hair floating, his breath escaping in a stream of bubbles.

When he came up again, the door was open, a dim grey rectangle in the dark.

He floated away from the spreading fan of light spilling through it. Carrying a candle, Theophano walked into the bathhouse.

The light danced on the black water, picking out the ripples he left in his wake. She started around the pool toward the cabinets on the left, saw the clothes piled on the edge of the pool, and shrank back.

"Who's there? Who is it?"

"Hagen," he said, seeing she was frightened. He went closer to the light, so that she could see him. "It's only me, Theophano."

"What are you doing here? What a presumptuous man! This is the Basileus's place."

"I like to swim." He went to the side of the pool where his clothes lay in a heap. "I'm glad to see you, anyway—I have something for you."

"For me?" Eagerly she came toward him; he gave her a quizzical look and on his arms boosted himself smoothly up out of the water, and seeing he was naked she turned her back.

"Come with me," he said, when he was dressed, and taking her arm he steered her toward the door.

"What do you have for me?"

"The clothes you left behind you at the inn in Chalcedon."

"Oh." Her shoulders drooped; he could feel her disappointment by touch, through his grip on her arm.

She did not try to get away from him. They went out into the darkness, cool after the steamy warmth of the bathhouse. She lifted her free hand to brush her hair back from her face. The top of her head came barely to his chin. He wanted to put his arm around her, to shelter her in the curve of his arm. Climbing the uneven steps to the next terrace, he thought that over, and at the top he moved his hand down her arm and took hold of her hand.

She glanced up at him, but she did not pull away. "The Basileus sent you to watch John Cerulis, I thought."

"He is going nowhere for a while." He led her around the end of the building where his quarters were, to the courtyard on the far side, where a line of bushy trees gave them some privacy. In the quiet, there, beside a little flowering tree, he kissed her.

She put her arms around his neck, her lips eager. Her body was warm against his. One part of his mind stood aloof from this, suspicious of her, but even as he fumbled at her dress, trying to find a way through the silky folds, her hand glided down over his back and across his hip and down his thigh and pressed up hard against his crotch.

From then on he thought only of getting her inside, in to the bed. She whispered some laughing, encouraging tease, her stroking fingers cupping the swelling bulge in his breeches. He lifted her up and carried her in through the door behind the curtain, her hair all down over his arm and his shoulder, and laid her on her back on the bed.

He lit a candle. She reached out her arms toward him. Their hands stroked over each other, pulling their clothes off. Kneeling on the bed beside her, he helped her lift her white silk dress up over her head. Trembling, hard and aching, he made himself wait for her, touch her where she needed it, kiss her little white breasts, his hands on her thighs, until she was ready for him. Her hand guided him inside.

It was wonderful. He was home again, a thousand miles from home, locked in her arms, her legs crooked over his hips, her whimpering cries in his ears. When he came, he bellowed with the force of it.

The candlelight flickered over her cheeks and her hair, the damp streaks of tears glittering down over her temples. He did not have to ask her if she had enjoyed it. Her pretty breasts and shoulders were flushed, no longer white as silk. She nuzzled close to him, her eyes closed, her face lifted, wanting to be kissed, and dutifully, already half-asleep, separated from her again, he gave her kiss for kiss, until they settled together into the narrow bed and dozed.

Theophano woke with the moonlight bright on her face. The candle had gone out. She lay beside him, his arm across her as he slept on. In the uncertain light, her sense of touch was of a higher power, and on the muscular slabs of his chest her fingertips traced the seams of old scars, long and straight as if made with a knife. She pressed her face against the mat of fine colorless hair on his chest.

He was waking up; his hands moved drowsily, stroking her sides. His palms were ridged with heavy calluses like horn. Both hands: she remembered the two-handed sword he had drawn on the porch of the church on the Chalcedon road.

When she lay still, her hands idle, her mind went straight to her meeting with Karros, and the prospect of facing John Cerulis again. She flinched even from the thought of that. What she wanted, this big quiet man could give her, and her urgent hands asked him, and his arms tightened around her.

He said nothing. He had not spoken since this began. She kissed his mouth, his throat, the scars on his chest. He pulled her over on top of him and they did it that way.

"Oh," she said, when they were both done. "That was good."

His embrace tightened around her slightly, his arms around her waist, his face between her breasts. She could feel him smile.

She wanted him to talk to her. It annoyed her that he said nothing, as if they were animals.

"Do you ever miss your own country?"

"I miss my brother." He shifted under her, his lips against her breast. Somehow she had expected that a barbarian would know nothing more of love than simply to get on and thrust; his tender skill amazed her.

"Did you do this with Rogerius?" he said.

"No." His tongue on her nipple was having an interesting effect between her legs. "Karros and his men broke in before we could do anything."

Gently he sucked and tongued on her breast. "Why are you doing this with me?"

"Must there be a reason? You are a man, I am a woman, we can simply enjoy one another." She would have done it sooner, had she known he was so good at it; she gasped, her thighs trembling.

"You'll forgive me, Theophano—" He kissed her mouth. "If I do not believe you."

Offended, she pushed herself away from him, her hands on his chest. "Then I shall leave."

Effortlessly he held her fast. "I won't let you."

"Why? Why do you want me? For pleasure—a surcease from care—"

"I've never met a woman yet who didn't want something for doing this with me."

"You have now," she said, angry. "In Heaven's name, Hagen, what sort of women do you have in Frankland?"

"None like you."

He pulled her down on him and kissed her, and they caressed each other; pleased, she realized that he would be hard again in a little while. He had the strength of a lifetime of hard work, country work, like a brute in the fields. She stroked the scars on his chest.

"What happened to you here?"

"Someone tried to kill me slowly."

"Oh. Well, he failed, for which I am most grateful."

"He was too slow. Rogerius got him."

"What—"

"Be quiet," he said. "You know, all you Greeks talk too much."

They made love with their mouths. He lit the candle and they made love in the light, sitting up. Straddling him, her arms around his neck, she thought, He will help me now, if I need him, and realized she was doing what he had said, expecting something in return for allowing him the use of her body. She promised herself she would never need him. She pressed her face into his white hair, wiping out the world.

Limp as an empty wineskin he lay there on his back with the warmth of the sun on his chest and did not really wake up; he was too relaxed to wake up. Yet in his dreams he knew she moved away, he heard her moving around the room, he heard her putting on her clothes.

Something clinked. That woke him up.

He turned his head and saw her standing over the pile of his clothes, feeling around in his purse.

"Oh, ho," he said, and sat up, swinging his feet over the edge of the bed to the floor. "That's why you did it."

She leapt back, dropping his purse onto the floor; the belt buckle clinked again. "No. No, it really wasn't—"

"You lose, this time, girl." He grabbed his shirt off the floor. "You gave me a good night's pleasure, and you're not going to find what you're looking for. Now get out."

"Hagen," she said. "I didn't—it was an afterthought. I really didn't—"

"Go on, get out."

"Hagen, please."

" 'Hagen, please.' " He sat down on the bed to pull his leggings on. She was dressed again, but he knew what she looked like, now, under her clothes, and she would never be covered up against his gaze again. "Get out. Go tell the Basileus that you failed again."

Her cheeks went ruddy, and her eyes blazed. Turning swiftly on her heel, she walked out of the room through the door on to the terrace. He went into the middle of the room, to pick up his belt, and stood there watching her walk away across the courtyard. She was straight and slim as a cypress tree, her silk dress flowing around her. Just the sight of her was a pleasure so acute he laughed. He put his belt on, ready for anything.

: 13 :

Ishmael spun the chariot wheel with his hand; the car was tipped up on one side, so that the wheel turned freely on the axle, wobbling in its orbit. He bent to see how it moved on the broad bands of leather that were supposed to cushion it. "This whole bushing has to be replaced, it's worn through."

"Yes, sir." His head groom crouched to see the bushing and nodded.

In the corridor outside the equipment room, in the open floor before the rows of the Blue team's stalls, some of the other grooms were dicing. Ishmael glanced that way; one of the grooms was Esad, Prince Michael's man, and although Ishmael meant to repair this car completely, he did not want his rival learning of its deficiencies. Esad had the dice. On all fours he butted into the center of the gaming circle, his voice high with excitement. Ishmael turned back to the chariot.

"The wheel is sound." He spun it again, his eyes on the rim, embedded with tiny grains of sand that sparkled in the light of the torch on the wall.

"Ho!"

The shout whirled him around, the hair on the back of his neck prickling up. The dice-players were scattering, their voices high and keen with fear. The big white-haired barbarian strode through their midst, kicking money and dice all across the hay-strewn floor, and walked up into Esad's face.

"Stay out of my gear!"

Esad scrambled to his feet. "My master dismissed you, pilgrim!" He waved his arm, and three of the other grooms leapt onto the barbarian's back.

The big man went down under their weight, half-buried under their bodies. Ishmael leapt up, shouting, enraged at the unfairness, and rushed toward the thrashing, yelling men. Esad yanked a short-bladed knife out of his belt and lunged.

Ishmael jumped toward him, but before he could reach Esad, the barbarian was heaving himself up onto his feet, bent double under the burden of the men on his back. He staggered away from Esad a few steps, reached behind him, and grabbing one of the men hanging on him he slung that body around and struck Esad down flat on the floor.

Esad's knife fell into the straw. He rolled over onto his hands and knees and scrambled toward it again. The barbarian had fallen, two men still punching and kicking on top of him. Ishmael got hold of one of these and heaved him away from the barbarian, and the white-haired man surged up to his feet, bucking off the other groom, and from his belt drew forth a battered long sword.

"Stop!" Ishmael flung himself on the barbarian's arm.

The white-haired man whirled around to face him, the sword raised between them; in this man's face Ishmael saw a cold murderous intent that shocked him. Even Esad never really tried to kill anybody.

"I mean you no harm," Ishmael said, and to prove it let go of the barbarian's sword arm. "You can't fight here, not with a sword, you'll get in terrible trouble."

Behind Ishmael, several feet pounded away down the aisle. The white-haired man straightened up. With a snap of his wrist he put the sword back into its scabbard on his hip. Seeing at a glance that Esad and the other grooms had discreetly left, Ishmael backed away a step, giving this man some room.

"Thank you," the barbarian said, and put out his hand. "I guess I lost my temper."

Ishmael took his hand. "My name is Ishmael—Mauros-Ishmael, they call me. I am one of the drivers."

"My name is Hagen."

They shook hands; Ishmael liked him at once, the hard grip, the straightforward look. Michael had said he was one of the Empress's spies, which was tantalizing in itself.

"Don't worry about Esad and the others," Ishmael said. "Once they get used to you, they'll leave you alone."

The barbarian laughed, putting his head back, his blue eyes snapping. "They'll learn to, one way or another."

"I can see that. Come on to the tavern. I'll stand you a cup."

"Done."

They went up out of the Hippodrome, on to the street past the Imperial menagerie. The bear-keepers and lion-tamers were feeding their charges, and as Hagen and Ishmael walked by, the archways resounded with the roars and growls of the great beasts in their cages under the walls. Most of the whores had gathered to watch the feeding, their backs to the street and their customers. As the two men walked by, one of the whores saw them and turned and whistled and flapped her skirt at them. A fortune-teller cackled at them from an alleyway by the tavern.

"I saw you race," Hagen said.

"You mean you saw me lose," said Ishmael.

"However you want to put it. You looked pretty good to me. Only one team can win at a time, right?"

They went into the tavern, half-empty in the middle of the day, and Ishmael steered the big man to his favorite table and called to the wench to bring them cups. Ishmael dropped onto his chair, leaned forward, his elbows on the table, and stared at the big man opposite him.

"Do you know anything about horses?"

"We don't drive horses the way you do. Even the harness we use is different; we use a collar, not the breastplate."

"Do you think I can beat Prince Michael?"

The barbarian smiled at him. "I would love to see you do it."

"You've met Michael?"

"Oh, yes."

"What do you think of him?"

"I think he's an arrogant swell-headed cheat."

" 'Cheat'!"

The barbarian shook his head. "He made fight-talk at me, to impress—somebody. When there was no possibility of a fight between us. That seems like cheating to me."

Ishmael jacked his eyebrows up and down; this assessment was too small to fit the Michael he knew. "Well, that's interesting." The wench was coming, with a jug and two cups, which she put down on the table between them.

"Mark it against my name," Ishmael said.

"Master," the girl said. "The old man says you owe too much."

"Damn him." Ishmael's neck felt hot and rough. "He does this every time I come in here. Tell him that I will pay him when I am paid."

The barbarian put his purse on the table, a leather bag that clinked. "I'll pay it."

"No." Ishmael thrust out one hand to stop him. "They know me here—they'll take my word, damn them, or as the Son is equal to the Father, I'll take my custom elsewhere."

"I'll tell him," the wench said, and left.

"Damn them," Ishmael muttered. He pushed his hair back with both hands. He was supposed to be paid by the Prefect of the City, who was master of the games, but they still owed him for the last two races he had driven. The barbarian was watching him, a little smile on his lips.

"It's not especially amusing to me," Ishmael said.

"No—I was not laughing at you—I was thinking of something else."

"What?"

"Nothing. A girl." The barbarian picked up his cup to drink.

"I'm sorry, I've forgotten your name."

"Hagen. Hagen the White."

"Well, I can see why that is. Do they pay you when they are supposed to?"

"They? Who?"

"The Basileus."

The blue eyes were sharp now, the smile still curving his mouth. "The Basileus pays me nothing. Not money, anyhow."

"Oh. I heard you were one of her spies."

Hagen laughed out loud. "No, no, no. I am only on my way home. I have a little business here to do, and then I will be gone."

"Oh." Disappointed, Ishmael drank his wine, and reaching for the jug poured another cup for himself and for Hagen, but as he reflected on it he realized that Hagen was not telling him the truth, since mere passersby could not stable their horses in the Hippodrome. Of course a spy could not reveal himself at once, or at all, if he could help it.

"Where are you coming from?"

"Jerusalem. The Holy Places. I was on a pilgrimage."

"Really? I've never been outside of Constantinople, myself."

"That's not a Greek name, is it? Ishmael?"

"My father came here from Nicaea. My grandfather from Aleppo, my great-grandfather from Medina. All men are citizens of Rome, as the saying goes."

"This is not Rome."

"Well, I am here, nonetheless."

"I'll never understand you Greeks. How—"

Abruptly the big man stiffened, looking past Ishmael, and in his eyes there blazed the same cold killing fury that had been in his face in the stable. Ishmael wheeled in his chair to see what had so taken his attention.

Karros was in the doorway, John Cerulis's man. He saw Hagen at once, and whirled and ran.

"Thanks for the wine," Hagen said, and bolted off his chair and out the door.

Ishmael leapt up, so quick he bumped the table and tipped the wine jug over, and raced to the door. The wench got in his way and he dodged around her.

They were gone. Looking up and down the crowded street, he saw neither Hagen nor Karros. He swore under his breath. The barbarian had secrets to hide, after all, and must work for the Empress, since at least one of his secrets concerned Karros. Standing on his toes, he searched the solid stream of passersby, but he could see nothing of Hagen or Karros. He would have to wait and see what happened. Dissatisfied, he went back into the tavern, to finish his wine.

Out of breath, Karros ran down the side of the street where the traffic was lightest, cut through an alleyway that stank of cat-piss, and crossed the Mesê, fighting his way through the crowd. On the far side, between the fluted columns of the walkway, he stopped and searched the street for the barbarian, but the big man was nowhere in sight.

Karros blew out his breath. He had outrun him. Relaxing, he sighed, smoothed down his coat, and hitched his belt up, his lungs cooling slowly. He might be getting fat but he was still fast on his feet. Soothed by that knowledge, he went around the column and walked into the arms of the barbarian.

He screamed; when he turned to run, a big hard hand clamped over his mouth, and a knife appeared before his eyes. In his ear, the rude accented voice said, "This is for my brother, Greek."

"No!" Karros screamed into the barbarian's palm; he clutched the other man's wrist with both hands, holding the knife away from him. "Let me talk—let me talk—"

The knife pricked his nose. "You killed my brother!"

"No—no—I didn't—"

Roughly the barbarian jerked him around to face him. "Then who did?"

"Theophano!"

The big man's head jerked up. His hands slid away from Karros; he retreated, shrinking back away from him. "What?"

"It was Theophano, as God forgives all sinners, I swear it, it was Theophano." Karros's mouth began to work at top speed. "It wasn't what you think—that business on the road. She is two-faced. She serves the Basileus but she serves John Cerulis, too, my master—she's really his thing, the Basileus thinks the other way around but the more fool she."

The barbarian was moving, closing with him again, and the knife rose through the light and shadow, the blade flashing. "Keep talking."

"She was only pretending to be escaping from us—it was for the Basileus's sake, a play, to fool the Basileus. I'm telling you, she killed your brother—she stabbed him from behind, in the neck."

He saw, in the wash of expression across the barbarian's face, that he made sense of that. Karros licked his lips, wanting to get away from that knife; his eyes followed every move of the blade, fascinated by it, the play of light along it.

"Listen to me. I'll prove it to you. She will be at my master's house tonight. If you come there, you'll see her—I'll let you in, you can see her sitting at the table with him."

The barbarian shut his mouth tight. Bad temper hardened all the planes of his face, his eyes like flint, his lips bloodless, but at least he put the knife away.

"All right, then. Take me there."

"Tonight." Karros put out his hand. "You know, maybe you could work for my master too—he can use a good fighting man. Hah? Think it over."

"Bah." The big man struck violently at his hand. "Tonight. I'll come to the back gate, the one by the myrtle tree."

"How do you know about the myrtle tree?"

The barbarian struck at him again, a short vicious punch in the chest. "I know a lot, more than you think. Don't try to fool me. The myrtle tree, at sundown." Glowering, his shoulders bulled forward, the big man strode off, out toward the Mesê. Karros watched him go into the crowd; he could see him for a long way, since he was a head taller than anybody else. Karros's heart was racing again. He was short of breath again, although he had not run at all. He thought, I'm getting old for this. On shaky legs he made his way back toward the palace of John Cerulis.

John Cerulis went to mass in the chapel of his palace, wearing his best coat, all worked with gold and pearls, as near to the imperial as it could be without the purple. He knelt down on the floor and asked God for help in achieving his purposes, although he knew it was God Himself who blocked him—for what other force could deny the throne to one who so obviously deserved it more than any other?

Outside, surrounded by his retinue and clients, he distributed money and bread to the poor, who came every day into his courtyard to receive his largess. They came to him, one by one, and kissed his hand, and bowing they all praised God for his wealth and his generosity, and then sent their own prayers hurrying up to God in favor of John Cerulis.

When that was done, he went into the reception hall of the palace, and there, seated in a chair covered with the pelts of leopards, smiling, ever smiling, he heard the petitions of his underlings. They came to him with flatteries and promises and begged him for his help, in gaining office, in buying land or selling licenses, in making marriages, in dissolving them, and if their oratory was clever, and quoted Homer in appropriate ways, and built up from subordinate phrase through subordinate phrase to the fully rounded climax, he granted what they wished.

He sat there in his gorgeous coat, his scribes beside him scribbling, his ministers behind him murmuring his praises, his clients before him praying for his purposes, and who seeing him would not know that he was truly emperor—in all but the diadem?

While halfway across the City, she who wore the diadem went on, hour by hour, moment by moment, using his place, spending his treasure, wasting his power.

In the middle of an oration, in fact in the middle of an elaborate period so contrived that John had lost track of the subject, a servant hurried up to him, knelt down beside his chair, and said a name to him.

He sat bolt upright. What a fool she was, the whore, to put herself again in his power.

The rhetorician before him was decorating his speech with gestures as stylized as the figures on his coat. By the force and variety of these ornaments, John Cerulis guessed the man was near the summit of his discourse, and he made himself wait (smiling, smiling) until the end should come, when he might cut short the reception without any undue excitement or conjecture. Yet his hands itched, his legs shivery, thinking of his sure revenge.

The speech ended in a pile of phrases. He did not grant the request, because, at the last, the orator lost control, and mixed his metaphors so atrociously that the scribes all sighed over their scribblings and the ministers all sniggered.

At a gesture from their master, the heralds marched forward and dismissed the gathering, in the name of God and John Cerulis. A page lifted up the master's cloak from the chair, so that he could rise without its weight upon his shoulders; another page went ahead of him with the rods of office. They went back through the palace and into his private apartments.

In a room carpeted with rugs from Persia, where icons framed in silver hung on the walls, there stood Theophano.

He stopped when he saw her, arrested by her beauty; he loved beauty, although not as much as he despised people who betrayed him.

"So," he said, and went forward into the center of the room. A snap of his fingers brought his servants leaping to divest him of the embroidered coat and belt of links of gold. Under it he wore a long white tunic, which they embellished with a vest and several necklaces of garnets and lapis lazuli, and a page brought him his chair and held his clothing straight so that he could sit down without wrinkling it. Theophano watched all this calmly. She was pale as candle wax. Her hair was so black it shone blue in the daylight.

Once he had held her in his arms, and fulfilled that passion which in him was so sensitive a taste that he had believed it doomed forever to disappointment. For that alone he let her live a while.

He said, "As the huntress Artemis goes forth upon the mountains of Taygetus, Theophano, so you have come among us here, outshining all my handmaids."

She turned her head slightly, her eyes upon him, and for a moment was silent; he began to be disappointed in her, but then she spoke, and her words were both apt and Homeric.

"Alas," she said, "what kind of people have I come among? Are they cruel, savage, and uncivilized, or hospitable and humane?"

He stretched out his hand to her and took her fingers in his, smiling in delight at her knowledge of Homer, her lovely voice, her excellent form and figure. "At any rate," he said, "you are among a race of men and women, Theophano."

"Then I need not break off a branch to hide my nakedness," she said, and smiled, and tried to free her hand from his, but John Cerulis held her tight.

"Yes," he said, "Nausicaa herself was not as lovely as you, laughter-loving Theophano. Now tell me why you so foolishly put yourself in my power again, after betraying me as you did."

"I never betrayed you," she said. "It was Shimon and Targa who betrayed you—they forced me to go away with them, when I would have cleaved to you, my only Emperor."

He lifted his head at that, his spirit elevated by her words, although he believed nothing she said. He regarded her from head to foot, charmed by her perfection of taste. Her dress of white silk, decorated across the breast and down the sleeve with gammadions of gold thread, was of an elegance so restrained and pure a man of lesser refinement would have thought it plain. He said, "And now you have brought yourself to me, to suffer for your sins against me, hmm?"

In his hand her hand was cold as the fire in the heart of a jewel. She said, "I have brought you that which you most desire, John Cerulis."

"Ah?"

"I will give you the gift of purple boots, if you will harken to me, and let me live."

His grip tightened, almost a spasm of the fingers. He drew her close against his knee. "Yes? What trick is this, laughter-loving one?"

"No trick, sir. The Basileus hates me, suspecting me of what is the truth, that in the weighing out of hearts I have found more value in your cause than in hers. My life's thread lies in the shears now, and every breath may be my last. Yet I will breathe my last among those who serve the true Emperor."

He laughed at this, at this dissembling innocence, moved to a rare affection, although he believed it no more than he believed anything else. She was here now, in his power. He would keep her alive as long as she amused him, and if she did indeed have some hidden knowledge of the usurping whore Irene, he would extract it from her as he chose. He had ever yearned for an ear inside the inner circle of the Empress, her women, and Theophano, willing or not, would give him what she knew.

"Tell me, then," he said, "what you believe to be of value to me."

"You know of the holy man in the desert," she said.

"Oh," he said, disappointed; the holy man was old news.

"You must convince him of the justice of your cause." Her cheeks suddenly bloomed with a subtle delicious color, more perfect than any jewel to complement her clothes. "He will preach your cause to the people, and the people of Rome will rise up and make you emperor."

"I see little hope of that, divine beauty."

"I can tell you this, John Cerulis, that the Basileus dreads more than any other course you might pursue that action which I have described to you."

He sat silent a moment, letting this suggestion mature in his understanding. The holy man was out in the desert, somewhere off to the east. It was tedious to leave Constantinople; nor did he believe that any serious advantage could be achieved outside the walls of the City, and the holy man would be dirty and probably obnoxious of manner. Rome was full of holy men, a new one every month.

He smiled at her. Relaxing his fingers, he let his hand fall to his knee, and she stood before him, unfettered, yet bound to his merest whim. He meant to see her die. Unfortunately, once she was dead, the pleasure would be over, and so he would prolong the anticipation a while, whetting his enjoyment.

He said, "We shall see, my lovely one. We shall see."

She bowed to him. "I await the moment when the diadem is on your head, beloved of God."

"I should think," said the City Prefect nervously, "that the honor of competing would be enough."

"Do you," Ishmael said. "God, what gives you that notion? When do I get the money, then, if not today?"

The Prefect looked around him, his mouth twisted. "Can't we talk about this someplace else?" He waved his hands at Ishmael as if the charioteer were shouting at him, and looked around for some escape, but Ishmael would not be put off. He knew the ways of the Imperial officers, and he needed money desperately, now, the landlord threatening to put him and his wife and babies out, the bakers refusing to sell them more bread on credit. He glared at the City Prefect.

"I need at least some of it now. Today, this afternoon, now, here."

The Prefect shook his head. "Everybody wants money, everybody thinks I have control of the purse. Why don't you talk to Nicephoros?" His voice was bitter. He nodded across the terrace.

Ishmael looked where he was indicating. The whole court was gathered here, on the pavement before the Chalke gateway into the Palace, where the Caliph's emissary would soon be received. Already a hundred people crowded the semicircular area between the gate and the scaffolding, which was supported at the back by the wall of Saint Stephen. The Basileus would appear on the scaffold, now shrouded by heavy purple curtains. Ishmael sighed.

"Take me to Nicephoros."

"Can't this wait?" The Prefect wrung his long soft hands. "Heavens, if you only knew how many people are in your position—"

Ishmael got him by the arm and applied force. "I don't care about them. I'm tired of being hounded by tradesmen."

The Prefect fell still and with an air of limp resignation he let himself to be maneuvered through the crowd. The Treasurer Nicephoros stood among a little circle of courtiers, listening to a joke being told; as Ishmael and the Prefect reached him, he was venting a mechanical, uninterested laugh. The Prefect touched his arm, and the tall Syrian turned.

"Ishmael." Nicephoros put out his hands, smiling, and grasped the driver's hands in a firm warm welcome. "How wonderful to see you again. You've heard, I'm sure, of the wonderful news?"

The Prefect opened his mouth, his eyes sliding from Ishmael to the Treasurer and back again, but before he could warn Nicephoros, Ishmael stepped down hard on his foot. "Has the Basileus assigned the next race, then?"

"Saint Helena's day. Truly auspicious, isn't it? You're sure to win."

Ishmael smiled at that, triumphant, the power in his hands. "Well, then, you'll have to give me some money."

The Treasurer's smile slipped an inch. The Prefect said, "He wants to be paid, Nicephoros."

"Does he really," Nicephoros said, his lips quivering. "What a novel idea."

"And if I am not paid," Ishmael said, "I will not race. How does that feel in your money bag?"

"Aaaah." Nicephoros shot a bitter look at the City Prefect. "What do you wear the belt for, anyway? Can't you do your job?"

"He made me bring him here to you." Nervously the Prefect's hands tapped on his belt of office.

Nicephoros faced Ishmael again, his smile quite gone, his eyes narrow, and the great wedge of his nose like a prow before him. "How much do we owe you?"

"Eight hundred irenes."

It would barely pay his debts. The Prefect muttered in surprise at the amount, but Nicephoros only stared at him a moment longer, his thick lips pressed firmly together. Ishmael met his eyes, struggling for patience. They would not please the crowds without his team; there would be trouble if he did not race. He hoped the trouble would be worth eight hundred irenes.

Behind him abruptly a ram's horn blasted, and he jumped, his nerves wound tight. Nicephoros grunted. "Well, not now, anyway," he said, and swiftly he turned to his position in the ranks of officials waiting for the Caliph's ambassador. Ishmael pushed back into the thick of the crowd. He was not supposed to be here and had no place assigned and he was wearing ordinary clothes; he stooped a little to conceal himself behind the people around him.

Swiftly the others were reaching their appointed spots on the pavement. They straightened up like statues, a dense-packed crescent of glittering coats facing the Chalke gate. The horns blasted again, their round soft notes rising like curlicues of sound that echoed off the high walls of the gate before and the chapel behind the crowd. Drums began to throb an even beat. Unconsciously Ishmael stiffened to attention, his arms at his sides, his head high, conforming to the posture of those around him.

The gate flew open, and with an ascending flourish of the horns, a thunder of the drums, rank on rank of foreigners marched through.

There seemed to be hundreds of them. In rows of eight, they marched through the gate, snapping their knees high with each step, and divided into fours and swung to either side, making room for the next row. Their robes were bright green; the hilts of their curved swords sparkled with jewels and gold. On their heads they wore soft folded cloth hats topped by ostrich plumes. Steadily they filled up the pavement, and when at last they were so packed in that only a narrow path was left, they stopped, turned their heads toward the gate, and in one great voice shouted something in their uncouth language.

Borne on the shoulders of six huge, naked slaves, the Caliph's ambassador entered, sitting cross-legged on a pile of carpets. The slaves carried him forward to the foot of the draped scaffold and stopped. The Caliph's man stood up. He wore jewels and silks worth a small kingdom; his hat carried an emerald the size of Ishmael's fist.

The drums paused. The horns rang silent. Everybody waited, breathless, while the music faded from the air.

There was an instant of perfect silence, and then the drums beat out again, the horns blasted. Fluttering like wings, the silk curtains swept to either side, and all across the packed terrace, gasping, the people fell to their knees.

On top of the scaffold the Basileus stood, a blaze of gold in the afternoon sun. Supported by her women on either side, great wings of gold extended ten feet from her, and behind her, fans of gold rose up above her head, catching and reflecting the sunlight, until she was so bright the eye hurt to see her. Ishmael, with all the others, fell on his face on the paving stones.

"Augustus, Chosen of God, Equal to the Apostles!"

She blessed them. Ishmael received it thankfully, knowing it would transform his life. His heart grew great with delight and gratitude that she was his Basileus, overwhelming these simple barbarians. Turning his head, he saw the Caliph's emissary gaping at her, and now even he sank down on his knees as if dazed, and like a great tower falling before a conqueror, he went down on his face at her feet.

Then from the scaffolding beneath her came a thunder of voices, giving forth praise of God and the Basileus, and glorifying Heaven with a hundred tongues. Ishmael's spine tingled. He thought that God Himself must sit upon the clouds to view this spectacle.

Through the Chalke now came the gifts the Caliph had sent to her, the Basileus. Crowding back to make room, the onlookers saw carpets spread out on the pavement, tasseled in silk, colored as wonderfully as jewels and flowers, and on these heaps of soft carpets, caskets overturned to spill streams of gold coins upon the ground, piles of emeralds and rubies, sparkling like the eyes of angels. And now, roaring, two great cats on gold leashes paced in through the gate, one patterned all over with clusters of dark spots on a golden ground, and the other streaked with black stripes on a field of dusky white, and these also were stationed on either side of the growing, glittering pile of tribute, and now through the gate, enormous, the ground shaking, came an elephant with tusks of ivory banded around and around with gold, and on its back great baskets woven of gold, each filled with flowers formed of gold and ivory and gems, and these too the Caliph's man offered up before the Basileus, as an homage to the Chosen One of God.

Ishmael buried his face in his hands. He trembled with pride. His City was the center of the world, his Basileus was ruler of the world: see, even the barbarians knew it! When those around him raised their voices in praise of her and God Who ruled through her, he joined them, his throat thick with gratitude and pride.

Afterward, when the formal reception was over, and the crowd had dissipated somewhat through the gardens and pavilions of the Palace, and the servants to the Empress were shoveling the gifts into boxes to be taken off to some treasure-house, Nicephoros came to him with a purse.

"You'll race?" the Treasurer said, looking sour.

Ishmael's hand sank, weighted down by the money in its leather pocket. "Of course I'll race," he said, irritated at the insinuation. "I would race for nothing. I would race for a handful of mud. But I must feed my babies." He stuffed the purse inside his coat, safe from pickpockets. With a glance at the scaffolding, now bare and bleak, stripped of its purple, he turned back to the Treasurer. "Don't tell her I ever said differently, either."

Nicephoros snorted at him. "If you race just for the money, Ishmael, you will never win."

"I don't do it for the money, I told you that." Ishmael went away through the Chalke; inside it, between the gate into the Palace and the gate onto the Mesê, a crowd of barbarians was gawking at the mosaics on the walls, depicting some long-dead general's triumph over other barbarians, far away. Ishmael did not linger. He went out on to the Mesê, his hand protectively over the bulge in his coat, and hurried off to pay his landlord.

: 14 :

Hagen sat on his heels beneath the myrtle tree, eating a handful of dates he had bought from a vendor on the Mesê. He had come early to his meeting with Karros because he had half intended to find a church along the way and pray a little and straighten his mind out. Many things bothered him. He could find no ground of confidence to stand on. Karros's story about Theophano made sense in some ways—the wound in Rogerius's throat had certainly come from behind him—and nonsense in others; but if she had killed Rogerius, Hagen would have to kill her, and that knotted up his guts, just thinking of it.

He had never killed a woman. He supposed a woman's flesh would give way as easily to the blade of a knife, her veins would open as wide and gush as red. It wasn't that. It was the memory that rose irresistibly of her lying in his arms that turned his belly to a rock.

This place was Hell. He had died and gone to Hell, and its name was Constantinople, where no one was what he seemed, where lies and truth were intermixed, and where people he did not understand were using him for purposes he could not fathom.

What had she said—"I know all, and you know only your small part." Yet Irene's own handmaiden betrayed her; Irene seemed to him a foolish old woman, in spite of her large ideas and the fierce energy of her looks.

There was some great design here, of which he saw only little pieces, and what pieces he was given were placed before him—as what, baits? Traps?

Theophano. The only evidence he had that she was betraying Irene to this John Cerulis was Karros's word. When she had lain in his arms, he would have sworn his life away that she was honest—that he saw her as she was. If she had killed his brother, he would have known it, somehow, seen it in her eyes, tasted it in her kiss—

And if Karros really had killed Rogerius, then this would be a trap, luring him here, and Theophano would now be back at the Palace, doing what she would be doing, if she were honest.

He could not pray. God did not approve of vengeance in any case and would not help him, and now here came Karros. Hagen stood up.

The other man was rosy with smiles; he put out his hand in greeting, which Hagen ignored. "I'm glad to see you. Very glad to see you. My master has been told of your coming."

Hagen watched him covertly, pretending to look all around him; Karros was leading him in through the gate, crossing the little kitchen court, smelling of basil and mint. A pile of broken terra-cotta pots covered a wooden table under the overhang of the myrtle tree. "I hope I'm to get dinner out of this, at least?" If Karros had lured him here to kill him, the Greek would have to act soon, while they were alone. He could already hear the voices of many people, in the building they were approaching.

"Dinner? Yes, yes, of course. I have every hope of being able to offer you a permanent place here with us. My master is most generous, and very powerful—he may be emperor one day, who knows?" Karros clapped him companionably on the back. Hagen moved sideways away from him, hating this false friendship, expecting to see a knife at any moment in Karros's hand.

They went into a large, well-lit hall. Rows of sofas crossed and recrossed it; Hagen had seen how sometimes the Greeks were made to eat lying down, although he marked that, everywhere, the great people sat up properly to a table in chairs. It was no different here. At the far end of this room was a long table, set with tubs of flowers and plates and ewers of silver and candlesticks of gold, already blazing, although no one sat yet in the chairs lined up on the far side of it.

Karros gripped his arm, and Hagen tensed all over, ready to jump. "You'll have a cup," the fat Greek said, and a little boy in a red coat appeared with a silver tray, on which stood several cups of glass and a big brass ewer in the form of a rooster, the feathers of the wings and tail deeply outlined in the metal. Karros beamed across this offering.

"Go on, taste it. It's marvelous wine. My master has the best of everything, we dine like kings here."

Hagen poured a thin stream into a cup and took it from the tray. The boy bowed and backed away, and turned to offer the wine to others in the hall. Could it be poisoned? Hagen did not see how. He looked down into the cup, uncertain.

"Go on," Karros said. "Drink." He put out his hand for the cup, and when Hagen gave it to him, he drank half of it. Giving it back, he waved it toward Hagen's lips. "Go on. Feel safe."

The wine was so dark it looked black. He drank a swallow and then another, thirsty.

"It's very good."

"I'm glad you like it," Karros said. "My master is very rich, you know. Of far greater birth than that upstart Irene—you know she's only provincial nobility? Isn't it a scandal? My master lavishes his wealth on those who serve him. I have chests of gold he has given me as rewards for my efforts in his behalf. I'll show them to you, if you like."

Hagen finished the wine; it was a very fine drink, and he looked around for more of it. "How does he pay for you, Karros—by weight?" He stopped the boy as he passed and took the ewer from the tray.

Karros laughed, a cracked note in the tone; yet he would not be insulted. He said, "If you join us—"

"I am joining no one," Hagen said, with emphasis. "I am King Charles's sworn man, my fealty is not mine to give away again."

"Hah hah hah." Karros's belly bounced. "Ah, well, if you are so in love with this barbarian king of yours. Come on, I'll show you my master's palace."

"You said Theophano would be here."

"She is here. Probably my master is enjoying her at this very moment."

At that Hagen's guts churned; a heat of rage rose through every vessel into his brain, and he nearly knocked the other man down. Slow behind his temper came his reason, dismayed; he thought, What is she to me that such a mention of her makes me reckless? If she lies with someone else, what does it matter to me?

It did matter. He knew two things at once: that he was going to kill both her and John Cerulis, and that he was getting an erection. He pulled the front of his shirt down and followed Karros on through the palace.

"Irene is as wily as an old cat," Theophano said; she had learned not to refer to the Basileus by her titles to this man who wanted so much to be emperor. She watched him through the corner of her eye. He made her skin cold just being near him; sex with him was like the embrace of death. "You will never be able to secure her person, except under the most extreme circumstances, an armed assault, perhaps. A riot of the general."

"I have no desire to secure her person," said John Cerulis.

He raised his glass and studied the color of the wine, swirling it to release the fragrance, and sniffed the developing aroma. One of his eyebrows quirked.

"The wine displeases you," Theophano said.

"I had hoped for better." He dispelled a sigh vibrant with regret; his perpetual smile carved deep lines and folds into his face, a mask of good nature.

Theophano looked away from him, her spirit sinking. Their table faced the hall, now busy with his hangers-on, gathered to have their dinner. None of them would eat until their master had finished. They sat on the rows of couches talking, laughing, exchanging kisses and ceremonial touches of the hand. She lowered her gaze to the table.

On the plate before her a steamed fish lay in a bed of olives, caviar, boiled egg, and clotted cream; she could not bring herself to eat it. She leaned her elbow on the arm of her chair and stared off across the room.

"I understand there has been a schedule of races posted on the gates of the Hippodrome," said John Cerulis. "Perhaps this year she shall see at last the overthrow of the superb Michael."

She said, "Michael has a few years left to him of the ultimate mastery. And Ishmael must buy his own horses."

She was repeating phrases she had overheard from others more expert. The races were not a passion of hers.

"Surely men besides Ishmael can challenge on the track? I understand the Greens are bringing in a team from Caesarea that's very well thought of."

"I—"

Her voice broke off. There, across the room, two men were coming in through a side door, and her heart leapt. That white head could belong to no one but her Frank.

"What is he doing here?" she said.

John Cerulis looked in the direction of her interest. "Oh, yes—

Karros has told me about this barbarian. I understand he is numbered among the legions who have bivouacked in your bed."

She slid an oblique half-pitying glance at him. She understood why he would have preferred she had no basis for comparing his prowess. "One must sample a great many wines, Patrician, to develop a discerning palate."

Her gaze returned to the Frank. He should not be here; surely he was overstepping his instructions from the Empress, coming into John Cerulis's presence. She hoped he would not make trouble and jeopardize her mission a second time.

Yet as she watched him cross the room, she remembered lying with him, the tenderness of his kiss, the ardent energy of his hands and body. Seeing him again was like waking up, like coming alive. She found herself beginning to smile and schooled her expression to decorum, but she did not take her eyes from him.

In her ear, John Cerulis said, "He has been told that you murdered his brother."

She started all over. Hagen was coming straight toward the dais, Karros a step ahead of him. Now suddenly his approach caused her real alarm. He was an innocent, a baby, in the hands of John Cerulis, and he had the list. If John could manipulate him—subvert him—

They stood before the dais now, and Karros, with many obsequious bows, was making Hagen known to his master. Hagen did not speak. He looked at Theophano once, just once, his eyes like cold iron. She saw hate in his eyes, and looked away, her face blazing. How could he believe that she had killed anyone, much less Rogerius, who had saved her life?

"Frankland," John was saying, through his eternal fixed smile, "and where, if a man may ask, could that be?" His hand came groping toward Theophano and took possession of her fingers. "To this Roman, the world ends at the land walls."

Karros said, "It's off in the north somewhere, Patrician. Somewhere north of Italy, I think."

"I'm sure this fellow is capable of speech," John said. "You, barbarian, favor us with a few words. Your purpose in Constantinople?" He lifted Theophano's hand to his lips and pressed a kiss to the tips of her fingers.

Hagen's features had no more expression than a rock. He would not look at her. He said, "I have been on pilgrimage to the Holy Land, I am going home now, Patrician."

Theophano pulled on her hand; it distressed her to have the big Frank see John Cerulis paying caresses to her. John held her fast. He said, "And you are seeking employment here?"

"I am going home," Hagen said. "Nothing more, Patrician."

Now his gaze did flick toward her; their eyes met for an instant. His look was like a blow. He hated her now. John Cerulis was nibbling on her fingers. She could do nothing, say nothing, to tell Hagen that this was all a piece of theater. And he was going. He was leaving, and taking with him the image of her in another man's arms.

Watching him go, she calmed a little, enough to wonder at the depth of her feelings for him. Amazed, she thought, Am I in love with him? She had enjoyed so many men, but she had always been able to walk away, before.

John Cerulis let her hand go. She sank back into her chair, her head tipped forward, struggling with her thoughts. He hated her, because of John Cerulis. Because of this serpent beside her. Her hatred for John Cerulis blazed up like a blast of Greek fire; he was evil, in the most evil of ways, in that what he said and did bore no rational relation to the truth. For him there was no truth, only convenience.

She raised her head, looking out across the hall, her mind falling quiet, the confusions and doubts sinking one by one away, only the cold decision left. She had never killed anyone, but she intended to kill John Cerulis. She would rid the Empire of him, once and for all.

"What is this?" said her intended victim, outrage in his voice.

She startled. But it was not Theophano who had drawn his anger this time.

In through the masses of the supper guests, a very dirty man was coming. From head to toe he was disgusting. His clothes were filthy rags, and his feet were bare, and his face and hands and all other visible skin were smeared with mud and dung. As he came in across the room, all those within fifteen feet of his passage shrank away from him. Their voices stilled, and the silence spread like ripples through a pond, until, when he reached the front of the room and stood there before John Cerulis, the entire room was still.

John pressed a scented napkin to his nose and mouth. "Who are you?"

Theophano's stomach turned. The man's stench was appalling; she had never smelled anything so awful. Beside her, John Cerulis lifted his hand, and from the side of the room several of his guards rushed forward, holding their noses.

"Where did you come from?" John demanded. "Who let you in here? Speak!"

"Stop where you are," cried the filthy creature. "If you lay hands on me, know that you obstruct a messenger of the Basileus!"

Theophano bit hard on her tongue, to keep back a burst of laughter. It was one of Irene's jokes. She moved her head as far away as possible from the source of the odor. John Cerulis was pale as paper; his hand with the napkin dropped to the table.

"You come from the Palace?"

"Indeed," said the filthy man. "She who rules the world has sent me here, John Cerulis, to command your attendance on her at the first of the qualifying races in the Hippodrome, to share the Imperial box with your Basileus and with the ambassador of the Caliph."

The filthy man spat on the floor, grinned, turned, and walked away. No one spoke. Even the servants recoiled from him as he passed through their midst. Reaching the door, he went out.

John Cerulis was absolutely still. The insult had peeled away his smile; he looked as if he had just swallowed a needle that was stabbing him even now in the bowels. Slowly he lifted the perfumed napkin to his nose and inhaled.

"She is the Devil's own daughter."

Theophano kept her mouth shut. A gesture from John brought his fat bodyguard Karros leaping up to his side.

"Go," John said, in an undertone. "Destroy that—thing, before he can boast of his offense to me. Go!"

Karros saluted him and strode off, his hand on the ornamented hilt of his sword. Slowly John's head turned, sweeping his gaze across the room, looking, Theophano knew, for anyone who was laughing at him.

No one spoke; all struggled to look enraged for their master's sake. Theophano looked away from him. There, among the line of the guards, was Hagen, his hand covering his mouth. She guessed he hid a smile. She glanced at John, and found him watching her with eyes that glittered like a dagger blade.

"You think to see me humiliated."

"Oh, no, Patrician, I—"

"Well, you are wrong. You and your upstart mistress—know this, foolish one. I shall never sit there in her company and be condescended to! I shall never join with other lackeys in increasing her pride! Not I!"

"You cannot refuse the command," Theophano said.

"I can—if I am not within the City." He sniffed the perfumed napkin again, his gaze still burning on her. "And so I shall leave the City. We shall take up your suggestion, laughter-loving Theophano. We shall go to find this holy man who will make me emperor."

"As you wish, Most Noble."

"And in the country," he said, showing his eyeteeth in a nasty smile, "many things may happen, hmm? And be hidden from all but the eyes of God. Hmm?"

"Are you threatening me?" she said evenly.

"I have no need to threaten, lovely, foolish Theophano. As you yourself said, your life is between the blades. And the blades are closing. Closing. Perhaps the wild uncouth barbarian can be persuaded to entertain us all with his revenge on the murderess of his brother? A public execution? Hmm?"

His smile grew wider and more unpleasant; he reached out with one hand and stroked her cheek lightly with his fingernails. Against her will, she turned her head, looking across the room, toward the wall where she had last seen Hagen standing.

He was gone. John Cerulis's laughter, like glass breaking, clattered in her ears. She thought again of slaying him, but her mind would not confine itself in those comforting daydreams; her rebellious mind turned ever toward Hagen. She wondered if she would ever see him again. She longed to see him again, even if it meant her death. She leaned back against the back of her chair, torn with anxious longing.

It was Esad who, especially decorated for the task, had taken Irene's invitation to John Cerulis. As soon as he got outside the nobleman's palace, he knew someone was following him.

He looked around over his shoulder into the dark street and saw nobody, and his steps quickened. When the order came for this, he had thought it funny; the heavy purse that accompanied the order made daubing himself with horse dung a relatively harmless inconvenience. Now he knew he should have thought twice.

He moved through the narrow twisting streets toward the Forum of Theodosius, greatest of the wide squares that were strung like beads along the Mesê; the street was lit at night with rows of torches, and there, he thought, his heart jumping, he might find some safety. Behind him footsteps pattered on the stone, pursuing. He broke into a run. The footsteps ran also, coming closer. Panting with fear, he dashed out into the center of the great square, deserted now that night was come, and whirled in a circle, looking all around him.

On the roof of every shop, a yellow smoking torch flared. In the light, he saw only the broad flat pavement, a few wagons, a scattered heap of donkey dung. Then from the unlit lane he had just left, a tall figure stepped.

It was the white-haired barbarian, and he was coming after Esad with a look of purpose on his face. In a pell-mell rush of memories, Esad felt again the whip around his throat, the heavy hands on his body, and whirled and ran up the Mesê.

The barbarian was chasing him. The barbarian was gaining on him. His lungs on fire, his mind white with fear, Esad raced up the wide street, between the colonnades and the yellow torches, up toward the Palace. His eyes darted from side to side, looking for a *cursor*, for anyone who might help him, but the great street was deserted; among the fluted columns only shadows moved. He stumbled and went flat on his face, his knees and hands scraping over the pavement, and the barbarian caught him.

He screamed. The barbarian hoisted him up onto his feet and held him fast.

"Don't be stupid," the barbarian said in his ear, and shook him hard. "I'm trying to help you. God's blood, you stink."

Esad flung off the heavy hand on his arm. "Help me! What are you chasing me for?"

The barbarian smiled at him. "Let me walk you back to the stables. Or better, to the baths. Pagh!" He held his nose.

"I don't need you!"

"You don't? Well, then, I'll be on my way, which happens to be the same way you're going, isn't it."

Esad cast a look over his shoulder. The street swept down behind him into the broad square of the Forum; he could see nothing menacing there.

Except, now that he looked, a man who had not been there before was walking innocently along the side of the Mesê, and while he watched disappeared behind the columns. He faced front again.

"I don't believe you," he said, loud. "Not even John Cerulis would dare lay hands on a messenger of the Basileus."

The barbarian said nothing, only walked along beside him, a few feet to the side, out of the stench. Esad was used to it; he mucked stalls for a good part of every day anyway. It had seemed such an amusing thing, when the order came, and the purse was heavy, a month's pay in silver. Surely nobody would harm an Imperial messenger.

His back crawled. He could not resist looking behind him again.

Now the street looked entirely empty. But columns lined it, the walkways on either side where the jewelers kept their shops, and any number of men might hide there, even with the streetlamps lit.

"I don't need you," he said again, to the barbarian.

The white-haired man didn't bother looking at him; he smiled wide as he walked.

If someone were coming after him—Esad glanced over his shoulder again—surely John Cerulis would send a pack? He thought of the two times he had taken the measure of the barbarian; his fingers went to his neck, still tender from the lash. On the big man's hip the long sword hung, its hilt wrapped in worn leather, like any common tool.

"Why are you doing this for me?"

The barbarian said nothing for a moment, striding along beside Esad, his arms swinging loose at his sides. Finally, he turned to look down at the groom.

"I don't know. I don't like you, I don't like your master, but I don't like the man behind us a lot more than I don't like you."

"I don't understand you—can't you speak properly?"

"I don't understand it either. I wish he would jump me and get it over with."

"I thought you said it was I he's after."

The barbarian said nothing more. They were coming to the great square before the Palace wall, rising sheer and white into the night sky. The Mesê ended at the Chalke, and before the huge bronze doors they stopped. The barbarian looked behind them. The Mesê swept away from them into the City, a ribbon of marble blue-white in the moonlight, studded with torches.

"Good night," said the barbarian, and walked away. Esad gaped after him; the ignorant, arrogant peasant, he was actually going in through the Chalke, banging on the bronze to wake up the half-drunken gateman. Esad shook his head, considerably uplifted by this evidence of the barbarian's inferiority.

A sound behind him startled him; he jumped a foot, and then, as if his reason lost its balance, he was overcome with fear. He ran all the way down the wall street toward the Hippodrome door, and dashed inside, into the warmth and safety of the barn.

Karros watched the two men from behind a statue on the Mesê. When the white-haired barbarian went in through the Chalke, leaving the filthy groom alone and vulnerable, Karros almost went after him, but the groom sprinted away before he could get within striking distance. Karros relaxed, leaning against the pedestal of the statue, his eyes reflective on the Palace wall before him.

He had been right to come alone. He congratulated himself on his craft and foresight. Had he brought any of his men with him, they would have seen that he was afraid of the barbarian, he would have lost stature in their eyes.

As it was, being alone, he enjoyed a comfortable latitude of choice.

Of course he had been wise not to attack the groom, in spite of his orders; outnumbered two to one, he would have been mauled. Not even John Cerulis would have expected him to take on two men by himself.

Anyway, he could manage John Cerulis.

It was the barbarian who caused him problems. Karros had to kill him—this business of walking the groom back to the Palace, that proved it, proved he was no friend of John Cerulis. It proved as well he meant to stand against Karros in everything. But he was tough, the big man. To kill him, Karros had to catch him drunk, his back turned, his breeches down around his ankles, his shirt pulled over his head, his sword fifty feet away. Karros had not gotten where he was by taking unnecessary chances.

Make friends with him. Then kill him.

He padded away through the Forum of Theodosius, through the City sleeping and quiet. It was cold, for mid-June. Karros began to think of a cup of heated wine and his fur slippers. In an alley behind the fishmongers' stalls, he killed a cat and smeared the blood along his sword blade, to prove to his master that he had slain the filthy groom, and went happily home again.

: 15 :

The public baths were in the Zeuxippus district, below the Hippodrome on the western slope of the City. The front entrance was always swarming with whores and fortune-tellers, and the City Prefect, anonymously hooded and cloaked, made his way around to the little door at the rear where the privileged could go in undisturbed. A knock brought the porter to admit him; he dropped a coin into the discreetly cupped palm and went by him and down a corridor to the disrobing room.

The great building in which the baths were housed was one of the oldest structures in Constantinople. The murals on the wall of the disrobing room showed people in styles of dress that no one had worn since the days of Justinian and Belisarius and the Reconquista. A number of other men were taking off their clothes there, but none of them was Nicephoros. The Prefect, with the help of an attendant, stripped himself to the skin, wrapped a white cloth around his loins, and walked down the slippery puddle-strewn corridor to the first of the three bathing rooms, the warm room.

An earthquake in the reign of Phocas had ruined this part of the ancient structure, and the tepidarium was much newer than the rest of the bath. The walls were sheathed in slick white tiles with a narrow band of blue around the top and the bottom. Wooden benches along all four sides allowed men to sit down and chat or daydream or even read while their bodies got used to the warmth. Now there were so many men in the tepidarium that the Prefect could not find a place on the bench, and his health requiring that he allow his flesh to warm gradually, he was forced to spend this period walking slowly up and down the center of the room; his only consolation was that exercise and stringent diet had kept his body smooth and slim and he could be proud of the figure he cut. He let his towel drape itself attractively over his hips and kept an eye out for amorous homosexuals, although this being the middle of the day anyone with a prurient interest would, by unspoken custom, be expected to keep still.

He noticed, through the tail of his eye, a number of appreciative glances at his excellent legs and shapely chest and arms. His spirit buoyed by this, he went on into the caldarium, the hot room.

This room, much larger than the tepidarium, was dominated by the enormous pool in the center, kept so hot that the greenish surface of the water released a constant mist of steam into the overheated air, and droplets of water condensed instantly on his flesh. Skylights in the roof let in enough light to give the place a milky luminescence. Through this swirling mist of steam and veiled sunlight the other men moved like shadows; their heads bobbed in the bath, and along the sides, on the benches, they seemed like parts of the wall.

The Prefect gave his towel to an attendant and walked down into the water. The heat made him gasp. Bravely he forced himself down until he was submerged up to the neck, and turned around three times, saying the appropriate prayers to Saint John, the patron of the baths, before he climbed out again and with a sigh of relief sat down on the bench.

Almost at once a body hove through the mists and dropped down beside him with a grunt. It was Nicephoros, his towel tied around his waist. Dressed, he always looked lean, perhaps a function of his height and his bearing; without the disguise of clothes his body was shapeless and pudgy, his abdomen a round womanish bulge covered with hair, his arms droopy with flab. The Prefect shook his head.

"Nicephoros, you ought to take care of yourself."

The Treasurer stretched out his legs. "I haven't the leisure." He twitched and shifted on the bench, settling himself, emitting little groans and grunts as he moved. The Prefect fought off a stab of the mild alarm that had nagged him since Nicephoros's request for this meeting; he reminded himself of all the good things Nicephoros had done for him.

"Ah." Nicephoros sighed, leaning back against the wall. A river of sweat streamed down his chest and over the side of his belly, sweeping the black hair flat. "I should come here more often."

"You should. And perhaps leave off those sweets that the Empress—"

"Peter," Nicephoros said, "if I were you, I would not take unnecessary liberties with my tolerance of insult. I want to know what you did with the money with which you were supposed to pay the charioteers."

The Prefect stiffened; he felt as if a blow had fallen on his back. Swiftly he looked around him. No one was near enough to eavesdrop. Facing Nicephoros again, he tried his smile on.

"Nicephoros, you know my budget has been curtailed. There is no money for anything."

"Peter, don't lie to me. The money for the charioteers was there. I looked it up. You had it, but you did not pay them, and now you have it no longer. Why not?"

"I'm sorry, Nicephoros. I don't know what you're talking about."

"Really."

"And I'm offended that you take advantage of our friendship to broach such a matter with me. Don't you trust me?"

"Hunh," said Nicephoros, and wiped his face on his towel.

This response encouraged the Prefect; he kept up the attack. "If you are accusing me of something, Nicephoros, I would be very pleased if you would come out and say so, or better yet—"

"I am not accusing you, dear boy," said Nicephoros, shifting on the bench again, and shooting a furious look at the Prefect. "The Basileus has asked me to find out what you are doing that makes it impossible for you to deal with her face to face."

The Prefect shut his mouth. He swiveled his face forward, toward the bath, the green water, the wraiths of rising steam.

"I must say, Peter, I do owe you a certain gratitude, since in misuse of your office you left sufficient evidence that I wasted very little time in uncovering the truth."

"Nicephoros, I swear to you—"

"I know you keep a very fine house, Peter, is that it? When the rest of the City suffers through hard times, you could not lower even a little your expectations of life?"

The Prefect said nothing. Bitterly he stared at the bath, reminding himself that this confrontation was no doubt inevitable, but why did it have to be Nicephoros, whom he trusted? He would rather have been called before the Parakoimomenos, or the Basileus.

Not the Basileus. He raised his eyes to the ceiling, pierced with skylights, from which the light fell in sheets through the tendrils of the steam.

Nicephoros's voice rolled through another fierce sarcastic question, rhetorical rather than interrogatory, and launched itself on another. The Prefect began to feel physically assaulted; his flesh trembled, and he wished he could leave. Abruptly he realized that everything Nicephoros was saying was true: he had committed a terrible crime against his City, his Basileus, his God, and his family, and he lowered his face to his hands and wept.

Nicephoros stopped talking. They sat side by side, the Prefect struggling for mastery, and the Treasurer giving him the silence to do so.

"The races," said the Prefect finally, lifting his head. His eyes burned.

"I beg your pardon, Peter."

"I lost it on the races, Nicephoros. I never meant it to be so much. I lost a little at first, and then I thought I saw a sure winner, so I bet enough to recover my losses, and I lost that too. And on and on—I couldn't stop, Nicephoros—I meant to repay it—"

"Then repay it." The Treasurer leaned toward him, urgent, his dark eyes full of Oriental fire. "Pay back what you've taken from the service, and I will go to the Basileus and say you are blameless."

"I can't, Nicephoros—it's thousands and thousands of irenes."

Nicephoros's blazing black eyes remained on him a moment longer, before the Treasurer swayed away, gripping the bench on either side of him with his hands, and shifting his bulk on the bench. "God, these seats are hard."

"Nicephoros, if I could!"

"You can," said the Treasurer. "You can sell something. What about your villa in Blachernae?"

"The villa is not mine, it belongs to my wife."

"Get her to sell it, then."

He could not tell his wife. He could not begin to explain something like this to his wife.

"Nicephoros, you could loan me the money, couldn't you? Everybody knows you have millions."

Nicephoros gave off a rough burst of laughter, his gaze elsewhere. "Don't ask me for that, Peter. I didn't embezzle funds and bet it all away."

"I'll pay you back. I promise."

The Treasurer swung toward him. "You will pay back the City treasury. Within the month. When you have done so, you will come to me and tell me, and I shall go to the Basileus and exonerate you."

"Oh, Nicephoros, please—"

The other man was getting up. With a motion of his hand he cut off further speech. "Do it, Peter."

"Oh, now, Nicephoros, you really—where are you going? Please! Can't we talk about this a little more?"

"I will not speak with you again, Peter, until you come to me with that which I have already required of you. Good day."

The Prefect licked his lips. Nicephoros was moving past him, lumbering, his skin shining with sweat; he fumbled with his towel and dropped it and, groaning, bent to pick it up. The Treasurer's body was a ruin. How then could his mind be whole? How could he inflict something like this on a friend? The towel bunched around his loins, Nicephoros went away down the long side of the pool, splashing through puddles. The steam veiled him. His dark head disappeared through the door at the far end, into the frigidarium. Lowering his eyes, the Prefect stared at the dancing green water of the bath for a long, long time.

Abdul-Hassan ibn-Ziad, the Caliph's emissary to the Roumis, knew his hosts well. He did not intend, this time, to fall prey to their tricks and duplicities, and therefore, one hour after his entry into Constantinople, he took himself, alone, and with a heavy purse, to the chambers in the Daphne where lived the Grand Domestic, the Parakoimomenos, John Melissenes.

Ibn-Ziad amused himself with the truism that his subject was certainly doubly corrupt, first by virtue of being shaved, and second by virtue of being Greek.

The Parakoimomenos, naturally, kept him waiting—not long, only a few moments, just long enough to imbue him with the understanding of who was attending whom. Ibn-Ziad kept his temper, which was the key to dealing with these people. Restlessly he paced through the antechamber in which he was confined, and pleased himself with his own patience.

He had never been in this part of the Daphne before. It reminded him of a harem, of his grandfather's harems, in fact, although his grandfather, who in the name of the Caliph had ruled Islam from the Indus to Gibraltar, had never lived quite as well as this; it was the lavish use of satins and silks, the gleam of gold and the clutter of small objects on every flat surface that made him think of the seraglio. He walked slowly by the shelf of books along the windowless wall, where a collection of miniature figures absorbed his attention. Just toys, they were. He had seen Persian chessmen as elegantly made. Yet he could not keep his hands off them; he picked up a tiny gold cock, only an inch high, captured in the act of crowing up the dawn.

When he touched it, it moved. Startled, he dropped the thing onto the carpet. Feeling like a fool, he stooped and recovered it, and found its head was loose, and at a touch came off: inside was some sort of scent.

He laughed at himself. Tricked again.

"Most excellent messenger," a voice said, behind him, and he wheeled. In the doorway was the tall supple form of the eunuch, bowing to him.

"Hail, Parakoimomenos," said ibn-Ziad, and advanced to meet the Empress's officer. In the middle of the room, facing each other, they bowed several times, exchanging ceremonial courtesies in the Greek language.

"I am ravished by the divine opportunity to serve the most excellent grandson of the great Vizier Yahya. Permit me to express my most abject apologies that you were made to wait on this undeserving personage."

"Yet my few moments here in this room have reawakened my delight at the treasures of Constantinople."

"Words cannot express the joy with which I receive your kind praises. We exist merely to make you familiar with the ways of civilization."

Ibn-Ziad's smile stiffened at that; words leapt to his tongue assuring this ball-less epicene that in Baghdad too men lived as well as God allowed them, but before he could speak, the eunuch was ushering him on through the antechamber into a small sunlit room beyond, where a marble table stood, strewn with papers and books. This room was as lavishly appointed as the one he had just left; the walls were painted with a frieze of dancing women, trimmed with gold and carnelian. Through the window behind the table, veiled by diaphanous silks, the breeze from the garden entered, perfumed with flowers, and made musical by an occasional ripple of laughter: some child played out there.

The Parakoimomenos handed him to a chair. "My dear sir, I am impatient to know in what way I may fulfill you. However my services may help you, please, inform me now."

Ibn-Ziad, in this elegant room, felt his confidence slipping. Had he brought enough money to bribe this creature whose very walls were made of gold? Gathering himself up, he took his purse and set it on the table.

"And what is this?" said the Parakoimomenos, pressing his hands to his clothing, as if to restrain a snatch at the money.

"That," said ibn-Ziad, "is to insure that I have your help in my endeavor here."

"My help." The Parakoimomenos took his chair on the far side of the table, leaned forward, clasped his hands together, and fixed his eyes on the Caliph's man. "Please. Explain further."

"I am here to advance my master's purposes—to take home the tribute to which he is by treaty entitled, and to incline the policies of the Basileus in his favor."

"Ah. And you expect my help in this?"

"I am prepared to make it very lucrative for you to do so."

"Ah."

The eunuch's long white hands came unclasped, and the fingers pattered busily over the clutter of papers before him. In the back of his mind ibn-Ziad noticed, with satisfaction, that they used Baghdadi paper here.

"My dear fellow," said the Parakoimomenos softly. "I am afraid you misunderstand us here. First of all, your objectives, if I may be so bold as to characterize them, fall in the realm of the Basileus's barbarian policy. I am merely the keeper of her household, nothing more, and therefore of no use to you in your efforts to sway her in your favor." The long flexible fingers swatted suddenly, contemptuously, at the purse. "Even if I were so deluded as to accept a bribe."

"Ummm." Taken aback, ibn-Ziad sank deeper into his chair.

"But let me put your mind at rest, my dear friend. You need not resort to such methods here. We are men of good will here. We desire what you yourself no doubt desire—the honorable and just relationship between our two powers."

"Unnh," said ibn-Ziad.

He felt his face glowing with embarrassment; he wondered where he had gotten the notion that a man as rich as this one would succumb to an offer of money.

"However, my good man, while I have you here, allow me to read with you the schedule of your visit with us."

"Very well," said ibn-Ziad loftily.

"I have the list here." In all that welter of paper the Parakoimomenos put his hand immediately on the slip he wanted. He cleared his throat.

"This afternoon we hope to amuse you with a reading of poetry in the rose garden. Afterward, a tour of the sacred relics in the Chapel of the Virgin—"

Ibn-Ziad picked up his purse and restored it to its place under his robes. "Excellent," he said. His head buzzed.

"And we shall have the honor of your presence at a state dinner in the Triclinium. Tomorrow—"

There followed a calendar of entertainments and events at which he would be expected to appear: an accessory to the glory of the Basileus; a witness to the power of those whom he had come here to dominate. He felt Constantinople closing in around him, slick and smooth as a golden cage.

We have conquered you, he thought. Beaten your armies, seized your provinces—some of them, anyway. You should fall down on your faces and beg our mercy. Instead—

The Parakoimomenos was still rumbling on through his schedule. "And then you will attend the service at the Church of the Holy Wisdom, where the Basileus will—"

"Wait," said ibn-Ziad, trying to catch hold of this slick surface of protocol. "When shall I have the honor of speaking candidly with the Empress?"

The eunuch drew back, his eyes widening. "I speak your pardon, my dear prince."

"I require deep speech with the Empress, at once. Concerning the payment of the tribute which she owes us."

"Concerning the tribute, you shall speak this very day to the Treasurer of the Empire, the great Nicephoros." The Parakoimomenos lifted his piece of paper again. "After the ceremony in the Holy Wisdom—"

"No," said ibn-Ziad stubbornly. "I must speak face to face with the Empress. My lord the Caliph—"

"Well, of course," the eunuch said, and put his paper carefully to one side. "You are expected to attend on the Empress at the Hippodrome, for the races. A very great honor, I can assure you, and one at which, surely, the moment may very well arise during which you might exchange a few words of relaxed conversation with the Basileus."

"The races," said ibn-Ziad. He remembered the Hippodrome from a previous visit, the excitement, and the thrill of competition. "Very good. Is it to be a championship race?" He remembered, belatedly, what they called it. "A race for the Golden Belt?"

"Alas, no." The eunuch spread his hands. His face, pale and smooth, with the noble sweep of brow like a cliff above the mild kindly eyes, was grave with regret. "Unfortunately in the course of your visit with us only part of the challenge series will be run. But we expect an excellent race. Besides the divine Ishmael—"

"Ishmael. Is there an Arab driver?"

"Ah, no, a devout Christian, I fear. Although of Syrian and Arabian ancestry, I believe. You know that Constantinople attracts to her bosom men from all over the world who desire the challenges and rewards of civilization." The Parakoimomenos's hands began to move, busily sorting through the papers and small objects on his table. "There is an Arab team in this series, however."

"Really," said ibn-Ziad.

If he was to spend his days touring churches and viewing relics and listening to foreign poetry read, the horse-race at least would be something to look forward to. And if one of the teams were Arab—

"Yes, there is a new team coming in from Caesarea." The eunuch lowered his already mild voice. "It's widely known although not officially accepted that the driver is of the persuasion of Islam." The eunuch's eyes darted toward the corner of the table where the heavy purse had lain. "If I were you, my dear, I would take your money and bet it all on this Caesarean team. I understand they are certain to win."

"Hunh." Ibn-Ziad sat back.

They would use him to glorify themselves; he would have to stand there and watch the Basileus proclaimed master of the cosmos, and have his presence seem a testimony to her power. But a horse-race was something else, something he could understand, something he could use. He smiled at the Parakoimomenos, and the eunuch smiled in answer, rather too warmly, as if he saw into ibn-Ziad's mind.

"Thank you," said ibn-Ziad. "You have served your Basileus and me with honor, and I am grateful to you for your help."

"I am overwhelmed by your generous praises." The Parakoimomenos bowed over his table. Ibn-Ziad left.

From the window the Parakoimomenos watched him go. It amused him that ibn-Ziad, wanting to bribe him, should have been so straightforward about it; a Roman would have made a gift of the money, or a challenge. The Arabs were children, after all.

And being a child, ibn-Ziad would be easily guided by knowing hands. It was unfortunate that the Basileus, the adored one, had chosen to place him into the hands of Nicephoros, who would not make use of the opportunity, save for the most pedestrian and obvious purposes.

He needed another guide, did ibn-Ziad, one who would introduce him to Constantinople in ways deeper than mere words. One through whom the Parakoimomenos could achieve purposes of his own. The eunuch slipped his tongue between his teeth, considering his possibilities, and called for a page.

"Most noble Parakoimomenos." The page bowed to him.

"Send Prince Constantine to me," said the eunuch.

Irene woke in the deep of the night, her bed shaking all around her. She sat up, her arms out to support herself. The bed quivered a moment longer, the hangings trembling, and from the darkness of the room came the wails of a frightened page; beneath the cries of the child and the shushings of another woman the rumbling voice of the earthquake died away.

"Ah." Irene swung her legs over the side of the bed. "Helena! My robe." She enjoyed earthquakes; this one left her with a residual excitement trembling in her veins; she knew she witnessed an arcane detail of the divine purpose. Helena came up to her, a robe extended in her hands, and swirled the gauze around her mistress's shoulders.

"Come," Irene said. "We'll go up to the Kathismus—see what damage has been done."

Helena yawned. "Mistress—it was only a little tremble. Nothing will have fallen, except a few tenements—" The page-boy, still shrieking, clung to the woman's nightdress with both hands, and now Helena bent down suddenly and caught the little boy's wrists and gave him a sound shaking of her own, more ferocious than the earthquake. "Be still! Stop thinking of yourself, little brute—you are of the Empress's train, comport yourself accordingly."

The boy screeched. Irene, gathering the robe around her, made for the door.

The guard was gone from the door into the Kathismus, the stair-tower that led to the Imperial box of the Hippodrome. Trailing her maids, Irene went swiftly up the stairs into the open air. The silk curtains had been removed until the next race; the moonlight poured down into the open box, bleaching the marble blue-white. The guard was there at the front of the box, looking out, and when the Empress burst in through the door from the stair, he wheeled, dropping to his hands and knees.

"Ah!" She walked straight past him, ignoring him. "See what the

Hand of God has brought upon us, to warn us of the fragility of life, and His awful power over us!"

The women crowded around her. They leaned out into the warm summer night. Out there, beyond the great dark curve of the Hippodrome wall, the City spread away from them, the Mesê a white river along the spine of the ridge, and on either side of this white stream, great golden flowers bloomed in the night, tossing heads of flame. The earthquake, as usual, had started fires in half the crumbling tenements of Constantinople.

Beside Irene, her tiring woman Ida began to pray. Helena was grumbling again about being pulled from her warm bed; the others were silent, or weeping. Irene raised her arms out. The scene exhilarated her. The leaping flames tinged the sky a sultry red, and fired volleys of sparks into the wind; from the deep stirring darkness out there came the faint wails and cries of people trapped in catastrophe. She pressed herself against the cold marble rail, her heart pounding. Out there, the only real truth was manifesting itself once again, the ordinary lives of ordinary people were dissolving in the rhythmless, irresistible tides of the cosmos.

Beside her something pressed against her; she lowered her hand, unwilling to take her eyes from the death and life flaring in the dark before her. It was Philomela beside her. The child laid her cheek against the Empress's hand, and Irene stroked her face quickly, reassuring her.

The fires would burn all night; at this time of the year, with the overheated winds from the east, and the water level falling in every fountain in Constantinople, there would be little anyone could do to put them out. Irene beckoned to the guard, still prostrated beside her feet.

"You. Send to the City Prefect, have him call the *cursores* out, to keep order and help prevent the spreading of these fires."

"My Basileus commands." The guard raced away down the stairs.

As he went down, he passed someone coming up, and Irene turned, now, to face a party of men squeezing into the Imperial balcony. Startled, the guard saw that the Caliph's ambassador had somehow found his way here, surrounded by his men.

Ibn-Ziad pushed forward to the rail, and looked out across the City; his breath hissed out through his teeth in a sigh of relief. The Empress watched him calmly.

Now he turned; he swept her a bow, his long Arabian sleeves fluttering. "Augustus. Allow me the luxury of apology after the fact—I knew of no other place from which I could assess the damage done by the restless earth, and did not expect to find you here as well."

"Your apology is needless, grandson of the great Yahya," she said. "Rather, I am pleased to see in you one who enjoys the cosmic play as well as I."

" 'Enjoy,' " said ibn-Ziad blankly; he turned toward the City again. The faint red hue from the fires danced along the beaked profile he presented to her. "God, God, I thought the whole world was falling into pieces."

The Empress laughed, delighted at this childlike awe. "Yes, God is wonderful in His exuberance."

A gust of the summer wind blew the smell of smoke into their faces, and the screams and wailings of people suffering. A glowing cinder floated through the air, a flake of red-gold that quivered and glowed as it fell. Ibn-Ziad reached out his hand suddenly and knocked the ember away from the Empress's arm.

She said, "Have no fear for me, sir. Jesus Christ is my protector." She smiled at him, who faced her now, his forehead furrowed up with thought. "In my City, also, you need fear nothing, ibn-Ziad, and no one."

As she spoke, she put out her hand and pressed his, to comfort him, as if he were a child, and he moved a little closer to her. His face turned toward the City again, and when he looked back toward her, something in his expression had changed, the nakedness of his fear covered with a clothing of intention.

He said, "Lady, by the Hand of God, we find ourselves together; perhaps now we may discuss those broad questions of policy I am charged with in my embassy here."

"It is the middle of the night, my child," she said. "Yet, if you have questions that cannot wait for my ministers' answers, I shall hear them."

"We require the payment of the tribute—"

"Ah, no." She raised her hand, palm toward him. "Talk about that with Nicephoros."

"And there is the matter of the border raids—"

"I know nothing of that."

"And the trade in silks—"

"Is a matter for the Prefect of the City and his staff." She turned away, back toward the fires, smiling. "Also you will have to meet as soon as possible with the Grand Chamberlain, who has some issues to take up with you."

Ibn-Ziad was silent a moment. Perhaps he had learned what she was trying to tell him. Down there in the City, in the Zeugma district, the fire was spreading; the flames glittered on the waters of the Golden Horn.

He said, "I have seen the Parakoimomenos."

"Excellent."

"I tried to bribe him."

"You did!" Stunned, she wheeled toward him, although he was still facing the dark City; she wondered what sort of fool he was, to reveal something like that, which not even the Parakoimomenos himself would have told her. "And did he accept?"

"He told me, lady, to bet it on the horse-races." Now the young Arab swung toward her, and he was smiling. "So I have a challenge for you, lady—one in which we shall be matched, as it were, in single combat."

"Combat, my dear boy!"

"Not your arms against mine, but your team against mine. I am told the race to which I am invited pits against one another two splendid teams, one Christian, the other Arab. I shall place my wager with you on the team from Caesarea, if you will take up your end of the ribbon, and wager with me on Mauros-Ishmael."

"Done," she said, and put out her hand to him.

He took her hand, and bent over it in a flirtatious sort of bow. "Charming opponent." He pressed a kiss to her fingers.

"Excellent." The whole idea was delightful to her; she told herself to give some present to the Parakoimomenos, for putting the seed into ibn-Ziad's mind that had grown into such a pleasing flower. A combat: a challenge.

He was going; he cast one last look over the rail, down into the City and the fires, and with another bow backed himself out the door to the Kathismus stairs. Irene swung forward again, to watch the fires.

Her hands struck the marble rail with an ebullient emphasis. The one problem with being a woman was that there were few such moments as this, a single combat. And it was a single combat, even if by surrogates. She leaned against the rail, yearning for race day.

: 16 :

In the morning the City still seemed to be trembling. The streets were full of people, standing in clumps, talking, their eyes whining with excitement and fear; every church was packed with prayermongers. Hagen rode past one of the places that had burned: the space between one street and the next lay in a heap of fire-blackened trash, a masonry corner still erect, a pile of bricks, some roofing tiles, stinking of smoke. A dozen people were picking through the ruin, some looking for loot, some for dead friends. There was a sheet on the side of the mess, with some bodies on it.

Hagen imagined that the ground beneath Constantinople had opened, and flames from Hell shot up to the surface. He shivered at the vision.

He passed by John Cerulis's palace and saw the courtyard clogged with wagons, some already loaded, others being piled up with boxes and jars. Swiftly he went away up the Mesê toward the Sacred Palace.

Nothing here had toppled. No sign of fire here. The precinct of the Empress, perched on its hilltop above the sea, was as inviolate as a piece of Heaven. He went inside, feeling safer there, and set out to find the Basileus.

The morning room was finished, the candles in the ceiling light all lit. Irene walked around beneath them, frowning up at the hanging lamp. It had seemed more interesting in the planning than it looked now.

"Well, I think it's charming," said Helena. "And at last the room is clean."

Irene paced up and down the carpet, restless and dissatisfied. "I'm hungry. Send for wine and cakes, Ida. And I want some music. Oh."

She had forgotten that Theophano was gone, who played the lute. Disappointed, she sank down on the sofa and drew little Philomela into her lap to be caressed; the child beamed at her.

"Were you afraid when the earth shook, my dear one?"

"Oh, no, mama," said the little girl proudly. "I never even woke up."

All the women laughed.

"And you've done your lessons for today?" The Empress stroked her face over the child's shining hair.

"I have finished the whole of Homer now."

"And your music?"

At that the warm flesh against her own stiffened and drew back. A cloud passed over the child's expression, and she burrowed her head into Irene's shoulder.

"I cannot play the lute, mama, I cannot!"

Helena swooped down on her, hands out like pincers. "Don't do that! Naughty girl, you wrinkled her dress, and see—" She pulled the child away and leaned down to smooth the disturbances in Irene's silk stola.

"That white-haired man is here," she said, under her breath.

"He is?" Irene sat bolt upright. "Very good. Send him in. There, Ida." The serving woman was bringing her a small plate of Cathayan ware, a slice of apple cake on it. Irene's mouth watered.

The big Frank came into the room. Somewhere he had acquired a Roman tunic, under which he still wore his barbarian leggings and boots. He looked curiously around the room a moment before he went down on one knee before Irene.

"John Cerulis is leaving the City," he said, without preamble.

"Oh? When?"

"Very soon. I was there last night when he announced it. He will surely be gone before the day of the next horse-race."

Irene cleared her throat. It was preferable that few people know all her thoughts, especially in the matter of John Cerulis. Beside her, Ida knelt, feeding her the cake bite by bite with a spoon, and Irene turned to the woman and took the dish from her hands. "Thank you, I will do that. You may go for a while. Take Philomela in and listen to her practice the lute." She swept the room with her gaze, and the other women stiffened, poised for her commands.

"Helena, to the looms, if you please, you know how important that is. Zoe, you may have the afternoon to yourself, to spend with your child."

"Thank you, mistress." Murmuring, they came one by one to kiss her hand and cheek and one by one they left, their feet silent on the dense carpets. Left alone with the big Frank, Irene held out the dish to him.

"Here. Eat this, it is too sweet for my tastes."

He took the plate and with his fingers broke off a corner of the cake. "Did you send Esad to him to command him to the races? That was funny."

"He is a fastidious man. I thought to have a little joke at his expense."

"You went too far—he is leaving Constantinople because of it."

"Is he. Yes, perhaps you are right, I went too far. Where is he going?"

"To find that holy man they are all talking of. Daniel, his name is."

"I know about Daniel." He was eating the cake; crumbs lay on his pale beard.

"Do you know this? That woman of yours is with him."

"My woman? You mean Theophano?"

"Yes."

Irene lay back in the heap of cushions behind her, curling a tress of her hair around her forefinger. "And what do you make of that?"

"I don't know. She was sitting beside him at dinner—" His gaze broke away from her; swiftly he consumed the remainder of the cake, and held the little dish in his hand, staring at it, not seeing it, frowning. He muttered, "He was holding her hand."

"You believe that she has betrayed me?"

"I told you, I don't know," he said, growing angry.

"Now, now, my man, I will remind you that I am Basileus."

Unimpressed by that, he grunted at her. He set the dish down on the floor beside him.

"Well, then, Hagen," she said, amused by his spirit, "if you will not honor me out of good manners, consider that at a word from me, you would be publicly eviscerated in the Hippodrome, and all your splendid strength and courage would go for nothing."

He brushed the crumbs off his beard. "Yes, I know that, Augustus. What do you want me to do?"

"Nothing, for now. But I will know where John goes, and what he does when he gets there, and as for Theophano—"

She wound the tress around and around her finger, watching him, wondering how much he needed to know. She said, "Theophano is in my service, even when she seems to betray me, as now."

"Oh?" Still on one knee, he laid his forearms over his upraised thigh and stared at her. "Or is she in his service, even when she seems to betray him?"

"Yes, there is a certain classic symmetry to the problem. In either case, it is essential that she be returned to me, when her work with him is done, whether she wishes to come or no."

"How will I know when her work is done?"

"If she is honest, then she will tell you herself. If she is not—" Irene pressed her lips together, considering the possibility that Theophano might indeed have betrayed her. The Frank believed she had. Or feared it: they had shared a bed once, perhaps the feeling between them ran stronger than a simple tumble. She said, "If she is to be numbered among my enemies, I shall know of it. If she refuses to be saved, take her anyway."

"Yes, Augustus."

That title came more easily to his lips with each use. In time, she knew, he would kiss the floor at her feet.

She said, "When she first encountered you, my Hagen, Theophano was in possession of a certain list of names, which concerns me deeply. She lost it in the course of her escape from John Cerulis. It may be that she is now attempting to recover that list."

As she spoke, she saw in his face a flash of understanding, of hidden knowledge, and she thought, excited, Oh, yes, he does have it. At once she had the sweet sense of the roundness, the fullness of truth; God measured everything, lost nothing, intended all, and everything was going as Irene wanted, now, with very little effort on her part, a proof of the correctness of her course.

"And here," she said. She took the garnet ring from her thumb and held it out to him. "You have served me well, with no thought of reward; I find you an honorable man, and am most grateful for it. Let this token show your Basileus's estimate of you."

He slid the ring onto each finger of his left hand until it fit one. "Augustus," he said. He did not seem grateful, just satisfied. That was how to handle him, ornaments and praises of the simplest sort. And he had not denied that he was her man. She nodded to him.

"You may go."

Ishmael drove two blacks and two greys, not by choice but by accident, since he had picked the horses out not for their color but for their physical skill and strength and speed. The inside wheeler was black, the inside flanker a dapple grey, the outside flanker a darker grey, the outside wheeler black. They were nearly of a height, and when they stood together in their harness, the chariot at their heels, their manes tossing like a sea wave from their necks, they were as beautiful as the horses of Achilles, that wept over Patroclus.

The two grooms held the ribbon before them. They were practicing starts on the outside of the track, since Ishmael anticipated winning the first heat.

"Hoo!"

Their great hoofs slammed into the sand, showering the car and the driver with sharp little particles, and bolted forward down the track. The outside wheeler, the fastest of them, got out a little ahead of the others but a touch of the rein brought him back into team. Ishmael let them run the length of the track before he gathered them in, and then they did not want to slow; they fought the bits, their heads thrashing from side to side, and the full glossy manes all spilling together in a welter of silver and black. He wrestled them to a walk and at a sedate pace took them once around the track, their necks bent to the bit, their feet dancing.

In the first row of the Hippodrome seats, directly below the Imperial box, Prince Michael sat, watching, his hands fisted together and resting on the rail before him. Ishmael tried to ignore him. Yet he could not but lift himself up straight, his shoulders square, as he drove past.

At the stable gate, he stopped his team, and the grooms came up to hold their heads. Ishmael got down out of the car. "Leo—" He held out the reins, and the apprentice took them and climbed into the car. He would take the horses at a canter around the track until they were tired. Ishmael stepped back, watching them, unlacing the leather cuffs on his wrists.

He was standing near the rail in front of the seats, and after a few moments Michael appeared in the row of benches behind him, moving casually down through the grandstand toward him. Ishmael kept his back to the Prince, but he was aware of the presence of his rival as if Michael's approach were preceded by a marching troop of drums and horns.

The Prince leaned up against the rail beside him. "When does this new team from Caesarea get here?"

"I don't know," Ishmael said. He wiped his hands and face on a clean towel and tossed it to one of his grooms. The horses galloped by; the two drivers watched, their heads turning in unison.

"They look good," Michael said. "That outside wheel has muscled up very nicely."

"He's a strong goer," Ishmael said.

"He didn't look like much of anything when you bought him," Michael said. "Just a big rack of bones. You've got a nice eye for a horse."

Down the track, walking the wrong way of it, came the big Frank. Ishmael watched him, prizing what Prince Michael had just told him; had any other man praised him, Ishmael would have suspected some hidden motive in it, but Michael always said exactly what he thought.

The Frank moved over to the rail, to get out of the way of the horses, and watched them gallop by him. Ishmael nodded toward him. "There is that—what's his name? Hagen. Has he had any more trouble with Esad?"

"The impression I get is that Esad has trouble with him."

"Have you talked to him at all?"

"He's a barbarian." Michael laid his forearms on the rail, his eyebrows down over the bridge of his nose. "What would I have to say to a barbarian?"

Ishmael said nothing to that; Michael cared about nobody who did

not race, in any case. Hagen was coming toward them, obviously meaning to speak to them.

He walked straight past Michael, came up to Ishmael, and said,
with no amenities, "I need your help, if you don't mind."

Ishmael straightened up. "If I can, certainly. What's your trouble?"

Now Hagen looked at Michael, a look full of hostility. The Prince
put his head back, staring down his long patrician nose at the Frank,
which was less easy than usual for Michael, Hagen being taller than
he was.

"Your little doings are of no concern to me. Good day, Ishmael."
Michael turned, leaving, and as he went he snapped his fingers in
Hagen's face. "And an excellent good day to you, too, barbarian." He
sauntered off, his arms swinging at his sides, and a strut in every step.

"Toy hero," Hagen said, under his breath.

"You're wrong about that," Ishmael said. "You're dead wrong
about him, all ways."

Hagen murmured something that Ishmael did not hear; perhaps
it was in his own language. Ishmael tried to see Michael from this big
rough-talking outlander's point of view—was it the Prince's manners?
his fine clothes, his title? what annoyed Hagen? He wondered, suddenly, what the big Frank's home was like, what other Franks were
like.

The white-haired man was digging a piece of paper out of his
shirt. "Can you read?" He laid the paper down on top of the stone
railing.

Ishmael smoothed it down with his fingers. The paper was much
used, ripped in the creases, and the ink smudged. He read quickly
down the names listed on it. "Nothing but the names of various men
of the Empire." He tapped a name midway down the paper. "This is
the Prefect of the City, who pays me."

"You mean, they are officers of the court here?"

"Some of them."

Hagen was frowning, his wooly white eyebrows pulled together,
his hard blue eyes focussed on empty space. "Hunh." He held the list in
his hand and stared at it as if he could force the letters to speak to him.

Ishmael thought, What a trick it is, to read. He is a clever man in
his way, yet this piece of paper converts him into a brute.

Hagen leaned against the rail, still directing his full attention to the paper. Ishmael picked his nose. Up in the stands, a movement caught his eye, and he looked that way to see a little group of men walking along the upper level. One was Constantine, Michael's uncle, who had been assigned to escort the Caliph's ambassador and his party around the City.

Hagen was folding up the list; he slid it away into his clothes. "I have to go away for a while," he said. "Can you watch over my other horse for me? He has to be taken out and run, or he'll break the stall down."

"I'll do it."

"It's not too much trouble? I hear you are to race again soon."

"Yes, in a week or so."

"Good luck, then. I hope I am here to see it."

Hagen put out his hand, and Ishmael took it; the barbarian's strong grip reminded him, oddly, of Prince Michael. He thought, They are much the same, Michael and this man, and that is why they contend together. At once, perversely, he found himself wishing that the barbarian contended with him.

"Where are you going?" he asked.

"Away." Hagen smiled at him and started off toward the stable.

Ishmael rushed along beside him. "Damn it, Hagen, don't you owe me more of an explanation than that?"

Hagen made a sound in his throat, half-laugh and half a groan of despair. He shook his head. "If I understood the least of what is going on, Ishmael, I would talk to you the night through over it." He stopped abruptly and stared at Ishmael, his face fretted. "Your Greek women—do they ever tell the truth?"

"My wife is Arab, like me," Ishmael said. "I never let her out of the house, she has nothing to lie about. What women do you mean?"

"This Empress. And there is another—"

He broke off, looking away, and as suddenly as he had stopped he was walking off into the stable again. Ishmael followed him, his curiosity like a maddening itch.

"The Empress is a Jezebel," he said. "Everybody knows that. About this other woman—"

"I don't care about her," Hagen said, his back to Ishmael, and went fast away into the gloom.

: 17 :

Theophano waited for a chance to kill John Cerulis, but it did not come. She was never alone with him anymore. Whenever she was in his company, one or another of his guards was always nearby, usually the despicable Karros. When she was away from John, one of his aunts, an elderly chatterbox, attended her, and every move Theophano made was watched.

In the morning after she saw Hagen, while she was still brooding over her stupidity in falling in love with a barbarian who hated her, John Cerulis with a modest retinue of three hundred people set out from Constantinople. By barge, they crossed over the narrows into Asia, and there took the road toward Sinop. Theophano rode in a chair with the aunt, Eusebia, who was embroidering silk in an oval frame, and maintained a constant level of incidental gossip. Clearly she was not there to draw Theophano into idle revelations, but simply to keep watch over her.

They spent the night on the shore of the Euxine. The great mass of servants threw up tents, lit fires, set tables out and with them chairs; over a hearth of clay bricks, John Cerulis's cooks made them a meal that was a mockery of those to which he was accustomed.

In the largest of the tents, Theophano sat on his left at the high table, which was placed up on a wooden dais covered with brocades and Persian carpets. The dinner was elegantly served, and she liked the meats, which, simply roasted on spits, had an unexpectedly delightful robust flavor; but the bread was a crime against humanity, and there was no fish at all.

John Cerulis sat there with his smile white-lipped, his eyes glassy. A fine wheaten pancake, stuffed with a terrine of wild game and garnished with a tart cherry sauce, revived his color somewhat. Then, when the wine for the fifth course was poured out full of sediment, he wheeled around toward Theophano and snarled, "You look like an urchin, you know—fading away into a shade of yourself. You could at least mind your appearance for my sake."

She raised her eyebrows at him. She knew how she looked. Resigned to death, she had no fear, and her hatred made her vicious.

In an idle voice, she said, "Really, Patrician, I wish you would send for some of your bully boys, and have me torn limb from limb, or boiled in oil, or otherwise performed on, to provide me with that much entertainment at least. I vow I have seldom been so bored."

"This was your idea, laughter-loving Theophano!"

"My idea!" She eyed him, leisurely, looking down her nose at him, in the way she had often seen Prince Michael wither people. "I merely suggested that you enlist this holy man in your cause. It was your idea, if the decision can be glorified as an act of mind, to leave Constantinople."

"Oh? And what would you have done, in my place?"

She considered that. She meant to kill him, anyway, so it did not matter if she told him anything useful.

She said, "I would have accepted the invitation. The Imperial box is the only place Irene goes where she is not surrounded by her guards. You could have planned your assault on the government for the beginning of the race, when most of Rome would be interested only in what was going on on the racetrack, and then at the proper moment, seized her person, and forced her to resign the throne in your favor, and the whole of the City would be gathered there in the Hippodrome to hear her do it."

John Cerulis's mouth formed a reflective pout. He thought a while before he spoke, and when he did, he gave her a slight bow of his head.

"An excellent scheme. You should have been born a man, Theophano."

"My God," she said, suddenly close to tears. "Do you mean a compliment? What a fool you are, Patrician. To be a *man*—you think you mean, to have everything; don't you? But what is a man in this world but a tool—God uses him for His Glory; the City uses him to maintain itself. A woman may at least have love—she may bear children —but a man! Pagh!"

She spat on the plate in front of him. A gasp went up from every throat in the room.

"Give me no such insults, John Cerulis. I will be only, and ever, what I am."

She stood up, even as John Cerulis with a jerk of his arm summoned his guards forward. "Stand aside." She put out her hand to stop them. "I shall be happy to leave. Never have I been so abominably served."

She marched straight toward the door, moving fast, so that the guards had to break into a trot to keep pace with her. That night she slept in a storage tent on the ground.

All the next day, she rode in the chair beside the aunt. The dust of the road and the heat and boredom rubbed over her nerves; she felt flayed. The aunt's empty chatter was maddening.

All this was John Cerulis's doing, torturing her. The only way to escape from him was to destroy him. She longed to kill him in some slow and painful way, but she knew that would be impossible—she would have to be swift, and certainly she would die, too. Resigned to that, she slumped on the cushions dully considering ways to end his life.

Beside her, the aunt said, "Oh!" and twitched.

"What's the matter?"

"Ah—I am clumsy." The aunt had stuck herself with one of her embroidery needles; she put her bleeding finger into her mouth. Intrigued, Theophano watched as the needle, fallen onto the old woman's black silk skirt, slid like a silver streak down into the cushions. Eusebia fussed to herself; she had gotten blood on her work, and with many recriminations and laments she unhitched it from the hoop and packed it away.

Theophano slid her hand down into the cushions, shifting her weight, as if trying to get comfortable, and found the needle. Carefully she hid it away in the cuff of her sleeve.

Hagen took his bay horse and rode after John Cerulis, not in the caravan's track but on the hillside above it, out of the dust. Once or twice, his way took him down out of sight of the great train, but he found it again each time without difficulty.

The road led along the shore of the sea, between the pebble beach and the round dun shapes of the hills. There were no trees, only twisted, wind-curried shrubs and stretches of blowing grass. On the high peaks, stone towers stood, and once, in the far distance, he saw a village or a small town, but the only natives were a few sheep and goats, grazing on the rocky hillsides, and rushed off into hiding by boys with sticks when they saw the caravan coming.

Hagen saw Theophano in her chair, some crone beside her; he followed as close to her as he could, for a long time, watching her.

That night he slept by himself, on the hillside above the camp. In the morning he went down to the road, which was curving inland now, away from the sea. The road was choked with horses and carts, servants on foot and others leading donkeys; Hagen worked his way through this pack until he found Karros, riding a big chestnut gelding with a blaze face.

Karros did not see him until Hagen was almost stirrup to stirrup with him, and for an instant the fat Greek's face went pale as a ghost's. Quickly his welcoming smile jerked up into place. "Ah, my friend Hagen! Good to see you, man—good to see you." He leaned out to clap Hagen on the arm, as if they were the oldest of friends.

Hagen hitched himself around slightly in his saddle, scanning the people around them. Theophano rode just ahead of them in the chair, the curtains drawn now against the dust. As they went farther from the sea, the sun burned hotter, and he guessed in a little while the dust would seem less a problem than the heat inside the curtains. He faced Karros again.

"I've come to take up your offer, Karros."

"My offer," the Greek said blankly.

"You said your master would make me one of his guards."

"I did? Oh. Yes, of course, I forgot. Well, certainly, he can always use a good fighting man." Karros's eyes fell to Hagen's sword, hanging in its leather scabbard on his hip. "I'll take you to him when he stops."

He produced another of his jovial grins and hearty backslaps, and turning to the men around him called them closer and said their names, and Hagen's name. None of the others seemed as pleased as Karros was with Hagen's sudden appearance in their midst. They were an ugly bunch, Hagen's age and younger, awkward on their horses, in their leather armor. Karros wore the red rosettes on his shoulders, his insignia of rank, perhaps. Hagen found his eye drawn again and again to the red patches on Karros's shoulders. They reminded him of Rogerius.

In among this band of soldiers were the men who had killed Rogerius. Even if Theophano had killed his brother, some of these men had wounded him.

He kept his eyes away from them. He was afraid if he looked too closely he would recognize the men who had stood there with Karros on the porch of the church on the Chalcedon road, and if he recognized them, he would strike.

He dared not attack them now. There were too many of them, too many other people around them. Had he been sure of taking Rogerius's killers with him, he might have taken the chance anyway, but there were too many questions unanswered.

He could feel the suspicion of him in the men around him. He could feel that Karros meant him no good. Now he was riding in among them, alone, vulnerable. But he had to see Theophano again.

They picked up their companionable chatter around him, these Greeks in John Cerulis's guard, talking about women, horse-races, fighting, getting drunk, whom they hated and whom they feared. Hagen said nothing. He rode in their midst inside a well of silence, his eyes straight ahead, avoiding their looks. He had been long in the City, confused by the ways of the City. Now he was coming to a fight, and he understood fighting. Impatiently he wished the time away until the moment when he took his sword in his hands again.

When they stopped for the night, he went off by himself, and hid the Greek paper under a rock in the desert.

The embroidery needle was three inches long. Theophano poked it through a piece of leather, to make a grip, so that she could hold it well. Throughout the afternoon, as they rode in the heat and the dust toward the eastern horizon, she thought how to strike, to kill John Cerulis.

If she pushed it through his chest, she might not get it deep enough to kill him. Yet the spot in the throat was so small, she could miss that entirely, and yield her life for nothing.

She felt her own throat, hunting for the pulse. There, just below the jawbone, a little in front of the ear. She wished she had a knife.

At sundown, when the caravan stopped to camp, and her bearers carried her chair up to John Cerulis, she found Hagen there.

Karros had brought him, the pig. While John sat in his opulently cushioned travelling chair, Karros bowed double before him and indicated the tall Frank, standing silent at his heels.

"Patrician, I present to you, again, my good friend Hagen the barbarian, who seeks to enter your service."

"Does he," said John Cerulis. He leaned his head on his fist, his gaze wandering to the woman at his side. "I believe you have the acquaintance of this fellow, laughter-loving Theophano?"

Hagen was ignoring her. She could not take her eyes from him. From the instant she saw he was there, all the other people in the world disappeared for her. The minutest detail of his appearance—the curls of his hair, the arch of his collarbone visible through the neck of his shirt—absorbed all her attention; the effort necessary to keep her head brought a fine sweat to her hands.

She gave a brittle little laugh. "Tut, Patrician. I do not make the acquaintance, as you put it, of the lesser orders. I have had use of him." She smirked at Hagen; nervously in her lap she drew the fingers of one hand over and over through the grasp of the other. "Bought any splinters lately, pilgrim?" If John Cerulis ever guessed how she felt about him, Hagen would surely die.

There were a number of people within earshot, and all laughed, even John Cerulis, at her silly jibe. Hagen stabbed a nasty look at her. Against her will, her hand rose a little toward him, palm up, an appeal she swiftly suppressed.

"You, barbarian," John said; a servant was bringing him water in a silver bowl, to refresh his face and hands, and he leaned over it, his hands raised before him in a sort of parody of prayer. "What brings you to me?"

"Your man Karros tells me that you are a worthy master, Patrician."

"I repay faithful service with a lavish hand. I am also swift to punish failure." While he spoke, a servant bathed his hands and dried each finger with a scented towel. "You would look well in the uniform," he went on, inspecting Hagen from head to foot, "but what knowledge can you have of Homer? There's good and bad in everything."

He allowed the washing of his face. Karros said, "I can vouch for him, sir—a valiant fellow. We crossed swords once on the Chalcedon road."

Theophano laughed at that. John Cerulis lifted his face from the towel with an inquiring look, and she said, "That's not how I remember it." Her eyes on Hagen, she said, "Patrician, you should dispose at once of this Frank, who is surely the agent of the Empress."

Hagen's eyes opened wide, a blue fire, and the look he gave her was murderous. It did not matter that he hated her, so long as he was safe from the curse of a connection with her. John Cerulis's face was lively with interest in this game. He leaned over the railing of his chair, his gaze going from the one to the other of them.

"Obviously you know this lady, barbarian."

"In any language," Hagen said, "I know a cunt when I see one."

From all those listening, a titillated gasp went up; Aunt Eusebia fell backward into the cushions in a swoon, and John Cerulis twitched as if he had been struck. Hastily Karros said, "Here, here, the Patrician abhors coarse language."

Theophano said, between her teeth, "Kill him, my lord." She could see that everything she said inspired John to do the opposite.

"Now, now," said John smoothly, "we are in the country, after all, where standards are somewhat different. Let us not be hasty." He smiled at her. He carried a slender rod of wood in his chair, to direct his bearers, and picking it up he poked gently at Theophano's bosom. "He frightens you, doesn't he."

"Not in the least," she said, too loudly, and became much interested in her clothing.

"Karros, allow your new friend to enjoy the hospitality of your fire." John's stick nudged and nudged; she refused to try to fend it off, and abruptly he jabbed her hard in the crotch. At the pain, she whined, and Hagen, leaving with Karros, heard it and looked around; over the heads of the fat bodyguard and John's servants and her bearers, his gaze met hers. There was no yielding in his look, no warmth, no friendship; it was as if he struck her with his eyes. He went away. Theophano sank down onto the cushions, her hand to her bruised vulva, suddenly near tears.

Karros stayed nearby the Frank all the rest of the evening, although the big man provided little in the way of conversation. Karros wondered if he had not the Greek for it, or if he were merely stupid.

It was the others who inclined Karros to favor him. The other guards were suddenly treating their fat officer with a good deal more deference, now that they saw Hagen with him.

Karros mentioned a few more times about their meeting on the Chalcedon road, and how they had crossed swords and come off equally, which, as he worked at the memory, did not seem so far from the truth.

The other guards were impressed with that. He knew why: they were toy soldiers, he and his men, having little exercise of their ability in John Cerulis's cause save the bullying of already frightened people and the guarding of their master's person at ceremonies. Hagen was something else, something from a darker, crueller world, where people actually had to fight for their lives.

The brother had been that way also. With a twinge of fear, Karros remembered the fight at the inn in Chrysopolis; he and his three underlings had surprised the brother naked and engaged in sex with Theophano, and yet the Frank had come off the couch with a sword in his hand and taken on all four of them, and had Karros not fallen down and feigned death and gotten behind him, the Frank might very well have won.

This other one, Hagen, believed that Theophano had done that. Another reason to keep him close by Karros's side, since two of the men who had been in that room at Chrysopolis were now sitting across the fire from him. Karros did not trust them; he trusted nobody, in fact. He began to watch for the chance to kill Hagen.

Nothing occurred that evening, or all the next day's march, while Hagen rode silent in their midst; but that next afternoon, late in the day, when they stopped again to camp, Karros decided to do something.

Hagen had gone off by himself. Karros and his guard were setting up their part of the camp on the sandy floor of a dry wash, whose throat was choked with squat twisted shrubs, and taking out his short sword, Karros gave a dramatic war cry, and plunged into the midst of these warped little trees and began to hew at them.

"Ah, ha! I'll match swords with any of you—watch!"

With a single blow, he hacked through one of the shrubs, throwing the gnarled top fifteen feet through the air. Hagen was just coming up along the top of the wash's bank and the branches nearly hit him.

"Come on," Karros called to him, with a broad and friendly smile. "Show off your strength and skill to these City men!"

Hagen did not move, but the other guards rushed into the shrubbery and began to beat at the brush with their swords, uttering yells and whistles of excitement, crowing in victory when one managed to break off part of the little shrubs, which were tough even if they were small. Bits of green boughs flew through the air and sprinkled the sand. Karros howled, dealing a death blow to a little bush.

"Come on, Hagen—join us! Show us your power!"

The Frank went to the sandy ground at the mouth of the wash, where the fire was laid out, and sat down with his back to the battle in the brush. Now one or two of the other guards hooted at him.

"What's the matter—afraid of a few sticks?"

Hagen kept his back to them. Karros paused, breathing hard, his hands splattered with bits of green and sticky sap. If he could lure the Frank into this mock fight, in the course of the mêlée he could get behind him and strike. A hamstring, or a neck shot, or even a good solid blow to the right arm, and Hagen would be at his mercy; it would take little to set all the others on him at once, and kill him in a few seconds.

"Come on, Hagen!"

The Frank did not move. The other guards were leaping into the brush now, screeching; half the dense thicket had been cut down and lay in ruins on the dry sand. Karros plunged deeper into it, his sword raised. Something alive squealed and ran off at his approach, and he flinched back a moment, his scalp prickling up.

The other guards were nagging and taunting Hagen now in strident voices. The battle with the shrubs had aroused their fighting spirit. A few of them even went down to the fire and danced around him, waving their swords in his face and whooping at him, and kicked sand on him. Hagen ignored them.

Dark was coming. Slowly the guards' killing frenzy subsided, and they drifted down on to the sand and finished building their fire. Hagen had not moved at all; he sat there with his shoulders hunched, his knees drawn up to his chest, staring into the darkness, and later, into the fire. Karros walked by him, once, close enough to brush against him, and the Frank ignored that too.

Had it been all bluff, then? Karros remembered, now that he thought back, that in his doings with Hagen, the barbarian had never really proved any prowess. Karros had reacted, rabbitlike, to the smell of danger the big Frank gave off. Maybe it was just a front. Maybe there was nothing behind it but the common fears and inabilities of ordinary men. Men like Karros. Maybe he was no better than Karros. The fat man beamed; he felt as if a heavy mantle of foreboding had fallen from his shoulders. Hagen was nothing. Karros had dealt with people like him many times. The brother, now: he had slain the brother. He went around the camp, throwing out his chest, buoyant with relief.

Hagen sat by the fire, thinking about Theophano. Every word she said to him struck him like a dart of fire; yet everything else—her looks, her acts, and John Cerulis himself—all pulled the other way entirely.

She had betrayed him to John, telling him that Hagen was the Empress's agent. That alone ought to make her Hagen's enemy. And yet he remembered, over and over, the little gesture of her hand, the palm raised, the fingers softly cupped, a sort of plea, quickly hidden.

He sat by the fire, trying to sort this all out. John was engaged in a sort of struggle with her—no, not a struggle, a game, a cat-and-mouse game. Prodding her with his stick. If they were lovers, or even conspiring together, he would not jab at her like that.

She had gasped in pain, once. He had not seen why. The low cry from her lips had gone all through him like needles.

She had betrayed him. If John thought him the agent of the Empress, he would not live very long in this camp.

And then there was Karros.

He had gone away from the camp, when the caravan stopped, and made water in private, and hid away the Greek paper where no one could find it, and gone back to the camp to find Karros and his men happily butchering a clump of little trees.

That had struck him with a peculiar force. His grandfather, whose soul had not belonged to Christ, had worshipped trees—not such puny pitiful things as these, but the great oaks and ashes of the north, the children of the supernatural Tree that was the world's axis. Hagen understood Karros's purpose; he understood also what sort of warrior it was who would draw his sword to club down a stunted tree.

There were no trees left here, only statues of them, he thought, remembering the white columns of marble along the Mesê. They had no warriors, either. Hagen suspected a connection between these two things, a conclusion that satisfied him very well; he thought no more about it.

: 18 :

"You've been to Baghdad," ibn-Ziad was saying, surprise in his voice.

"As a young man," Nicephoros said. He bowed his head to avoid an overhanging palm frond. They were walking through the palm garden, near the Phiale of the Greens. "I studied at al-Ghazi's school of arithmetic for a few months, before I took up the belt of Imperial service."

"I was under the impression that the rest of the cosmos had nothing of value for Constantinople."

Behind these two, the Parakoimomenos walked with his arms folded, listening; at the sarcasm in the Arab's voice, he smiled. Nicephoros of course, took no amusement from the envy disguised in the remark.

"I learned much at the school of al-Ghazi."

"Then you must also have learned that we Arabs keep our word to friend and enemy alike. The tribute due us from the Basileus must be paid."

"Ah," said Nicephoros.

They were walking along the foot of the palm garden now. It was the full of the day, the day after the earthquake, and the intense humid heat characteristic of such phenomena pressed down upon them like a lid. All around them, in pots and jars and wooden boxes, stood a hundred different kinds of palm—some tall, some small, some bushy—some full of fruit, their shadows like black daggers sharp on the ground.

"If you people are having some difficulty with your finances, we can arrange payment in separate allotments, but we must have what is due us, or we give offense to God."

"I understand your position perfectly," said Nicephoros.

Ibn-Ziad was a large, jocose man, his habits of mood betrayed by the great webs of laugh lines spread around the corners of his eyes and the deep marks at the corners of his mouth when he smiled—an optimist, over all, the Parakoimomenos suspected, one easily induced to believe that what he wished for would befall him, because of his special place in the love of God.

They were slowly climbing down the palace grounds, toward the Pharos, where in the little Chapel of the Virgin that stood next door they were supposed to view the sacred relics. From the palm garden a short flight of steps fell to the next level; beside the steps stood a statue of Venus, and ibn-Ziad paused to admire the figure. Beside him, Nicephoros allowed himself one of his rare smiles.

"Lovely," said ibn-Ziad, and sighed, his hand moving toward the statue, which was three-quarter size, the goddess standing with her head turned over her shoulder, her pert little breasts coyly shielded by one curved forearm.

"You people deny yourselves much grace and pleasure when you will not allow your artisans to form figures," Nicephoros said. "It is a gift from God, to gaze on something lovely; it directs the soul outward, and gives it rest from its constant labor of self-examination."

"We believe it blasphemy," said the Arab. "Yet such objects as I have seen of the works of the pagans stir my heart."

"Perhaps," said the Parakoimomenos, moving up beside the others, "our friend prefers women of less impermeability."

"That, too," said ibn-Ziad, and released a hearty laugh that shook his handsome clothes.

Nicephoros scratched his nose. "Our guest surely will have no difficulty in cultivating the females of his choice. We should be going in."

They moved on, descending the steps. On this level, in the curve of the pavement, their attendants awaited them; the heavy sun-drenched air seemed to stir sluggishly around them, making walking a labor against nature. Beyond the cypresses along the edge of the terrace, the lighthouse rose, its fire transparent in the sun. They made their way toward the chapel, with its sets of fluted columns all around, and its dome of silver.

The Parakoimomenos fell back to walk beside Nicephoros. "Are we not giving a dinner party for our guest this evening? Some companion could be found for him. That woman of the Empress's, Theophano—"

"I think," said Nicephoros, between his teeth, "he should be allowed to secure such companionship for himself."

"Excuse me," said ibn-Ziad, and moved on, out of earshot of the two men and their argument.

"A man needs a woman," said the Parakoimomenos, and bowed.

"How would you know?" Nicephoros said. "He does not need a pander. Nor does he need a heavy-handed effort at seduction, by you, by Theophano, by anyone."

Turning on his heel, he walked on after their guest, now the center of a sedate crowd, moving in through the double doors of the chapel. The Parakoimomenos stayed where he was. In spite of the rage in his heart, he smiled; he promised himself that when the day came of Nicephoros's downfall, he would know who had arranged it. Drawing himself up to his full height, his face smoothed free of any expression, the Parakoimomenos went after the others at a pace designed to keep a distance between them.

Ibn-Ziad loved Constantinople. He had been coming here now since his boyhood, when he had accompanied his father on an informal embassy to the court of the Emperor Leo. Every time he came here he felt more at home.

Certainly he was at home in the Chapel of the Virgin. Several other foreigners had joined their little group, and a guide in the clothes of a Christian priest was supposed to be escorting them about, but before they had set eyes on the first of the wonderful objects in the Treasure Room, ibn-Ziad had begun his own discourse.

He could not help it. He knew these relics, now, as well as any Greek, and he loved showing off to his hosts and lording it over his fellow barbarians. The looks of amazement and wonder on the faces of the Romans spurred him on. He would show them they had no monopoly on knowledge.

"Ah," he said. "The rib of Saint Paul. The reliquary"—he paused, to allow those in the mob around him unfortunate enough not to recognize this word to grasp its meaning—"was designed in the time of Justinian, was it not?"

The guide bowed with a flourish. "The most excellent Lord Ambassador flatters us with his knowledge."

Ibn-Ziad bowed; around him with a rustle and a hiss of silk the others bowed too. They moved on through the magnificent room. After the blasting heat of the day, the cool stone of the chapel made this space a blessed sanctuary. The marbles of the floor and the walls were wonderful in themselves, dark brown veined with white and gold in the exuberant patterns of nature; God's paintings, ibn-Ziad thought, sentimentally. In cases of glass and polished wood, set around this room, the relics of the Imperial collection were displayed, chips of bone and wood surrounded by goldwork and enamel, little vials of crystal clasped in filigree, all set off on cushions of velvet and subtly lit by lamps whose direct glare, shielded off by screens of perforated gold, was reduced to a reverent glow.

It was this that was most Roman, to ibn-Ziad: these small masterpieces, this attention to detail, this elegance. They went from one case to the next; sometimes he let the guide talk, but usually he pushed himself forward, delighted with what he knew, and expounded at length on the finding of the True Cross by the mother of Constantine the Great, and on the miracles wrought by the little bottle of the Virgin's Tears, stoppered by a huge diamond. The others listened with such attention that he felt himself released from all inhibitions; he knew himself the most assured of orators, and when he was done, they burst into applause, and he felt the heat rising into his face, and could not restrain his smiles.

But when they had seen everything, and the others were gathering at the doorway, ready to be whisked off to another gathering, ibn-Ziad went back by himself, and stood looking through the glass at the wonderful reliquary of the True Cross: a tiny replica of the chapel itself, with doors that really opened, and goldwork so ornate and finely done he had to squint to make out the details.

While he stood there, Prince Constantine came up to him, and stood waiting, a little to one side, to be noticed. Ibn-Ziad turned to him, smiling.

"Good afternoon to you, sir. I trust you have some happy news for me?"

Constantine's mouth curved into a grin, and he winked. "I have the girls, the room, and the wine. When will your official duties be over?"

"Ask the Parakoimomenonononono."

Constantine laughed outright; the two men shared another knowing smile. Ibn-Ziad straightened, putting his shoulders back, his head high; it soothed the lingering bruises in his pride to make fun of the Parakoimomenos, and he turned to look for the tall eunuch in the crowd that still filled the far end of the chapel. Suddenly something else, something much more vital and amusing, leapt into his mind.

He turned to Constantine again. "That race—remember? You told me—some Arab team is coming to race in the Hippodrome?"

" 'Some Arab team.' I did not tell you."

"One of you did." Ibn-Ziad plumped out his chest and bounced on his heels. "From Caesarea, it is."

"Oh, yes."

"Well, I have engaged the Augustus in a wager. That ought to make the moments with her more compelling, don't you think?"

Constantine grunted. "You've bet on the Caesareans? How much?"

"Unimportant. I gather I shall not lose, in any case?"

But Constantine did not smile reassurances at him; Constantine was frowning.

"I'm sorry?" Ibn-Ziad said stiffly. "I've erred, in some way?"

Constantine shook his head. "No, of course not. A wager is a wager, isn't it? Gambling's a matter of taking risks."

"I was under the impression that this Arab team would sweep all before it."

Constantine's eyebrows jerked up and down over his nose. "The Caesarean team is in the race with Ishmael—Mauros-Ishmael, you saw him, yesterday, do you remember? In the Hippodrome, the blacks and greys."

"Ah?" Ibn-Ziad said, alarmed. Who had told him of this race? He could not remember; someone had told him that the Caesarean team would surely win.

"Of course, everybody has a chance," said Constantine. "And the Caesareans are supposed to be very good."

Ibn-Ziad stared at the Prince with a hostile look. Now he saw the pitfalls beneath the velvet cushions and honeyed words and the instant fulfilling of his pleasures. Somehow he had been lured into this wager, and now it seemed that he would lose.

He pulled up his chest again, thrusting out his chin. He did not mean to lose.

"My dear Prince," he said. "Surely some way could be found to assure that my team reaches the finish line ahead of all the others."

"Aaah."

Now Constantine's smile began again, slow as flowing oil, and his gaze met the Arab's. With a wave of one hand, he bowed deeply in ibn-Ziad's direction.

"Whatever you wish, my lord."

"See that it is done," said ibn-Ziad loftily.

Nicephoros had walked through the chapel with the others, looking at the relics; he enjoyed the displays, and he always hoped that the mere proximity of so many sacred objects would work some small miracle in his heart and give him peace.

He had no peace. The confrontation with the City Prefect in the baths of Zeuxippus had left him sore and low of mind. He liked Peter and knew the other man liked him, and it disturbed him that the Basileus should put this friendship in jeopardy by making Nicephoros into the Prefect's harpy. Beyond the simple fact of having to deal with his friend's crimes against his office there was the undeniable truth in Peter's own argument that Nicephoros could loan him the money to make all right.

Nicephoros could not phrase in words his reluctance to do this; it was a black pressure in his mind that nagged at him, the thought that he ought to rescue his friend, the suspicion that the Basileus rather expected him to do just that, beneath those sentiments the hard ugly unwillingness to do it.

All this soured everything he did. He could find no solace in his numbers anymore, no pleasure in the simple performance of his duties, no joy in Christ. Besides, he knew that the Parakoimomenos was plotting against him.

Now the eunuch was talking to ibn-Ziad, on the far side of the Treasure Room. Beside him stood Prince Constantine. Nicephoros's eyes rested on this trio, and almost against his will the upwelling suspicions and fears of a lifetime spent at court swelled up through the dank distempered depths of his mind and flooded all his thoughts.

They were plotting against him. The Basileus was behind it. She wanted his disgrace. Why did he go on? Nothing he did worked out properly anymore. He turned away, his heart sick.

Nearby him, also waiting for this part of the tour to end, was one of the other foreign visitors; this was a monk, clearly, by his tonsure, his cassock of some coarsely woven grey stuff, his hands, folded before him, innocent of any ornament. Above the cowled neck of his garment his head was close-cropped where the hair grew; his face was leanly made, the skin weatherbeaten, the eyes wide-spaced and clear as an animal's, as if he had no thoughts to veil.

The severe and simple aspect of this person was so at variance with the others that Nicephoros on an impulse drew near and with a gesture and a bow said, "Allow me, Father, the honor and privilege of making myself known to you—I am Nicephoros, the Imperial Treasurer."

The monk faced him gravely, with no change of expression. His eyes were pale as water. It seemed as if nothing could surprise him. But when he spoke it was in Latin.

Nicephoros gritted his teeth. He knew no Latin. With a few more gestures and another bow, he expressed this sad fact to his new companion, and the monk, by his look, was not inclined to mourn the loss of conversation. Nicephoros would have ended it there.

Unfortunately the guide had seen him attempt to speak to the barbarian monk, and the guide, his functions usurped by ibn-Ziad's extraordinary exercise in self-expression, was eager to be of use. He rushed up to the two men and pattered out a string of Latin to the monk.

The barbarian responded in a low voice, which the guide translated.

"He is a monk of Eire, my lord—Hibernia, that is, at the edge of the world."

"Hibernia," Nicephoros said. That had never even been part of the Empire; it was so far away the waters of Ocean totally surrounded it, as if God, having made the world and drawn back to observe His craftsmanship, had let drop a bit of the leftover clay into the sea. "What in God's Sacred Name is he doing here?"

Another exchange between the guide and the monk, during which Nicephoros heard his name spoken. The monk faced him and bowed once and lifted his hand and made the Sign of the Cross over him— made the barbarian way, left to right, with three fingers.

"He says," the guide told him, "that his monastery was destroyed by an assault of the Northmen. He is here to ask the Basileus to give his order a place to build a new monastery."

"Here? Why not Rome? Who are these Northmen?"

The guide and the monk spoke together a moment.

"He says that his order had some dealings with Rome in the past that left them unwilling to discuss matters of faith with those people. He says that this being the center of the world, we shall be safe from the Northmen for a long time yet."

Nicephoros searched the barbarian monk's face, curious against his will: this seemed the sort of man who would live at the edge of the world, the wind from the abyss tearing at him, the darkness ever ready to overcome him; surely there was no room in that gaunt implacable face for any ease or pleasure in life. He said, "Who are these North-men?"

"He says," the guide said, after some more gabble with the monk, "that they are wolves from the sea. They come from the fogs, from the night, and from the storm, and set upon all things in their path, and all things in their path they devastate utterly. They are God's chosen instruments for the destruction of the world, and surely, he says"—the guide smiled, his teeth gapped—"they will come upon us one day, at the end of things."

"Hunh," said Nicephoros.

He faced the room again. Somehow the simple words of the monk had transported him. The room was oddly strange now, as if he had just been somewhere else. The splendid marble walls, the glass cases glowing in the diverted luminescence of the covered lamps, the low ripple of conversation—all seemed so safe, so ordinary, so cultivated, and so fragile; abruptly he shivered all over. In his imagination he saw these walls burst apart, this whole place shaken to the roots, while through every yawning crack rushed a wild ravening pack of wolves.

The vision made him sick to his stomach; he turned away. A few words to the guide transferred his best wishes and hopes to the Irish monk, whose cool pale gaze remained on him. Nicephoros thought, He will never reach the Basileus. Even if he did, what use would they be to each other?

Nicephoros turned around slowly again toward the Treasure Room. Marvelous, splendid, unbroken, unbreached, it surrounded these people caught up in their mundane conversations, preserving them from the greater all-encompassing truth. Was life possible only by insulating men from reality?

What reality? It was his low mood that brought him to such cankered daydreams. Nicephoros turned on his heel and walked out of the room, out on to the terrace, into the blasting sunlight of the day.

"He wants me to fix the race for him," said Constantine.

They were standing on the edge of the rose garden, just outside the Daphne; from behind the Parakoimomenos came the boisterous laughter of a good party. Ibn-Ziad's voice was clearly audible through the open doors, shouting exuberantly to another celebrant. They had already seen tumblers and jugglers; in half an hour, there would be women in to dance.

"Can you do it?" the eunuch asked Prince Constantine.

"Ishmael needs money. Probably he could be talked into it, yes." Constantine smiled at him.

The Parakoimomenos sniffed, disinclined to this little exercise in amending the possible. "I don't think so, really, my good man, do you?"

Beside him, Constantine moved, a short, fierce gesture swiftly brought under control, and said, between his teeth, "You know, we could all profit a little from this. Why not? I say. I mean—it can't hurt, really, can it? If she loses a wager—what does that matter?"

The Parakoimomenos raised his hand. He had just thought of a context in which Constantine's proposal acquired the overtones of an act of God. Even now, from the merry-making behind him, came the voice of the City Prefect, full of good humor, answering ibn-Ziad's remark.

"Gambling is a sin, my prince. A vile and corrupting sin, as some among us have only too great occasion to know. However—perhaps—in the circumstances, it might be preferable if ibn-Ziad did win his wager. Yes. Do what you can."

"Excellent," said Constantine briskly, and strode away, back toward the lights and the music.

The Parakoimomenos stood there a while longer. The evening was very warm and the roses yielded up their perfume in heady vapors, and everywhere in the purple twilight insects whirred and chirruped. Someone else was coming out of the party, out on to the terrace.

This was Nicephoros. Tall and angular, the Syrian came up to the edge of the terrace, reached in through the opening in his coat, drew out the arbor vitae, and relieved himself into the bushes. He ignored the Parakoimomenos, but the eunuch watched him steadily.

His clothes arranged again, Nicephoros turned, and the rivals faced each other. Nicephoros was looking surly and half-drunken. The Parakoimomenos remarked that he and the City Prefect, always friends before, were avoiding each other now. The Treasurer grunted.

"What is wrong—have you forgotten your quill?"

The eunuch's head snapped up at the insult. Nicephoros walked heavily back toward the party again. A cold hand closed around the heart of the Parakoimomenos. He had been a fool, before, when with a method of success at hand, he had held back from it. The City Prefect would fall, and Nicephoros with him. The eunuch swore it to himself, on the testicles he had lost in infancy, when his family determined on a career for him in the civil service. It was the holiest oath he knew. He did not go into the party again; instead, he went away by himself.

: 19 :

"You know what the law says," said the City Prefect, and tapped the owner of the ruined tenement on the chest with his staff of office. "You let entirely too many people live here—what were you running here, a cattle yard?"

He jabbed his ivory staff toward the blackened shell of the tenement on his left. They were standing on the waterfront; behind him was the harbor, a teeming human hive. The sunlight blazed on the waters of the Golden Horn, and on the sweating bodies of the lines of slaves and criminals working to unload the ships at the quays. Piles of goods stood along the side of the street, spices and cloth, wood and furs and grain. The groans and songs of the workmen reached his ears, and the screams of the gulls, fat tenants of every jetty and pile, gross with life.

Before him the tenement was a silent pit, a place of death. Inside the huge brick shell nothing remained. Most of the debris had been cleaned out of it already, and all the bodies; more than four hundred people, men and women and children, had died here in the fire. The Prefect imagined it with more detail than he wished for: the earth shook, knocking down the cooking pots; the flames caught on the desiccated wood of the floors, and raced on, through tiny crowded room after tiny crowded room, through ceilings and floors, through straw ticks and shabby blankets, through hoardings of coal and oil and wine, through blazing hair and eyes and skin.

His stomach turned. He faced the tenement owner again.

"Where else can they go but to such places as these?" The landlord made a face, bland, not worried; probably, the Prefect thought, he had friends in high places. And the first day of the month was just past: he had taken in all his rents. "The City is crowded with poor—where else can they live?"

"You are supposed to keep to the limits of the law."

"I can't be here every day. The families already here were taking in other folk to stay with them."

"And you are supposed to see they do no cooking in these premises. That's how this happens—they make fires in their rooms—"

"Look," said the landlord, beginning to frown, his forehead bent into sweating creases, "I brought in the priests when they were built, I had verses written on every joist and upright. The place was safe as a church! Some great sinner lived there, that's why it happened—God rid us of some horror in the earthquake."

The Prefect crossed himself. A little crowd had gathered to watch this confrontation, and now, at the landlord's words, they began to murmur.

"God's will, it is God's will." They sounded satisfied, their uncertainties reduced to a platitude.

The Prefect straightened, hearing, in this, the voice of popular wisdom, and looked out over the black scab of rubble, reaching back to the next street, rising steeply past warehouses and more tenements, probably belonging to this same man, certainly also overcrowded, every room crowded with the wretched poor, every room stinking from the smoldering coals of the little fire in its iron pot, waiting to be kicked over, tumbled over by another trembling of the earth, to set the whole place blazing like a torch.

"The will of God," the people in the crowd were whispering. "It was the will of God." Some of the old women knelt down, in their black shawls, and began to pray.

The Prefect did not understand the will of God anymore. He saw no divine purpose in the frying of four hundred people. He saw no use in anyone suffering, especially since in everyone's suffering, he saw the mirror of himself.

In this man before him, smiling nervously, saying, "God did it, not me," he saw himself as well, a corrupt and wicked man. Raising one hand, he said, "Rebuild it," and turned away.

Turning, he saw, beyond the dissipating crowd, an elegant cur-tained chair, which he recognized as much by the long train of re-tainers behind it. He stopped. The bearers were squatting at the poles, but now, at a command perhaps from inside, they straightened up, lifting their burden to their shoulders, and advanced toward the City Prefect.

It was the Parakoimomenos. The eunuch drew back the curtains, sighed, and breathed deep of the inrushing air.

"The heat is quite unbearable. I am on my way to the Blachernae, and saw you here, and since I must have a word with you—may we?"

"Certainly," said the Prefect. "Tell me how I may be of service."

"You were greatly of service last night, I understand. Ibn-Ziad is full of your praises."

"He is a fascinating fellow, for an Arab."

"You know he has made a wager with the Empress, on the out-come of the next race—between Ishmael and the Caesareans, in fact."

"I heard him say so last night."

"Good. Then my task is a simple one. The Empress requires some object, for her wager, some piece of beauty that will amaze a caliph."

"Of course."

"Your taste is exquisite, your knowledge of the City's resources infinite—can you find something?"

The Prefect bowed in answer. He was very flattered to be chosen, but not surprised.

The Parakoimomenos smiled at him, a conspiratorial gleam in his eyes. "The object must be perfect, since it will certainly find its way to the Caliph. If you take my meaning."

The Prefect said "Ah."

With a gesture, the Parakoimomenos signalled his bearers to lift him away. "I shall leave it to you, sir. Good day."

"Good day, my dear Parakoimomenos."

Swiftly the red chair swayed away into the passing crowd; the eunuch's retainers hurried after it. The Prefect stood where he was. His mind was torn. On the one hand he was sorting rapidly through a mental index of possible art objects; it should be, he knew at once, a piece of that extremity of artifice that had as its goal the exact reproduction of nature. Another part of his mind was saying, They have fixed the race.

Turning, he began walking slowly back along the street, toward the harbor office at the far end, where he was to meet with several of his staff. He knew every goldsmith in the City. Only a few specialized in the sort of exquisite pieces he was thinking of, and only one of them produced work of highest quality.

If they had fixed the race, then all he needed to know was who ibn-Ziad was betting on.

His steps were coming faster and faster. His breath felt short. He lifted his head. He could get out of this. One last bet and he would be out of this. And once he had evened himself up again, he would never ever bet again, God witnessed it; he swore it. Striding at top speed toward the offices, he allowed himself the easy luxury of a blissful smile.

Ishmael took Hagen's black stallion into the Hippodrome and let it run. No blood stock, still the horse was a good mover, and his opinion of it was rising as he worked with it.

While he was following after it with his whip, to keep it moving, he saw Prince Constantine come down out of the stands and cross the sand toward him.

Constantine had worn the Golden Belt, some years before, and older men than Ishmael said he had been a great driver; Ishmael had never seen him race, and did not believe it. He watched Constantine through the corner of his eye. The black horse skittered away across the sand, its tail stuck straight up in the air and its nostrils flared, and when Constantine passed by, it sprinted away with a flat spray of sand spurned up by its heels.

"You have some use for this donkey?" Constantine said, as he came up to Ishmael's side.

"It isn't my horse," said Ishmael.

"That's a relief to know."

Ishmael trailed after the stallion, which had gone on around the turn at the far end of the racecourse. Constantine strolled along at his heels, whistling between his teeth.

"I understand you have problems with money."

"Why is that of interest to you?"

"Oh, I don't know. I could help you out with it, perhaps."

"You could."

They rounded the curve, and seeing them the stallion leapt into the air, all four feet off the ground, and executed a body-screwing buck in the air.

"I happen to know how you could make yourself a good deal of money," Constantine said.

"Really? How?"

"If you let the new team from Caesarea win your race."

Ishmael spun around and faced him. "I don't believe it. You're suggesting that I throw a race?"

"It's just a qualifier. You can always qualify in the next round. You'll make it into the race that matters."

"I don't believe it."

"Certain people I know would give you a sizable sum of money right now, and you could make a lot more, betting against yourself."

"I'm not that desperate, Constantine."

"Think about it," Constantine said, smiling, and walked away across the track toward the seats. He didn't even have the grace to look embarrassed. Ishmael rubbed his hands together, his thoughts tossed.

It was true he needed money. Everybody needed money, even the Empress, or so rumor had it. He wondered if this were one of her plots—if she needed money enough to gamble for it.

The black horse jogged down the track, and Ishmael dragged his feet after it. It was true: he could let the Caesarea team win, and still qualify in the next round. And who would be hurt by that? The Caesarea team was probably good, everybody said so, all the rumors, all the advance talk. A lot of money. Constantine had not said how much. Ishmael owed money again to his landlord, to the tradesmen. His wife needed cloth to make garments for herself and the children, and she wanted other things, a few pieces of furniture, a rug. She had complained for months that a man as important as Ishmael ought to live better than he did.

He was tired of being poor. He was tired of having to wait for money, and then when he finally did get it, all of it flowed away at once to pay the debts accumulated while he waited.

A lot of money, Constantine had said. Thousands of irenes, perhaps. He could pay all his debts and still have money in his purse for months to come.

If he were caught—if word got around the City—

It was Michael he thought of, what Prince Michael would think of him, if he found out.

Constantine was a prince also, and this was Constantine's idea. No. Someone else was behind it. Who? The Empress.

Unlikely. If the Empress wanted to fix a race, she would not go about it with a simple bribe, that could fail so easily, and expose her to scorn as well as failure.

He wished Constantine had told him how much money.

Morose, he caught the black stallion and led it away into the stable. His grooms were cleaning stalls and chattering back and forth; ordinarily he would have joined in their banter and jokes, but Constantine's offer tied his tongue. That was all that occupied his mind, and he could not let it out to the grooms, with their loose tongues, and their compelling interest. He went out of the Hippodrome and walked down past the baths to his house.

His wife gave him dinner, complaining about the cost of lamb. She was a slender, doe-eyed girl, younger than Ishmael, with a voice as musical as a lute, even when she sighed and fretted. Since their courting he had taught her to depend on him, and now there was no question of exposing her to the realities of things like this.

Eating beans and onions, he thought of bringing home a big bag of money; she would never ask him where he had come by it, she would buy the rug, the furniture, buy lamb for every meal. Even if she suspected, she would say nothing.

He almost made up his mind to go to Constantine and agree to it, but then his son came in, shouting, a wooden sword tied to his waist, and rushed up to his father and hugged him.

Then Ishmael knew he could do nothing dishonorable; he would never be able to face this boy again, this treasure of his life.

But then when he went back toward the Hippodrome, the landlord accosted him in the street, demanding money, and his certainty came unlocked again. He spent the afternoon watching the farrier trim his horses' feet and chewing over the whole proposal.

In the evening, Michael came down to the stables. He always visited his horses at night, while they were eating their hay, like a mother kissing her babies to sleep. Ishmael was sitting on a pile of straw, mending a bridle with an awl by the light of a torch. The grooms had all gone home, or to the tavern, much the same thing; Ishmael was unwilling to go either place and have to talk.

Unfortunately Michael wanted to talk. He sauntered past, his hands on his hips. "This new team from Caesarea arrives tomorrow."

"Oh?" Ishmael said, and fastened his gaze on the bridle.

"When you've done with that, come and have a cup with me. Maybe I can give you some winning advice."

"I don't need any advice from you about driving horses."

"If you think that way, you'll never beat me. Put the bridle away, you have grooms for that. Come down and drink with me."

"I can't afford it," Ishmael said.

"I'll pay it. I don't mind supporting the lower orders, it's the obligation of the aristocracy."

"Never mind," Ishmael snarled at him. "I'll drink with my own kind, Prince."

He was remembering Constantine, a prince, offering him money to do evil. He wondered if Michael knew about it. He had always thought Michael was honest, but the bribe had come from his uncle, after all.

"You're surly tonight, Ishmael," Michael was saying. "Do the Caesareas have you a little worried?"

Ishmael stabbed the awl into the bridle, his mind churning. He was sorely tempted to ask Michael what he knew of the bribe, but if he did that, would he not condemn himself a little? They had offered the bribe to him—maybe they thought him weak. They knew he needed money. And why should he not have money? Michael had everything he needed, the horses, the grooms, the living, everything he needed, for nothing. For an accident, for God's inscrutable reasons. Why should Ishmael not narrow the gap between them a little?

He realized he was staring straight at the other charioteer, but saying nothing, and now Michael grunted at him, his lips twisting.

"Very well, Ishmael. Good night." He walked stiffly away across the Apron.

In the morning, the Caesarea team entered Constantinople, and half the City came to see them. They were high-steppers, four matched chestnuts, with manes the color of spun gold. Ribbons and banners festooned their car. The driver and his supporters had paid boys to run ahead of them and cheer, and so all the way up the Mesê the wild clamor of a crowd greeted them.

In the Hippodrome stables, they took over an entire aisle, between the one where Michael's horses were kept and the palace side. The driver was a big, round-bodied man with a full black beard, who walked up and down through the Apron, swearing at his grooms as each horse was led by, and complaining about the size of the stalls, the quality of the straw, the ill light, the stink of the torches. With new horses in the barn, every beast was neighing, stamping, kicking the partitions and the doors, and Hagen's black horse got loose somehow and rampaged up and down the aisles, snorting and whinnying until the walls echoed.

With his grooms' help, Ishmael cornered the black horse and got a bridle on it, and he was leading it back to its stall when the Caesarea driver crossed his path.

"One of yours, there?" The Caesarea driver leered through his curly black whiskers. "I thought your team was supposed to be good."

The black stallion danced sideways, pinning its ears back, and Ishmael hooked his arm around its head, his hand on the bone of its nose, holding it down. He said, "Get out of my way."

"No," the Caesarea driver said, in a booming voice; everybody in the barn turned to hear him. "You get out of *my* way, little man, on the racetrack, come race day. You mark me there!"

He strutted off, into the circle of his team-mates, who surrounded him with cheers and backslaps and adoring gazes. Ishmael led the black horse swiftly away. Prince Constantine's bribe turned to a handful of ashes. He didn't care now if his landlord kicked him into the street, he was going to run the Caesarea team off its wheels.

The lute was out of tune. Nothing of this daily horror of the music lesson was as tedious as tuning the lute. Philomela hunched her shoulders. She sat on a marble bench under one of the mulberry trees, awaiting Helena, and the lute lay beside her, pearwood and silver symbol of the sublime, and of woman, and source of so much misery for Philomela.

She had, however, a piece of currency, with which she could buy a day's freedom from this torture; she made up her mind that this would be the day. She loved the Basileus, but the lute was impossible.

She raised her head. Already in the midst of her childish roundness a longer, more slender shape was forming, and sometimes, tentatively, like putting on a mask, she tried out the expressions and attitudes of a woman; she was *turning*, the Empress told her, as if it were some private female rite, like the antique mysteries. Turning into what? she wondered. Now she saw, coming through the mulberry trees, the tall sedate figure of the chief lady-in-waiting, and a voice in her mind said: Not that.

Picking up the lute, she played triplets across the strings, as if for the first time she noticed that it was out of tune, and bent studiously over the instrument, her brows knit.

"Well," Helena said, arriving. "No need to ask what we'll do with this half hour."

She sat down on the next bench, under the next mulberry tree, and dropped her hands into her lap like something she could now forget about.

Philomela played with the silver screws. "I'm afraid I'll break a string, Helena."

"Tosh. Watch your manners, my girl."

"Yes, my lady."

Viciously she twisted the screw tighter and tighter, but the string would not break. Her courage wound up as well; she began to play the coin that would buy her escape.

"My lady, what does *fix* mean?"

"You silly girl. You know that. To mend something that has broken."

"Well," said Philomela, over the lute, "it must mean something else, because a race can't be broken, can it?"

She kept her head down; she did not see the older woman's re-action to this, but Helena said nothing for a long while, in itself a telling clue. Finally there was a rustle of silk, and a vanguard of per-fume, and Helena sat down beside her. "Where did you hear this?"

"I heard some men talking. It was just gossip."

"What men?"

"I'm sure I don't know who they are, Helena. Just some men."

"Oh, the villains," said Helena.

She took hold of Philomela's wrist and led her up onto her feet. "Come along."

"But what about my music lesson?"

"I think today, you imp, you will be excused the music lesson."

Irene heard Philomela's story with her back to the child and the lady-in-waiting; she was glad of it, because her hands began to tremble with the violence of her feeling. They had bought the race; they had put forward a challenge to her, and she had accepted it honorably, and then they had cheated her.

"Perhaps," she said, and was surprised to hear her own voice say-ing it aloud.

"The child may be making it all up," said Helena. "You know how her imagination breeds when she is idle."

"No," Irene said. "She would not lie to me. Would you, Philomela? No."

The girl faced her, chin up. "I'm not lying, mama."

Irene waved at them. "You may go. Thank you for bringing me this news."

When they had gone she let go of her passion in a single furious oath, and struck at a hanging. How dare they! Men, who trumpeted of honor and glory and the nobility of risk; men, who strutted their superiority over women. It was all a sham. She had always known it. They feared her, they pranced and paraded and talked Homerically but when she came face to face with them, they went craven and had to buy a victory.

Well, what could one expect of an Arab.

She paced up and down, rubbing her hands together; in less than an hour she had a meeting of her council, to hear news from the campaign against the Bulgars. To buy the race, ibn-Ziad would have to buy Ishmael, the champion of the Greens. The whole fix then turned on whether Ishmael could be bribed, crippled, or otherwise destroyed.

She did not know if this were possible, but Michael would know. She went out of the Daphne and, alone, walked down through the great descending sweep of the Palace grounds toward the Bucoleon.

It was early afternoon, and most of the people of the household were inside, resting after dinner, and getting out of the sun. It was another ferocious summer day, hot and windless as a furnace room. Irene had always disdained to let the weather affect her; she walked at a quick pace down the gravel walks and the shallow steps of the lower gardens. Now directly before her stood the lighthouse, a great cracked column, raising its bronze tray of coals forty feet above the very tip of the headland. Below, the sea lay like wrinkled silk. To her left was the Bucoleon Palace.

Michael himself sprawled in the sun before the fountain, on his stomach; one of his slaves was massaging oil into his back. Irene stood a moment watching him. He was a sort of talisman for her; he had won the Golden Belt for the first time in the same month that she arranged the overthrow of her son Constantine and raised herself to the ultimate power, and in all the Empire his power over the crowd was rival only to hers. Yet they fit together well. He wanted nothing save great horses and opponents who would push him to his best, and the multitude needed a hero, to fix their hopes on.

She said, in the dialect of Athens, which she had not spoken in years, "Well, well, sister-son, why spendest thou the hours of the sun in idleness? Up: thy days are short, the night cometh."

Michael lifted his head, twisting to look toward her, and the slave bounded backward a yard and dropped to all fours. The Prince lolled on his elbow, drawing his sheet across his nakedness.

Irene went forward half the distance between them, and stood looking down at him. She said, "I need your opinion, my darling, but what I must tell you to derive it will ruin your supper, I think."

"Ah?"

"Would it be possible to bribe Ishmael?"

"Ishmael!" He sat up, his face vivid with bad temper. "Who has tried to bribe Ishmael?" Now suddenly he breathed deep, and across his face walked a look of sudden understanding. He lowered his hands to his knees. "Oh—yes."

"He can be bribed?" she said, in a steady voice.

Michael flung her a dark look. "God, it was a fine day, before you brought your games of power into it."

She snorted at him. Her hands hung at her sides; unlike him, she needed no physical agency to express her power; she stood before him shining, shining in her golden coat. "You made yourself a false world when you cut the games of power out of it. Answer me."

"No. God! God! The amount of gold has not been dug up, Basileus, that would compensate Mauros-Ishmael for the loss of a single race. But it's been tried—I see it now, I understand it, now, how he's been acting."

She smiled at him, radiant. "Then you believe him proof against corruption."

"As I know myself."

"Thank you." She turned and walked away.

The sun was blazing in the western sky. She had her council meeting, and the hour was slipping by; she hurried her steps, climbing back up the mount of the clifftop. Under her heavy clothes her skin had melted into a sticky slime of sweat. She went up through the palm garden and had to stop at the next level, at a fountain, to catch her breath.

Her legs were quivering. She had felt this before, and remembering she gathered herself, willing herself to continue, and made for the Daphne like a hare going to den.

At the edge of the paved court just outside her private entrance, a number of women had gathered. She went in among them blindly, burrowing toward the door, and they scattered. Their voices clanged in her ears. She could not catch her breath, and the booming of her heart was like the tramp of oncoming footsteps. She reached the door and slipped inside.

The pain hit her. It came down like a hawk from the center of the sun, dug its claws deep into her breastbone, and crushed its weight in on her. She reached her morning room and fell onto the sofa there.

Helena came. Dear Helena.

"Oh, my God, my God—"

She shut her eyes. When she lay still it went away. It always did. It would go away now, if she could lie still long enough.

It clutched her still, a weight like an anvil on her chest. She felt the women around her, murmuring, and Helena bustled them all away. Helena had the hands of an angel. The medical instincts of Asclepius. Around Irene there fell a healing silence, and a sense of safety. She shut her eyes, lost in the pain.

The Parakoimomenos said, "But it's been over an hour."

The others turned their white faces toward him, and no one spoke. In the corner, Nicephoros bent over the chess game, dreamily moving the knight methodically over the squares.

"Where are the women?" The Grand Drungarius marched back and forth in the center of the room. "The Lady Helena surely will know—"

"Helena will say nothing." The Parakoimomenos strode forward. Taller than any of the other men, stretched and thinned by his deformity, he seemed like a wax figure, supple with the heat. Nicephoros looked quickly away, his stomach turning over.

"We must demand to see her." In the center of the others, the Parakoimomenos wheeled around, his heavy Hunnish coat flaring at the hem. "If she is—God have mercy on us—if she should—pass on—"

"No."

Nicephoros got up and went forward, unwilling to hear any of this. "She is the Basileus. We must have faith in her as we have faith in the Empire itself. She will tell us what she wishes us to know."

Even to himself, these words were a feeble wail against the storm. He put his hands to his face. Could she be dying? He had seen her at breakfast, when they talked of applying pressure to the monasteries to give up some of their treasure. She had seemed well, even hearty. He had seen people die of cholera in less time than had elapsed since he had last seen her healthy; in the depth of summer, when the plague raged, strong young men went from full bloom to blackened corpses in twelve hours.

But not Irene. Not Irene.

She walked through their midst, through a silence that her footsteps, cushioned on the carpet, only accented. She touched none of them. Nicephoros thought, Did she hear?

"Parakoimomenos." At the end of the room, she wheeled, her clothes swirling around her, glittering in the sunlight coming through the window behind her.

"Yes, Augustus," said the eunuch.

"Tell me, my angel—have you still an Empress?"

She had heard, then. Nicephoros hunched his shoulders closer to the carpet.

The voice of the Parakoimomenos was half an octave higher than usual. "Augustus, Chosen One of God, you alone are the Glory of the Empire—"

"Silence!"

There was silence.

"I am the Basileus," she shouted, and behind Nicephoros someone whined.

The Parakoimomenos babbled, "Augustus, Chosen One of God, we meant only to—"

"Silence!"

Nicephoros's cheek pressed against the carpet. He thought, She would not be so enraged if she were not also frightened, and his heart sank. Was she losing her call? Cautiously he lifted his head to look at her.

She stood there in the blaze of sunlight, her golden clothes so brilliant his eyes were dazzled. Towering over him she might have stepped down from Heaven. She lifted one arm and he quaked at the threat.

"I am Basileus," she cried, again, and they all answered her.

"Hail, Augustus, Chosen of God, Equal of the Apostles, hail!"

She lowered her arm, mollified. Now, blinking, Nicephoros could discern her features, behind the veil of golden light; he saw her magnificent eyes, wide and bright with life, and was angry with himself for doubting her.

"You may rise," she said.

With the others, he lifted himself up onto his feet, grateful that she had recovered her temper; it unnerved him to see her unnerved.

Now, as was her custom, she came among them, going from man to man, greeting each, and touching each. She looked into Nicephoros's face, and smiled, and he lowered his eyes, warmed by her acceptance. Her touch on his arm was a pressure he felt long after she had gone past him.

She reached the Parakoimomenos. She did not lay her hand on him, nor did she smile.

She said, "My angel, was it not your idea that ibn-Ziad and I should wager on the outcome of the race?"

"Yes, Augustus, Chosen One of—"

"Then since you have an interest perhaps it would amuse us both to wager, each other, on the race?"

"Augustus—"

"I shall take Ishmael, and you the Caesarean team."

"Augustus."

"Yes. And the wager, my angel—"

She reached out and plucked at the belt around his waist, made of links of gold, the belt that signified his office in the Imperial service.

"The wager is your belt, my angel."

"Augustus, I—"

She drew herself up, fierce. "Do you accept?"

"I—" The eunuch was white as ivory, and now suddenly red as a new baby. He whispered something.

"Louder!"

"I accept!"

"Excellent." She turned again, going back to her place. Behind her the members of her council stood rigid, all eyes on the Parakoimomenos. As one man they shifted, moving away from him, isolating him as if he showed open sores and rang a little bell.

She faced them, an icon, glittering. "Let the Council begin!"

: 20 :

The Basileus blessed the people, and the parade to the first heat began. Smiling, she sat down in her chair at the front corner of the Imperial box, her women gathered around her, little Philomela on her lap.

Two pages with garlands of flowers came in through the door in the back of the box, and bowed and strewed the flowers over the floor, and with a flourish they turned to usher in their master. With a braying of horns, the Caliph's emissary entered.

He wore a magnificent long coat, with a sash of gold lace, a turban of many folds on his head. Prince Constantine, escorting him, seemed very plain by contrast, a figure of provincial nobility. The Basileus watched gravely as they filled up the box with their male talk and strutting. Their comradeship had made her more than suspicious. Three or four of the ambassador's own servants hurried around, putting cushions on their master's chair, and when he sat down they ranged themselves behind him.

All but one, who brought up a little casket of silver, which his master took and set upon his knee.

"My part of our wager," he said, and tipped up the casket lid.

All who saw it gasped, all but the Empress. The box was top-full of jewels, mostly polished but unset, mingled with pearls as luminous as the moon. Irene put out her hand and dug her fingers into the glittering mass and, lifting her palm, let the gems trickle back into the box; it was a nice way to be sure the whole box was full. Across the lovely pile, the Caliph's man smiled at her, his eyes bright as the gemstones.

"Helena," said the Empress, and raised her hand.

The waiting woman came forward, carrying something covered with a velvet cloth. Irene nodded, and the cloth was whisked away.

There on a branch of green jade sat a golden bird, its eyes made of ruby chips, and its beak and claws of alabaster; green and blue enamel covered the wings. Irene touched the key at the base of the branch, and the bird turned its head, spread its wings, and opening its beak began to sing.

The Caliph's ambassador forgot his smile. His eyes popped out of his head, and all his followers cried out in admiration, their hands raised.

"A miracle!"

"A small example of the work of our artisans," said Irene. The little bird was winding down, and Helena turned it off and set it on the stool at Irene's right hand.

On the track, the teams were approaching the ribbon. Irene leaned forward to see, her hand on the rail. Through the tail of her eye, she saw how Constantine and the Caliph's ambassador gloated over the prize she was offering them. She smiled, for her people's sake, her eyes keen, unblinking, fixed on the teams below her.

Prince Michael watched the race from the stable gate. He hated to see other people race and usually did not bother, but he wanted to see for himself if Ishmael had been bribed to throw the race to the Caesarea team.

As they came up to the ribbon, his guts knotted with envy, his fingers twitched, and he almost turned away, unable to bear seeing someone else do what he so longed to do. He forced himself stolid. His moment would come. He stared at the teams at the starting ribbon until his eyes ached and each figure dissolved into a blur of dancing light.

"Yaaaah!"

The ribbon fell. As the horses lunged forward, the crowd let go a roar that seemed to rock the Hippodrome.

Michael shouted, unaware of it. With half the grooms and the apprentices, he rushed forward on to the sand to watch the cars fly away down the track.

The horses reached the curve and whirled around it and were gone from sight. Michael pressed his back to the wall, his gaze pinned to the near turn, where they would appear again. From the crowd came wave on wave of cheers. It seemed like hours before the horses thundered around the curve and shot down the straightaway again.

The Caesarea team was in the lead, racing on the inside track against the spina, the driver plying his long whip with a fury. Their pale manes and tails streamed on the wind; their red-gold hides were darkening with sweat. Half a length back, their heads even with the Caesarea driver, were Ishmael's flying greys and blacks.

Ishmael did not use his whip. He leaned forward over his chariot's rail, the reins gripped in his fists, his feet braced against the floor, and called his horses by name. They heard him. Their ears flicked back to catch his voice and, inch by inch, they gained on the golden chestnuts.

The other two teams were out of the race. But they did not pull up. One behind the other, they raced along the inside track in tandem, the ground widening steadily between them and the back of Ishmael's car. Michael gave a little shake of his head. The two slower teams would be a problem in a couple of circuits. Then they hurtled around the curve at the far end and were gone again from his view.

Michael swung his eyes to the near end of the track; he held his breath. The men around him were swearing in pleading voices, calling their teams around the track. The crowd screamed in waves. The roar of their voices dimmed a little, and swelled again until his ears rang with it.

Around the curve they came, the golden chestnuts still ahead by scant feet. Ishmael's team was surging. With strides that skimmed the sand they charged forward down the center of the track, bidding to take the lead.

The Caesarea driver flung a quick look at Ishmael, and he went to the whip again. His horses rallied. The spume flew from their necks; their heads stretched out flat, and they held off the blacks and greys into the next turn, where the change in the track gave them a moment's respite. Many lengths behind, hopelessly outdistanced, the other two teams struggled along.

"It looks as if the Caesareas are going to take it," said someone behind Michael.

Michael said nothing. There had to be at least two heats, after all. The crowd was screaming again, and here came the leaders again, flying around the turn. If Ishmael were throwing the race, this was where it would be evident to the expert eye.

The Caesarea team bore out as they swung around the turn, and carried Ishmael out with them. They were head to head now. The chestnuts were tiring. They swung out into the middle of the track, down the straightaway, but racing on the far outside Ishmael could not seize the lead. Locked in their battle, the two teams wheeled into the far curve and vanished from Michael's view, and as they went, the other teams rolled around the near turn, their drivers whipping away.

They knew they had lost; they were slowing, taking it easy. Michael whistled under his breath. The howling of the crowd changed a little, sprinkled with laughter, buoyant with abuse.

With the two slow teams still wheeling down the straight, the leaders raced around the curve again, coming up behind them. The

Caesareas had regained the lead by nearly half a length. Surprised, Michael let out a yell. Ishmael was throwing it; he was giving the race away, leaning back now, his reins slack, and his horses faltering off their top stride. The Caesareas shot out to the front, going like an avalanche.

But the losing teams now blocked his way. The black-bearded driver howled and lashed out with his whip, and the two slow teams swerved out toward the middle of the track, trying to give him room. The crowd shrieked. Michael whooped, delighted, seeing now what Ishmael did. As the two slower teams veered out, the Caesareas lost their rhythm; they staggered, and Ishmael, who had brought his horses down evenly, given them some rest, and gathered them up together again, suddenly reined them around to the inside track and shot between the spina and the Caesareas, between the fading last-place finishers and the curve, and seized the lead by six lengths.

Michael roared; he pounded his thigh with his fists. "What a driver!" He laughed and waved his arms, forgetting who he was, forgetting who might be watching, and when Ishmael swung around the near curve and raced the last straightaway, the clear winner, Michael started out to meet him.

He remembered; in time, he collected himself. He put his shoulders back and sucked up his gut and with his head high he stood there by the gate, while the grooms and apprentices streamed past him and ran crowing and leaping and cheering to meet Ishmael and bring him home again.

"Good racing," Michael said evenly to Ishmael, and the other man grinned at him, baby-wide. They went into the stable.

The Caesareas came next, their heads hanging. Like all great racehorses, they knew when they had lost, and felt it sorely. Their driver swore and snarled at his grooms.

"He cheated. He cheated me! I want the race run over."

"Win the next heat, then," Michael said, and hiding his smile went away into the darkness of the barn.

The crowd was settling down. A troop of jugglers rushed out on to the track to entertain them during the interval between heats. Irene sank back into her chair. One of her women brought her a cup of wine, and she lifted it in a little salute to the Caliph's ambassador.

"A great heat," said the emissary coolly. He threw an instant's harsh look at Prince Constantine, who was looking intently somewhere else. Irene's smile widened a little. She wondered what corrupted her cousin Constantine.

"Of course, this Ishmael is of Arab blood," the ambassador said.

"He is a citizen of Rome," Irene said.

"We shall see if it has diluted his ability."

"Or concentrated it, perhaps?" Irene's eyes were on Prince Constantine. Smoothly she said, "Although Roman citizenship, or even noble blood, is hardly proof against bad judgment and sin and treachery."

Prince Constantine cleared his throat. "It's just a horse-race." He looked away over the rail of the box, toward the jugglers. "Here comes a Roman worth the name," he said, and pointed.

The crowd had seen him, too, and lifted their great voice in a thunderous welcome for their darling. Prince Michael was driving his team out on to the track.

"The Golden Belt," said Irene.

The champion drove his team with one hand. With the other he held aloft the insignia of his place, his belt of gold links. At arm's length over his head he held it. The horses snorted and frisked out with their forefeet, objecting to the sedate pace, and he let them out a little, sweeping down the middle of the track, their great necks curved to the bits, their tails high.

The crowd loved it. They screamed his name, and the names of his horses; they swayed and swung their arms as he passed, as if the wind of his passage bent them like young trees, and a rain of flowers pelted the sand in his track. He made one more circuit of the track and slowed by the gate, but the rapturous uproar of the people brought him back again, and again he gave them what they wanted.

"They say no driver in the memory of man can rival this one," said the Caliph's man. "Would that I could see him race."

"Stay, and you will," said Irene. "When the qualifying races are done, and we have a field to send against him."

"When?" Constantine said swiftly.

"I shall decide," Irene said, smiling.

"Here they come," the Caliph's man said, excitement in his voice, and craned his neck.

From the stable door the teams issued forth, all in a line; the last-place finisher came out first. Cheers greeted each of the teams, but the acclaim for the first three was nothing in comparison with the shrieks and pleas and screams of praise that thundered forth when Ishmael's blacks and greys appeared.

They lined up at the ribbon, and the crowd hushed.

The race began. The teams flew down the track into the first turn, and there the slower teams clogged up the inside going. The two outside teams surged forward into the middle of the straightaway, racing wheel to wheel, head to head.

The Caesarea chestnuts, inside Ishmael's team, had the short of the track around the curve, and came out on the other side leading by half a length. Ishmael's horses fought back, inch by inch, along the straightaway, and again, entering the curve, the teams were head to head.

Once more, the inside track carried the Caesarea horses into the lead; once more, on the straight, Ishmael's horses won back the lost ground. The other teams were out of it. This time, wisely, they pulled off to the side and let the leaders fly by them.

Twice more the two teams raced around the track, flying along side by side, stride for stride, the distance between them widening in the curves, only to shrink away to nothing on the straightaway. The crowd screamed and roared Ishmael's name. His horses responded, and in the fifth circuit, as they wheeled around the curve, Ishmael's horses lost only half a length. The chestnuts were lagging. In the next straightaway, it was clear, Ishmael's team would pull ahead.

The Caesarea driver saw that too; he looked around at the black and grey heads beside him, and raising his whip he lashed it once across the rumps of his chestnuts and then swiveling around he flogged Ishmael's horses across their faces.

The crowd shrieked in pain, as if the whip fell on their own eyes. Ishmael's horses staggered, tossing up their heads. Irene let out an oath, starting up from her chair, her hands clenched tight. Alone, the winner, the Caesarea team crossed the finish line, and Ishmael's horses walked across.

Irene sat down again. Hard-eyed, she glared at the Caliph's man. "What is this—to win at any cost?"

The ambassador shrugged. "It is a form of war, is it not?" Beside him, Prince Constantine edged away, his face averted.

"We shall see how well such tactics succeed," Irene said. "My heart is still with Ishmael."

"Yes," said the Caliph's man smoothly. "Your wager, however, may soon have another owner—what horses could recover from such a blow?"

"We shall see," Irene said.

The outside flanker, the dark grey, stood between Ishmael and its groom, its head hanging; the whip had laid open the skin of its face between the eyes. Ishmael stroked the trembling body with both hands. He had only a few moments to get the horse ready to race again.

"Get me a brush. Are the others recovering?"

The grooms answered him from down the aisle; all the other horses were unhurt. The grey's groom brought him a brush, a pail, and a soft cloth. Ishmael began to clean off the sand clinging to the sweaty grey coat.

He talked to it as he worked, reminding it of the courage and pride of its ancestors, and of its own triumphs, and the horse's ears flicked back and forth, listening. Slowly its shivering stilled. Its head hung, its blood dripping down its cheek. The groom came with a cloth and cleaned its face.

"He cannot race. How can he race half-blind like that?"

Ishmael was on his knees in front of the horse, brushing its forelegs. "Get me a scarf." He ran his hand down the long tendons at the back of the slim black legs, feeling for heat, for bows, for other signs of breaking down, but the horse was sound enough.

In the next aisle, he heard the Caesarea driver's loud voice, fuller and louder now with victory. Ishmael's lips writhed away from his teeth, and he swore under his breath; the horse lifted its head up, snorting, at the change in his tone of voice. Ishmael stood up. He put his arms around the long slender neck and pressed his face to the flat cheek.

"You will win. You will overcome him. Remember your father, who ran on the track until his heart burst. Remember the great Kharayyun, your great-great-grandfather, who raced eight heats in a single day."

The horse nickered, and its neck bent, recovering the proud arch of its kind. The groom brought the scarf, a yard of yellow silk.

"We have to start hitching up, if we're to go out for the last heat."

"Hitch them," Ishmael said.

"Ishmael, he will never race again. His spirit is broken."

"No. Look at him."

The horse lifted its head; the skin split wide over its broad forehead, the blood clotting in ridges and lumps. The flies were swarming toward it. Ishmael waved them away. The groom murmured to the horse and put out his hand, and the beast switched its ears forward, and pawed at the ground.

"You may be right."

"I am right."

"If you're wrong, you'll ruin the whole team."

"I will race," Ishmael said, between his teeth, "and I will win! Now do as I tell you, hitch up the other horses, and come back for this one when I call you."

The groom went away down the aisle. Ishmael turned to the horse, which was trying to rub its injured face on its foreleg.

"Hey, hey, old one." Ishmael laid the silk scarf over its face, covering both eyes. "You need no eyes. You have run on that track a thousand times, and you know who you run with. Trust your brothers and trust yourself, and give me everything you can. Forget your face, old one."

He knotted the scarf securely around the horse's head, and under his hands, to his relief, he felt the horse pick up a little, its head rising, its ears swiveling back and forth. Again, it lifted its forefoot and pawed at the floor, and it snorted and nudged Ishmael's body with its nose.

He put his arms around the sleek dark neck and hugged it, and said into its ear, "Harken to me, to the reins, old one. We shall win again, you and I and the others, if you but keep faith, and we will break those bastards' hearts when we do it."

The horse nickered again. Ishmael led it back to the rest of the team.

Getting into the car, he was as nervous as the first time he had ever raced. He gathered up the reins into his hands, separating and smoothing the leathers between his fingers. His heart pounded. It was madness to do this; the horses, so abused, would certainly shrink from the Caesarea driver's whip; he would make a fool of himself and destroy his team. He lifted the reins and spoke to them.

They responded. Bred for courage as well as speed, they loved challenge, and at the sound of his voice they went forward toward the gate, into the great wedge of light, and on to the track.

When they drove out on to the track the crowd surged up onto its feet and thundered their applause, and that, too, spurred the horses; even the dark grey, its head wrapped in the yellow scarf, began to dance.

Eagerly they rolled forward down the track. They loved the cheering crowds as much as the crowds loved them. Ishmael could feel their weariness leave them; their heads rose, and their mouths pulled and worked at the bits. Ishmael reined them down, talking to them.

The Caesarea driver was outside him, having won the last heat; the other two teams had withdrawn. Ishmael faced the long straightaway, the sand like chips of gold, the heaving, waving, screaming crowd.

"Get out of my way when I go for the lead," the Caesarea driver said, and laughed.

Ishmael gave him a long, disfocussed look. He lifted his reins, and the ribbon fell.

The horses sprang forward. For an instant he felt the outside flanker hesitate, but the horses on either side of it steadied it and gave it heart, and it strode forward with a new strength and rhythm. They raced even with the Caesarea team down into the turn, and there Ishmael gripped his reins and drew back slightly, to keep even with the outside team.

The Caesarea driver roared. He flexed his whip and laid it onto the heaving backs of his chestnuts, and bending sideways he flogged at Ishmael's horses as well. They took the attack. With the whip burning on their bodies, they raced on, ignoring it, keeping in team, their great hearts carrying them, now, as much as their legs. They whirled around the curve and down the straightaway, and Ishmael kept them even with the Caesareas, head to head, although now he could have taken the lead.

The other driver knew it, too, and shot a wild-eyed look across the space between them. He leaned over his horses, urging them on. Matched stride for stride, they hurtled down the next straightaway and into the turn.

As they raced into the curve, that happened which Ishmael had been waiting for: the Caesareas began to bear out slightly, too tired to hold the track. He yelled. With his fists straining at the leathers, he drew his horses off line also, and shouting to them to keep pace he pulled them straight across the track, driving the chestnuts next to them out across the Hippodrome.

The Caesarea driver saw what was coming. He flailed away with his whip at Ishmael's team; he raised the whip and struck at Ishmael himself. The long lash wound around Ishmael's waist and chest and caught, and the Caesarea driver was yanked off balance.

He dropped the whip; he dropped the reins. Wailing, he clung to the rail of his car as it lurched madly across the sand, and the horses, brought up close to the outside wall, veered hard back toward the inside. The car's wheels caught. Ishmael whipped the chestnuts off his own team, and running ragged, out of team, headlong and maddened, the Caesareas swerved off again, and the outside horse ran into the wall.

The horse collapsed. The others were yanked down with it, and the car, going too fast to stop, smashed into the heels of the horses and flung the driver face-first onto the sand.

The crowd screamed with delight. Roaring, on their feet, they cheered Ishmael on around the track, as alone he raced, his horses at a steady, leisurely gallop, their heads high, their tails like banners, until they crossed the finish line, the winners.

In the evening, Michael sat in the courtyard of the Bucoleon, by the fountain, eating his dinner; a single manservant attended him. As he was drinking his wine, his uncle Constantine appeared, coming toward him past the fountain.

"What are you doing here?" Michael asked coldly.

Constantine stopped. "You sound as if you don't want to see me."

"I don't."

"But—what—"

"Did you try to bribe Ishmael to throw the race?"

Constantine's eyes blinked several times. He ventured a false, humorless laugh. "Who told you that? Ishmael? He's a liar."

"I don't want you around here or around my horses or my grooms anymore, uncle. Get out."

Again, the cracked laugh. "You can't mean that."

"I do mean it. Get out."

"But—"

"You corrupted the races," Michael said, a heat of temper rising in his blood. "Even if you failed, you brought suspicion on the races. Now no one will ever see another horse-race without wondering, even if just for an instant, if it's been fixed. You slandered me. Get out."

Constantine's face was turning red, and his lips quivered. He said, "Aren't you being a little sanctimonious, Michael? I mean, surely, a little tolerance—"

"Not for me!" Michael sprang up and advanced on his uncle, his fists clenched. "I will not suffer any stain on my name, Constantine; my honor must be perfect, or it is no honor!"

"Your honor! It's just a horse-race, Michael—"

The Prince slapped him across the face, twice, three times, four times, as hard as he could. "Get out!"

Constantine staggered back a step under the blows; his eyes shone bright. He said no more. Turning on his heel, he walked away into the darkness. Michael sat down again, trembling all over; he wished his uncle had fought back, so that he could vent this violence that welled in him like the irresistible urge for sex. He lowered his head between his knees, bereft.

: 21 :

John Cerulis had dined alone in his tent every night since the unfortunate spectacle where Theophano insulted him before everybody. A row of servants stood by the table, some with dishes in their hands, others with towels; the whole tent was swimming with the aromas of food. Karros bowed deeply before the man in the chair.

"Command me, Patrician."

"Tomorrow," John Cerulis said, putting down a spoon, "you will go ahead of us and find this holy man and bring me back a report of him."

"As you command, Patrician."

"You may take your new friend there with you. You, barbarian, what name do you go by?"

"Hagen," the Frank said. "In my country they call me Hagen the White."

"How imaginative. I understand you have been much in the company of the racing teams—have you the acquaintance of Prince Michael?"

Hagen was silent a moment; Karros elbowed him, trying to nudge him into speech, and the barbarian moved sharply away from him. Finally, in a meditative voice, he said, "Somewhat."

"Then perhaps you know the meaning of certain mysterious actions of his? The yellow color he wore at the last race, for instance?"

Karros said, "Oh, Patrician, this one won't—"

"Silence!"

Hagen put his hands on his belt, his head to one side. "The scarf on his arm?"

"Yes, yes. I am convinced it is a signal of some sort."

"A signal," Hagen said; there was some undercurrent in his voice that Karros could not identify. "Yes, of course it is, didn't you know? Patrician."

John Cerulis leaned forward, intent. "You do know?"

"They are fixing the races," Hagen said. "That's what the signal is. To make money on the bets."

Karros clenched his teeth together, wondering why he had not heard of that; John Cerulis's face shone with discovery. A moment later he frowned.

"They cannot make money if Michael wins."

"No, no, no," Hagen said, contemptuous. "The yellow means the fix is off. A red banner means it's good."

"Ah." John Cerulis's face cleared, bright with understanding. He turned toward Karros with a motion like a snake striking. "Why could you not discover that? What's wrong with you?"

"Patrician—I was diligent, I asked everyone I could—"

"Keep your lips together, you pig, you offend me with your excuses. Go! I don't want to see you again before you have done my bidding properly for once."

Karros chewed on his moustaches, humiliated. With a curt gesture to Hagen, he marched out of the tent, past a little train of servants bringing in the next course.

Darkness had fallen over the camp. They walked off through the camp, circling the cooking fires in a ring at the center, and moving through the little groups of people busy with their own dinners. Karros turned to Hagen.

"How did you know that? About Michael."

Hagen walked on a few steps before he answered; he said, "I thought it was common knowledge."

"Certainly it was not common knowledge." Karros grabbed his arm, stopping him. "You made it up, didn't you? You lied to him!"

The Frank shrugged his hand off. In the dim light he smiled with a flash of white teeth. "Don't touch me, Fatty."

He walked away through the dark, passing between fires, his shape black against the leaping flames. Karros looked back toward his master's tent; the lamps inside illuminated the silk of the walls in circles of red and white and yellow. He knew if he went back to John and accused Hagen of lying that his master would think it only backbiting jealousy. He wanted to know something about Michael and now his wish was satisfied.

Yet in a way the lie soothed him. Hagen was shifty, a liar, a cheat like everybody else. Not brave, just big. Karros puffed himself up, feeling better all the time. He went off after Hagen, toward the guard's fire.

Before dawn, Hagen got Karros up out of his blankets and against the fat man's protests put him on his horse and went off down the road to find the holy man. The camp with its swarms of people bothered the big Frank; a long hard ride struck him as a distinct relief, and he wanted action.

He rode along far enough from Karros to discourage any conversation. The day dawned very fine, the sun rising up through a haze along the horizon, and the heat of the first level rays promised a broiling afternoon. Hagen strapped his cloak behind his saddle. Later, as the sun climbed, he stopped and took off his shirt.

Karros rode up beside him while he was doing that, and with one hand up to shield his eyes scanned the road ahead of them, winding off through the low featureless hills. "He can't be too much farther on."

Hagen nodded toward the horizon. A thin dun smoke overhung

the fold between the hills where the road disappeared into the distance. "That must be what we're looking for." He glanced at Karros, beside him. "What are we looking for?"

"A desert preacher named Daniel. He's been stirring up something of a sensation, calling for a new breaking of the images. My master thinks he may help turn the mob against the Basileus." Karros puffed up a little, smoothing down his moustaches with his thumb. "If you show some manners, who knows? You may serve an emperor some day, barbarian."

"God grant it." Hagen picked up his reins; the sun was bringing out the sweat on his shoulders and back. They rode on along the dirt track through the hills.

The dust cloud thickened as they went on, and in the early afternoon they began to meet the vanguard of a rabble army, people on foot spilling down the road toward them, poor folk by their rags and weathered looks, who were gathering up whatever they could find on the ground they marched over: roots and fruit and flowers, firewood, a few stray goats they managed to catch and kill. At a steady trot, Hagen and Karros moved deeper into this mass, and the crowd thickened around them, filling up the road, forcing them to ride off to one side. Then at last they came in sight of the holy man.

He walked down the center of the road, surrounded by people who sang and waved their arms and danced. A heavy ragged mantle was his only clothing, and that scarcely enough for modesty. He walked with a staff. His beard was long and yellow and matted with burrs and thorns, his hair a tangle down his back. As he walked people rushed up before him to throw flowers in his path, and when he had walked on them other people ran into his wake to snatch the flowers up and kiss them.

Hagen drew rein on a rise above the road, watching the holy man walk by. He said, "There he is. Who are all these others?"

"Disciples," said Karros.

"Shall we take him back to Cerulis?"

"By the Son's Corruptible Body," Karros said, aghast. "He is a messenger from God! Do you think we could drag him off before even such as my master with impunity? Barbarian!"

"I guess not," Hagen said.

"You barbarians, you live in darkness." Karros turned his horse. "We'll travel along with him a while, he'll stop to preach soon, probably."

Hagen followed him. This holy man confused him. He had heard of wild preachers before, men who went into the wilderness and came out with their eyes full of fire and the word of God leaping from their lips; in Frankland, when Pepin ruled, a man from Bourges had gone around claiming to be Jesus Christ, come again to redeem the world, bringing judgment and eternity to the faithful and the false. He had gathered a band of followers and lived a life of robbery and rape and murder until the local count destroyed him. Hagen saw no use for John Cerulis in this Daniel, only danger.

Yet he remembered how passionately the Greeks argued faith, and how ardently they went to church, and it occurred to him that the word of a ragged old man might bring an emperor down.

The Empress is a fool, he thought, to let this happen. Of course she was only a woman. If Hagen had worn the crown, he would have sent someone long before to slit this old man's throat.

When he thought of killing, he thought of Theophano.

She hated him. She had thrown her darts at him, the last time they met, with a savage will to hurt. She had tried to have him killed. He turned that idea over and over in his mind, because her obvious dislike of him inclined John Cerulis in his favor. If she meant that—

What was she doing with Cerulis anyway, since they despised each other?

He remembered when she spoke to Cerulis, her face clear and implacable as a saint's, and the little motion of her hand, asking for something, withdrawn even as she extended it. Over and over in his mind he saw that half-expressed appeal. She had called for his death; she had begged him for help. His mind thrashed, torn in opposite directions.

His body knew no such turmoil. His body loved her, and the more he thought of her, the more his body trained itself in sympathy for her, muscles and tendons, bones and blood, like the strings of a lute tuned to one harmony. He flung his head back, his eyes shut, his face lifted to the sun, sore with longing.

Karros said, "There, he's begun."

The two men reined in their horses. Below them on the road, the holy man had stopped, and his followers were swarming around him. He raised his arms and began to speak to them.

In the hot still air his words carried well. He spoke of God's love for each of His children, and of the lack of faith that kept His children from Him. How from lack of faith the children thought they needed other than God. They made themselves houses, they covered themselves with costly robes, they put up idols to worship and built their lives of the material dross of the earth, while around them, like the burning sky itself, God spread His all-encompassing love and was ignored.

They needed only God. God alone would save them. If they yielded themselves up to God, they would enter Heaven at that moment.

Hagen murmured in his throat. Before he realized it, he had gone down halfway to the road, his horse responding to the shift of his weight in the saddle as he leaned toward the preacher. Karros came after him.

"Excellent, is he not?"

Hagen shook himself out of his fascination. He told himself the world was more complicated than that: you could not simply give everything over and walk naked into Heaven.

The holy man's followers gathered tight around him, praying, and many began to chant. They linked arms and swayed back and forth in an undulating union, their voices raised, and the old man went up and down before them, blessing them, calling to them by name to denounce sin and give themselves to God. His voice was remarkable, soft and yet carrying, flexible as silk. Hagen wanted him to speak to him, to know his name, to call him personally into Heaven; he longed for that peace, for that certainty, and that finality.

Not yet. Rogerius's soul still cried unappeased from the grave. Theophano—

She was stronger than the holy man. Thinking of her, he brought himself back from the brink, from the old man's influence like a chasm before him.

"Let's go," he said to Karros, and wheeling his horse he galloped away over the thorny hillside.

"You must be bored," Theophano said, "to deign to seek the company of a mere female."

John Cerulis leaned on his elbow on the side of his chair, with his little rod tap-tapping on the frame. "I am thinking of ways to deal with you, Theophano—I wanted to have you before me as I try them out in my mind."

He swung the rod sharply out and cracked her arm with it. On the far side of her chair, Aunt Eusebia put down her embroidery, lay back, and shut her eyes. Theophano smiled. Deep as the bone, her arm hurt where he had struck her.

She said, "I do wish you would proceed with more pace, Patrician. Your company and this enterprise have become tedious in the extreme." Her fingers slipped into the cuff of her sleeve, where the needle was hidden. If she could lure him a little closer, he would be within reach; she would strike then, and go on striking until he died.

"There is Karros," he said, "and your wild beast of a lover." He gave her a languid sideways look, his tongue between his lips. "He looks as if he has fleas. Worse than fleas. Did you trade one itch for another, my heart?"

"He is a man in all his parts," she said, "which is his shame as well as his glory, since being a man he is coarse and stupid and without grace. You know, Patrician, by a simple amputation of that member which seems of no use to you anyway, you could become at least the image of a woman, if not the perfection itself—"

The rod struck; she saw it coming and did not dodge. The hard round of wood met her cheekbone with a force that snapped the stick in half. Unmoving, she stared at John Cerulis and took the pain like an honor. He looked away. His neck was red.

The two horsemen were nearly upon them. Theophano leaned against the cushions behind her, her face throbbing. Already she could see the swelling below her eye. Soon she would be ugly, misshapen as a witch. She felt drained, almost drugged, a lassitude like death itself creeping through her limbs. For days she had done nothing but ride in the chair, her body collecting the dust of the road, her hair unwashed and uncombed; the thought that she would die like this, her beauty ruined, brought her almost to tears. She took the needle in her fingers, ready to use it at the first chance. Then suddenly something large loomed between her and the sun.

It was Hagen. She blinked up at him who had ridden in between her and John Cerulis. On the far side of the Patrician's chair, Karros was greeting his master with fulsome stupid compliments. Hagen looked down at her from his great height, his face unreadable.

It infuriated her that he should see her this way. She snarled at him, "The servants' train is over there."

"This one's for sluts and back-stabbers?"

The needle in her hand pricked her fingers. He was between her and her victim. Her face hurt. She said, "You are in my sunlight, pig."

He glanced up at the sun and moved more exactly between it and her. Now she was shielded entirely from John Cerulis, and she said, "Patrician, this man offends me."

John made no answer. He was listening to Karros's report of the holy man. Hagen's horse edged closer, while Theophano formed a scathing insult in her mind, and suddenly his hand shot out and pinned her wrist against the wooden frame of the chair.

She made no sound. She wrenched at his grip but could not move him, and quick-fingered as a wool-picker, he took the needle out of her hand.

At that she moaned in despair. Lifted her eyes to glare at him, and found him smiling at her, with his eyes more than his mouth. When he let her go, his fingertips minutely caressed the inside of her wrist, where the pulse beat.

She sat straight again, her eyes averted, in a panic. He had taken away her only weapon. Yet he had smiled at her. He loved her still. Or perhaps he hated her so much that disarming her gave him the deepest pleasure.

"Tell us your impression of the holy man, barbarian," said John Cerulis.

Hagen kept still a moment, which Theophano had seen he was accustomed to do, when directly questioned; perhaps he was translating to himself, although his Greek was much improved.

"Well, speak up, fool," said John.

"I trusted him," Hagen said. "I thought he meant what he said."

"That's hardly remarkable."

"It is, among you Greeks," Hagen said.

"You have a most unpleasant manner of address, which I advise you to reform, if you wish to serve me."

Hagen said nothing, one hand on his hip; he looked amused rather than threatened. On his left hand, on the little finger, was a garnet ring she had not seen him wear before.

She said, "Get him away from me, Patrician, before I vomit all over both of you."

Hagen said, "I'm leaving. The female smell here is making me sick."

He rode off ahead of them, leaving in the space between her and John Cerulis a roil of acrid dust. The would-be emperor gave her a cold look.

"This holy man does not sound worth so much effort to me. And I find, Theophano, your value as entertainment declining. After we have met this desert Christ, I think we'll have one more spectacle of you—I know a certain act of theater, employing a brass bowl, a rat, and a pot of coals—you've heard of it? You would surely give us a fine performance."

"Naturally I've heard of it," she said, furious, and near to tears; her needle, her needle. He was within her reach now, and she might have killed him, but she had no weapon now. "You haven't the gift to think of novelty, have you, John?" She lifted her face to the sky. "God, I only want to die, now, before I must go another day without my hair washed."

"We shall grant your wish," he said. "After the holy man has disappointed me tomorrow."

Daniel slept under a thorn bush by the side of the road, wrapped in his mantle. Around him his followers slept, a crowd of nearly one hundred, some having tents, some having servants to cook meals for them, some having wine, so that they kept the holy man awake half the night, and in the morning, when John Cerulis came, Daniel was brim full of the wrath of God.

With his staff in his hand, his garment clutched around him, he stood on the road watching the nobleman's train approach. A raucous mountain wind parted his beard and flapped his mantle against his legs, where fading purple scars remained from his struggles with the Devil. A solid mass of bodies spread around him in a cresent; his followers also watched the coming of the men from Constantinople.

There were more of these than there were people around Daniel.

They all rode horses. One in their lead carried a great banner of silk, and others played on drums and cymbals and flutes; in their midst a man with silver hair was borne along in a cushioned chair.

Daniel recognized this man at once: the Emperor was coming to him, to seek his wisdom, to find his way to God, and so lead all of Christendom home to Heaven.

He thrust out his staff, and in a terrible voice shouted, "Halt! Stop where you are, and let the Emperor come to me on foot."

At the bottom of the slope, the gaily clamorous and colorful little army came to a stop. In excited voices the riders called back and forth to one another.

"He named him the Emperor!"

"The Emperor!"

"It is an omen—the holy one took John Cerulis for the Emperor!"

Daniel heard them, and pressed his lips together, vexed with himself. His neck prickled up in a damp rash. He wondered if the others had heard, if they would doubt his words henceforth. The man on the chair was being carried nearer. Now at the very foot of the hill he was struggling to get up from the confines of his silken pillows, and a little crowd of men in leather armor hurried forward to help him. Braced on their hands, he climbed to the ground.

He thrust off the helping hands of his guards. Slipping and stumbling on the rough ground, he plunged up the slope toward Daniel. He fell once and rose again, stepping on the hem of his silk tunic. One of his jeweled slippers came off. He reached the top of the hill and flung himself on Daniel's feet.

"I am the Emperor. I am the Emperor." He clutched Daniel's ankles, weeping, and tears splashed onto the holy man's bare feet. "I am the Emperor!"

Daniel thrust at him, furious and confused. But now there were others coming toward him, their hands out, reaching for him. They fingered the welts on his legs and arms and ripped off pieces of his mantle, and in their midst the silver-haired man stood with a face that glowed like a lamp, crying, "I am the Emperor!"

In the desert, by himself, Daniel had felt God in him, but now he shrank from himself, desecrated by these hands on him. Their din in his ears made thinking impossible. Who was this man, if not the Emperor? If he was not the Emperor, why had he come out riding to meet

Daniel? Had God sent him? Did God mean him to be proclaimed? Or had the Devil sent another temptation? Why would God not answer him? If God were truly with him—

At that suddenly he lost all sense, and fell down in a swoon, there at John Cerulis's feet.

From head to foot they bathed her; she had only to stand still and let them do it. They heated the water in pots over the fire and strained it through Gaza cloth and perfumed it with scents of attar and almond and lime. They washed her hands and feet, each finger and toe by itself, and rubbed fine oil into her skin to soften away the harsh dry desert scale.

She lay down on her back and they rinsed her hair, running the water through it like a warm sweet-smelling river, every strand floating free. They dried her hair with heavy towels and then finished with a sheet of silk until her hair shone glossy and blue-black, curling damply at the ends.

She sat before a mirror of polished silver and saw herself beautiful again. They painted her face with the finest cosmetics, putting blue and violet around her eyes, and the hue of roses in her cheeks and on her lips, and they curled her hair and arranged it with combs and flowers of cloisonné, and put on her robes of costly work, and on her feet slippers of velvet.

The only imperfection was the great bruise on her cheek, which even the dense Egyptian color could not quite hide.

She sat there admiring herself in the mirror, thinking that she was ageing very well; at twenty-two she still had the vivid look of youth. Carefully she turned her head to one side, to hide the bruise. While she was experimenting with various postures, John Cerulis came into the tent.

"My heart," he said, and standing behind her with his hands on her shoulders he bent to touch her cheek with his lips. "I forgive you everything."

Even Theophano could not turn her mind that fast; she had to struggle against the bitter words that the mere sight of him brought like bile to her lips. In the mirror their faces were side by side.

She said, "The holy man serves, then?"

"He has named me emperor," John said. He straightened. His hands pressed together before him, he paced away through the tent, his face assembled into an expression of lofty contemplation. "God has sent this man as a messenger, to urge the City to cleanse itself of the defilement of the usurper Irene, and to place upon the throne of Constantinople one who is worthy of the diadem."

He crossed himself. Theophano looked deep into her own eyes in the mirror.

"And you shall be my empress," he said, and laying his hands again on her shoulders he stooped to put his cheek against her right cheek. "You have proven yourself to me, and I accept you as my mate."

"I think we are a match," she said.

" 'A match'!" he said, surprised. "Well, perhaps— More of an ornament, I thought, but, yes, I suppose you might see that as a match." His voice was smooth again, the fiery edge of conviction oiled over. "Come along, now, we must dine together tonight, to celebrate what you have given me this day."

They went into the largest tent and sat down side by side, his guards in a double rank behind them. She did not see Hagen among them. What would he make of this? She wondered if she could get a weapon from him. Now that John trusted her again, she would have no trouble killing him, if only she had a knife. The first dishes were presented, the cook leading his assistants past the table, each with his spoon held upright like a lance in his right hand, while in their train came the servants with platters and bowls. The soups, one clear, one slightly thickened, were excellent.

A troop of acrobats came out, twirling and flipping. John leaned on his chair, looking bored; he took one bite of the bread and spat it out.

"Why can they not bake a decent loaf?" He beat his fist on the table. "What use to be emperor, if I must eat like a peasant?"

"Flay the chef," Theophano said. The bread knife was certainly sharp enough. It was six feet from her, and he was in the way, but now he was glowering at her, peevish.

"Your face is very poorly dressed, my dear."

"It's the bruise," she said. "It's black as an African, there's no help for it."

"I insist that you sit on my left, then, so that I need not be required to see it every time I look at you."

"As you wish, Basileus."

Moving to his left would put her directly in front of the bread knife. She rose, and a flock of servants rushed in to take her chair and rearrange the table. As she was sitting down again, Hagen came in.

He stood on the far side of the acrobats, and John Cerulis saw him. "There," he said, and wiped his lips with a napkin. "I have a little surprise for you, Theophano, a token of my change of heart toward you." With a gesture he sent away the acrobats, and Hagen walked forward.

"Welcome, barbarian," said John Cerulis. "You remember that I told you I punish failure with an unerring hand. Karros!"

The fat man bustled around the table to Hagen's side and bowed down. His voice boomed out round as his belly. "Yes, Patrician!"

"Lately you have been a disappointment to me, Karros. I ask you to discover Michael's secrets, and you fail; I send you to recover my property from a mere girl, and you fail. Then you kill this man's brother and thereby engage his interest here, although he is utterly bereft of refinement, deserving of no place in my society." John leaned forward, his chin thrust out. "The only way you can avoid death, Karros, is to kill this Frank for me!"

Hagen backed up quickly into the middle of the tent, looking one side to the other, his hands out. Theophano's fist clenched. He wore no sword, only the dagger in his belt. Karros strode toward him, and Karros drew his sword from its scabbard and brandished it.

"Don't run away, barbarian!"

Karros charged, and all around the tent people screamed and shrank back, their hands raised. Theophano stood up, her teeth set in her lip. On the carpets at the middle of the tent, Hagen's feet made no sound; he leapt backwards away from the wild horizontal swing of Karros's sword, jumped sideways to escape the returning stroke, and ducked under a third. At John Cerulis's order, the other guards ran swiftly around the table and formed a ring of bodies around the fighting men.

Karros stood still at the center of the space, panting, the sword raised above his shoulder. Hagen moved swiftly around him, bouncing on his toes. When Karros turned to follow him, Hagen lunged.

Karros's sword hissed through the air past the barbarian's white head, and whirling he caught the fat man's forearm. The sword flew from Karros's grasp. Hagen yanked on the arm, and the fat guard, off balance, wobbled and swayed to one side, his back to the Frank. Hagen crooked one arm around his neck and held him still.

He twisted the fat man's arm up between his shoulder blades and put his mouth to Karros's ear. The tent was utterly quiet. Everybody heard him say something in his own language, and then, in Greek, "This is for my brother, Karros." He jerked hard with his arm around the fat man's neck. There was a muted crack, and Karros sagged down to the carpets.

Into the shocked hush, John Cerulis fed the little pat-pat of his applauding hands. Theophano sank down into her chair again; her legs were shaking so violently she almost fell. Hagen stood over Karros's body.

"Does this mean I take his place here?"

John Cerulis's smile widened with genuine amusement. "Oh, no," he said. "You are entirely too dangerous. I like the men around me to be a little softer and more malleable than you. Besides, as she says, you are certainly the agent of the Empress. My guards, kill him."

The guards hung back an instant, unused to orders direct from him, and Hagen jumped. Karros's sword lay on the carpets midway between him and the table, and he reached it in a single leap and snatched it up. With a yell, the guard, twenty strong, closed on him.

He let out a roar that raised the hackles on Theophano's scalp; he laid around him with the sword like a man swinging an axe at a tree. The guards in his path gave way and he rushed through the gap in their line to the table where the dinner's next dishes were waiting. The guards behind him reached him. Their swords struck at his back and his head. Wheeling, his back to the table, he met each blow with his own blade, fending them off in a flurry of ringing strokes. The guards could not reach him through the flying iron blade; he knocked aside their assault, and once or twice he counter-struck and each time killed a Roman soldier.

They withdrew a few steps, the guards, their eyes glassy. He bounded up onto the table, sweeping away the meats in their sauce, the wine opened up to breathe, and a tremendous sound came from him— if words, then surely not in Greek—as if he were a great brass vessel that the wind boomed through. Theophano thought, amazed, that he was laughing.

"Come on, tree-killers!" He whirled the sword over his head and slashed the air before him. "There's not a Frank alive who can match swords with me; do you think twenty of you Greeks dare even try?"

The guards launched themselves forward again, and again their blows cut and slashed at him. From the back of the pack, three or four suddenly whirled and raced out the door of the tent. Theophano held her breath until her lungs throbbed. Only a few feet behind Hagen's back was the wall of the tent; they would kill him through the cloth. He battered at the swords before him; she saw him cleave down through the skull of the man directly before him, and the brains blurted out, grey and white.

They swung at his feet and he leapt in the air and the blades whipped harmlessly by, and landing light on his toes he struck behind the blades and another of the Romans fell. Then, without a pause, he swung around. His sword hacked into the tent wall, and made it bulge around some form behind it, and through the rending silk and canvas came a horrible scream.

The guards retreated again. There were bodies all over the carpet now, bleeding into the Persian roses. On the tables, Hagen leapt up and down like an acrobat; he swiped at the air, three or four mighty blows that whistled and hissed.

"You see, Basileus," he shouted, "your soft and malleable men are no use to you! Now, hear me, Basileus—"

He wheeled and swiped at the tent wall again; Theophano could not see that he struck anything. The guards hovered nervously in a semicircle halfway across the tent from him, and at every move he made they flinched.

He faced John Cerulis. His face was bright as a flag. "I have a certain piece of paper, Basileus, that these women will do anything to possess—"

"No!" Theophano screamed.

"And if you kill me, Basileus, you shall not have it either!"

"No—"

She wheeled toward John Cerulis; she flung herself on her knees beside his chair, clinging to his arm. "You don't need it now. You are Emperor already—"

His face was sharp as a knife blade. He said, "You have the list? Yes, of course, I see now that you must have had it, all along."

"Hagen!" Theophano got up from the ground. She clambered up onto the table, going for the bread knife, and at a sharp word from their master, the bread cook and the assistant saucier jumped on her and dragged her back. She hung on their arms, gasping. Throughout the tent, now, people burst into excited talk.

John Cerulis said, "Silence!"

He stood up, lifting the corner of his mantle over his arm, and arranged the folds properly before he spoke. The tent quieted.

"You have the list?"

"Yes," Hagen said. "Not here. I will give it to you in exchange for my freedom and that girl."

"Your freedom only. The girl does not concern you. She was not responsible for your brother's death."

"I'll decide that," Hagen said. "She was there, and she brought your men down on us."

John stood a moment in thought, his eyes distant. Theophano imagined that the arms around her relaxed a moment, and she lunged forward, but they seized her again. John looked down at her.

"I regret this, Theophano. Really I do."

She began to weep. He would kill her; he would give up the list. In the grip of many hands, she went out of the tent.

Hagen had the list hidden away in the desert. He took Theophano and one of John Cerulis's trusted men away to retrieve it. They left the camp at once. Hagen had no interest in remaining very long in John Cerulis's range, now that they were enemies.

He put Theophano on his horse and swung up behind her. She had said nothing to him since she broke down weeping over the list he was trading for their lives. With his arm around her waist, he held her tight against him and galloped away into the desert, John Cerulis's knight beside him.

To keep anyone from following, he moved fast, staying on the road. The moon rose, a sickle among the stars. No one spoke. The night was full of a wild rushing wind, and when he stopped to let his horses breathe, he thought he heard hoofbeats down the road behind them, but it might have been the wind.

He raced on, although Cerulis's knight protested at the pace, and left the road to cut off a loop of it that went around a hill. Hagen led the other man up the steep slope and down the far side at a dead run.

Now the horses were blowing hard and hot and worn, their hides steaming. He reached the road again and dropped their pace to a walk, and a mile on came to the place where he had hidden the list. Dismounting, he fished it out from under a rock and gave it to the Greek knight, who took it without a word to him and rode away.

Hagen gathered up his reins. From the saddle, Theophano looked down at him, the moonlight faint on her face.

"You have just condemned those people to death," she said. "They were friends of the Empress among John's supporters, and they will all die now for your deed."

"Come down here," he said, raising his arms to her.

She slid down from the horse and stood before him; her fragrance made him light-headed. When she put her hands on his arms he nearly cried out at the luxury of her touch. She lifted her face to his.

"Go back," she said. "You could overtake that man, without me to weigh you down, and have the list again."

"I made a bargain," he said. He closed his arms gently around her, her warmth against him now.

"A bargain with the Devil!"

"I don't betray my word, girl. Not even to men who betray theirs as a matter of course."

"Hagen—" She clutched his arms, her face tipped up, and now tears streamed down her cheeks. "He will kill those people!"

"I don't care about them," he said. "I only care about you." He tightened his embrace around her and kissed each tear and then at last he kissed her mouth.

Her arms went around his neck. For an endless moment the world fell away from them; there was nothing left but her, sweet and pliant in his arms, her kiss as fierce and full of passion as his own.

"I love you. I love you."

"Oh, my man," she whispered. "What a man you are—"

The wind rose, harping through the thorny brush, and whirled around them, buffeting them like a great hand that urged them on. Reluctantly he stepped back, his hands sliding down her arms. "We have to get out of here."

"If we get back to Constantinople before he does," she said, "we can warn them. Some of them. I have some of their names."

He lifted her up onto the saddle, the wind blowing her cloak flat against her back, and taking the reins in one fist he vaulted up behind her. She turned, her hands out to him, and he leaned toward her and they kissed again.

He heard the whistle in the air an instant before the blow struck. It knocked him out of the saddle; he hit the ground so hard his senses left him for an instant. He struggled up, fighting for his consciousness. He was unhurt. He reached his feet, shaky still, and looked around.

His horse still stood in the road, too tired to run away, but there on the ground beyond it lay Theophano.

"Oh, God—"

She was trying to rise. The arrow pierced her back like a bolt that bound her to the earth. When he lifted her up in his arms she sobbed with pain.

"No—save yourself—"

The sibilant hiss of another arrow sounded behind him, and he heard the thunk as it hit the ground. Another came, and another. He leapt onto the horse and kicked it into a gallop down the road.

In his arms, she cried out with pain. The arrow was still lodged in her back. He knew every stride of the horse was an agony. Ahead the road curved, and he forced the weary horse on past the bend and turned it sharp off the road and up the steep rocky slope.

Halfway to the peak, he reined in. From here he could see a long way, and he dismounted and laid her down among the rocks and bent over her, shielding her with his body.

He knew she was dying. He knew by the bubbling in her throat. She said, "Take this."

She fumbled at her slipper, and he took it from her foot. Inside it was a thin piece of silk, which she pushed at him. "Take it—to the Basileus. Tell her—"

He cast a quick look around them; down there on the road, a line of horsemen was coming into sight around the curve.

"Tell her—that here, obedient to her law—"

"Theophano!"

"I fell."

And she was dead, gone, slipped away like a sigh, leaving behind nothing he could cherish. The slip of silk crushed in his fist, he bent over her and let his tears fall like burning coals onto the shell she left behind.

More arrows thudded around him. He tore the shaft from her back, slung her over his shoulder, mounted the horse and went on over the hill.

Tired as it was, the horse kept on, and Cerulis's soft and malleable men did not. Dawn came as Hagen crossed a ridge and rode down on to the sandy slope before the sea, and there he buried Theophano.

He sat down on the ground beside her grave and looked out across the sea. The rising sun brushed gold over the tops of the waves, but the darkness still lay in the folds, so that the sea rolled toward him in curls of light. Hagen sat there, his sword in his hands, and wept like a child.

He wept for himself, who had lost his love, his wife, his dearest heart, but he wept also for Theophano, who deserved life so much. He cursed God, for arranging the world in such a way that good people died at the hands of evil people who then went on and on, enjoying life. He beat at the ground with his sword; he scrubbed his wet face dry and rubbed the salt tears from his eyes and a moment later gave himself up to fresh torrents of grief.

At last, his passions dead from overwork, he sat there limply staring at the sea. The sun was risen now, and its heat blasted him; the brilliant light lay on the water's restless surface like a sheen of oil. There was no wind. As he sat there silent, the small birds and flies and creeping things that lived in the brush began to move around again and sing and eat and dig, the ants around his feet, the hawk in the air.

He understood his own courage; he relied on his strength and skill, and if he lost anyway, he knew God was against him. Her courage mystified him. Alone, a mere girl, friendless, weaponless, in the grip of a cruel enemy, she had fought on, using whatever weapons she could find—a needle, the knife she had tried to reach in the last moments before he led her away. She had never cringed.

He laid on his knee the scrap of silk she had given him and stroked it smooth with his fingers. She had written on it in some faint ink, letters barely recognizable. Suddenly he found himself kissing it, a wrinkled dirty bit of cloth, and fresh floods of tears erupted from him;

he howled and rolled on the hillside. He lay on her grave and willed himself to die.

He did not die. Gradually the intensity of his passion subsided into the dull ordinary apprehensions of the moment. The shadow of the hawk glided over him; he realized he was hungry. The dust made him sneeze.

It was the list that sent him on, to do what she had bidden him. He found his horse, eating wild lilies in a crevice near the sea waves, the sweat dried on its sides in long white lines like a map. He mounted and turned its head toward Constantinople.

<h1 style="text-align:center">⁘ 22 ⁘</h1>

The silk was crumpled, and the names on it barely readable. Irene rolled it around her finger.

"Why did you send her? Why did you send her back to him?"

She glanced at him, where he knelt in the middle of the room, his voice pleading, as if Irene could call her back from the dead. She had never thought to see him again.

She said, "I thought it was necessary."

His head swayed from side to side. He had come straight here, and his clothes were dusty and his white hair rough and uncombed. He said, "She told me to tell you something. It sounded like something from a story. That here, according to your law, she fell."

"Yes," she said, and her throat filled, painfully tight. "From a story. And very fitting."

Her hand fell to his shoulder. "I'm sorry, Hagen. I loved her too. Remember this: she chose this course. She understood the importance of success and accepted the risk of failure. She gave herself for the Empire. We must be proud and honor her even in mourning."

His hands covered his face. In spite of his filthy condition, she gathered him up into her arms, and bending she pressed a soft maternal kiss on the top of his head.

"Be patient," she said softly. "We shall have our revenge. I promise you, we shall see John Cerulis suffer for what he did to her and to us."

Under her hands he shuddered. She stroked his hair, wondering at his depth of grief. It infected her; tears came to her eyes and spilled in rivulets down her cheeks. She pressed his heavy head against her, thinking with hate of John Cerulis.

In the afternoon, bathed, dressed in fresh clothes, Hagen went by ferry across the narrow water to Chalcedon, and found his brother Rogerius's grave and knelt down before it. He crossed himself and said some prayers and told Rogerius that Karros who had murdered him was dead, and spoke in his mind to Reynard the Black, his father.

Revenge, his father's spirit replied. Revenge, revenge.

That no longer satisfied Hagen. The old, tried way now seemed to him too simple. When he thought of Theophano he did not want to stain her memory with blood.

Revenge, he heard his father say. Blow struck for blow taken. It is the only way.

But there was more to it than that. What had caught Theophano up in its coils and crushed the life out of her would not be destroyed by a course as narrow as that. Something was at work here that went beyond his understanding, and it touched close to his notion of the very nature of evil. He could not see it, but he smelled a monster here.

Under this dirt his brother lay, and he put his hand to the mound, now softly sprung with new grass. "Sleep," he said. "Sleep, brother." He laid a stone down beside the head of the mound, a token of his visit there, and walked away across the churchyard to the gate where he had left his horse and sword.

It was a hot day. The Caliph's ambassador was sweating in his heavy ceremonial clothes, in spite of the two servants busy with their fans around him. Irene was sitting down; she had long experience of the Imperial harbor below the Bucoleon Palace, and had made them place her chair at the corner of the L-shaped wharf, where the breeze from the sea flowed in through the break in the protecting breakwaters. She smiled at the ambassador.

"You will convey my deepest respects to your dear master, whom I love as a mother does her son."

The ambassador had caught sight of his barge rowing briskly up to the wharf through the moored vessels of the Imperial home fleet. "I shall tell him so, Basileus." He bowed, his eyes turned to watch the barge. He was in some haste to go, she knew, because he had lost all his ready money betting on the Caesarea driver in the Hippodrome. She beckoned, and a page-boy hurried forward with a little velvet-covered box.

"My dear lord." She gestured toward the box. "A little present from us, in token of a happy visit."

He took the box, straightening; under the folds of his turban his face was damp and pink. When he opened the box a wordless exclamation slipped from his tongue.

"Permit me." Irene leaned forward and touched the key in the base of the mechanical bird, and dutifully it flapped its enameled wings and sang.

"Basileus," he said. "Your generosity far exceeds any of your predecessors; let your name be written in jewels and gold forever." He bent and kissed her hand.

He would have to give the bird to Harun, the Caliph, and the sight of it would inspire others of the court of Baghdad to want such marvels, which could be made only in the factories of Constantinople. She sat back, smiling. The cool breeze from the sea crossed her face.

"Make haste, sir, your barge awaits."

The Caliph's man paused only a moment longer, and his eyes met hers; he formed a wicked little smile under the edges of his moustache. "Most excellent of women, let me offer you my sympathies in your trials. I hope when I come back it is to fall once more at your feet, and not those of John Cerulis."

His eyes sparkled. He was showing off. She lifted her hand to cover her mouth, hiding her own smile.

"Be certain of it, my lord."

With a crash the gangplank fell across the gunwales of the barge and the edge of the wharf. In the stern of the wide flat craft, a little group of musicians burst into a skirling wild tune, and all the sailors stood up straight in respect. The Caliph's man walked up the plank and on to his barge, the plank was hauled in and stowed, and to the boom-boom of a skin-drum the oars stroked up and out and down, bearing the barge off across the quiet water. Its course divided the square shape of the Imperial harbor almost in half. Nosing out the opening in the breakwaters, it met the open water of the Golden Horn and the drumbeat picked up.

The Empress sat where she was. The breeze here was cool from the water and this place was quiet and when she went back into the palace, high on the cliff behind her, she would face worried people and treacherous ones as well.

John Cerulis was marching on the City, not with an army, but worse, a fiery-eyed prophet from the wilds who had proclaimed him emperor. Every eye in Constantinople was turned on her now, speculating: had she lost her call to the throne of Christ? Any false step now, any mistake, any sign of weakness, and they would turn on her, as they had turned on so many before her, and tear her to pieces.

They, less one. Now, from the next wharf of the Imperial harbor, another barge was sliding out toward the opening in the long grey lines of the breakwater.

This barge was bigger than ibn-Ziad's. Bright with scarves and gold-embroidered silks, crowded with servants, it passed by the Empress as she sat there alone on the wharf watching. She did not raise her hand in greeting. Nor did the Parakoimomenos, seated—enthroned —on a canopied chair in the front of the barge, facing the stern. Perhaps until the very last he wanted to keep his eyes on Constantinople. Perhaps he was merely loath to look upon Lesbos, the place of his exile, before he had to. Like the whistling Memnon he sat there with his hands on his knees, staring away into the empty air, as he glided by her. The Empress waited until he was gone before she laughed.

⦂ 23 ⦂

Late in the afternoon, when everybody else was busy with preparations for the evening meal, Nicephoros, the Treasurer of the Empire, put a cloak around his shoulders and by himself went out a little gate at the back of the Hippodrome. In the lanes and alleys there, where the Imperial bear-keepers kept their beasts in cages and the City's prostitutes walked up and down hissing and jeering at men passing by, a chair waited. Nicephoros got in, and the curtains were drawn, and the bearers lifted him up on the supporting poles and sped away.

Nicephoros settled back into the depths of the chair. The cushions smelled musty but he did not open the drapery to let in the sweet air. He tucked his cloak around him and sunk his head down into the folds of his hood, his mind full of crossing thoughts.

He knew himself the victim of his own subtlety. All his life, he had guessed that things were never what they seemed; that the events on the surface of reality, like the shadows of clouds gliding over the earth, were merely the transient effects of the higher verities, often shown in contradiction and equivocation, to deceive the foolish. He had learned to see things in their opposites, to find truth in lies, confusion in understanding, and faith in skepticism. For the sake of argument, he could assume any possible viewpoint, and long ago, he had forgotten what it was he really did believe.

He knew, for example, that John Cerulis was a wicked man, from the point of view of the Empress; to John Cerulis, of course, the Empress herself was a monument of wickedness, and if he was right (and Nicephoros had potent evidence to favor that position), then the Empress's viewpoint was in itself a wicked one, and John Cerulis, being wicked in the eyes of wickedness, was good.

At that even Nicephoros's wonderful flexibility failed; it was not possible to see good in John Cerulis. And now he was bringing this image-breaker to Constantinople, this Daniel, this Jeremiah, this poison-toad, this saint who hated saints.

The chair swayed and bounced along on the shoulders of the bearers. Reaching the City gate, their chief spoke to the gate-keepers, and passed along a piece of money, and they were admitted to the world outside the walls. Now Nicephoros did lean forward and open up the curtains a little.

He had left Constantinople by the Gate of Charisius, in the north end of the City. Here, the road ran up over hills and meadows and past groves of many-legged olive trees, curving slowly to meet the great forest that began miles off and ended, no one knew exactly where, in the snowy wastelands of the north. The little plain outside of

Charisian Gate was still near enough the City to be populated by Romans, who had built their villas here and there among the groves, and on this undulating plain, facing the City like a little army, John Cerulis had brought his retinue and his holy man for the first engagement against Irene.

Nicephoros could see the camp the moment he opened the curtain. It lay on higher ground, ringed with bonfires. His bearers took him there at a steady trot.

It was for the sake of this holy man that he had come out here, leaving the protection and comfort of Constantinople. John Cerulis had been plotting against Irene for years, with no success, but the holy man Daniel was another matter entirely.

The urge to break images was nothing new. For many years Irene's immediate predecessor and his father had waged a full-scale war against icons, saints, and monks, disrupting the Empire and causing the enemies of Rome to rejoice. Nicephoros had seen people roasted alive for praying to images of the saints; he had sat in the Hippodrome on that terrible day when thousands of monks and nuns were herded into the arena at the points of swords and ordered to pair off and copulate then and there to save their lives. He had watched in horror as men with buckets of whitewash and plaster covered over paintings and mosaics in churches, and he had wept when people—mostly women, it was women who loved them best, the images—when people fought and died to save the figures of eternity from an untimely destruction.

The iconoclasm had been grotesque and vicious, and the Council that ended it was the greatest triumph of Irene's career, that moment in which her skill at handling men had found its finest work. Now here came this Daniel to start the madness up again.

Or to bring down God's righteous wrath on Constantinople for worshipping idols.

Nicephoros pinched the bridge of his nose between thumb and forefinger. He loved Irene; he did not want to doubt her. That also made him wary. He had learned long before that those ideas to which he was most passionately committed were likely to be wrong in exactly the degree of his devotion to them. He trusted only those thoughts that he had subjected to the full blast of his doubts and suspicions—in short, he felt himself most liable to be right when he was least enthusiastic.

None of this seemed to him the sign of a whole mind. That was when he concluded that his subtlety was killing him.

The bearers slowed, coming to the pitch of the road. He looked up at the camp on the hill ahead of him. Soon he would be within that ring of fires, and it occurred to him, again, as it had when he first considered coming here, that he might have some difficulty getting out again, and in his mind he reviewed those means of persuasion available to him, in case he had to induce John Cerulis to let him go.

He had money; he lived frugally, and saved his salary; but money would not move John Cerulis, whose family owned half the European Empire. He had knowledge and understanding, since Irene had over the years given into his hands most of the administration. He had Irene, who, whatever her feelings toward a servant who had gone behind her back as Nicephoros was doing now, would surely prefer to deal with him herself than leave him to her worst enemy. If none of these tools served, he thought, uncomfortably, he belonged to John Cerulis.

He told himself this, but even now, as the bearers carried him up toward the circle of bonfires glowing in the darkness, the great billowing silk tent in the center like the center of a monstrous rose, his heart began to beat faster, his mouth went dry, and his stomach fluttered. He was entering an unknown and incalculable future, where the rules he had always kept no longer worked. He was outside Constantinople; anything could happen.

"Take this name, and go into the City, and slay."

The two soldiers knelt on the carpet before him, their faces down between their hands, their noses to the ground. Their mutters of assent were muffled in the heavy rug. John Cerulis, sitting in his new throne before them, waved his hand to the scribe kneeling at his left, and that man copied off the next name. They took it and backed swiftly off on hands and knees toward the door.

"How many more?"

The scribe counted swiftly. "Thirteen, Augustus, Chosen of God."

John Cerulis rose, restless, and paced off across the tent. He longed for the comfort of his palace in the City but he could not leave this work to others. The list had shocked him. There were names on that list he had thought were bound to him forever—men he had entrusted with the most crucial work, the innermost secrets of his career. He could have faith in no one—that was the great lesson of Theophano's list.

Soon, very soon, they would all suffer the consequences of betraying him; he did not mean to enter into his City until all those who had turned against him were dead.

"Bring in another."

But before the next group of soldiers entered, a page came in, flung himself on the ground at the feet of the rightful Basileus, and begged permission to speak.

"Yes, yes."

"Augustus, Chosen of God, the Treasurer the Most Noble Nicephoros is without, craving audience with you."

"Nicephoros!" John wheeled around, triumphant.

Of all the men who served the usurper Irene, Nicephoros was the most indispensable to her. If he were coming to join the cause of John Cerulis—

He said, "Bid him wait." In dealing with such men it was essential to convince them that they were unimportant. He measured his steps back to his throne and sat down.

More soldiers came in and prostrated themselves, and the scribe copied off the next name and they took it away, to write it on their swords. John sent for wine. He had dined tonight better than he had on the long trek into the country, because being so close to Constantinople he had ordered bread brought out from the City's ovens, and the wine had been permitted to settle.

"Bring me Nicephoros," he said, and the page ran out.

The Syrian came in, his silken clothes still crumpled from the ride out from Constantinople. He walked across the high-piled Persian carpets and stood before John Cerulis and doubled up in a deep bow.

"Greetings, Most Noble, and welcome back from your journey."

"Nicephoros," said John, "your face is an offense against God. Unless you hide it from me, I shall take measures to have it removed."

The dark features of the Imperial Treasurer never changed. He said, "Patrician, I reserve the ultimate obeisance for her who wears the purple boots."

John Cerulis gripped his robe and yanked it up and thrust out his foot, shod in a buskin of dark red-blue. "Prostrate yourself, Nicephoros."

The other man did not move. He said, "I shall suffer martyrdom gladly, Most Noble, to preserve my soul. It is blasphemy to do the Imperial honors to one who is not Basileus."

John Cerulis pressed his lips together; he had gone too far, insisting on the prostration; he reproved himself for leaving no graceful way out of this. He had no intention of killing Nicephoros, whose brain was a great mine of invaluable information, necessary to the functioning of the Empire.

While he was examining his possible courses of action, the door blew back and Daniel stormed into the tent.

"Ah," said John Cerulis, and relaxed. The holy man would get him out of this. "God's messenger to me makes his appearance. Come forward, holy one."

Daniel strode straight up past Nicephoros and glared into John Cerulis's face. "How dare you have me confined!"

"For your own protection, holy one," John said, smiling. It amused him to see the scruffy old hermit rant, and certainly it proved him authentic, a real Jeremiah. "There are those who would take your life on the very sight of you, for what you have done."

"I will not be confined!" The holy man hopped up and down, his clothes slapping his bare legs. "I must be alone—I must have space, and the clean wind, and the open sky, or I cannot pray. I cannot pray inside this camp!"

John turned his gaze on Nicephoros, standing off to one side now, his gaze fastened on Daniel. "You see the messenger from God, who has named me emperor."

Nicephoros was looking the old man keenly up and down. Finally, lowering himself to his knees, he reached out and tugged on Daniel's robe.

"Holy one, I ask the blessing of the Lord's fool."

Daniel wheeled around. He was bony as a poor man's mule, and his clothes hung on him with no grace. He frowned down at Nicephoros's bowed head, but after a moment he raised his hand and made the Sign of the Cross over the Syrian.

"God have mercy on you, who are greater than you know."

John Cerulis made a rude sound with his lips. He lifted his hand, and from the back of the tent a brace of his guards came forward.

"Remove the holy man to a quiet place where he can pray for our success."

Daniel spun around, looking for a way to escape, and the guards closed on him from either side. Nicephoros skipped out of their way. One gripped the old man's arms against his sides, and the other got hold of Daniel's knees. The holy man shrieked and flung himself bodily against their hold, but he was old, and light, and the guards carried him off like a bundle of air. Daniel's screams and half-articulate curses sounded long after he had left the tent.

"The holy fit descends on him at odd moments," John Cerulis said to Nicephoros.

He did not hide his smile. He enjoyed shaping Daniel to his own meanings.

Nicephoros had regained his feet. He said, "I am surprised at your confidence in him. He does not seem to view you with any ardent affection."

"God is in him," John said. "And he has done what God meant of him, when he acclaimed me emperor. His blessing on you disposes me to favor you, Nicephoros—if you join me now, I will promise you that you will keep your lucrative position in my court."

Nicephoros bowed to him, his hands describing graceful flourishes in the air. "I must give the matter the thought due such a weighty decision."

"No," John said. "You will decide now, in this moment, or the possibility of decision will pass you by."

He leaned against the arm of his throne, striking the casual, confident pose of one who had no doubt of his success, no doubt at all. He said, "I do not need you, Nicephoros. It matters only if you choose rightly, and join me. If you choose wrong, then that, and you, will matter no more. Now, choose."

The Syrian stood motionless before him, his hands pressed together. His great wedge of nose filled up his face. His silence wore on, and John stiffened, straightening up, irritated.

Before he could speak, Nicephoros said, "Then you will not stop me from leaving, if I choose to abide with my lady."

John bit his lips, furious. He almost called for his guards, to take this stupid fool and stop his mouth with mud. Yet it was true, surely, if God were with him, that the rejection of such as this stupid Syrian did not matter. He showed his power when he showed it did not matter what Nicephoros did.

He let himself fall back into the cushions of his throne. "Go," he said. "Prepare yourself and your despicable mistress for the inevitable. Take back into the City the message of God and this holy old man and your Basileus: Your days are numbered, your sins are soon to be avenged. Go. Go. Go."

The Treasurer backed away, bowing, to the tent door, and was gone. John unfisted his hands. What a fool that man was! And such a fool could not be valuable, could not have necessary knowledge. His death alone could give him consequence, the wrong kind, the eternal damnation of one who had defied the will of God.

He said, "Put his name on the list."

"The Basileus commands," said the scribe, and his pen scratched.

Nicephoros reached the Palace in the black of midnight. He went quietly through the courtyard of the Daphne and across a garden to his apartments in the back of the Magnaura Palace and went in the little rear door. His chambers were dark and empty, the three servants having long since gone to their beds, and he passed by memory's guide through the lightless outer rooms to the room where he slept.

There, shedding his coat in the dark, he groped along the table by the window for a lamp and a firebox to light it. The tabletop was cluttered with books and papers; he swore, not finding what he was looking for, and as if his words had kindled it, a flame burst into life in a corner of the room.

He whirled, cold all over. The fire grew and steadied, a pale nimbus, shining on the side of the bed, the marble table there, the pillows stitched with gold thread, and sitting among them, perched up comfortably on Nicephoros's own bed, the Empress Irene.

Seeing her he froze, sick; he knew he was caught now. He blinked at her. She stared calmly back at him through the shivering white light, and finally, for want of something better to do, he prostrated himself.

"Very good," she said, and put down the lamp she had lit.

"Chosen of God—I am most honored—I cannot tell you the glory, the delight I experience at the sight of you—"

"Be quiet, Nicephoros. I don't want to hear it. I want to know your impressions of the holy man."

"I—I—"

"You did go out to see the holy man?"

"Augustus, I would never think of—"

"Oh, but you should have, Nicephoros—your career and your very life perhaps depend on it. If you have not gone out to see for yourself, you have disappointed me, Nicephoros."

He raised himself up on to his knees, her voice calming his rabbity heart. She trusted him, surely; had he ever betrayed her trust? Relieved, he realized he had not, and he faced her, more assured.

He said, "Augustus, I lay open my heart to you, and you see therein both my deep and fleeting thoughts."

"Perhaps." She smiled; there was something humorless and awkward in the smile, but he shunted that out of his mind. "As a method of retrieving your invaluable opinions, however, this reading of hearts is less efficient than direct speech, Nicephoros."

"I saw an old man, much abused in John Cerulis's company, who gave me a blessing."

"Oh? No more than that? No aura, no miracles? He has not elevated John Cerulis several feet above the ground?"

Again, he detected something brittle and unhappy in her tone. Carefully he chose words.

"Augustus, Equal of the Apostles, I cannot tell anything with an absolute degree of certainty, but I know that he and John are not friends. John uses force to control him. If, perhaps, John somehow manufactured him—"

"He does control him, though."

"Oh, yes. He is very confident, he let me go with no trouble about it."

Her smile widened, suddenly genuine, intimate, and kind. "Although you defied him, my heart?"

Nicephoros bowed down, grateful that she had drawn this conclusion for herself.

"Well," she said, "excellent. Yet I foresee some danger in the coming days. Already John's men are doing his filthy work in the City.

His enemies will die, and many innocent people as well. I advise you to find a bodyguard, Nicephoros, someone who can defend you at close quarters. My Frank has come back. He is well suited to the task, a man of great strength and courage, who has proven himself surprisingly dependable. I suggest you hire him to protect you."

"Basileus, I accept your wisdom." Or was she giving him to the Frank to be quietly assassinated?

"You have done well, Nicephoros." She slipped off the far side of the bed; the darkness enveloped her, and he waited, his ears straining, while she stole away.

Just as he was preparing to rise, convinced that she was gone, her voice came from the darkness. "Nicephoros."

"Basileus," he said, surprised.

"I will confess, my heart, that I did not come here expecting to find you off at the holy man's court, but to convey some very unpleasant news to you."

"Ah?"

"Your friend Peter Karrosoulos, the Prefect of the City, is dead."

Nicephoros's mouth opened; his breath exploded from him in a grunt, as if he had been struck in the stomach. He said stupidly, "Dead? Truly?"

"Oh, yes. He hanged himself."

"Oh, God. Oh, God."

"He had lost heavily at the races, using money that was not his. I am sorry, Nicephoros."

Nicephoros sagged forward onto the side of the bed, struggling with this. He said, "But the month is not yet over."

There was no answer. She was certainly gone now. Heavily he raised himself up off the floor and sat on the side of the bed. Suicide. He hanged himself! His hands rose to his throat; he imagined the condition of mind in which the Prefect had taken rope and wound it round and round his throat.

He deserved it. Corrupting his office like that. His own weakness destroyed Peter Karrosoulos, Prefect of the City.

Oh, but who did not have weaknesses? Nicephoros's head tipped back, his guts churning. Was he not also handsome, and charming, and kind? Why was it so common that a man's weaknesses destroyed him, and so rare that a man's virtues lifted him to greatness?

It was the Empire, he thought, the Empire, waiting like a basilisk for the missteps of men, waiting to devour them all.

His mind flinched from that, but his soul leapt like a flame. The Empire to which he had devoted his adult life now seemed to him like a horror. The Devil made it, to seduce men from God. The Devil built here a promise of order that was fulfilled in a chaos of disorder—an illusion of peace in a history of warfare. Men came and laid themselves upon the rack of Empire and were broken. Like the Prefect, like Nicephoros himself, they pursued the vain dream of a sane and liveable world, when they should be giving themselves up wholly to God.

Then into his mind sprang the memory of the Irish monk, whom he had met in the Chapel of the Virgin. Especially he remembered the monk's gaze, clear, aloof, and invulnerable. He longed for that detachment, proof against pain. He thought, I will become a monk.

At once the idea crystallized into a certainty. When this crisis was past, when the Empire was safe again, for the moment, and the Empress safe, for the moment, Nicephoros would retire into a monastery.

He let out his breath. Sitting heavily on the bed, he gathered his tumultuous feelings and stuffed them back inside his tormented heart. There, ahead of him, now, the promise he had made himself shone in the distance, beyond the work and fear and struggle, a goal to be waited for, to be striven toward, a refuge and a reward.

That decision, somehow, brought all else into line with it; the time between now and then became suddenly manageable. He sighed. The bed beside him was creased and wrinkled where she had lain upon it, waiting for him. He bent suddenly and pressed his lips to the seamed cloth.

"Sir."

His housekeeper, a Circassian slave, stood in the doorway with a lamp.

"Sir, is there anything I might do?"

"I would like a cup of wine," Nicephoros said. "Before I go to bed."

"Yes, sir."

"And ask the Ethiopian woman to wait on me here."

"Yes, sir."

The Circassian went out. Nicephoros sat still, his hands between his knees, and thought again of the City Prefect. What a fool, what a poor fool, Peter, oh. His eyes swam with tears. His shoulders hunched. The Ethiopian woman would ease away some of this pain. Some of it would never leave him. Like an old man, slumped there on the side of his bed, Nicephoros waited, fighting against tears.

: 24 :

Wretched and despairing, Daniel knew that he was beaten. The task had overcome him. He had lost the sense that God was with him—that God was in him, working through him. He had failed.

He had not supposed that his burden would be easy, but he had assumed it would be possible. Maybe that was his first mistake.

In the desert it had seemed so real. In the desert under an open sky, God had spoken to him in a clear voice. As men built houses to keep out the wind and the sun, so men made images and performed rituals that divided them from God. If people would simply tear down all forms and structures, they would rejoin God; and the universe, rent with the first sin when Eve took the apple, would be whole again.

It had not occurred to him, until too late, that there was more to it than that. That people filled the space around them with images and forms to protect themselves against other people. That when he went among them, they would build their defenses around him, too.

He prayed all day long, begging God to take him back again. When he was too tired to pray, he cried, lonely and heartsick.

In the desert he had run over the rocks, shouting the praises of God. He had felt God all around him there, surrounding him like the air, an active and boisterous presence. He had moved through God, breathed God, touched Him in every rock, seen Him in the flash of the lizard diving under cover of a ledge, in the high soar of the vulture in its endless wheeling search. He had eaten God, shit God, exhaled God, and every day had been the first day of Creation, when the earth rejoiced and there was no sin.

Then he had decided that he had a mission to the rest of men, and now it was all gone.

This John Cerulis came to him and wanted him to preach, to say thus and so, words that meant nothing to Daniel. These alien words, like blocks of stone, made a wall around him, like mirrors they turned his own face back to him, putting himself where he had been used to finding God. Out of false faces the people around him spoke to him, and there was no truth in them, no honesty.

It had all begun with the appearance of John Cerulis—with that mistake on the road, when he had thought he saw the Emperor coming.

"You must denounce Irene," John Cerulis told him. "She pretends to be Basileus, and she deserves the worst. A mere female! Yet she has dared to lift her eyes to the supreme power, and surely it is blasphemy to claim to represent the divine Son of God in the body of a woman."

Daniel rubbed his face with his hand; he did that a lot, touching himself, reassuring himself that there was a boundary between himself and this world around him. He did not understand what John wanted, although it had repulsed him to learn that the Basileus was a woman, and he agreed with the notion that such a thing was blasphemy. Sometimes he suspected that he had walked down that mountain road into a devilish world made up from the jealous wicked mind of the Fiend to seduce him, a world in which everything was the exact opposite of the divine plan.

John Cerulis, cruel and frivolous, ruled this world. Daniel hated John, as the owner of a precious vessel of gold might hate an ugly noisy child with dirty hands that smeared everything it touched with sticky fingerprints.

He made no protest anymore. Too unhappy even to complain, he blamed himself for his arrogance and his failure, and knew he deserved whatever came on him. When they gave him a new robe and took away the mantle he had worn for years, he accepted this as penance for his sins. He ate the rich food they brought, although he knew it was gradually replacing his spiritual essence with a perishable and rotting dross that corrupted his flesh and withered the strength of his soul. He did everything they told him, because he had lost God, and nothing else mattered.

He went out one day before a multitude of people and spoke the words John Cerulis had given him to speak, although they were rough and ugly. He called the anathema down on the pretender Irene, who had sullied the throne with her unclean female presence, and released everyone from their oaths of allegiance to her, and he called on all good true Christians to rebel against her, and put the rightful emperor on the throne, John Cerulis.

The people spread out before him in a great mass, filling the whole meadow, all the way to the road and past the road, in among the olive groves. In the distance stood the tremendous wall of the City, its towers and golden domes shining in the sun. Daniel spoke from a high wooden platform, with Cerulis's soldiers standing all around the edge. The crowd before him covered the field from side to side with the flutter of their clothing, the pale dots of their faces, a great murmurous mass. His words evoked no more excitement from them than from a great wind-rumpled field of daisies. But as he looked, he began to discern individual faces among them: here a woman with great dark eyes below the severe line of her headcloth; there an old man leaning on the shoulder of a boy; here a little child in a colorful coat, a doll clutched in its arms; every life another gift from God.

He began to talk to them. His voice came faster and higher in pitch and he paced back and forth before them, pointing and waving his arms at them, calling to them, pleading with them to answer him.

He told them of the wonder of God, the ecstasy of union with Him, the necessity of giving up everything that got between them and Him— their homes, their work, their families—all must be thrown away, he told them; nothing mattered save the delight of finding God.

Here and there they began to respond to him. Grunted monosyllables erupted from them, yells of assent.

"Walk out of this false life," he cried. "Your deliverance is within reach. All you must do is recognize it. Come to God. Come to God, Who loves you."

Now they were shouting, their arms raised toward the sky and toward Daniel, calling to him. He reached out toward them, loving them, and they shouted his name. He began to weep. He wanted them; he wanted God's love for them. The tears in his eyes blended out distinctions between them and he saw them as a single creature, that begged him to lead them on to Heaven.

"See," he cried, "how God calls to us! See—"

Now, suddenly, through eyes washed clean with tears, he saw in the

sky a vision, a white city, a mass of towers and walls and domes that
floated in the blue of Heaven above the earthly City of Constantinople,
and he flung out his arm toward it.

"See the City of God, descending from Heaven! God is coming to
earth—God will lead us into His heavenly City—"

Now they saw it too, and screamed. They wheeled around toward
it, floating in the sky among the clouds, and many bounded to their
feet and ran toward it. The sun struck the glistening heights into a
dazzling white, the domed rooftops mounting toward Heaven; and if
some were shouting now that it was only a cloud, they saw without
the eyes of faith. Most of the crowd saw it. They howled and wept and
prayed to be led away to it, to the City of God, and Daniel went to the
edge of the platform and started to climb down toward them, to lead
them there.

From all sides, the soldiers rushed at him, pulled him back onto
the platform, and flung him down on his back. One of them stood on
his hands to hold him. John Cerulis's spokesman hurried forward to
tell the crowd that Daniel would enter the City on Saint Febronia's
Day, a week away, to preach again, and they wrapped Daniel up in a
cloak and bundled him off like a roll of carpet, to put in storage until
they needed him again.

Ishmael's wife was still on her knees, swaying back and forth, praying
and crying. Ishmael touched her shoulder. She unnerved him, when
she was like this, outside herself like this; he could not reach her. He
bent down to put away the wine flasks and the remnants of their lunch
and to collect his small son and daughter, playing on the trodden earth
near their mother.

He understood his wife's passion, because he had felt it too, and
it still shook him. This holy man knew God. At first Ishmael had
doubted him, when he spoke against the Basileus, in the beginning;
he had been disappointing to one used to the great preachers of the
City. But when Daniel began to speak about God, then Ishmael had
heard the truth ringing through his words. He had felt that Daniel
was speaking to him alone, out of all the hundreds gathered there, and
every word had fallen like a drop of acid on Ishmael's corrupted soul,

burning through the dead layers of lies and sin, down to the stinging quick.

"He knows God," he said, to those people around him, who were also getting ready to leave. Like his wife, many throughout the crowd were still deep in their prayers. Those who heard Ishmael nodded in agreement.

"He knows God. He has God's words in his heart and on his lips. What a wonderful sermon! He drew down the City of God from Heaven with his sermon."

"But—the Basileus—"

At the mention of the Emperor, everyone turned away and fell diligently to the work of packing their belongings and urging their loved ones home.

Ishmael hooked his hand under his wife's arm and elevated her to her feet. His son and daughter were dashing around merrily getting underfoot and calling down disapproving looks from the people around them. Ishmael thumped and shouted them into obedience and they started back toward their City.

Walking, Ishmael turned his eyes to the sky. All day long, great white masses of clouds had been rushing up over the horizon, and still they came, floating past the sun, brilliant in the sun's light. The Heavenly City that had appeared for a moment among them was gone.

His heart was breaking. What the holy man had said rang over and over again in his mind. Go to God—give up everything but God— a wave of guilt washed over him. Since his victory in the Hippodrome, he had been stuffed fat with pride, as if he grew enormous with it; he had been to church only once, and then had not kept his mind on his prayers; he had come here today for his wife's sake, not his own. The victory had seemed enough, a perfection needing no other.

It was not enough. Even now he ached for the next race, to prove himself again, this time against the champion, against Michael, his rival. To win again. To overcome other men again.

His head hammered. Thinking of the Heavenly City, he walked on, going at top speed, pushing his family before him, hating himself. Daniel was right. He had turned from God—he had made a false God of victory. The snow-white City in the sky was not for him. But oh! how he wanted to go there, to walk out of this life with its toil and hardship and constant care. He was close to weeping now; careless of his wife and children, he strode forward through the gates into Constantinople.

Hagen had seen Nicephoros before, once in the company of the Empress, other times around the Sacred Palace; he had no idea what honors were proper to such an officer, and so he did nothing, neither bowing nor saluting him with his hand. Nicephoros also did nothing and said nothing to greet him, and they stared at each other a long moment, as if the Treasurer had not sent for Hagen to attend him. Finally the Treasurer sighed, sat down, and laying his hands on his thighs nodded to a chair opposite him.

"I understand in your own country you are a prince, and therefore I am somewhat reluctant to appear insensible to your honor, sir, yet circumstances constrain me to seek the use of your superior abilities in certain spheres of action."

Hagen did not sit. He saw in Nicephoros a nervous wind, like a horse that blew and jittered all over before the start of a race. Patiently he waited for the dark man to tell him what he meant.

"There are dead men all over the City today," Nicephoros said, and now rose, his nerves driving him into action, his hands rubbing together, his eyes restless. "Men of high birth, men of great station in life—men I would have thought invulnerable to such a savage purge as this. And I—I fear I may be intended to become one of them."

"Who is killing them?" Hagen asked.

"John Cerulis."

"Ah."

"He means to become emperor. He believes this holy man will make him emperor, and he is cleaning out all the—the—"

Nicephoros put his hands to his face. Hagen said, "Someone should go to the Basileus."

"Ah—what can she do? His men strike in packs, they say, like hyenas."

"Kill John Cerulis."

"Kill him!"

"If she gave me leave, I would do it for her—though it meant my life, I would kill him with my bare hands."

"Could you do it?"

Hagen shrugged one shoulder, smiling at this city man, this man of such power and such fear. "If you wish to badly enough, you can kill anyone at all."

"Ah, don't say that."

"I'm sorry."

"Will you protect me? I am told you are the greatest of warriors among your own fierce people. I need—I want—" Nicephoros sat down again, hunched forward, his face seamed with strain. "I am terrified. Yet I must go all over the City, every day, on the business of the Empire—I must have protection."

Hagen straightened up, surprised. "I shall have to ask the Basileus. She considers herself my overlord while I am here."

"She suggested I ask you to do it."

"Oh."

Now Hagen turned away, and prowled around the room, thinking about Irene with some irritation; she was managing him like a slave, which annoyed him, but more annoying yet was her inability in this crisis to do the right thing: to murder John Cerulis. He stood staring out a window, onto a deserted brick courtyard below, where stood some jars and bottles in rows, thinking that he might go now, out to the great camp on the meadow beyond the City, and find John Cerulis and put a knife in him, and reminded himself that this was not his City. He had forsworn vengeance for Theophano's sake, and there was no other good reason he could see why he should involve himself in this.

He swung around, facing Nicephoros, ready to refuse him, and saw in the Treasurer's face such a haunted look that his hatred leapt alive again. If the Empress could not or would not stand against this evil, someone should show her how.

"I will," he said. "I'll do what I can."

"Thank you," Nicephoros said, and now, to Hagen's surprise, he bowed.

In the morning Irene performed the sacred ritual of the well of Saint Stephen, carrying water in a procession around the Church of the Holy Wisdom, and sending off little phials to all parts of the City and to the rest of the Empire, to purify the altars everywhere. In the heat of noon she went into the little garden below the Daphne and there was served her dinner, and while she was there, the Frank Hagen came to her, and knelt down before her, and asked her to be allowed to kill John Cerulis.

"Is it so easy for you to kill another human being, Hagen?" she said. "Has the death of dear Theophano taught you no respect for life?"

"He is killing everywhere," Hagen said. "This isn't a murder, this is the uprooting of a weed, Basileus."

That amused her, but she did not laugh, not wanting to seem frivolous; the issue was a serious one, after all. Her women were moving around her, serving her a selection of dishes in the Arab style, the Caliph having sent her a new cook along with the menagerie. She had sent back the leopard and the tiger but kept the cook. Little Philomela sank down beside her and laid her head on Irene's knee, and the Empress fed her a stuffed onion.

"Hagen," she said, "God chose me to be Basileus. God will protect me and those whom God desires to live. Those who have lost God's sanction, those will die, and John Cerulis is but an instrument. So it is with evil; foul though the intent, the act cannot but be the will of God."

Out there, beyond the low wall at the edge of the garden, she saw someone walking; for an instant her eyes followed him. It was Prince Constantine, whom she had not punished for his triflings with the horse-race.

She said, still watching her cousin, "You know, Hagen, you are in many ways still a boy, impetuous and narrow. When you have come to my years, you will see how little one must interfere with the flow of things. What is meant, will be, my dear. Success in life is a question of finding out what is meant, and then fitting oneself to God's will."

She smiled at him. Hagen did not look convinced; he was standing up, his hands against his thighs, his face rumpled with dissatisfaction.

"Are you going to guard Nicephoros?"

"Someone must," he said.

"Excellent. Leave the rest to God, Hagen. Have faith." Now she was too amused not to laugh, and she did laugh. "Didn't you listen to the holy man?"

He grunted at her. "Give me leave."

"You have my leave, dear one."

He walked away; she leaned on her elbow on the side of her chair, watching him go, his long shapely arms accented by cuffs of silver on his wrists. She decided to get him some jeweled rings for his upper arms, perhaps some sort of collar. He was wearing the garnet she had given him. She loved garnets, light-shattering, imperial. The women hovered around her; one was daubing scent inside her elbow, a whiff of rose, of almond, the aromas of fine poison. Her gaze drifted across the wall again, but Prince Constantine was gone from sight. She smiled, thinking again of fine poison.

Ishmael loitered in the Apron, watching the grooms and stableboys rush in and out with buckets and nets full of hay and leather measures of grain, back and forth down the aisles full of horses. His head was throbbing. He had drunk himself to sleep the night before. His wife had nagged him out of bed this morning and so he had come down here, but there was nothing for him here, not anymore.

Down the aisle behind him, a horse was fretting and neighing, but it was Folly, Michael's inside wheeler, who was crazy anyhow, and it had been going on since he got here; he paid no heed. Ever in his mind he saw the City of God descending, pure white in the sunlight, its towers and rooftops, its streets of solid gold.

Behind him a man shrieked. That brought him up, his back prickling, whirling around.

Down the aisle from Michael's horses came the groom Esad, screaming. "Constantine!" he bellowed, running past Ishmael, and seized a horse-boy by the shoulders, spun him toward the door, and shoved him.

"Go get the Prince—get Michael, damn you, fast!"

The boy raced off. Esad rushed to the wall and tore a whip and a leadrope down from their pegs.

Ishmael leapt up. "What's happening? What's going on?"

"Constantine!" Esad ran into the aisle again with the whip and the leadrope, and Ishmael, with a dozen other men, hurried after him.

Two of the torches in the aisle had gone out. Only the one in the blank wall at the far end burned, and against its fitful light the tossing mane and head and neck of the horse Folly were framed in a stark silhouette. Esad raced to this horse's stall, the rest of the horsemen on his heels, and flung open the door.

The horse charged. It was notoriously jealous of its stall and could not bear even its groom inside for very long, but Ishmael had never seen it so furious as this. Esad wasted no time. Two steps into the stall, he dropped the leadrope and laid on the horse with the whip, and the great beast reared up into the air, striking out with its forefeet, its eyes glaring, ashimmer, in insane fury.

Then someone behind Ishmael screamed "Constantine!" and pointed.

Ishmael saw it at once. There behind the horse, against the wall, half-buried in the straw, lay a motionless body, facing the door. It was Constantine.

Ishmael dashed into the stall, where the horse, towering over Esad, was squealing in piercing blasts. Its forefeet struck down through the air. Scooping up the leadrope from the floor, Ishmael darted to one side. The horse wheeled after him, its head darting, its teeth snapping closed on his arm.

Esad brought the whip down butt first over the horse's poll, and it let go, half rearing again, and lunging sideways away. Ishmael leapt on it. He whipped the leadrope around its neck and flipped another loop over its nose, and gripping the horse hard by the head he forced it down and dropped it on its side on the straw. His arm throbbed, where the horse had bitten him.

The others thundered into the stall and lifted Constantine out. The horse was trembling violently, its spirit outraged. Ishmael stroked its neck in a quick sympathetic caress, his fingers slipping on the scum of sweat and blood and grime that lay over the brute's skin. Constantine had been here a long while; and he was dead, certainly. What a fool, to have entered this horse's stall without a whip.

An instant after the thought formed, he suspected something deeper. He got up. Folly lay there shuddering on the straw, half-invisible in the dark, except for the mad white glare of its eye. Ishmael went out of the stall and locked it. Pulling up his sleeve, he inspected the bruise forming on his upper arm. The cloth had protected him from any real damage.

In the Apron a thick ring of men surrounded Constantine's body on the ground. Esad was kneeling over him, and there in the crowd was Hagen, the Frank.

Ishmael went up beside him, and the Frank said, "Him, too. God's blood, I don't understand this."

"What?" Ishmael looked up at him.

"There are dead people all over the City," Hagen said. "I don't understand how he fits into it, though."

Ishmael shivered from head to toe, chilled down to his soul. A surge of revulsion and dread ran hard on the heels of the cold. The Heavenly City blazed in his mind. He spun around and walked out of the stable, out to the street.

Hagen followed him; side by side they walked through the warm windless sunshine, each in his own thoughts. Finally Hagen turned to him.

"Was there any sign of murder—did he show a wound?"

"I didn't see," Ishmael said. There was a mob ahead of them, crowded around the great gate into the Hippodrome, and he bent his steps that way. "No, of course not; all someone would have to do is knock him on the head and pitch him in there with Folly. Everybody knows that horse. He would trample anything in the stall."

"Even Michael?"

"Michael. You don't think Michael had anything to do with Constantine's death? Look!"

They were coming up behind the crowd at the gate. There on the tall part of the planks hung a belt of gold links, with a huge oval clasp: Michael's championship belt. Ishmael's mouth fell open. Now he knew why the crowd was here. More, he knew why that which drew the crowd was here; his stomach churned.

"What is it?" Hagen peered at the gate where the great placard was nailed up; of course he could not read. "What does that say?"

"There will be a race for the Golden Belt," Ishmael said, his voice flat. "On Saint Febronia's Day."

"A race between you and Michael?" Hagen put his hands on his hips. "When is Saint Febronia's Day? Oh." He remembered, understanding on his face like the sun rising.

"She wants to take the mob's attention from this holy man," Ishmael said. "So she is proclaiming a race." He turned away from the gate and went off down the street. "Let's go get a drink."

"I think I undervalue her," Hagen said. "Can you beat Michael this time?"

"I'm not going to try," Ishmael said.

"What?"

Avoiding the big Frank's eyes, Ishmael turned into the tavern and made for his favorite table in the front of the room by the door. At least he still had credit here. It made no difference if he raced; they would not pay him anyway. Sitting down, he buried his head in his hands. How false the world was, how full of sin and disappointment. Constantine murdered, lying there in the straw while mad old Folly stamped and beat and kicked him to a pulp. All false, all sinful; he could bear it no more.

And time was coming to an end. The Heavenly City would descend, and take all those chosen of Christ up to Heaven, and the sins of the damned would drag them down to Hell.

Hagen put a cup in front of him and poured the pale red wine into it. "What do you mean, you won't race?" He sat on the bench with the corner of the table between them.

"Oh, God, Hagen—" Ishmael ground the heels of his hands into his eyes. "Yesterday—did you see it? In the sky?"

"I saw nothing in the sky but clouds."

"Your eyes are blinded with sin."

"One of us is blind, if you saw anything in the sky but clouds."

An unaccountable rage mounted in Ishmael's heart, red and hot as a flame. "What would a barbarian know about God?"

Hagen smiled at him, uninsulted. "You think this Daniel is bringing with him the Heavenly City. You know he is in the power utterly of John Cerulis, who is as wicked a man as any I have ever seen—"

"God chooses His instruments as He will."

"What sense does it make to choose John Cerulis?"

"You belittle God—you try to fit God into the puny human frame of reason! No! God's way is beyond our knowledge—" As he spoke, Ishmael felt mounting in his heart the almost unbearable longing for that wonder, a place where the iron claws of time and consequence mattered not. He shut his eyes again. "We are whatever God wishes of us."

Hagen snorted at him, sipped his wine, and pushed the cup at Ishmael. "Drink. You are too sober."

"God's day is coming!"

"You people here—you glorify everything."

"What does that mean?"

"Ishmael, listen. My grandfather was not Christ's man. He sacrificed horses on the solstice and prayed to oak trees. My father used to say, 'Leave a little for the old gods.' You people here, you have given up everything to Christ—"

"You blaspheme. Christ is all, we owe all to Christ."

"Maybe, but it strikes me that if Christ were everything, there would be no reason for Him to be jealous, and yet He is jealous."

Ishmael's temper burst like a blister. "You pitiful creature. You blasphemer—you want me to spend my soul on horse-races, when the end of the world is at hand! Some devil sent you—some devil speaks through you, to seduce me from the right way. Get away from me, Satan!"

As he spoke, he put Hagen away from him, by getting up, by running out the door.

In the street, it was no different; people bustled here and there, on their trivial daily business, all unseeing that the day of the Lord was at hand. He ran away down the street, the air itself an irritation, running away to the Heavenly City.

Michael knew who had killed Constantine, and he understood why. He sat down beside his uncle's body, laid out on the floor of the stable, there in the straw with the dung and the mud. The horse had beaten Constantine's bones to bits, inside the bruised casing of his flesh; his head was all misshapen. Michael put his thumb down on each of his uncle's eyelids and firmly pressed them closed.

It was unjust, somehow—she had taken advantage of the purge, of the horror in the City, to slip one more body in; nobody would care, so many were dying. Unjust and pitiful. And yet had he himself not cast out this kinsman? Constantine had violated what was sacred—his honor, his reputation and the reputation of the races, the only thing that mattered. Michael had given up his bond with Constantine; he had no right now to be angry that she had punished him.

He thought, In a world more like the Hippodrome, such things would not happen. He wished she had not thrown the body into the stable. Wished she had not used mad old Folly to do her dirty work. Yet there was a certain roundness to it, a fitness. He knew why she had done it. He told himself again it was no business of his, not anymore. Getting up, he walked away through the stable.

⁘ 25 ⁘

If the Empress spent her days in ritual and procession, Nicephoros her minister spent his rushing from one place to another, meeting with other officers, working out practical ways of meeting the demands of life in Constantinople. Hagen escorted him through the streets to a palace or a public building, and then lazed around outside for hours, half-asleep in the sunshine, bored and low of humor.

He supposed this was a fit punishment. If he had not given John Cerulis the list, people would not be dying now all over the City, and Nicephoros would not need protection.

He brooded on that, how it was his fault these people were dying, and his grey mood turned black. He felt John Cerulis like a poisonous vapor that was slowly spreading over the City. The Empress with her empty babble of God and doing what God intended could not stand against this infection; in the end it would destroy them all.

One afternoon, while Nicephoros met with other officials inside, Hagen stood outside on the steps, wondering if he ought not to kill John Cerulis at once, and tell the Empress later—thinking, too, of Theophano, who had sacrificed herself without hesitation for the greater good of all—and a woman passed by on the street.

She slowed; she gave him a warm look. He smiled at her, and she stopped at once and beckoned to him, nodding toward the narrow alley between the square two-story building where Nicephoros worked and the low flat-roofed warehouse next door to it. Hagen started after her, and she darted into the alley with such a teasing laugh that he broke into a run.

In the alley, she turned to face him, and with her hands pulled open the front of her dress. Out popped the most beautiful breasts he had ever seen, large globes perfectly shaped, with nipples as tight and pink as little pursed lips. He had them almost in his hands when it crossed his mind that this was all too easy.

At that moment his ear caught the scrape of a boot on a roof tile, almost directly above him. He flung himself sideways; as he moved an arrow zinged past his shoulder and shattered on the hard ground.

He rolled over and over until he came up against the warehouse wall at the side of the alley. The woman was scurrying toward the street. He slung his legs out and tripped her. She fell flat on her face with a scream, and rolled over; he got to his hands and knees and peered upward.

A man with a bow was looking down at him from the flat roof of the warehouse. Seeing Hagen, he raised the bow, drawing up the arrow to his cheek. Hagen leapt up straight at him. Catching the overhanging eave of the roof with both hands, he swung himself up toward the bowman, who shot.

The arrow flashed past Hagen's head, and the archer turned and ran, but as Hagen got up to his feet another arrow came from the side and took him through the forearm. There were two more bowmen halfway across the roof. He pulled the arrow out of his arm and flung it down.

The man directly in front of him was nocking another shaft, his face desperate. Hagen lunged at him. The other two raised their bows at him, and Hagen plowed into the man in front of him and took him cleanly off his feet. The bow clattered away. The archer struck with his fists at Hagen, but the Frank only lowered his head and heaved the bellowing soldier up across his chest, both arms tight around him, and charged across the roof at the other two.

Their bows swung level, side by side they drew back the arrows, but they hesitated, unwilling to shoot their friend to get to Hagen. The man in Hagen's arms screeched and kicked and pounded him over the head with his fists. Hagen's forearm hurt where the arrow had gone through it. He braced his feet and swung the man in his arms like a whip at the two bowmen before him.

The effort drove him to his knees, but all three of the Greek soldiers went flying. Like a fool the first to gain his feet kept on trying to use his bow, scrabbling for another arrow from the case on his belt, and Hagen staggered up and wrenched out his sword.

He shouted. The feel of the sword in his hands was like a jolt of strong liquor. The bowman, his arrow still unnocked, whirled to run, and Hagen struck him down, cleaving down into his head with the blade so that half his face fell off.

The other two men came at him from opposite directions, wielding short-handled double-bladed axes. The taller of these hewed at him, and when Hagen fended off his blows with the flat of his sword, the shorter man attacked his back.

Hagen dodged, running out from between them, and they dashed after him. He stopped and they ran to catch him between them again, and he leapt away. Like this they crossed the flat rooftop, going from side to side, a short dash, the two men splitting up to go on either side of him, another dash. The roof was sound, at least, but the two Greeks were clever and would not be run off the edge, and they were improving their tactics as he let them work at it.

The shorter one was quick but he always struck left. The tall one was slow. Hagen dodged again, waiting for an opening.

A yell from across the alley startled him; he jerked his head around to see, in a window of the second story of the building next door, a gasping shouting group of men, among them Nicephoros, watching the fight. They cheered as they saw him turn. Distracted, he stared at them an instant too long, and the man behind him struck.

The blow went short, and the Frank flinched from it, but the upper tip of the curved axe blade sliced across his back. He bolted off into the center of the roof, doubled up with pain, clutching the sword with both hands for fear of dropping it.

He yelled; he beat at the air with the sword, driving back the fear and weakness lurking in the wound. The two axes circled him. He howled again, jumped into the air as high as he could.

They came at him again, the tall one first, cutting high and low, while the little one scurried around and rushed at his back and yelled.

All his nerves jumped, but the shout behind him told him to expect an attack from the man in front of him. When the tall man lunged, Hagen hit him with a counterstroke across the spine that broke the tall Greek nearly in half.

Hagen screamed, triumphant, and jumped on the fallen man and hewed off his head. The little man turned and ran. Hagen started after him but his foot slipped on the blood and he went to his knees. Nimble as a tumbler, the little man leapt from the rooftop and raced away down the street.

Out of breath, Hagen made no effort to follow. The battle-rage that had sustained him ebbed swiftly away. His back hurt and his arm was bleeding a lot. Living in the City had softened him and he felt sick to his stomach. He walked over to look at the two men he had killed; one of them wore a lot of fancy rings, but he took nothing; he wanted nothing to remind him of this. He climbed down from the rooftop and went up toward the street.

The girl was gone. He growled, remembering her; he was in a mood now to bite those breasts off. Nicephoros was coming out of the door.

Seeing Hagen, he came forward, with both hands outstretched. "How badly are you hurt? Oh, my God, Redeemer of all. Let's get out of here. Chair! Chair!"

"I'm all right," Hagen said.

The cut in his back was painful but shallow. It was the hurt in his arm that felt bad to him, oozing, itching already.

Two of the City *cursores* were standing by Nicephoros's chair, talking to him, and when Hagen came up, they both stared at him. One of the bearers was bringing his horse for him and Hagen turned to mount.

Nicephoros said, "He was magnificent, I cannot tell you how courageous and great of arms he is. Achilles would have turned and run from him. His voice was the bellow of a volcano as it roars the fury of the Almighty."

"Come on," Hagen said.

The bearers set off at their smooth flowing trot. Hagen's horse was practiced at keeping pace with the chair, staying just to the left side of it, and went along without any urging of Hagen's.

"You were magnificent," Nicephoros told him yet again, just as jubilantly.

"They were Greeks," Hagen said. "You people have no gift for it."

He told himself that it had been a good fight. He had taken wounds, but they had set on him unexpectedly, and he had killed two out of three of the men. The last had fled from the prospect of facing him alone.

He was tired. Had he been forced to fight another few moments, he might have gotten too tired to do it. He was turning Greek: he was getting soft. His mood sank again, as if lowering clouds of menace pressed down on him. He thought again of John Cerulis as a vast stinking fog that closed down on the City and invaded through the breath. The sense gnawed him of business undone, of something owed, of something to be justified. Why had he given up the list to John Cerulis? He had held her in his arms for twenty minutes only before they slew her. His heart ached for her like a raw wound. He followed Nicephoros up to the Palace and the gate shut on him.

The physician put Hagen's arm to soak in holy water and plastered the gash on his back with a bandage on which an appropriate Biblical verse was written. While the Frank sat on a bench in the sunny little sheltered courtyard, he could hear Nicephoros in the room behind him, describing the fight on the rooftop to someone else.

"Never a move wasted! He moved more like a great cat than a man —it was beautiful, a sort of dance. Makes you understand why it was so popular, when it was part of the Games."

Through the door behind Hagen a tide of people spilled—pages, one with a fan, one with a sunshade trimmed with ostrich plumes, and after them two women in sumptuous dress, and a crowd of others Hagen could not see—he knew the Empress was coming. A moment later he heard her voice.

"Who were they? Did you recognize any of them?"

Hagen wiggled his arm in the basin of water; the wound felt good, drawing and tightening as it healed. His whole body ached, every muscle sore, and he was still tired.

Constantinople was corrupting him, yet he could not go. He had a debt here, an obligation. Over and over in his mind he rode double down that dark road, he stopped with Theophano for that last kiss. Over and over, the arrow came. She was gone; she had given her life for something else, something he did not understand, and he had interfered and made a nothing of her sacrifice.

Deep in this black daydream, he caught a dazzling glimpse of gold, and stood up to face the Empress.

"Let me kill him," he said to her. "I could reach him even if a hundred men surrounded him, and I would gladly die doing it."

Her eyes were brilliant green, more wonderful than jewels. She laid her hand on his arm and gently urged him down again on the bench. "Tend your wounds. You have earned our deepest gratitude. They certainly meant to shoot Nicephoros through the window, had you not acted."

"Give me John Cerulis."

"My boy, my boy." She put out one hand, and her people encircled her, one bringing a chair, another the sunshade, the others straightening her silken skirts and her sleeves and her hair. "You must have faith in God, Hagen."

"Maybe God wants me to kill this pig."

"I feel not, my boy."

"He is killing as he chooses, you know—he will take you when he chooses. Will you not defend yourself? Let me have him."

"Sin cannot have consequences of virtue. My champion is Christ Himself, as I am His Basileus."

Hagen's head sank down between his shoulders; he felt himself smothering in the soft luxury of this place, where a woman could be king.

She said, "When you were travelling with John Cerulis, did you find anything remarkable? Anything at all? Did you talk with him?"

"I talked to him once or twice." He struggled to recall what they had said. "He seemed interested mostly in his food and drink and poetry."

"Can you remember anything he said—anything at all?"

"He is a serpent. He believes nothing but evil speech. He—"

Now Hagen thought of something and laughed. He raised his head, his gaze meeting the Empress's, intense and smiling at him. "He wanted to know about the favor that Michael wore, in the race that time—a scarf he wore on his arm. I told him it was a signal that the race was fixed."

For an instant her eyes were wide and fierce; then, like water bubbling up, her laughter rose. "And he believed you?"

"Yes. He believes all poison, nothing healthy will he hold in mind, but all wickedness. I told him the yellow scarf meant there was no fix, but a red one meant there was."

She laughed, long and richly, and he saw again what a beautiful woman she was, and wondered if she had men. He guessed not. She would give no man that power over her. He imagined seducing her; she loved luxury and touching, it would not be so hard. Then again he imagined being seduced by her, and saw that it would be like being eaten alive, and in a sudden cool reality knew why she had no men.

She was watching him with a broad smile on her face. "I beg your pardon. There was an attempt to fix one of the races—did you know that? While you were away. Fortunately Ishmael would not be bought."

"Ishmael." He remembered Ishmael, wishing this world away, and saw a connection there.

"How do your wounds feel? Will you heal swiftly, do you think?"

He moved his shoulders, putting off useless considerations. His back hurt when he shifted. "God willing."

"God willing." She leaned forward and laid her hand against his face, a maternal sort of blessing. He bowed; when he raised his head again she was going.

Nicephoros said, "Here, at the top of the wall."

He started up the steps that climbed the inside of the huge land wall, with one hand holding fast to an iron railing bolted to the bricks. Hagen went up after him.

The wall was made of the same dark yellow stone and darker brick the rest of Constantinople was built of. It rose up out of a thicket of sharp-smelling myrtle, rising twenty-five feet high to a top surface broad and smooth enough to ride a horse on. Nicephoros reached it and walked along it, going the opposite way from the closest tower, toward the Sea of Marmora. He beat his arms around him as he walked; the night wind was coming up. Hagen went along behind him, wondering why Nicephoros had brought him here.

They walked about a hundred feet along the top of the wall. The sun had just gone down. The twilight was rising off the sea like a transparent veil. Here the wall broke steeply downwards, down a short difficult slope toward the beach, and on the outward side was nothing but thickets and overgrown trees and wild meadows, while on the inside were groups of little houses, surrounded by gardens and goat pastures, in which, now, as the twilight deepened, one window after another grew yellow with the light of lamps. Nicephoros stopped.

"It was here," he said, "that the Virgin Mary appeared on the walls,

when the Arabs and their fleet were besieging the City; she came to
warn us that the infidels were launching a surprise attack. You can see
that cove, down there, where they came ashore in little boats."

He pointed down the hillside toward the sea. Hagen nodded; he
had been at the siege of Milan, and he saw the possibilities of an attack
up this slope.

Nicephoros was looking from one side of the wall to the other, from
the wilderness to the City, his head moving steadily back and forth. He
said, "I have been thinking of becoming a monk."

"A monk!"

The Treasurer sighed. With one hand he rubbed quickly at his huge
arched nose. "I come here, you see, because to me this is the edge of
the Empire. Not—we have territories outside the walls, of course, but
they are ancillary. It is here that Constantinople ends."

Hagen put his back to the brambly wilderness and stared into the
great City. Here, close to the wall, the houses were sparsely scattered
among fields and meadows, but as the slope mounted, rising and falling
in a succession of hills that climbed toward the great summit of the
headland where the Palace stood, the buildings thickened and gathered
to a solid mass of worked stone and tile roofs and domes. Over there he
could see the Mesê, where now the streetlamps were being lit, starting
at the Charisian Gate. The smoky orange flames in pairs mounted halfway up the uneven slope, and as he watched, more appeared, rising
through the gathering dusk like a bed of fallen stars.

He said, "To me, this City is like a woman, who turns her back on
me, but flirts with me over her shoulder, and seems ugly and plain at
first, but becomes more beautiful than any other, and is good to me and
foul to me—"

He stopped. He did not want to say what he felt, that the City's
fascination frightened him. He thought of Theophano. In his memory
she was pure and white and good as the Virgin herself, who had come
here to warn her people against evil, and he ached for what he had lost.

Nicephoros was saying, "Indeed. Well: corroboration from an unexpected source. I too feel her to be an illusion."

He locked his hands behind his back, looking out over the land
wall into the thorny thickets and tumbled boulders. Hagen could hear
the surf on the beaches of Marmora, and he could make out also the
sounds of animals in the wild brush, the birds hopping from branch to

branch, the first faint piping of the night frogs and the little tree-toads. Above the brush, the bats whirled and dove after insects invisible in the gathering darkness, and something larger was crashing through the brush almost directly below him, browsing. A deer, or a wild goat, perhaps.

Beside him the Treasurer's voice began again, freighted with meaning.

"Life, my friend, is a castle of illusion. The only reality is death. We may strive against it all we will, and imagine great bulwarks of art and science and faith to put it off, but in the end it takes every one of us. Christ Himself could not elude death."

Hagen glanced at him, wondering; he saw the Treasurer's face fixed in an expression of fierce decision.

"Yet even Christ had to live in the illusion," Nicephoros said. "He lived thirty-three years upon this earth, awaiting the moment of His Godhead, and while He lived, He lived in the Empire."

At that he caught a quick breath, as if he had walked into something. Hagen kept still. In Nicephoros's voice more than his words he sensed a struggle going on.

"If one must live in the illusion, even when the reality is elsewhere, then what matters is the quality of the illusion. There is this, or that." He indicated first the wilderness, and then the City. "There is the brutish life of savages, or the rational, humane life of Christian men."

Hagen said, "You think too much, Nicephoros, and act too little."

"Ah, yes. One might expect such criticism from such as yourself, my dear barbarian—in your smaller sphere, you may brawl and blunder as you will, harming no one but yourself. But my failures are disaster for the Empire."

"Then why are you becoming a monk?"

"I—" Nicephoros lifted his arms and let them fall. His gaze swiveled from the wilderness to the City and back again. Finally he turned to Hagen once more, and his face was grave and eaten with doubts. "As long as she needs me, of course, I will stay."

"Nicephoros, if you give it up, if all men of heart and mind give it up, who will do it?"

"Clowns, and fools, and wicked sinners," said Nicephoros. "Which is very little change, it seems to me."

Then suddenly he was weeping. Hagen stepped back, surprised at the vehemence of the other man's tears.

"I am sorry." The Treasurer struggled for composure. "A friend of mine died recently, I am not myself." His eyes burned lunatic bright behind their gloss of tears. Under his breath, he whispered, "But I am alive! Alive."

Hagen looked toward the City again. He was resisting the impulse to touch this Greek whose passions contended so nobly, who struggled so stubbornly to make sense of the inconceivable. Beside him, Nicephoros, with a certain superb practicality, blew his nose.

"You drove the Arabs back," Hagen said. "The City will survive this, too."

Nicephoros was putting away his napkin. He said, "It was my fault the Arabs came at all. I am not much of a soldier—she gave me an army, and I lost it." He threw back his shoulders, lifting his chest, bracing himself into a manly stature, like putting on a uniform. "Well: let us go back. There is much to do before dinner."

"As you will, Nicephoros."

They went down from the wall; they went back into the bosom of the City, glowing with the lights of the evening.

: 26 :

Ishmael was not at the underground stable of the Hippodrome, nor at the tavern where the racing teams gathered; no one there had seen him for days. Hagen went down into the City and found the charioteer's house.

He banged on the door with his fist; there was no answer. He stood there staring at the blank panel, wondering what he was doing here: Ishmael was no matter of his. None of this was any matter of his. Yet he knocked again on the door, and this time, someone answered.

"Yes?" The door opened a crack. A woman peered out, covering her face with the flat of her hand. "Yes? Yes?"

"I am looking for Ishmael." He struggled to remember the rest of the charioteer's name, and it leapt into his memory, the reverse of his own. "Mauros-Ishmael."

"He isn't here. Go away."

"Wait." He stuck his foot into the crack in the door to hold it open. "Has he been here recently?"

"Go away."

"When was the last time you saw him?"

At that, she melted into floods of tears, and sank down in the doorway, and the door swayed open. Weeping, she huddled at his feet, and from behind her came forward a little boy, unmistakably Ishmael's child, who said, "My father has been gone two days, sir."

"Where is he?"

"Down to the holy man—down to wait for the Heavenly City."

Now the woman lifted her head, her face smeared and red. "He says we are no more married! He says I must do for myself now—he won't care for us anymore—" She sobbed. "The neighbors have given me bread for the children the past two days, but what shall I do now?"

She reached out her hands toward Hagen, who recoiled from the need raw in her face, her desperate eyes. "I have no money—not a crumb in the house—please—"

Behind her the boy stood, silent, watching him, and now beside him an older child appeared, a girl. They said nothing; they only stared at him over their mother's head. Hagen thought, They could die and no one would notice, here, and in his mind saw them swept away, whirling like fallen leaves along the great rushing torrent. He pulled the purse from his belt.

"Here. Feed them." He shook out coins, the money Nicephoros had given him for saving his life. The money bounced ringing off the stone doorstep. "I'll get him back." He turned and went long-striding off toward the street, to his horse.

Ishmael was half-drunk. There was nothing else to do but drink; he had lain here on this meadow grass for hours, waiting for some sign, for the holy man to come again and preach, for the Heavenly City to show itself again in the sky, but nothing had happened, except that more people had drifted down from Constantinople into the fields below the camp of John Cerulis.

He supposed he should be praying, but he could not. The world was rushing to its end, surely; there was no more preparing for it, only the final event itself. He wished the holy man would speak again. It was hard to keep his mind focussed on eternity without some help from God.

He lifted the leather flask of wine and drank again. His stomach hurt.

All around him were others waiting for the Coming of Christ, some praying, some talking, some asleep or eating or drinking—it seemed incongruous that these gross functions of the flesh should be necessary, now, but people could not be expected to become saints overnight. Ishmael did not watch the ragged man who was going from sleeper to sleeper, fingering their clothes, and taking little things away. None of that mattered anyway. The material would all disappear, in the Heavenly City; they would walk around in shapes of pure flame. He squeezed his eyes shut, imagining the city, its white streets, its vaulting domes and towers.

With his eyes shut, he swayed, half-lost in drink, but he did not lie down. If he lay down they would rob him.

Behind him a horse snuffled. The familiar stable sound cut through the haze of drink and the bonds of faith and touched the quickest part of him, and he gasped out loud. He had not seen his horses in days. He fought against the upsurge of anger at God, that finding God meant giving up his dearest love, and the struggle had him rigid and inward for a long moment, until Hagen sank down beside him.

"Ishmael."

"What are you doing here, blasphemer?"

The barbarian sat on his heels. He did not look at Ishmael, but turned his gaze forward, toward the camp of John Cerulis, and his jaw was set. His cheek was faintly pocked from some old disease. His pale eyes and his hair were bright in the sunlight.

He said, "I just left your wife, Ishmael. She is afraid, and alone."

Ishmael bit his lips. Oh, these were temptations of the Devil, to deprive him of the Heavenly City.

"I gave her some money," Hagen said.

Up there in that camp, somewhere, was the holy man who could call the City down; why would he not preach again? When he spoke, Ishmael was certain of everything.

"Are you a man, then, to let another man take care of your woman and your children?"

Ishmael flung himself sideways onto the barbarian, snarling; he attacked him so unexpectedly that Hagen went down flat on the soft ground under him, and Ishmael pounded him three or four times hard in the head. Under him the barbarian rolled over and flung him off. Ishmael skidded backward through the dirt.

"Fight! Fight!"

From all around the meadow people came running, joyful, toward this diversion. Ishmael got to his feet. Startled, he looked around him at the ring of cheering onlookers, urging him on.

Hagen was up on his knees, his hands at his sides. His hair was dirty. From the crowd a clod of earth flew at him, and he ignored it. Slowly he got up onto his feet.

"Your Heavenly City," he said, and spat.

Ishmael raised his fists at him, and the crowd screamed, delighted. "Kill him! Beat him up!"

Through the luxuriant silk sleeve of Hagen's stola, a crimson stain was seeping. Ishmael struggled with himself, trying to keep his temper up, but he saw now that the barbarian was wounded. And Hagen was going. His face twisted with contempt, he started toward his horse.

"Keep your damned dream, Ishmael."

"Wait," Ishmael said.

Hagen did not wait. He walked straight toward the horse, and the people blocking his way jeered and thumbed their noses and flew their fingers at him and yielded a way for him through their midst. The blood was streaming down Hagen's hand, dripping from his middle fingertips.

"Wait," Ishmael called, and went after him.

The Frank ignored him. Reaching his horse, he took up the reins and put his foot in the stirrup and mounted, and Ishmael got hold of the bridle.

"Can you make it back to the Palace? You're hurt."

"I don't need you, Ishmael." He closed his good hand into a fist and jammed it against his arm, to stop the bleeding.

"I'll go with you." Ishmael led his horse toward the road.

Hagen said nothing. There was the sound of tearing cloth; when Ishmael looked back Hagen was wadding up a pack of cloth against the hole in his arm.

"What happened?" Ishmael asked, when he and Hagen were sitting down in the tavern near the Hippodrome.

"I got into a fight."

The wound had stopped bleeding. Hagen sat slouched on the bench, drinking red wine. Ishmael had gone to the stable and seen to his horses, and now he meant to go back down to the meadow again, to await the Heavenly City, but surely it would not matter much if he stayed a little while, here where he had had so many happy times. He nodded to the tavern wench for a cup of wine.

"You will not race, then?" Hagen asked.

"I shall never race again."

"God, you're a fool, Ishmael."

"Shut up. You won't think me a fool, when the earth is being consumed, and you with it, and I am safe in the Heavenly City."

"That did not look like a congregation of saints down there today."

"God does not work according to the rules of men."

"That's what you told me before. When is Saint Febronia's Day?"

"Three days from now," Ishmael said.

"And then the holy man will enter the City preaching, and also the race will be run?"

"So."

"And on that day, John Cerulis will become emperor."

"No! On that day, all this shall fall away, and we shall become saints," Ishmael said.

But he had to struggle to believe it. Here, in this place where he had been so often, his certainties went otherwise than up to God. He shut his eyes. What a weakling he was, how his faith failed him. Or he failed his faith. He thought of his wife, depending on some stranger's money to feed her children.

The Devil did this to him—tormented his mind like this.

"Here is the Prince," Hagen said.

Ishmael straightened. Prince Michael was coming into the tavern.

The usual flock of hangers-on swarmed around him, but Michael seemed utterly alone in their midst. He walked upright as a column of marble, his eyes wide and fierce. Ishmael had seen him before, on the day before a race, and he always had this look, this soaring pride, this fierce intent purpose barely restrained.

Without realizing it, he stood up on his feet before the champion. Michael stopped to stare at him.

"Will you race?" he said.

Ishmael met his eyes, and made his tongue move. "I have given myself to God, Michael. I will not go back to Mammon."

Across the face of the Prince the dark anger flashed like a streak of lightning. "I should have known you haven't the heart for it."

That fell across Ishmael's soul like a lash, and he jumped up in his place, facing Prince Michael. "It's God's will, Michael—"

"God's will!" Michael snorted, contemptuous. "You should know by now, Ishmael, that nothing matters but the race." His gaze moved, going past Ishmael, and his voice changed slightly; now he was talking to Hagen, and there was a guarded respect in his voice. "Can you make no sense to him?"

Hagen grunted. He sat there with his arms laid across the tabletop, his cup between his fists. "No. Nor can you, if you think nothing matters more than horse-races."

"Oh? And if I disagree with you, will you hack me up with your sword, warrior? Is that more honest and just than the Hippodrome? You live in a simpler world than I do, if you believe that."

He turned to Ishmael again and their eyes met. Michael lowered his voice to a murmur. "If the Judgment comes, Ishmael, He will take you for what you are, and what you are best is in the arena."

"You speak with the voice of the Devil," Ishmael cried. He pushed through the cordon of men between him and the door; he had to get away from here; he knew if he lingered they would seduce him into it again, into that heat of struggle and uncertainty, death and power. Outside in the street, the sunlight was so strong he blinked and flung up his hand to block the glare. Half-blinded, he wobbled away down the street.

"Ishmael! Ishmael!"

His own name burned like a whip now. He flinched from the sound of his name. In his path a ragged dirty old man appeared, his head wrapped in a brown cowl, a bundle of herbs tied around his neck: one of the soothsayers.

"Ishmael! You will win. This time you will carry off the Golden Belt! I saw it—I saw the omens in a dream, Ishmael!"

The charioteer staggered; he ran down the street away from the old man, away from the tavern, going toward the Mesê, the way to the holy man. He had to reach the holy man, who made life so simple, so bearable. Who would bring the Heavenly City to him. He hoped no one had stolen his place in eternity. Swiftly he raced down the street full of people.

In the tavern, Hagen watched Ishmael go, and his heart fell. When Prince Michael came in, he had seen in Ishmael's face that he would return, take up the challenge, and be a man again. He glowered up at the Prince, who still stood on the far side of the table, watching him, his head back, aloof and arrogant.

"I hear you are a veritable Achilles," Michael said. "It bears some remembering that he was a barbarian also."

"Is there any way to bring Ishmael back to his right mind?"

Michael laughed. He pulled back a chair and dropped into it, half the table between him and Hagen. "Have no concern. When the horns call forth the Blues and the Greens, on Saint Febronia's Day, Ishmael will be there. He could not do otherwise and be Ishmael."

His hangers-on were still pressing close around him. He swung his head, driving them back with the force of his gaze, and when the area around them had cleared a little, he turned to Hagen again.

"Let me talk to you, Hagen."

That surprised the Frank, that Michael knew his name. He laced his fingers together. "Speak, Patrician."

"Prince," Michael said, correcting him. "We are Athenian nobles, not city courtiers with long fingernails and flowers in their underwear."

He stopped. A girl was bending over the table with a cup for him and a jug of wine; she fawned on him, but he did not seem to notice. Hagen watched him curiously. A man with no more consequence to his life than a game, he needed that overblown arrogance.

"What I want to ask you—" Michael lifted his head. "Do you know where Theophano is?"

"She is dead," Hagen said.

"Dead."

"John Cerulis had her killed. Why do you ask?"

"Oh, well. We were lovers once. I liked her. I noticed she was gone, but she was often gone, on errands for my cousin." Michael frowned, his eyes focussed on the empty space before him. All his strut and swagger left him; startled, Hagen saw that Michael was younger than he was by several years.

"She was such a beautiful girl," Michael said.

"Oh, yes," Hagen replied. "Almost as interesting as a horse-race."

The Prince gave a light, glib phony laugh. "Oh, it would have to be a hell of a horse-race."

Hagen swung at him. Smoothly Michael wheeled around, half rising from his seat, and his hand clamped tight on Hagen's wrist. It was like catching his arm in a closing door; Hagen could not move his fist an inch either forward or backward. Michael leaned into his face.

"Stop milling at me—I don't take that from anyone!"

Hagen's breath was stuck fast in his throat. Michael's strength amazed him; for a long moment, staring into the other man's eyes, he worked over in his mind a way to beat him, but then, sighing out his lungs, he relaxed, leaning back, his arm loose in the other man's hold.

"Let go of me."

Through the torn, stained sleeve of his shirt, the fresh blood suddenly bloomed. Michael saw it, and his eyes widened. Letting go of Hagen, he slid away into his seat again.

"I'm sorry. I didn't know you were hurt."

Hagen pulled his sleeve down. "You're strong, for a Greek."

"Therefore you want to fight me? God, you barbarians."

Hagen laughed, seeing this a new way, and shook his head. "I don't have anything to prove to you."

"Nor I to you," Michael said swiftly.

Hagen reached for his wine cup. "Whatever you say." Ishmael had told him that he was wrong about Prince Michael, and perhaps he was. It would be hard to be a man in Constantinople, with every breath prescribed by law.

"How did she die?" Michael asked.

"I told you, John Cerulis had her killed."

"And you are letting it go at that?"

Hagen raised his eyebrows at him. "Your cousin will not let me take him."

He raised his cup in a salute. "To Theophano."

"To Theophano." Michael lifted his cup in answer. They drank deep.

"She would never have gone home with me anyway," Hagen said. "She would have never liked Braasefeldt."

" 'Braasefeldt.' What a name. That's where you come from? What is it like?"

"Not like here."

In his mind, he summoned up the place, the dark swift-flowing many-fingered river, rushing through the fields and marshes, in among the wet knees of trees, and on the high ground, the hall, its doorposts made of the trunks of trees still rooted in the earth. He smelled the reeds and the river and the sea and heard the wind, and felt the icy cold of the winter mornings when the first sun brought the mist like wraiths up from the flat water.

"No, in truth," Michael said, "I doubt Theophano would have done well in your Brazen Field." He propped his elbows on the table. "Do you want to go back there? Why?"

"It's my home. I have things to do there—" His mill, his dike, his reclaimed fields, his ripening oats and hay, the wealth of which money was the counterfeit. "Besides, when John Cerulis is emperor—"

"John Cerulis will never become emperor."

"He is becoming so even now. All over the City, he is killing off the Empress's supporters, and she will do nothing. I talked to her of it and she gave me some drivel about God and faith—"

"She will overcome him," Michael said. He gestured, and a wench brought them another jug.

"She is a woman. What can she do against a man as determined as John Cerulis?"

Michael leaned toward him over the table. "Don't be a fool, Hagen. Don't think your balls are made of gold. My cousin may be a woman, but mark this: she was born the daughter of a poor provincial nobleman; she had no treasure, no friends, no education, not even a place in the City, but today she is Basileus. John Cerulis is rich, but he came into it with his christening, and although he has been plotting all his life, he has no more power now than he was born to."

Hagen reached for his cup. "As Ishmael says, the ways of God are inscrutable."

Michael shrugged. "Water always runs downhill. I see no need to find the hand of God in every river."

"You're a very reasonable man. I thought that was against the law here."

"I'm allowed to be, since I confine my use of it to horse-races."

Hagen was getting drunk. He reached for the cup again, wanting to be drunker. He had made a mistake about Michael; his passions had fooled his judgment. Now, finding the Prince's eyes on him, he lifted his cup in a little salute.

"Pax."

They drank.

⋄ 27 ⋄

In the morning, with the rest of the Imperial Service, Nicephoros heard mass in the Church of the Holy Wisdom, and saw once again the Crowned Christ before him in the person of the Basileus. Together with his fellows, he knelt down and put his face to the floor and worshipped her. Overhead, the great dome seemed to float upon the radiance of light that streamed through the windows, as if, when Justinian built this place, he made a union here between Heaven and earth.

In his prayers Nicephoros begged God for peace, for guidance, and for answers to his questions. His mind was in possession of a devil. Over and over the vision of the City Prefect, with the rope around his neck, presented itself to his inner eye; since the massacre had begun of John Cerulis's victims, the strangled man had come to mean the Empire, dying in the grip of a malevolent ambition.

I will become a monk, he repeated, a verbal drug to stupefy the action of his mind; yet this expedient served nothing; with clarity undimmed, intensity undiluted, the vision forced itself upon him, not as something complete and finished but as a riddle which he had to answer.

He had no answer. *I will become a monk,* he told himself, and shut his eyes, and longed for sleep, or drink, or opium to quell this dream.

After the mass he went into the vestibule of the church, where behind several painted screens of wood, the Empress's women were removing her diadem and robes of gold. Kneeling down, Nicephoros pressed his lips to the floor, and taking from his clothes a letter he offered it to the Basileus.

"What is this?" Irene looked at the oblong of paper in her hand.

"It was written by the City Prefect," Nicephoros said, in a steady voice. "It was conveyed to me by his executors, who found it among his other effects, addressed to me."

She gave him a sharp glance, opened the paper, and began to read.

"My dear Nicephoros," the letter began; Nicephoros had read it over and over, his friend's voice sounding in his ears. "When you come to read this, I shall be dead. You will blame yourself, but you are blameless—it was I who condemned myself to everlasting torment, when I corrupted my office.

"Now, at the extremity of my pitiful ruined life, I have yet one more crime to confess to you. Because, dear Nicephoros, you were wrong about me. It was not my misuses of the money from my office that made it impossible for me to face the Basileus. It was something far worse—the knowledge that I had joined in a conspiracy against her, and the fear that she, who reads men's souls as easily as men read books, would see what I was doing. Yes. I lent my support to the cause of John Cerulis.

"Why? I don't know. Boredom, I suppose. False pride, that a man should have to bow down before a woman. Love of intrigue. The inability to do well at my proper work. Who knows? I did it. So be it."

At that, the Basileus paused, and her eyes stabbed at Nicephoros before her; her face was harsh as a mask of the Gorgon. Nicephoros looked away.

"Now," she read on, "I will do whatever can be done to redeem my disgrace."

What followed was a betrayal of John Cerulis. The Prefect in three or four quick paragraphs described the inner workings of the entire conspiracy: the passwords, the payoffs, who had what power, and at what signal would use it. Where the treasure was; who his spies were. Everything was there.

"Too late, perhaps," said Nicephoros. "Yet he did the honorable thing, at the end."

"Too late," she said, in a meditative voice. She folded the letter. With a gesture, she sent away her waiting women, and nodding to Nicephoros drew him after her into the back of the vestibule, where a little window opened on the garden; outside, a mulberry tree was bearing fruit, littering the ground beneath.

"Had we known all this a week sooner," Nicephoros said, "we might have saved many lives."

"Perhaps." Her voice was still thin, restrained, concealing her anger, he thought. "Tomorrow is Saint Febronia's Day. Tomorrow John will enter Constantinople with his holy man. But every soul in the City will be at the Hippodrome, waiting for the race for the Golden Belt."

Nicephoros bowed in response. He kept silent, thinking that John surely knew this as well as they did, and when all attention was focussed on the horse-race, the moment would be perfect to seize control of the government, now decimated and half-paralyzed by the assassinations of the past days.

"He will strike then," she said, in her cool, tight voice, looking down at the letter in her hand.

"Indeed," said Nicephoros.

"Yet perhaps this last pitiable gesture—this effort at atonement— will not be in vain. Here, Nicephoros." She put the letter into his hand. "On the day of the race, you will take what this letter gives you. Seize John's treasure and his fortresses, confiscate all his belongings, in the name of the Basileus."

"Yes, Augustus."

"Then if John Cerulis and the Basileus should come to be the same, on the day after Saint Febronia's—"

She shrugged. Her face was hard, sucked dry, and older than he ever remembered seeing her. He stared at her a moment, shocked. He had not seen before how thin she was becoming. Her eyes were sunken in hollows of bone and failing flesh, camouflaged with make-up. The Parakoimomenos had said that she was sick. Nicephoros held his breath, fighting against the quivering panic in his belly: he saw death in her face.

She said, "Perhaps he would enjoy watching the race from the Imperial balcony."

"What?" Nicephoros said, startled.

"Issue him the invitation. This time, maybe, he will not decline it, if the messenger be clean." She laughed, a sound that raised the hackles at the back of his neck; her eyes were too bright, too intense, like a flame fighting against the wind. "He may watch the race from beneath the purple."

"Yes, Basileus." Had she gone mad, at the last? With the whole of her power falling to pieces around her, why would she invite the author of her misfortunes to a place of honor at her side? Now her gaze fell on him, and her lips smoothed into a gentle smile.

"Nicephoros, you old fool. Do you blame yourself for the Prefect's death? Yes, I see you do. What an old fool you are." She put out her hand and touched his cheek. Confused and miserable, he sank to his knees, the letter in his hand. When he looked up, she was going.

Ishmael waited until dusk fell, and stole up to the edge of John Cerulis's camp, spread out over the low crown of a hillock north of the City walls. A ring of bonfires, for which the soldiers had stripped the whole area of wood, lit up the border of the camp, and the guards were supposed to march with sword and axe along the spaces between each blaze. Of late, however, they had grown easy and confident, and now sat in groups around the largest fire, talking and drinking. Ishmael drifted around the outside of the ring until he found a place unguarded and walked into the camp.

Three large silky tents stood on the flat ground, and many smaller shelters filled up the sloping spaces. As he walked through the little city of cloth, a noise warned him, and he stood in the shadow to watch John Cerulis, the center of a cavalcade, march by on his way to his dinner. Tumblers preceded him, and flutes and drums, and John himself wore a tunic of cloth of gold that shimmered in the torch-light of the procession. Ishmael realized that this man believed himself already emperor.

He had given little thought to John Cerulis in this. If the world ended, of course, it did not matter who was emperor. But it was so hard to keep faith. The world was here, insistent, forcing itself in on his senses, filling up his mind with trivial things, like eating, and wanting his wife now, and, above all, the race, the Golden Belt, the challenge that he ached so much to meet. It had been days since he saw the Heavenly City, days since he heard Daniel, and he needed to hear him again, now, face to face.

He walked back and forth through the camp, stopping at each of the tents, and watching who came and left; if none, then he went in and looked, and satisfying himself that the holy man was not there, moved on. Most of the people in the camp were involved in feeding John Cerulis his dinner; nobody stopped him or even looked his way.

In the end, he found him, not under a roof at all, but in the back of the camp, near the latrines and the picketed horses, sitting with his back against a dead tree. Ishmael almost walked past him without seeing him. He stopped and stared at the old man for a long while, unsure, and afraid to speak.

"Who are you?" Daniel said, at last.

"I am—" Ishmael knelt down, his hands together. "Master, I am one who needs you desperately."

"Come closer."

Ishmael crept closer on his knees, and the holy man peered at him, frowning.

"Well? What do you want?"

"I want—"

He fell down on his face beside the holy man, and sobbed.

"I want the Heavenly City. I saw it, when you called it down— but now, I cannot—I have lost my faith. I need you to tell me again that the City will come, and that I can enter into it, and be safe and sure forever."

For a moment, silent, on his face on the ground, he waited for the reassuring fatherly words. Then something struck him sharply over the head.

He yelped, startled, and put his hand to his head. The old man glared at him. He brandished the stick at Ishmael again.

"You wretch. You want it made easy for you, do you? Do you want the City of God? Then come with me, boy, back to the desert, to the barren mountains. Eat thorns, and drink the alkali, let the sun burn you, the night wind freeze you—for there is the City of God! Not ease and luxury, boy, but suffering and death are the City of God! Pain and suffering and struggle and death!"

He struck Ishmael over the head again, and the charioteer crouched and flung up his hand to ward off the blows. The holy man lowered his staff. With a look of contempt he turned his face deliberately away from Ishmael and composed himself again in his inward thoughts, blocking out the world.

Ishmael straightened slowly. As if the blows had broken open the shell of illusion, he saw in a new way, fresh and clear. He saw how he had been gulled, or how he had gulled himself.

As the Heavenly City faded away from his mind, there rose up strong and irresistible another place, the Hippodrome, the crunch of the sand, the smell of the excited horses, the roar of the crowd, the passion of the race. He backed away from the old man, suddenly in a haste; with every second the lure of the Hippodrome grew stronger. What was he doing here, with the race only days away? At the edge of the camp, he whirled and ran.

Daniel escaped once, and ran away toward the wilderness, but John Cerulis's men caught him and brought him back to the camp. That he took for a sign that God had work for him yet in the affairs of the new emperor.

On Saint Febronia's Day he would enter Constantinople, and preach again to the multitude, and he decided to denounce John Cerulis then, and cause his downfall. But then John Cerulis summoned him before him and said that there would be no great entry into the City after all.

"The usurping female has proclaimed a challenge race in the Hippodrome for that day," John said, sitting in his ivory chair, smiling. "No one would come to watch you or hear you preach, and therefore it is a waste of time. I suspect, anyway, that your purpose in my elevation has been fulfilled. We shall keep you by us for the while, and when we have been crowned and enthroned, shall find you a quiet monastery to retire to."

"Why can I not go back to my mountain?" Daniel asked.

The Emperor's lean pale face elongated with his smile. "We feel perhaps it were better you did not have so much freedom. The temptations of the world might overwhelm your tender spirit. We shall see that your saintliness is properly maintained."

Daniel backed away, repulsed, as if the man lounging in the chair before him had been transformed into a giant reptilian slug. Another man came up to the new emperor and knelt beside his chair and whispered in his ear, and John laughed.

"She has played into my hands this time. The garrotte is closing around her neck, and now she has given me the last necessary fitting for it—on the day of the Challenge Race, she shall wear my crown no more!"

Daniel crept away out of the tent. No one bothered him, so long as he made no effort to leave. He went into the back of the camp, near the horse lines, and sat down under a poor wretched tree that had been hacked up by the soldiers, and thought deeply on his sins.

He had made this possible. He had proclaimed John Cerulis the emperor. Now God was reminding him, over and over, that it was his duty to rectify that evil.

While he was sitting there, God sent a messenger to him. In the shape of a townsman from Constantinople, an angel appeared before him, and reminded him rudely of the sermon he had preached, and of the delusion he had brought on the people of Constantinople. He sent the angel off with assurances of his own understanding and settled himself again to his plan for the destruction of John Cerulis.

On Saint Febronia's Day, not too early, because John Cerulis did not rise early in the morning, they set off to enter Constantinople. They went in by the gate at the foot of the Mesê. Daniel rode on a white donkey with a guard on either side to lead it. Behind him came the train of the new Emperor.

They went in through the gate, and a little crowd gathered to greet them sent up a thin piping cheer. Little children with garlands of flowers on their heads ran out to scatter a few rose petals on the street before Daniel and the Emperor, and music played.

Slowly they made their way up the Mesê. Daniel had never been to the City before and he gawked around him, amazed, at the broad white street, the rows of columns, the fora spreading out around him in great luxurious spaces of pavement and shops, fountains and statues. They passed a church with a roof of gold, and another from which music sounded. Steadily the road led them upward, toward the Palace, now visible on the highland, against the sky, a clutter of white horizontal lines, with the great dome of the Church of the Holy Wisdom a soft breast among the rigid angles.

Here, as the little parade climbed the last few yards to the bronze gateway into the Palace, they met the first real crowds; the stragglers on their way to the Hippodrome filled the last street they crossed, and some turned curiously to look at Daniel on his pretty donkey, and John Cerulis with his feathered parasol and swarms of hangers-on, but most of them went on shouting about the races, arguing, and making bets.

They entered the Palace through the great double gate of the Chalke, passing between mosaics of outlandish beasts and men in armor. There they were met by a little group of gaudy men who bowed and scraped to John Cerulis and escorted him away. Daniel was shuttled off into a chapel, with some of the guards, as a creature of no importance.

He went toward the altar. There on the domed ceiling was a great image of God, the ultimate blasphemy, as if God were contained within the form of a human; Daniel drew his eyes away. He felt contaminated by this place. Soon, he told himself, it would be over. He would recompense the Lord for the evil he had done, bringing John Cerulis here, and go back to the mountain, to the hard rocks and the bitter water and the hawks and the enormous sky. He sank down on the slates of the floor, waiting.

⋮ 28 ⋮

The crowd was boiling into the Hippodrome, a wild rush of bodies and noise, swiftly mounting the tiers of seats, filling up the lower reaches, and spilling steadily higher and higher along the sides. Hagen went up to the top level of the racecourse, where the broken statues stood, and worked his way through the chunks of worn marble, the bits of bodies and topless pedestals, until he stood above the Imperial balcony.

The great purple canopy floated above it, gripped at the corners on golden spikes, and buoyed up in the middle by the wind off the sea. Nobody was under it yet. He sank down on his heels to wait.

Whatever happened today, he meant to see John Cerulis die. It did not interest him who was emperor, but John Cerulis would not be. He meant to tear up this foul weed by the roots, and if it required him to die also, that was a fair price.

The crowd had taken up all the seats. Down on the oval of sand, several people were running up and down, pretending to be horses, as he had seen them do the first time he came to the races here. The people on the seats nearest him were eating food out of baskets, shouting to their neighbors, spreading cushions and robes on the hard benches.

This section was clearly one of Blues. Each wore his color on his arm, a flutter of silk, and some of the boisterous young men lower down the long swoop of the benches had brought a great blue banner that they strung up across their tier. From across the way came hoots and shrieks of derision as another group unfurled a long green banner in response.

Now the roar of the mob rose in a crescendo to a blast of sound. The Empress was coming out on to the balcony.

A glittering figure dressed all in gold, she blessed them all; her arms flashed in the sun when she made the Sign of the Cross in the air. Her people cheered her with lusty voices. Then behind her, coming out on to the balcony through the door at the back, came John Cerulis.

Hagen's hand slid down his side to his sword hilt. He had not seen the man who had murdered Theophano since that night in the tent when he killed Karros. The would-be emperor was dressed in spotless white, with gold embroidery and jewels on cuffs and neckline, and a dark red cloak over one shoulder, caught up in a big filigree brooch. After him, into the balcony, came an enormous man.

This man wore armor, and carried a two-handed axe. He looked like a giant from an old story, with his curly black beard and red headband. Hagen pursed his lips. This was going to be more of a problem than he had wanted. He crouched down between a marble boy and a bull's head, his eyes on the figures below him; they were so close he could hear the low melodious voices of the Empress's women as they made her comfortable in her chair. The little girl was there, Philomela, with a lute, her cheeks red.

The horns blew. The chariots were coming out on to the track.

Hagen stood up, his eyes keen on the little bouncing cars and the leaping horses. The roar of the crowd that greeted each one was like thunder in his ears. He had not seen Ishmael since the day in the tavern when he had said he would not race.

The first car that emerged carried the Green color, a wisp of a scarf in his leather cap, but was not Ishmael. These horses were matched bays, which jittered and pranced and reeled from the crowd noise like virgins at a wedding. After them came Prince Michael.

The voice of the crowd swelled and swelled until Hagen thought his ears would burst, and the enormous sound coalesced into a single roared name: "Michael! Michael! Michael!" The whole Hippodrome seemed to rock with it. Hagen's back prickled up; he had been a fool to think Michael was powerless.

Down there, on the track, the Prince urged his team in a quick burst past the leader, galloped them easily down the track, acknowledging the adulation of the crowd. He wheeled them neatly around at the end of the oval and went back to his place in line. On his arm, a red scarf waved.

Hagen grunted, wondering what that meant; he thought he had invented it, back in John Cerulis's camp, but here it was, actually happening, as if by force of mind he had brought it into being.

Someone had. His gaze slipped sideways, down to the only other person who knew of that, down to the Empress.

She sat there with her hands in her lap, smiling. He had seen matronly women at the court in Aachen sit like that, their tatting on their knees, smiling benignly on the antics of children. Michael had said she was capable of anything. Hagen had not believed it. Now he opened his mind to suspicion, and in that space, she seemed to swell and grow.

The crowd's voice dimmed an instant, and then shrieked up, piercing, wild, full of one name.

"Ishmael! Ishmael!"

Hagen jerked his head around; he looked down on the track, and saw the blacks and greys wheeling out on to the course. The driver raised his hand to the crowd, and Hagen, out of himself, beat his palms together, delighted.

The fourth team appeared, and the racers formed up a rank and advanced toward the ribbon, the horses' necks arched to the bits. They pranced and cavorted on their slim long legs, and the cars bounced after them. The crowd hushed its voice. Leaning forward, they hovered on the edge of their benches, waiting.

Ishmael leaned back, getting his weight into the leathers, and spared a quick glance sideways. The driver next to him was a novice from somewhere east of the City, who probably had no chance. Just beyond him, Michael stood in his car, his head high.

Their eyes met, Michael's and Ishmael's, for an instant. They straightened forward again, and all over Ishmael's body his skin tingled alive, unbearably sensitive. He could not keep from smiling. Before him lay the track; his horses were in his hands.

"Yah!"

The boy between him and Michael burst forward in a false start. Ishmael's horses leapt after him, and Ishmael reined them back. To the hoots and jeers of the crowd, the boy, red-faced, turned his team and circled decorously around the line and came up into his place again, between Michael and Ishmael. He mumbled some apology, and then, before anyone could speak in answer, the horns blasted.

The horses sprang forward. Ishmael was rocked back off balance, gasping, and nearly dropped his whip. On his left the boy was surging along even with him; just beyond him, Michael, also taken unawares by the quick start, was a little behind. The team on Ishmael's right had been left stock-still at the ribbon.

"Go!" Ishmael shouted. He gathered his reins, steadied his horses and urged them on. If there was an advantage here, he meant to seize it.

The sand splattered the front of the car. The lashing tails of his horses struck his wrists like tiny whips. They swept down on the curve, and he collected the inside horses and drove the outside wheelers on faster, and they whirled into the curve in a perfect line.

The boy was good at this as well; he held the curve as tight as Ishmael, but not as fast, and gained nothing of the track. On the inside, Michael was surging ahead, carried into the lead by the shorter distance he had to travel, and whirling into the straightaway they pounded down the track at full speed, Michael, the boy, and Ishmael, a dozen horses head to head across the track.

Ishmael screamed. He felt the power of his horses like an irresistible call. They flew down the center of the track as if the wind bore them, and at the far end, swinging into the curve, were half a length ahead of Michael and the boy.

They wheeled around the curve, and the boy, lashing his horses, overestimated their speed. They lost stride and faltered, and Ishmael shot out ahead of them on the one side and Michael surged to the lead on the other. The track curved around and straightened out before them again, and now, with the crowd howling and stamping its feet and screaming and weeping and pleading and raging in triumph, Ishmael and Michael went head to head down the straight, their horses flattened to their work.

Stride for stride they raced the length of the straightaway, and in the curve, they wheeled around in a spinning, sliding spray of sand, Ishmael's horses like a shadow of the team on the inside. He gripped the reins in fists as soft and pliable as clay, that yielded to every motion of the horses' heads, hands firm and strong as iron, that held them steady when they needed it.

He had never felt so alive. He knew he was going to win.

They rolled into the straightaway again, still head to head, and now Ishmael asked his horses for more speed, a little more, a little more yet, and as they gave it to him, calling up from the depths of their blood the strength and courage of generations of champions, he steadied their power and blended it together and asked, again, for more.

They answered him. By slow inches they crept into the lead. Ishmael saw Michael's head turn, noticing the blacks and greys draw past his own horses, and saw the champion bend to his work. He raised his hands, begging for more, and his own team responded. They dragged up the last of their strength, and for half the length of the Hippodrome, although they won back not an inch of the lead Ishmael's horses had stolen from them, they gave up not an inch more.

They raced into the final turn. Ishmael felt his inside flanker come back a little, and guessed the horse was tiring; he drew them all in slightly, to rest them for the last run down the straight to the finish line. Beside him, Michael's team surged up into the lead again. Michael was calling to them, pleading with them. Their ears swept back to catch his voice, and they strained for more speed.

Coming into the straightaway, they were head to head again, the

Blue and the Green, and the crowd surged to its feet. The noise was like an ocean that swept down on the racers. Ishmael felt the tremor through the reins as his horses shrank from it. He held them on line. He needed no whip. They turned into the straightaway and before them was the finish line, and they raced forward toward it, bringing from the last of their heart and muscle another swelling surge of speed.

Michael's team stayed with them, their heads bobbing in unison. Ishmael screamed and laughed and sang and wept, the fire of God dancing in his veins. The finish line swept toward him. Still Michael's horses clung to a hair's breadth of a lead. But now Ishmael's horses lunged forward, faster with each stride, flinging themselves at the victory. They swept out ahead of the Blue team, by a head, by half a length, by a full length, and charged across the line, the winners.

Irene sank back into her chair, half out of breath. "Ah, what a race."

"A thrilling finish," said John Cerulis, smiling. He drew his napkin through his fingers, his eyes keen on her. "Of course, one that you knew beforehand."

"I! Never. I would have thought no man alive could defeat Michael and his team."

John sniffed at her. "You dissemble to one with inner knowledge, Madame. I am aware that the scarf your worthy cousin wore predicated a loss on the track, and doubtless a great win at the bet-makers' expense."

Irene leaned back and laughed, long and richly. "Oh, no, my fool. You are in serious error there, although I know by what course you came into such a mistake. No, seeker of illusions. The scarf is a signal to my people, that your plot has been traduced."

"My plot! I assure you, lowly born one—"

"Hold! What is this?"

Irene leaned forward, her eyes caught on a motion on the track. The crowd was surging in its place, content as a fat man at a feast, but there on the golden sand, a strange figure had appeared, gyrating with its scrawny limbs, and shouting.

"What is that?" she said, and looking around her saw John Cerulis canted forward to see, frowning.

"That fool," he said, under his breath. "It is the holy man, Daniel."

Irene clenched her fist. All the many threads of this were drawing together now; she felt a tingle of alarm at this unexpected intrusion of some force she had not foreseen, that might wreck all her plans.

Down on the track, the holy man was reaching up his arms, was calling out, his voice thin and piping from his distance, and yet audible. The crowd hushed, and he began to speak.

"This John Cerulis," he shouted, "this man who wants to be emperor—he is no more emperor than any one of you!"

Irene glanced at the man at her side and saw his face harden. She refrained from smiling.

"I made a mistake!" the holy man was screaming. "When I proclaimed him emperor—that was not God's choice, but a mistake!"

Through the crowd, now, as voices carried on this message to those too far to hear it, a ripple of laughter spread.

"Denounce these wicked men!" the holy man was crying. "Come to God—give off the unnecessary trappings of pride and power and wealth. You need no City, no emperor—only God. These races with which they stuff your ears and eyes are tawdries, to deceive you!"

At that, the crowd growled at him. But Daniel heeded nothing; he danced up and down on his thin knobby legs, waving his arms.

"These champions, this Golden Belt—it is sin. It is work of the Devil."

Now the crowd's bad-tempered snarl deepened to a thundering roar of disapproval, and from the benches sailed a volley of missiles, pieces of fruit, empty wine flasks, pelting the holy man.

He kept on. Fending off the objects that struck around him, he shouted again, "God will give you life eternal, if you open your hearts to Him Who made you from the dust—"

Something hard hit him, and he went to one knee. Irene's stomach tightened.

He struggled up again, and his mouth opened, but the crowd now had scented his blood. With a howl like a cruel beast, they leapt to their feet. They tore off pieces of the benches and threw them at him; they hurled down their shoes and bottles, their apple cores and empty dishes.

He stood there, pleading with them, his voice now lost in their shouts and curses. Irene saw bits and pieces strike him, and although he tried to keep his feet, he sank down slowly to the sand. Still he tried to speak to them. But they heard nothing anymore, saw nothing in him anymore but a momentary amusement, a target for their blows. Long after he lay there motionless on the sand they flung whatever they could find down on his body.

"I sometimes wonder," Irene said, in a voice that trembled, "why I choose to lead these people."

John Cerulis smirked at her. "The problem will be yours no longer, after this day, lady."

"Will it? Even now, deluded one, my *cursores* are confiscating your palaces and fortress and all your wealth, because you have dared plot against me."

"Dared to plot," he said, unperturbed, "and dared to succeed, whore. On this day all the great offices of your power are in the hands of men sworn to uphold me."

"Really? I think not." She leaned toward him, fierce. Unlike this unruly crowd, now sinking into a sensuous somnolent murmur like a fed cat, she struck but one blow, and that one final. She said, "Ah, no, beguiled one. You thought that by slaying those on Theophano's list, you removed from my administration all those who supported me against you. But you were wrong, as ever you are wrong, murderer of women and babies. Theophano's list was not of your enemies, but of mine. I meant you to find it and use it as you did. You killed your own men in that purge. You rid me of all those I feared in my government. You destroyed yourself."

His face quivered, his lips colorless, his eyes shining suddenly wide and fearful. She leaned back, smiling at him. At that moment, a move on the ledge above him caught her eye, and she jerked her gaze that way.

It was Hagen, crouching there among the broken statues. Hagen, who glared at her now with eyes as hot and bright as molten gold. Hagen, who had overheard, and worse, had understood, that she had always intended Theophano to die.

She straightened up, tearing her gaze from him. After all, he was only a barbarian.

But her flesh crawled now. This was going wrong. Down there the Hippodrome attendants were picking up what was left of Daniel and laying it on a cart, and shoveling in on top the heaps of debris with which the crowd had slain him. Soon the race would start again. Beside her, at least, John Cerulis sat limp and white, a ruined man. She gripped her fists in her lap, her breath short. The race was about to start. Her temples pounded; she fixed her eyes on the golden oval of the track.

For the first time, Michael found himself missing Prince Constantine. When he realized that, he thrust the feeling roughly down again below the surface of his thoughts.

He was the champion. He might lose a heat, but he would not lose the race. The crowd was howling out there, whooping and screaming in a frenzy; he would bring them to their feet again, when he beat Ishmael.

Swiftly he went to his horses, whose grooms were leading them up and down the aisle. Esad was waiting for him and called him over.

"Look at him," Esad said. "He's gone lame again."

Michael's heart contracted. He went to Folly's head, and gripped the bridle, to keep the excited horse from biting him, and led him off a few steps, watching his legs. He seemed sound enough to Michael, although he stepped a little short, but then when Michael let him stop again, the horse shifted his weight on to three legs, and held his off foreleg slightly ahead of him, the toe pointing.

"He can't race again," Esad said. "Not like that."

"He'll race," Michael said.

He stooped to run his hand down the slender foreleg. At his touch, Folly leapt sideways, and he spoke to the horse in a soothing voice.

"He's not sound," Esad said. "You'll ruin him."

"He'll race. Two more heats, that's all."

"You can't—"

Michael whirled up; he thrust his face into Esad's, and the groom shut up. Michael glared at him until the other man looked away. Straightening, the Prince set his hands on his hips.

"Harness him."

Esad's lips trembled. He said nothing, but he made no move to obey.

"Harness him, Esad, or by God's Word, I'll do it myself."

The groom's shoulders slumped; he went away with the horse to the racks of harness. Michael walked forward, into the front of the stable.

The team had not given him what he needed, when he asked for it, in the first heat. In that drive down the stretch, with Ishmael's horses surging alongside, he had asked them for more speed and they had tried to find it for him but nothing had come. This time he would not let that happen. This time he would hoard their strength until the moment when he put Ishmael forever in his dust.

He would have the inside track of his rival, this heat, since he had finished behind him in the last. If he took the lead, he could control the pace. Ishmael had great hands, but Michael had the experience and skill to outwit him.

Behind him the grooms worked madly on the horses, rubbing their bodies clean and dry, picking up their feet to check for stones, inspecting the harness. Ishmael's grooms were doing the same thing, in the next aisle, and as Michael stood there, deep in his thoughts, Ishmael himself walked swiftly by with a pail of water.

Michael tore his gaze away from his rival. He could not bear to look at him—if Ishmael met his eyes, would he see there some contempt, some triumph—worse, some pity? Michael fixed his gaze on the ground.

He had demanded perfection from everybody else, from all who wished to serve him; he had tolerated no flaw. Now he had to meet that test himself.

From the track a man ran into the stable, shouting.

"They've stoned the holy man to death!"

"What?"

"That holy man! He came out and tried to preach to them, and the crowd stoned him."

"Haaaa."

Michael went a little toward the gate, to look out, and stopped himself. There was really nothing unusual in that—often there were public executions in the Hippodrome, between heats, and the holy man was surely a criminal, because this was the City of God. That did not matter anyway. What mattered was the race.

He saw it as a sacrament, this race. As Christ died for the sins of the multitude, so he raced with the hopes and dreams of the multitude on his shoulders. They could not win, so he won for them. That was why they loved him, and he meant to win for them today. It was simple enough. This was the real world, the track, the race. Everything else was merely an apparatus for moving souls through time into eternity.

Now the horns were blowing, calling him out to his epiphany. His horses were walking out toward him, each in its harness, the reins leading back into the chariot. He went to them, patted each one, spoke to it, and told it how they would win. Folly snapped at him, his old self again, wild-eyed. Michael climbed into the chariot and drove out on to the track, into the deafening cheers of the crowd.

<h1 style="text-align:center">: 29 :</h1>

Hagen watched from the statue tier; he saw the chariots line up for the start, and saw them burst forward down the track; but his mind was a wild whirl, and he cared nothing for the race.

He knew now why she had not let him kill John Cerulis and end the purge. He knew why she had sent him after Theophano, not to rescue her, but to die trying. She had known he had the list; she had thought he would die at the hands of John Cerulis's men, and the list would be found on his body.

To authenticate her false list, she had laid down his life, and Theophano's, and further back, Rogerius's too, indirectly.

John Cerulis was nothing, a poor clown, her dupe, her excuse for this game. It was she who was the stench of evil in this place.

Now slowly the screams of the crowd penetrated his fierce inward concentration, and he raised his head.

Down there on the track, the chariots hurtled along around the oval, spinning up the sand with their wheels. Michael was leading, with Ishmael close beside him, and the other teams in his wake. They reached the curve, and raced around it, Michael and Ishmael, dead even, because while Michael saved ground through the turn, he also slowed his team down.

The crowd knew it. They were not cheering now. They were

screaming for speed, for a real race, and their roars were ugly and outraged. The champion was falling; a new champion was rising from the
field; but they had already tasted blood this day, and now they were
dissatisfied with anything less. They wanted a real fight; they wanted
a war.

Michael heard it. As the teams rounded the curve at the far end
of the track, he urged his horses on, picking up the pace, responding
to the crowd; he gathered speed, and Ishmael stayed beside him, match-
ing his team stride for stride.

Now the crowd approved. Their screams of anger changed to
cheers and whistles. The horses flew down the straightaway. Rapidly
the two leaders pulled away from the third- and fourth-place teams, and
as they whirled into the turn, Michael on the inside pulled out in front
of Ishmael by half a length and more.

Ishmael's blacks and greys leveled to their work. Spinning around
the turn, they rocked the car behind them up on the inside wheel, and
Ishmael leaned out to hold it on the track. He lost more ground, bearing
out into the center of the track, and when the car bounced down on
both wheels again the horses set out after Michael on legs that skimmed
the sand like wings.

Michael heard them coming; he looked back over his shoulder, and
he went to the whip. His horses were straining into the harness. At the
touch of the whip they flattened out still more. Yet Ishmael was gaining
on them. Sweeping into the next turn, Michael glanced over his shoulder
again, and again he plied the whip, and Ishmael surged up on the
outside, drawing even with him through the curve.

As the track straightened out, the two teams raced together like
one great eight-horse hitch. For three strides, they ran like one another's
shadows; the challenge of the team coming up from behind them drove
Michael's horses to one last surge of speed. The crowd leapt to its feet,
swaying, screaming, a thousand thousand arms fluttering in the air, a
thousand thousand voices thundering up to Heaven.

For a painful stride, Michael's horses answered; they won back a
yard of the track, they thrust their heads in front, and held off Ishmael's
blacks and greys. Then the smooth flow of the horses' strides broke and
jerked; Michael's inside wheeler changed leads twice in two strides and
went down headlong onto the sand.

The horse's body somersaulted, slamming into its team-mates, and those animals fell too. The car spun around. Michael sailed out of it and struck the track among his thrashing team.

The horses behind him veered across the sand to keep from hitting the wreck. Ishmael's horses bolted nearly to the far wall. Still trapped in their harness, Michael's horses fought to rise and fell again and again into one another and onto their driver.

The crowd shrieked. Drawn by the smell of blood, the whole mass of the mob rushed down toward the track. Hagen stood up, his heart pounding, his palms slick with sweat. The grooms had run out to the wreck, and were cutting the maddened horses free; one horse ran dragging its traces the length of the track, met Ishmael coming around the far curve, and spun around and galloped along ahead of him. Ishmael stopped for nothing; he was making for the Golden Belt. He swerved out to avoid the broken car and the bodies on the track, and loped his team over the finish line.

From the momentary stunned silence of the crowd arose a mounting roar. The whole Hippodrome began to move. The people in the lower seats shoved forward, and the ones along the rail climbed over and rushed out on to the sand, toward the charioteers, the victor, and the dead. The whole great grandstand cleared; within moments, the whole racecourse was filled with people, fighting one another, screaming, struggling, a boiling cauldron of bodies. As if with Michael's death their order had failed them, the whole great mob ran wild.

Hagen held himself fast where he was. In the balcony below him, Irene sat in her chair, and John Cerulis still sat beside her. Whatever she had planned, surely she had not foreseen this riot, and it occurred to Hagen that chance, or God, or some laughing devil somewhere had just given John Cerulis one more run at the purple boots. If he could seize Irene now, in this tumult, he could take it all.

Even as Hagen realized that, the people in the Imperial box realized it also. The Empress's women rushed in to surround her, and John stood up and beckoned to his bodyguard, the huge barbarian with the axe in his hands.

This man lumbered forward, raising his weapon over his shoulder. Hagen shouted, but his voice was lost in the din of the riot. He saw the axe heaved up, and the Empress shrink back from it, and then from among the women the child Philomela sprang forward, her arms out, defending her mistress.

The axe struck her where her neck joined her shoulder and swept her to one side. Blood spurted across the balcony. The giant axeman strode on, his blade swinging, going at the Empress; and another of her women, and another, leapt forward bare-handed and with cushions to defend her, and was cut down.

Hagen roared. He drew his sword from its scabbard with both hands and leapt down into space, falling the five yards that separated him from the balcony. He landed on the balls of his feet on the rail and for a dizzy moment swayed, off balance, behind him a sheer drop into the boiling mass of the riot. Before him the axeman turned.

Above the curly black beard, little pig-eyes squinted at him. The axeman opened his mouth and let out a shrill yell and charged.

Hagen bounded into the balcony. The axe whistled at his head, and he dropped to one knee and let the blade pass by him. In the corner, the women packed themselves against Irene, a living wall protecting her, and Irene shouted his name.

"Hagen! Hagen!"

The black-bearded giant gripped his axe with both hands and cocked it back. His eyes blazed. With lumbering steps he bore down on Hagen, and again Hagen dodged the hissing sweep of the curved blade past his face.

He struck back, aiming for the giant's knees, and the big man dropped the axe neatly down and parried off the blow. The impact numbed Hagen's hands. He bounded backward and came up against the wall, with no place left to dodge, and this man, unlike the other Greeks, knew how to fight. A worm of fear gnawed at Hagen's heart.

Huge, leisurely in his confidence, the black-bearded man paced forward toward him. Blood dappled the blue-black metal of his axe blade. He lifted it up over his shoulder and struck again at Hagen.

Hagen saw the blade coming, and began to dodge, and even as he moved he read the feint. He dropped to his knees and the giant whirled the blade around in the counter blow. Hagen flung his sword up and the axe glanced off it and struck the marble wall behind him, and the giant yelled, startled. Hagen launched himself forward in a desperate dive for the big man's midsection.

He got inside the giant's arms, drove his knee into the big belly, and got his elbow around and slammed it into the unprotected throat.

The giant grunted. The axe clattered to the floor, and both men fell heavily among the carpets and cushions.

Hagen twisted, trying to get his sword up; the blade tangled in a fold of the rucked carpet. The giant swatted at him, backhanded, and knocked him sideways up against the railing.

Out of breath, Hagen wheeled around. The giant had found his axe again and was coming up to his feet. They faced each other across the width of the balcony, Irene and her women to Hagen's right, John Cerulis to his left. The giant lowered his head and charged.

Hagen wheeled around, trying to get out of the way, and swung his sword up. Through the corner of his eye, he saw John Cerulis move around behind him, and he flinched. The giant bore down on him. Behind him he knew John Cerulis was preparing to strike, but he could not turn to see; he faced the giant and swung his sword in a level two-handed blow, as hard as he could, his back itching, waiting for the knife from behind.

It never came. From the side of the balcony, shouting like a true warrior, Irene ran headlong, her hands out before her. With both outstretched hands she struck John Cerulis in the chest as he lifted his arm against Hagen, and she flung him backwards, over the rail of the balcony, down into the crowd below.

Hagen shrieked, triumphant; the axe hissed at his face, and he yanked his head back out of the way, and his counterstroke split the air like a bolt of lightning, cleaved through the giant's armor where the leather straps joined breastplate to back, and bit deep, deep into the flesh below.

The giant gasped. He went down on one knee, as the blood fountained up, and rolling his eyes back into his skull, he fell forward on his face at Hagen's feet.

Hagen dragged in a breath, his arms sagging; the sweat stung his eyes. He backed away from the great body at his feet and raised his arms to the Empress.

She said, "Once again you have proven yourself to me, Hagen."

"Hah," he said. He looked into the basilisk glitter of her eyes. "It is you who have proven yourself, lady. I know you now for what you are."

"Do you? And what am I to you?"

"You killed her. You sent her out to die."

"Theophano died for the Empire. No greater glory—"

"No," he cried; out of pain and grief, he sobbed. "No, she died for nothing—she died so that you could kill more—she died for the sake of a game you played with John Cerulis."

"You are a barbarian, Hagen. You do not understand."

"I understand," he said. "I understand that you have wasted the best and most noble of your Empire, and you will go on no more."

"Hagen, I will make you rich—"

He started toward her, determined to kill her, although his soul shrank from it. She screamed once, "Hagen!" and flung up her arm between them, and then with a thunderous pounding, the door to the balcony flew open and Nicephoros rushed into their midst, wearing a helmet and breastplate.

Nicephoros looked from her to Hagen, frowning, and reached up and took the helmet from his head. Doing so, he moved a little, putting distance between himself and his Basileus. Hagen lowered his sword, waiting.

"Basileus," the Treasurer said, in a neutral voice, "I have to report that the *cursores* have the mob contained, and the City is in order; all of John Cerulis's possessions have been seized to the throne."

"Excellent," said Irene. "Nicephoros, you have ever done my bidding, better than any other. Only—seize this man here, and I shall make you powerful before all but me!"

"Seize Hagen?" Nicephoros asked.

Hagen stirred. "Nicephoros, she betrayed us. She has betrayed us all. The list—the murders—that was her doing. She tricked John Cerulis into it. She caused it all."

Nicephoros's head swiveled toward the Empress, who stood there, fingering the brooch that fastened her cloak, her gaze hard and glittering on Hagen.

"You did this?" Nicephoros said, in a low voice.

"Nicephoros, seize him."

In a louder voice: "Did you do it?"

"I—"

"Answer me," he shouted. "In the Name of God."

She flinched from him. Her hand pulled on the brooch. "I am Basileus, Nicephoros—I can do what I choose!"

The Treasurer straightened out of his habitual slouch. Now suddenly he was taller than she, as tall as Hagen himself. His gaze was fastened on her with a new fierce energy. He said, "Then you are the hands on the throat of the Empire."

"Nicephoros," she said, in a voice that trembled. "Seize this barbarian."

"Not at your order, lady—you are Basileus no more." Nicephoros strode forward, reaching for the door into the stairway.

"Who, then?" she cried. "Him? This fumbling barbarian with his bloody sword—"

"I shall be Basileus," Nicephoros said. "For weeks I have felt the Empire calling to me, and have struggled against it, like Jonah in the whale, but now I understand, and I will obey."

He opened the door. "Guards! Come seize this woman."

"Good," Hagen said. "So be it," and he lowered his sword.

Irene screamed. As the blade dropped, she lunged, past Nicephoros, coming at Hagen so fast he could only recoil from her. Her full weight struck him. She had the great brooch in her hand, open, the pin between her knuckles. Shouting, he thrust at her, and the pin stabbed deep, deep into his eye.

The shock and the pain drove him down on one knee. He crossed his arms before him, to hold her off, but now the guards were there, rushing into the box, obeying Nicephoros's crisp loud orders. A tide of blood and the liquor from his eye swept down his cheek. Squatting there, he breathed deep, struggling against pain, and covered his eye with his hand.

She was shrieking; the guards held her nearly horizontal among them, while they unlaced the purple boots from her feet. She fought like a wild animal, scratching, kicking, biting at them. At last they wrenched the boots from her feet, and with the symbol of her power gone, her spirit left her also. She sank down, weeping, limp in the grasp of many arms. Hagen got up; his legs were shaking violently. His eye was destroyed. He watched them take her away, out of the Imperial box, into the Palace.

Nicephoros said, "God give you a fair wind all the way to Italy, Hagen."

"Fair wind or foul, I shall be back in my own home by winter," Hagen said.

The Greek physicians had sewn his bad eye shut with silk thread. It hurt only a little now. He stood watching his horses being loaded on to the galley—Nicephoros had given him two blood stallions, as well as the two he had brought from Syria—and the itch to leave was strong as a hunger.

"You will not think again and stay?" Nicephoros said. "There is a life of ease and pleasure for you here, and my eternal gratitude— mine and my people's."

"I'm going home," Hagen said. "Your life will not be one of ease and pleasure, I think, if you are to be a worthy Basileus."

"I will be as great as I can be. I shall not forget the cost of my diadem."

Hagen touched the patch over his eye. "We have an old story, among my people—of a god who gave his eye for wisdom. I won't mind, if it turns out I have gained some from this." He put out his hand. "God help you, Basileus."

Nicephoros shook his hand in a firm grip. "God go with you, Hagen."

He stepped on to the ship; half a dozen servants of the Emperor carried on his luggage and the gifts that Nicephoros had lavished on him. The horses were restless and he went to stand by their heads to calm them. When he looked back, Nicephoros and his retinue were climbing up the steps from the Imperial harbor toward the Bucoleon and the rest of the Palace, gleaming white in the sun at the top of the cliff. Hagen turned his eyes forward again. The sea leapt under the brisk merry breeze. At the far end of that wind was his river, his hall, the rest of his life, waiting to be taken up. He could never have married Theophano; she would never have lived there with him. He would have lost her no matter what he did. In his heart, that wound closed over and healed without scar. He faced forward now, into the future; eagerly he leaned into the wind going west.

The Basileus Irene died in exile on Lesbos in 803, one year after she was deposed. Later she was canonized a saint, in memory of the favor she had shown the monasteries.

Nicephoros became Emperor and ruled well for nine years. He was a good emperor, but a bad general, and when he led an expedition against the Bulgars in 811 he was killed, and his skull was cleaned and covered with jewels and used as a drinking cup for the Bulgar Khan.

Hagen returned to Braasefeldt, and there lived a long and happy life, marrying three times, and siring many children. He died peacefully by his fire, in the twilight of his years, with all his friends around him, and speaking of Constantinople.

A NOTE ON THE TYPE

This book was set on the Linotype in Granjon, a type named in compliment to Robert Granjon, a type cutter and printer, active in Antwerp,
Lyons, Rome, and Paris, from 1523 to 1590. Granjon, the boldest and
most original designer of his time, was one of the first to practice
the trade of type founder apart from that of printer.

Linotype Granjon was designed by George W. Jones, who based his
drawings on a face used by Claude Garamond (ca. 1480–1561) in his
beautiful French books. Granjon more closely resembles Garamond's
own type than does any of the various modern faces that bear his name.

Composed by Maryland Linotype Composition Company,
Baltimore, Maryland.
Printed and bound by Fairfield Graphics,
Fairfield, Pennsylvania.
Typography and binding design by Virginia Tan.